Devine Road

Volume I

*A Comedy of Sex, Politics, Religion
and Other Impolite Topics of Conversation*

Gabriel Coeli

PublishAmerica
Baltimore

ISBN: 1-4137-9736-9
PUBLISHED BY PUBLISHAMERICA, LLLP
www.publishamerica.com
Baltimore

Printed in the United States of America

To the late, great Zach D.
I climb the Mountain alone now, if at all.

Table of Contents

Book 1
The Mountain with No Name

I saw Eternity the other night
Like a great ring of pure
And Endless Night

All calm as it was bright.

And round beneath it,
Time: In hours, days and years
Driv'n by the spheres…

-Henry Vaughan, *The World*

From the highest plane in the material world down to the lowest, all are places of misery wherein repeated birth and death take place. But one who attains My abode never takes birth again.

-Bhagavad-Gita, Chapter 8, Text 16

For who knows not that Truth is strong, next to the Almighty?

-John Milton, *Areopagitica*

Untitled
Prologue

It is some night in the middle of winter, and it is snowing. This would not surprise you, if you live where it snows. But it might be a little out of place for you, a little much to wrap your head around if you happen to be a resident of, say, California. Or Saudi Arabia. Or the Galapagos Islands. Those kinds of places.

In some places on that wild and beautiful planet called Earth, little frozen flakes of water fall from the sky when the planet's axis is tilted away from the sun. Sounds incredible, but it's true.

In Katmandu, it snows in the winter. In Oslo, it snows in the winter. In Moscow, it snows in the winter.

On the Mountain with no Name, it snows in the winter.

It is some night in the middle of winter, it is some night on the Mountain with No Name, and the bottom half of my pants are soaked with once-frozen water.

I extend all appropriate salutations to the readers. I'm the Protagonist of this story.

I behold before me a beautiful man with a heavy black beard and skin as brown as the mouths of rivers. His single eye looks uneasy, unsure, twitches nervously. The man is clearly in pain. His body, like mine, is broken. And his spirit, like mine, seems to trudge on.

He's got a wicked-looking stick in his hand, and he's swaying from side to side. Why "wicked?" Indeed, why do I disparage his staff with such an unflattering adjective? Some kind of inborn prejudice? Early childhood canalization against staves? It could be that this wicked stick in particular just broke two of my ribs on the right side of my body, and I think that a blow I sustained not moments ago from that long, gnarled shepherd's crook may have partially collapsed one of my lungs.

Both sides of my tortured torso pound on my brain, screaming for it to pay attention, demanding that my body pass out or die or do whatever it can to stop the hurting. My brain, in its evolutionary-conditioned cerebral stubbornness, says no. It'll do what it pleases, thank you.

That is why my eyes work. That is why I'm breathing. That is why blood is still pumping. Because my brain refuses to surrender under the onslaught of this violence.

Or is it my soul that refuses to let go? Is it my soul that is keeping my body alive when it is so obviously broken?

Where, exactly, is my soul?

And why does it hurt as badly as the rest of me?

I have a fighting iron in my hand. It is a bar upon which rests a spiked iron ball. There is blood on the spikes. His blood.

How long have we been battling? Days or weeks? Years? Eras, whole epochs? Have ice ages come and gone, planets been born, stars died? Eternities? Has God added a few inches to His already impressive beard?

Minutes? Yeah, probably about six minutes.

All around us people stare. A beautiful feminine creature with red hair and perfect breasts is crying. A priest looks on solemnly. Four women and two Muses stand together and hold each other, comfort each other. Twin men that were felled by the very mace I hold lie at the feet of the Devil. The enemy of God has blood in his hair.

And surrounding us on every side are the stony faces of armored children.

I remember, suddenly, the face of a Japanese man, and remember, too, his *jisei*. His death poem. It was beautiful.

I remember Og, King of Bashan. He made the sun set at the end of the day.

I remember a gentle man with a big mustache and his four wives, and how they cried when he went on up the Mountain.

I look around me and I see the Mountain.

I stand in the middle of the Road.

Rain falls on the Road.

Did you know that if you were to set out on this thoroughfare, this mystical, magical Road and just follow it all the way to the top of the Mountain with No Name that you would find God at the end of it?

Devine Road is the only way in and the only way out.

Have you ever read the Bible? Remember Genesis 6:4?

A giant is brandishing a staff, and is brandishing it threateningly. He moves toward me, slowly. Very slowly.

I have a severe head wound.

So does he.

I have a broken ankle.

He has a broken elbow.

Our bodies are symphonies of color, and fireworks of blue and black and purple explode in hemorrhaging glory, celebrating our injuries. Our teeth would make a piano proud. It's been a regular punch-drunk lovesick sing-along.

My world is spinning out of the control of my perception. The ground is my ceiling. I hear wind rushing past my ears. I can't feel my face. There is blood in my eyes.

I duck as his staff soars over my left shoulder. He narrowly evades my sluggish attempt at reprisal. We both fall over.

We both get up.

We swing again and miss again.

We repeat.

I fall and can not get up. He rises, stands over me, raises his weapon for the final crushing blow and loses his balance. Then he falls over.

His head is next to mine, his face faces mine. He smiles and, feebly, expels a tooth from his mouth. It tumbles down his face and sticks to the bloody black quagmire that was once his noble and fatherly beard.

"Quite a conundrum." he says.

"Indeed." I retort.

Somehow we manage to laugh.

Somehow we remember that we love each other.

I find the strength to rise and help him to his feet. He wobbles, his knee buckles, and I catch him. When he is steadied, I step back and raise my weapon.

He cocks his arms like revolver hammers, preparing his staff for a blow I expect will kill me, if it connects.

I don't have the strength to dodge another attack. I do have the strength to propel my weapon right into him. I suspect that this blow of his will kill me.

But his guard will be just low enough that my strike will hit him at, if I pull it off just right, the same moment that his blow connects with me. I expect that this swing of mine will kill him.

I suspect that we will kill each other, now. Here at the end of our battle. Our duel. Here at the end of all things.

What will happen to the farmhouse?

What will happen to the Connection?

What will happen to God?

We swing and there is a connection.

A surge of pain fills my whole awareness as suddenly as it leaves, and an old world, a world that sprung to life with the cries of a woman and an infant boy, a world that lived nowhere but within the perception of one very real being, a world has ended.

I bless the name of God as the pain leaves my body. There was a world, and then there was none.

100 Devine Road
Chapter 1

Autumn, in the place that I lived, had its own distinct scent. I don't know if it was the same everywhere, if every region of the world had seasons with their own special smells, their own unique bouquets, their own soft and subtly seductive olfactory experiences. They might have. I don't know. I can hardly formulate conjectures with my available information, because I was never a traveler. Before traversing Devine Road, I'd never been more than a hundred miles from home.

Autumn, in the region of the country that I inhabited before moving to the Mountain with No Name, smelled of oak leaves and ozone and crisp, chilly air that mingled delicately with burning firewood and warm pastries. It was almost everywhere you went (besides downtown, which smelled more like smog and garbage and Lebanese food.)

If you happened to wander near my old apartment when I lived in it, you would have smelled the hearty mushrooms in the beef stroganoff or the sweet ham and ripe tomatoes I used for my famous rice and gravy. I loved to cook, and still do, though I don't suppose I find much time for it up here on the Mountain. I'm a busy man these days.

I stepped out of the front door of my apartment one day in a September long ago with one half of a turkey sandwich in my hand and the other half sitting uncomfortably on my stomach. I rarely made a habit of breaking fast within two hours of rising in the morning; inexplicably, it nauseates me and I end up with heartburn for the rest of the day. In fairness, I do drink gallons of coffee every morning and it rarely agrees with anything I've got in there, so we've had to strike a deal, coffee and I. If I wait to eat, it doesn't make me throw up or even want to. In return for this, the caffeine renders me able to function with some semblance of normalcy before noon.

This morning in question was a morning that I woke up ravenously hungry, too famished to go without *something* to eat. The trouble? I'd already had a pot of coffee to myself, rendering the faintest notion of breakfast a clear and flagrant violation of the Java Accords.

When I had taken the first bite of that fateful turkey sandwich, the characteristically docile Juan Valdez in my stomach became fighting mad and started rumbling and roiling and kicking around my gastric juices, biting the lining, punching the walls, shaking the floor and shouting obscenities in Spanish up my esophagus. I was distressed, disparate. Discomforted and disagreeable and disapproving and other words starting with that prefix.

So I kicked that squirrelly South American back with my only defense against these episodes of unadulterated Latin fury: Two shots of Pepto and a big glass of water. It provided little respite, but that was okay. All I needed was a smidge. All I needed was enough to set out for my big day.

Before I took even three steps out that door, I smelled autumn and it thrilled me, nausea or no. Fall is my favorite season by far because it possesses something I can't hope to comprehend and can only describe as magical, like bubble tea and space flight and Pachelbel's Canon. It has a kind of, well, to coin a phrase, it's a very simple elegance. Maybe I'll call it an 'effortless majesty' instead, to avoid a trite description, but none of that is important. What autumn really means is red leaves, and sunshine after rainstorms, and the bluest skies all year. And I love it.

This day was my first day of community college. I had a bag lunch, a pack of Camels, my car keys and a crumpled copy of my class schedule. A quick glance over my itinerary would reveal that tomorrow I was to report to my school for an Algebra course with a man named Daffron and an "Introduction to Sociology" with a man named Dallman. The day after that I would show up for English 101 with a woman named O'Neill and a fencing class with a man named Sheldon. Today, Monday, I had one obligation: A class called History and Moral Philosophy taught by a man with a German name that I had trouble pronouncing.

Hmmm. *Trouble* is a bit of an understatement.

His name looked like a line on an optometrist's chart. If I could have read it letter by letter, I wouldn't have needed glasses, which was a prize in itself. But if I had actually been able to *pronounce* it I'd have gotten a sticker and a lollipop. And everyone knows that stickers and lollipops constitute two of the Four Great Prizes of All Time. The third is four virgins to do with what you please, and you only get that if you've been *really* good. The fourth is your very own Partition. More on that later.

In my right hand I held all of my possessions but the keys: those were shaking and jerking and flopping around in my left hand like they were on fire. You see, my left hand has some nerve damage from a wound I received during a particularly traumatic number of years of my life spent on foreign soil. That is to say, I received some shrapnel in the worst way and now it doesn't hold things so good.

Maybe that's unfair. It works just fine, now that I've learned to live with it. Not so in the morning, perhaps, because it always hurts and feels weird in the morning. But, dear reader, you will likely hear very little about my left hand and its nerve damage again, because I've compensated and gotten past it. I am not disabled. I am not handicapped. Slightly impeded. On the other hand, I've got different fingers. That is all.

Back to the matter at hand (as opposed to the matter *of* hand): I couldn't keep my lunch and everything else in the left hand because of my morning shakes, which would have dropped them all over the place, so I fit everything I could in my right hand. Necessarily, I struggled with the keys and keys alone in the other.

With some effort, I got in my car that sunny autumn morning and fired the engine up. I pulled out of my apartment complex, drove eight blocks to Fourth Plain Boulevard and nearly got killed by a driver who decided that *now* was the time to get in the right turn lane (six feet from the streetlight) and *fuck* no she wasn't going to use her turn signal *thank you kindly*. Eventually, I made it (alive) to the college and found myself weaving in and out of the packed parking lot and finally settling in a cramped space that I'm not sure was a "space" at all but was nevertheless parking, even if it was a fortnight's walk to the college.

A large crowd had assembled in the commons, tumbling and oozing slowly towards its collective destination like a great heap of people molasses. That is to say, it was moving painfully slow. Five hundred or more people looking for the room numbers of their classes. At once.

I love and hate crowds like I love and hate snow, which, thankfully, is tucked at least two months from now into my least favorite season, winter. You see, with both crowds and snow, there truly is something beautiful about so many tiny individual pieces falling together into a cohesive form, but it's so cold and uninviting that I can barely stand it. Unless, of course, there's a snowball fight going on, which no one can resist.

I waded through the sea of people, vaguely wishing I could just Moses everyone to both sides and get what I needed: The room number of History and Moral Philosophy. True, I had more than an hour before class started, but I was anxious. I'm anxious about a lot of things. It's the kind of person that I am.

Unfortunately for the Protagonist, dear ladies and gentle gentlemen, God in His Infinite Wisdom stopped giving people cool magical powers in the first few years of the Common Era, so I was forced to force my way through with my arms and shoulders. This proved a mean feat; I'm a fairly big guy, and you're afforded leeway when you wear pauldrons so wide they don't always fit through doorways.

There were six desks, lined up in alphabetical order for teachers' names, A-D at one desk, E-H at the next, and so on all the way to U-Z, which, incidentally, had no one crowding around it. I went to the second desk (at least I could discern the first *letter* of the Professor's last name) and waited for five minutes or so until I got to a person sitting behind a giant paper filing bin. She was a kindly looking woman with dark eyes and brown hair and smile lines deep enough to fit quarters in. I liked her immediately. When she looked up at me, I said, "History and Moral Philosophy."

Her eyebrows raised a fraction of an inch and she reached into a small paper bag resting at her feet. "This must be for you." she declared.

"Huh?" Ah, that most eloquent of prepositions.

She produced a yellowed envelope that smelled of yak musk and mountain air and peach pie and extended it to me. I looked it over. My name had been carefully inscribed in calligraphic black ink on the front of it.

I took it from her hand and gave her a quizzical look; she both shrugged *and* smiled with her eyes (something only women can do, which I've never understood) and turned her attention to the next person.

I walked away from the desk, which I found easier than pushing my way to it, and puzzled briefly over the envelope. I carefully opened it, removed its vellum (!) contents and unfolded them. It had an address, 100 Devine Road, and a time, 1:00 P.M. on it. Under it was a finely drawn map of a maze of country roads off the freeway north of the town I lived in, with Devine Road clearly marked in red ink. I checked my watch and saw that I had forty minutes to get there, so I hurried away to my car.

—

At some point during my drive, I turned my radio on and tuned it to the jazz station just in time to catch the last snatch of "Georgia on My Mind" by Billie Holliday. It was nearly over, so I let the song finish, then turned my radio back off and rolled down my window and just listened to my car and the cars around me.

There is something therapeutic in the sounds of driving. Listening to your car, the whine of your engine, feeling the set of the gears when you shift the transmission, the heater roaring blisteringly hot air on one side of your face and the chill fall air tantalizing the other side. Listening to the *zips* and *zings* of cars whipping past you or passing you or getting passed by you. It sort of makes you feel like you're part of something, part of all those drivers. Like a cell in a body, a part of that big, fire-breathing organism called traffic. I tried to revel in it because it was a simple pleasure, and it's the simple things in life that add up and eventually become the big things. I've long said that every major event in life is made up of that which is considered trivial.

Then again, I've long said that nothing is trivial.

The highway stretched out and wound around hills and trees like a great black adder beneath my wheels. Cars snaked around me and I snaked around them. A bus slithered by me in reverse. A motorcycle hissed as it passed me. Some dickhead in a Dodge Viper cut me off. You can think of lots and lots of allusions to those limbless, forked-tongued vertebrates when out on the road and it's kind of funny to think that the traffic system, one of the paradigms of modern society, can be likened in every facet of its existence to a serpent, the traditional symbol of deception and evil.

And sex.

Maybe the road is trying to tell us something.

It was a day of busy traffic, if particularly swif -moving, which is my favorite kind. Traffic like this means that thousands of cars are sharing the same stretch of road at high speeds and not having to slow or brake or swerve or kill each other. It always makes me happy to see so many people being responsible at the same time. Never mind that fucker that cut me off a mile back, he'll get his someday. I don't have enough time or energy to take part in revenge. Karma's got its own methods of dealing with miscreants without me mixing it up and anyway, *my* payback might be a bitch, but karma is a real fucking mean cunt.

After exiting the freeway and traversing a labyrinth of winding unpaved country roads that seemed to go nowhere (from the look of things, wherever they went would have *had* to be designated just that: nowhere), I came at last to a small marker that said 'Devine Road: Next Right'.

So I took the next right, considering myself well advised, and after five or so miles of quiet, pastoral scenery, cows and all, came to a straight, steep incline leading up some kind of hill or mountain, the higher elevations of which were shrouded in a heavy veil of fog. My car arched up and began to climb, climb, climb. It would do quite a bit of that before the drive was over.

Before long, my vision was enfolded in the miasma of that obscuring wall of clouds hovering around this Unnamed Mountain I was climbing, and I was surrounded on both sides by mist-choked green and black pines. I drove through the thick pall and under the stoic gaze of the giant conifers for nearly ten minutes, unable to see even twenty feet ahead of me, though it was midday. It made me nervous, of course, as nervous as anyone ever is when driving in conditions such as these, but there was also something beautiful about it, so I tried to relax and enjoy it. Simple things.

Some miles later, the road started to swerve dangerously. I found myself hugging every corner and being threatened with a deadly fall off of a cliff on my left, then right, then left side. Precipices loomed on all sides.

I slowed down, realizing that I was taking the road way too fast, and stuck my head out the window for a big whiff of the forest. Forests, if you're not really inclined toward them or can't remember the last time you went hiking, smell fantastic.

But I didn't get that big whiff of the forest. What I got was a blast of cold, cold ozone and another subtle fragrance my nose was skimming off of the top of the fog. A rather perplexing and rich Moroccan spice. My eyebrows shot up involuntarily and I almost took the next curve too quickly, which would have sent me veering off into a cedar abyss, but I jerked my emergency brake up so loud it yelped and slammed my wheel hard to the right so that I came to a screeching, skidding stop on the shoulder of the road, perhaps sixteen inches from my death.

I waited there for a little while, if only for my heart to finish its drum solo, then wiped a fine layer of perspiration from my hairline. It seemed like on this road I was constantly riding the accelerator down to the floor, playing with death or perhaps just teasing it with soft, absentminded brushes. Earlier I had been tempted to just let it go and drive the Mountain as fast as I could, but my near-miss had presently sapped the courage out of me. If I was going to die, it wouldn't happen on the way to some class. Hell, no. I intended to either go out in a blaze of some ill-conceived, violent glory or to be found mysteriously floating ass-up in a bathtub full of milk and Cheerios. Either seemed fitting.

I started back up and made special efforts to watch my speed. After dozens more curves and inclines and swoops and turns and hills and sunken grades, my car at last tipped up at a forty-five degree angle and began climbing, climbing, climbing. My ears plugged up and a yawn seized me, if only to blast, a little painfully, the pressure out of my aural canals. I went up and up.

At length the road plateaued off and I shot out of the clouds into clear, brilliant sunlight so suddenly that it hurt my eyes. Phone lines that I didn't recall seeing at ground level ran the length of the road, from where I was to, say, ten miles ahead, where another steep incline sent them shooting up and over a high cliff wall perhaps fifty or sixty feet tall. There were two cliff walls, actually, one on each side of Devine Road that ran east and west all the way to each side of the Plateau, where there were high stone walls on either end running from the top of the Plateau to the bottom, unbroken but for the craggy cliffs, the easternmost of which had a colossal stair carved by nature or giants into it. It led to a ridge and a massive cave that split the cliff face in half. The western one had small, carved areas on it, like rock art, but it was much too far away for me to discern their precise shape.

A large forest leaned up against the face of the twin plateaus and embraced Devine Road for a time before the thoroughfare bridged a small river and slanted up on a ramp leading through a jagged canyon that separated the two plateaus. It carried on for some distance before leveling with the higher elevation, where it appeared to transmute into an unpaved gravel road that ran flat for another twelve or so miles until it came to a drastically sharp incline that led farther up the Mountain. That incline was shrouded in deep fog, like the road to this first Plateau was, and small punctures in that misty canopy filtered dramatic fingers of stony gray light to frame the path with a subtle, 'divine' sort of illumination. Like when you see the shafts of light piercing the great big cumulus on the horizon you feel like God is smiling at you, even though you stopped believing in God before you stopped believing in Santa Claus.

(Go on, admit it. The concept of a big old Guy in the sky who sends you to Hell for having premarital sex is harder to swallow than a big old guy at the North Pole whose belly jiggles when he laughs and who loves Coca-Cola. You know why? God doesn't give you presents.)

Looking at that heavenly display, that Devine light that illumined Devine Road, I felt suddenly compelled to continue driving, onward and upward, to skip my class (not the last time today I'd have that impulse) and just Excelsior! to the summit. In my head the peak was sharp and beautiful, a jagged edge of Clorox-white broken glass puncturing the ionosphere. The air was cold and crystal clear. The sky was bluer than B.B. King.

Then something struck me as odd. I knew of no such mountain in the vicinity of where I lived. Certainly I'd never seen it on the skyline. How far away from home was I? And was I late for class?

The phone lines, supported by the occasional tall metal tower, went up the furthest incline leading to Bog knows where and disappeared into that second round of intense fog action, hanging like the laundry lines of the Information Age. I imagined washing the Internet and hanging it out to dry on those lines. That made me chuckle to myself. The Internet could use a good scrubbing.

I slowed my car when I came to a quaint little yellow farmhouse on the left, nestled between two phone towers standing like giant banal monoliths in the natural sea of soft brown wheat and emerald grasses, waves of which broke silently and passively around the towers only when the wind ran her gentle fingers through it.

Oh! And the wildflowers! Thousands of them, like a Thomas Kinkade painting, every color of the rainbow and many that the rainbow discriminates against, thrown in spades all throughout the fields, mottling the austere earth tones of the grass and wheat with brilliant, vivid color. I took a deep breath. This was incredible. Wow, this was incredible. I remember thinking that I would chart the time it took to get back to the city from here so that I could look into building a house here someday.

With some effort, I wrenched my attention from the festival of reds and blues and magentas and golds (etc.) and placed it back on the geography of the road. On my right was a narrow dirt path leading to what might have been an old, gray-bricked church of some kind. Possibly a monastery. I didn't know how to tell the difference. There was a steeple and a cross on top to remind everyone of how the Romans killed their criminals and Never Mind That Jesus Lived but Isn't It Just Great That He Died?

Hmmm. That farmhouse seemed more likely to have a class than the church, though why I thought that I could not say. At any rate, I looked for an address. There's usually an address on the mailbox.

Hell, they didn't even have a mailbox.

Unable to locate any semblance of an address, I pulled into the driveway and resolved to see if anyone was home who could tell me if this was 100 Devine Road and if not, whether they knew where to find it.

When I stepped out of my car, I suddenly made eye contact with a man perhaps ten years older than I, with shorter, lighter hair and black eyebrows, leaning anxiously on one of the legs of the phone towers and scratching at his torso furiously. He looked like he had a terrible itch, like he'd just made love to poison oak, like his chest was on fire and he was trying to put it out. He wore a brown leather coat, a white button-up shirt that was left lazily open over a white undershirt and expensive designer jeans. None of these were spared his merciless fingernails, tearing and scratching to get at those itches.

K'ung Wu.

Those words reverberated through my head, loudly and suddenly. Chinese, it sounded like.

What the hell?

I looked again at the man in the brown leather coat and was stricken by a new and terribly odd sensation, like the strange Asian words in my head had given me new eyes by which to perceive this person scratching himself on that phone tower. For some reason, when I looked at him, I saw pain. I saw deep, deep suffering when I looked at this man. But I did not see it *in* this man. I saw it *of* this man.

I saw in my mind's eye a flower wilting in a sweltering sun. I suddenly remembered the name of a serial child molester I'd read in the newspaper. I felt like a widower surviving his only son. I thought of police brutality, of the Inquisition, of the Ku Klux Klan. I had a vision of a French beach drowned in thick crude oil.

I saw her face again.

A creeping violence started billowing in the back of my brain and firing crackling fingers of electricity in every which way, directing lightning into every one of my limbs. My adrenaline flowed. My fists clenched. I was taken by rage. And I had no idea why.

I lowered my shoulder, just like high school football, and ran at this man in the brown leather coat.

His face went from startled to panicked to utterly terrified in about a half second, and he suddenly took off at a full run away from me, across the road, and far away, fast as his legs could carry him. You might find this very strange, and I surely did, but God help me, I didn't pursue him. I just laughed. I didn't know what else to do.

I chuckled until it caught up with me what I had just done. That was one of my classmates. Oh, shit. How do you explain something like that to a teacher?

"Professor, it was my subconscious understanding that this man destroys things of beauty, so I attacked him." I could say.

"I'm calling the cops." He could say.

More than a little mortified at my own behavior, I walked up to the house and rang the doorbell, more because I had no idea what to do than for any other reason. That's not to say the idea of jumping in my car and driving home didn't cross my mind. It's just that the G.I. Bill is picky about not paying for classes that "veterans" (I'm still not old enough to consider myself a veteran, even if I'm the legal definition) refuse to attend, so I had to try and go, even if I'd just screwed myself out of an education. Boy, if the Army got wind of this…

The farmhouse was Georgian, two stories tall, painted yellow with white trim and sporting lots and lots of mullioned windows. A large, Southern style porch ran the diameter of the first story and tall Roman pillars Atlased a second-story veranda. There were iron balconies around some of the rooms and it had eccentric double fan front doors painted white and flanked by similarly bleached pilasters; ornate balustrades littered the multiple slopes of the roof.

I estimated from the size of it that it was a five-bedroom house. Probably had a study and a dining room separate from the kitchen, perhaps an anteroom, too. It certainly had a basement.

It was a nice house, but it would have been nicer if it wasn't *yellow*, for God's sake.

I rang the doorbell three more times. When no one answered, I knocked three sharp raps on the leftmost of the two front doors which was (though heretofore unknown to me) ajar before I applied this new pressure to it. It swung open. I heard footsteps so I waited and looked inside the house from the doorstep. Nothing exciting, of course: Simple country décor, no television (I found that somewhat unusual) and a large fireplace. A black piano with dandelions in a white vase situated on top of it.

A painting, another depiction of Jesus Christ, that mystic power house betrayed twice by his followers, Judas and then His Church, stared me right in the eye. There was an almost accusing hint to His gaze. I diverted my attention. At least that painting showed Him alive and healthy, but the look on His face was almost as disturbing as the crucifix was graphically unsettling.

Hmmm. Couch, ottoman, loveseat, recliner. Lots and lots of shelves with lots and lots of religious statuettes, Buddha and Jesus and Shiva and more, like a really eclectic collection. No soot in the fireplace, but there was wood there. The house smelled of Salisbury steak.

It looked like a farmhouse. Looked like every farmhouse I'd ever seen or heard of. Cozy, comfortable and incredibly boring.

Not much longer than half a minute later, a tall, well-dressed man rounded the corner and stopped in his tracks. I remember thinking immediately that he was Oriental, but something was strange about his appearance. I'd look at him and swear he was of East Asian descent, but then he'd suddenly look perhaps Greek or Italian to me, and then Asian again.

He looked me up and down with a puzzled expression on his face, then looked as if he remembered something and turned his head to the side, and inexplicably looked Middle Eastern. Another man dressed the same way and of the same height and of the same subtle Oriental countenance and who was in fact the first man's identical twin came around the corner and gave me the same silent examination.

At this point and under this much scrutiny, I was feeling a tad uncomfortable, so I spoke up. "I'm just looking for 100 Devine Road," I asserted, "And was wondering if I'd already passed it."

They both looked surprised and the first one bowed to me and pointed at the phone tower, pantomiming a leaning man, and then a dropped shoulder. When I saw that he was reenacting the event with the man in the leather coat, I (nervously) tried to communicate, wordlessly, a little of what happened, but the other twin interrupted me. He pointed me to the unpaved foot trail across the road that led to that old, red brick abbey and tapped his wrist, where a watch would have been had he been wearing one. It didn't take him long to become aware that I did not understand a thing that he was trying to "say," wordlessly, to me, so he stopped with the sign language, presently, and paused in thought for a moment, looking a little frustrated at the failure of his onomatopoeic endeavor.

When it appeared that he had made up his mind about whatever he was deliberating about, he looked at his brother, and his brother looked back. He eyed me, smiled proudly, and disappeared into the living room. Before long he had produced a piece of paper from the coffee table, upon which he had drawn an arrow, and was holding the impromptu directional device high and in the direction of the Abbey. Deciding that these were the best directions I was going to get, I took my leave of the twins and set off for the church, dearly hoping that these strange people had pointed me to 100 Devine Road.

The abbey/monastery/cathedral, I thought, was decidedly Catholic and probably Dominican; though I'm admittedly a layman on both architectural and monastic matters, and what I was to eventually see rather obscured that precursory assumption thereafter. But I'll keep pace with my narrative.

I walked in through the front gate, a high arch with thirty-one flavors of vines crawling between and over and through and hanging from the once-polished stone bricks that the arch was composed of. The gate was the only entrance through the twenty-foot high walls (also dark gray bricks, the color of a raining sky) that surrounded the Abbey and its courtyard, which was a long, flat, grassy front yard with rows of ficus trees (professionally taken care of) skirting along the edges of a cobblestone walkway that formed the image of a Celtic cross. The protruding arms of the path stretched from the west wall to the abbey and was proportionate to the shape of the cross in its extensions north and south, and in its middle was a small green hill with a stone obelisk jutting up from it like a rhinoceros' horn, an obelisk that looked unflinchingly like the Washington Monument, only it was perhaps as tall as me, and certainly no bigger.

I ventured into this walled courtyard bewilderedly, because I was looking upon hundreds of monks garbed in distinctly different vestiges, huddling in scattered circles all across the grounds. I walked past a group of orange-robed monks who looked North African and dressed like Hindus, and they were all whispering and pointing, seemingly arbitrarily and suspiciously at the other groups of monks, first at a group of brown-robed Franciscans, then at a group of Buddhists dressed similarly to them, then at any of the several other groups, then back around to ones they had pointed at, all in nothing resembling any kind of sensible order. Looking around, I realized that all of the other monks were doing exactly the same thing, and I stopped to scratch my head for a moment, but a quick, subconscious check of my watch informed me that my class was to start in exactly five minutes ago, so I resumed and redoubled my pace. I walked up to the huge double doors, noticing a huge plaque above them that read '100 Devine Road'.

I pushed open the doors at the exact moment that the abbey bell tolled a single, clear note. The two distinct and different pitches that were creaked by each of the doors (in stereo) joined harmoniously with the bell and created a stunning major chord so precise and so beautiful that a chill ran down my back and halted my steps. As if this was a cue, the group of Franciscans standing nearest the door began singing *Jubilate Deo*, and was joined almost immediately by all the other monks in the courtyard, with each scattered little circle launching into song. Within seconds it became a competition, each order trying to sing their own faith's hymn louder than the others. This naturally culminated in a great roar that swelled in volume so suddenly and became so incredibly unpleasant to listen to that I covered my ears and swiveled on my feet, incredulous, to stare at this cacophonous choir.

Then a very strange thing happened, if anything stranger than what I was witnessing could have happened: The monks seemed to align in thought with each other in simultaneous fashion; those that were off-key shifted their pitch, those with differing tempos slowed or sped their songs to match each other, and soon every hymn sung by what seemed to be every monastic order in the history of religion swirled together into a single chorus and formed a perfect unison. They were singing in rounds, in dozens of different languages, harmonizing with each other, weaving a single musical show of worship to their God and their gods and their forces and powers. I was suddenly overcome by emotion, so beautiful was this display, and I uncovered my ears and stood there in the open threshold for some time, enraptured.

I saw then, in that small ring of grass at the foot of the Washington Monument a white flower that I had not seen on my way in. As I stared at this flower, this small wonder amidst such a great one as the monks were creating before my eyes, I saw out of my peripheral vision a woman slowly entering on the far side of the courtyard.

She was a woman with a dark complexion and heavy black eyebrows like sentries keeping vigilant watch over her soft brown eyes, with long, beautiful hair as black as her lips were red. She wore a backless white dress that fastened at her shoulder and ended just above her knees, a dress that reminded me of a painting I had once seen of Livia of Rome. The curves of her body would have given Euclid a massive coronary.

It was her.

It felt like snow melting down my back. My stance shot straight up, my spine stiff as a board. I was assaulted by a sudden terror. My fingers tensed around an imagined rifle, my eyes filled with horrific images of bodies charred, windows destroyed, families shattered, and parents broken. My ears rang with the sound of an explosion. My nose registered seared flesh and burnt hair. Little glistening beads of perspiration addled my forehead and trickled down my nose.

My God, the kids.

She was beautiful. So beautiful. The most beautiful woman I'd ever seen. And I knew why I was so terrified of her. I was terrified because the woman was *her*.

This woman walked slowly but deliberately toward the white flower and knelt beside it, and suddenly it seemed to me as if the monks sang not their exultations to Heaven but began to sing of her instead. She smiled demurely, looked at me, then lowered her face very near to the flower and whispered words I could not have heard had there not been hundreds of voices exalting her. She paused, as though the flower was replying, then uttered another soft declaration and rose to her feet. She locked eyes with me a second time, held my gaze for the length of time it takes a man to inhale sharply, and turned and began walking out of the courtyard at the same slow, deliberate pace she had entered. The closer she got to the exit, the lower the monks' collective volume became, until she had disappeared from sight, and one lonely voice, one voice out of the multitude that had been rejoicing, could be heard. It was a Benedictine monk, and he sang these words, then his voice, too, fell silent:

Nil sine Deo.

Then, as if expectant of me in some way, every monk in the courtyard turned to look at me, not accusingly or inquisitively, just distinctly expectant of me. I didn't know what to do. I was still in the grasp of my mania, still frozen in fear.

She's dead. She can't be here. That woman just looks like her.
That woman looks just like her.
You need more therapy. You're delusional. Get your head together, man.
I turned without a word and ran in, slamming the doors behind me.

Once inside, I saw that I was indeed come to an abbey and not a church (I guessed at the difference.) I was in a great hall of some sort, with high, arched ceilings and what seemed like Byzantine (again, I'm no expert) architecture. Tens of gigantic rectangular windows on the east wall spilled sunlight in shafts that cut through the dusty air, down onto a massive tapestry (to call it a 'rug' would be like calling the song those monks had sung not forty-five seconds ago a 'ditty') on the floor. The tapestry was the entire length and width of the great hall, with a great, seamless image embroidered into it that seemed to start at the top right corner and end at the bottom left. At the top right was a man standing alone on an island, below that was the same man facing seven lamps on the seashore, then the next 'segment' depicted a second man clothed in light, giving the first man some sort of instructions. I realized shortly that this massive floor decoration was a portrayal of the Book of Revelations from the Christian New Testament, masterfully crafted, thread by thread, in astounding detail. I became at once grossly fascinated, almost forgetting *her*. Almost.

Of course, I'd *almost* forgotten about History and Moral Philosophy, too, but not quite. It's just that I was such a mess from seeing that woman that if I had inclinations towards skipping class before, I was now intent on it for sure, if only to give myself a chance to calm down, take a day off and look around this place, see the abbey, maybe check out that forest up north.

I was definitely going to examine this tapestry. It was the most beautiful piece of art I'd seen in my whole life. It was incredible. And a perfect diversion from that upsetting vision in the courtyard.

Why was this happening to me? Was I hallucinating? Maybe I needed to schedule some more appointments with the shrink.

I knew I could get away with playing hooky. I can lie when I have to and I'm quite proud of the simple yet nearly irrefutable excuses I can make up off the top of my head. Not the most desirable quality in a human being, but it comes in handy in a pinch, like when you're postponing your higher education to stare at the floor.

—

The Protagonist of *Devine Road* Presents
How to Lie

There are really only three ways to lie, and one way not to lie. All involve strict adherence to the tenets of the eleventh commandment in order for success.

1) Tell it short and vague. If questioned, give similarly vague answers and act testy, like now is not a good time to be asking you details about the subject in question.

2) Tell the truth, but make it sound so incredulous that they'll come up with a story *for* you and leave you alone. Warning: This is difficult to accomplish.

3) Choose a recent event that is true and that the recipient of the lie is privy to and pretend that it is so monumental, so catastrophic, so incredibly upsetting to you that you just can't focus on what you're talking about. This is known as avoiding the subject altogether by way of bait-and-switch, and is only a half-lie.

Equally important to these rules is to remember that a lie never be too complex. It is also important to remember never to forget Father Luke. More on this later. If a lie is too complex, something may come tumbling out of your mouth which was totally non-essential to the fiction and may throw your entire story into the shadow of doubt. Minimize your risks.

Of course, the eleventh commandment is "Thou shalt not get caught."

—

Not that I needed to lie. After all, I was suffering from some mania here, something I'm sure Dr. Schreiber (the psychologist) wouldn't be surprised by. I've got some major PTSD, he says. It's a good thing I got out of the Army when I did, he says.

He would help me explain it to whoever was asking if I decided to skip a few classes.

Ah, self-justification. You vicious enemy of humanity.

As I stood in awe of that great work, that beautiful tapestry, a short priest with short dark hair named Father Luke walked out of a door on the east side of the room and breathed labouredly as I walked all over the room, examining and reveling in each separate section of the tapestry. When I finally noticed him, he walked over to me lazily, though deliberately, with some speed that belayed his relaxed posture and the most obscene, offensive, ridiculous crocodile smile hanging lopsidedly on his face that you could ever *hope* to formulate in your imagination.

That smile is a smile I would see many times in my life and a smile that would never cease to amaze me. It was brilliant and ostentatious and crude and refined and a million other adjectives all at once (including confusing.) If it made a sound, it would sound like pants unzipping.

He had dark eyes and a huge mustache and managed to look proud and noble even with that crazy grin, even despite that massive, gaudy hood ornament on his face that was so cheap and tawdry I couldn't have bartered it for a *Keep on Trucking* tattoo.

At length he spoke, and betrayed his absurdity with a hard voice so rough and gravelly you could have shoveled it. "If the *monsieur* has not already realized, each segment is done in a different art style, either emulating a period or a great master." He was French. *Really* French.

I had noticed the differences in art styles, but I pretended I hadn't, so that he would tell me about them. He seemed to appreciate that as he cleared his throat and loosened his little white collar, which served to ease his breathing and soften his voice somewhat.

"For instance, in this particular segment," he pointed to a small patch on the tapestry to show me where to look, "the Enemy, depicted as a dragon with multiple heads and crowns on each of them, is done in a style reminiscent of the Surrealist Dali. Over here, the congress of the one hundred and forty four thousand anointed is made to resemble Pre-Raphaelite portraiture. Shall I go on?"

I nodded in the assent and he explained every event in Revelations and the corresponding emulation used in the tapestry. It was incredible.

"Who did this, Father? I mean, who made this? It's incredible!"

"Ah, you have my gratitude for your kind compliment." Replied the priest, and he had a surprised look in his eyes. "I have spent the last thirty years of my life weaving it myself. A labor of love, like this abbey."

"You built the abbey?"

"No, of course not." He laughed condescendingly. "But did you know that on the back of every brick that went in to the construction of this place are the letters YHVH? That is the old Hebrew name for God, and though it is impossible to see, since the embedding is on the back side of each brick, those who built this abbey felt it fitting to dedicate the abbey in such a way to the Man. Jehovah." His eyes flashed for a moment, like blue electricity cavorting carelessly through stripped copper wires.

"The Man?" I asked.

"Nothing. It is nothing." He said abruptly.

"Okay." I changed the subject back to the art. "You did this tapestry all by yourself?"

"Indeed."

"I don't know what to say. It's incredible."

The priest folded up his horrible alligator and put it in his magic bag of smiles, produced a Bel Air smile and positioned it on his face. It reminded me of a mustard stain on a Hawaiian shirt. "Ah, now you're being redundant." he said softly.

I smiled coyly. "So, is there a Persian flaw?"

Father Luke laughed/snorted, suddenly misplaced the smile and didn't bother looking for it. He had plenty. "A Persian flaw? I daresay not! *That* was an overtly arrogant device implemented in Iranian tapestry because nothing, they said, could be perfect but God. Which implied that they were capable of perfection but deferred out of respect, not inability. There are times when the hubris of mankind astounds me."

I tried to hide a smile of my own as he cleared his throat. "So, is my little distraction the reason you are nearly two hours late for your class?"

I looked at him and on his lips now was a Fatherly smile. Uh-oh. I was in trouble. He knew. And now I was in trouble.

Lie? Gonna have to.

Wait a damned minute. Lie? To a priest? *You*, dear Protagonist, are a godless savage, nay, an uncultured *slut*. Tell the truth.

"Well…" I started sheepishly. "That, and the monks outside, and the twins in the farmhouse, and the woman in the white dress and the man in the leather coat, I suppose."

"A man in a brown leather coat?" he asked.

"Uh, yes."

His eyebrows furrowed. "Man. Not men?"

"Right. Just one."

"Thank you."

"For what?" I asked. The priest did not reply, only looked in a sort of half wistful manner out the window.

I inhaled. "Okay, you're welcome. Uh…I don't suppose you would happen to be my instructor, then?"

"*Moi? Non, non*. Your instructor is in his classroom, and has actually been waiting for you to arrive before starting class."

I slapped my forehead. "Oh, no. You've got to be kidding me. I held up the whole class?"

"Indeed. And I'm sure if he knew I was keeping you held up here with my idle chatter he would be even less happy than he's sure to be. So go down that stairway…" he pointed and I took note, "…take a right and then enter the second door on the left. He is waiting."

"Oh, man." I groaned. "Maybe I should just skip class. I know I'd be upset if I had to hold up a class two hours for one student."

"He will *not* be upset if you have a good excuse. Tell him that I waylaid you and prattled on about this ridiculous blanket and that you lost track of time. If you say it that way, it's not lying. I did talk to you about my tapestry, and you have at some point today lost track of time."

"Wow, Father, thanks. Uh, I'll be back up to talk to you again when class is over."

"Are you sure?" he replied.

"I promise." I said, though I shouldn't have. More on this later.

"Well, feel free, when class is over. In the meantime, get moving." he said.

I actually broke out in a run, following Father Luke's directions, down the stairs, to the right and second door on the left. When I opened the door (a little too fast; I was in a hurry) I was hit by yet another surprise: I was the only student in the class.

Now, it's possible that you may have thought of this already, may have guessed that I was the only student in this class. A reasonable assumption. This *is* fiction. But *you* have the advantage of objectivity. You bought this book (or are standing reading it) in the fiction section of your local bookstore, possibly even in the fantasy area, if that is where this book has been relegated to, sandwiched between two paperbacks by authors named Anderson and Chidester with heroes sporting Olympic bodies and giant swords alongside scantily-clad women fighting dragons with "magic" (whatever the hell that means to fantasy authors) on the cover. You can swallow silly notions like the protagonist of the story being the only person in a community college class, because you have the advantage of being able to suspend your disbelief in order to enjoy fiction *qua* fiction.

Couple that objectivity with the fact that people really don't get to feeling like they're anything special after they wake up one morning around the age of ten and realize that the world, contrary to what they believed when they went to bed the night before, does not revolve around them. At any rate, I certainly wouldn't imagine that an instructor would sacrifice two hours on a Monday (and much less entertain the idea that someone would pay him!) to have a class with me and only me. Ridiculous. Preposterous. I'm just *me*. Nothing special.

The room was small, with fifteen desks in three rows of five and a large green chalkboard on the back wall. There were no windows, busts of Whitman, Emerson and Thoreau on pedestals lined up against the east wall and there was a roaring fireplace on the west. At the head of the room was a small wooden table and placed on top of it were a bronze globe, a cup of pencils, a shiny red apple and my instructor, a smallish dark-haired fellow with a brown sports jacket covering a black button-down tucked formally into his dark khaki dungarees. He had a retroussé nose, a jutting chin, crow's feet around his eyes, liver spots on his hands and a bright gold band on his wedding finger. He was perhaps fifty, with salt-and-pepper hair and a thin black mustache. I would have liked him just from his appearance if the scowl on his jowls didn't make me feel like a puppy who just shit on the carpet.

I closed the door behind me and was formulating an apology when he looked me solemnly in the eyes and said, with a deep Corn Belt accent, "Don't apologize."

So I didn't. He looked me over head to toe and wrinkled his face in a manner that didn't remind me so much of disgust as much as it reminded me of mild distaste mixed with disappointment. Like the first time your uncle caught you smoking his cigarettes out behind the garage. The look faded, and he spoke again. "What's your name?"

I told him, and received a second look identical to the first. Then he told me to pick a desk and get comfortable.

I did, and thus began the greatest experience that I had ever had.

I sat in amazement as my teacher opened, in that rusty saw accent of his, with a discourse on morality, on cultural mores, on childhood canalization. He examined in detail a great many philosophies, from utilitarianism to absolutism to Western society's sexual ethics and burned them all at the stake. Despite his scornful countenance, none of my questions were subjected to disgusted looks or superior snorts no matter how silly I felt asking them. My inquiries were met with patience and understanding, with hard facts where he could provide them and pure logic where he could not. When I was ready to move on, we did so.

He put great men of history on trial and questioned their stories, their motives, their outlooks, their accomplishments. He scrutinized Hammurabi, Christ, Napoleon and Mao. He interrogated the legacies of Julius Caesar, Abu Bakr, Genghis Temujin Khan and Alexander the Great. He subjected Keats, Tennyson, Eliot and Dante to stress tests; Gustave Dore and Michelangelo's artistic capabilities were under the hot light. Mozart may or may not have been as great as he was. Was Freud a fraud? Should Plato even be remembered? Was he ever more than a vessel for the words of Socrates?

I still don't know how long I sat in that room; it had no windows, so the sun was no compass for the hours spent. It felt like it could have been three months that I sat and listened to him talk. It felt like it could have been my whole three and a half years of high school.

He discussed military theory for a time; this I was able to interject on. I'd learned enough in the Army and he seemed pleased that I had spent time in the service of my country, so we had talked about it. I told him that I'd served in the Middle East, fighting a war I didn't believe in but was nonetheless forced to fight, told him I had to take lives of people whose lives I didn't feel justified taking away. I did not tell him about her.

He explained to me some reasons that war exists, what makes it tick, why it makes us tick. I understood his words, but could not agree. I will never fight again. I will never be a soldier again. Not after two tours in Mosul.

We continued on and I learned more about history, moral philosophy, economics, religion, astronomy, literature, culture, sociology, art, music, psychology and a dozen other subjects in this one session than I could have hoped to learn in years of academia.

I didn't take a single note; he didn't ask me to. He sat at the head of the class and invested in me the soil of knowledge, fertilized it with understanding and perception and then sowed the seeds of wisdom. When he had finished speaking, it did not compute with me for nearly two minutes. I was still in shock. His words had transformed me in a way I did not think it was possible to be transformed. I was smarter, or at least better informed, but this was not his gift to me. I felt as if my entire mode of consciousness had altered, sitting in that room. I felt like a blind man that could suddenly see. Like a layman that could suddenly *think*. It seemed like I had never been able to think before and that my instructor had taught me to *think*.

"Did you hear me, son?" He spoke again, cutting the silence and staring at me intently. His voice was at once as down-home as Southern-fried collared greens and as polished as a Broadway actor. He chewed on his words lazily, but there was a high end to his cant that wore a sense of refinement like a veil. If his accent could have been photographed, it would have looked like a New England bourgeoisie snoozing in a star-spangled hammock strung between two willows on a humid Mississippi evening. "Yours, now, if you want it." He continued. "Your own perspective, yours for the taking. Not anyone else's. Not defined through what you've lived through, certainly not defined through the occupation of soldier or sailor, or through the philosophies of violence.

"I have showed you the door to your cell, albeit the door that leads to a new, limited freedom in a new, slightly larger cell, but you are growing now. I have shown you that you are wearing fleece that is over your eyes but underneath your blindfold, and have positioned within your reach a knife with which you can slay your stagnation, if you would do it.

"I can not push you out of your box, son. I only hope you will leave of your own accord. But know this: If you do leave your box, you will want immediately to know how to get out of the brand new, wide and wonderful box you've stepped into and how to get to the next size. You can not. It will take time and effort and love and life and experience and an obsessive honing of the Eight Great Virtues of the Perfect Man. *I* will give nothing to you but the assurance that there is a door to your next cell and that you are capable of finding it. And though you will never see me again, on the eve of every one of your discoveries of every one of the keys to every one of your new, larger cells, you will think of me. That is, until the last time, when there are no more boxes and no more cells and no more blindfolds. You will be free forever."

His eyes suddenly seemed to be able to perceive my soul. "Do you want to take that step, son?"

I nodded, unable to say anything.

"I thought so. Listen carefully. Tomorrow, you will throw every moral, every belief, every ethic and code of conduct you ever held dear and throw it out the window. You will then salvage what was actually good, you will throw out the other ninety-nine percent and you will tend your own garden from that day forward. You will be your own man, your own identity, not 'the sum of your experiences' or the product of childhood conditioning or just another proprietor of superfluous and deadly societal prejudice. You will be *you*. You!

"Then, one day long from today, something strange will happen. You'll wake up and life will suddenly be as soft sunshine on your face, as a cold glass of water on a hot day, as a warm blanket on a winter's night. Like lasagna after a hard day at work. Catching a fly ball at a Sunday afternoon baseball game. Breasts as pillows. Sand between your toes. Nothing profound, nothing powerful, nothing suddenly life-altering. You will simply perceive in life an effortless majesty that you never understood before, because you'll understand that happiness was a prison, an insidious prison, a merciless opiate that you were dying without. You'll understand on *that* day that you are no longer dying without it because *you don't need it anymore*. You, my young friend, will have fulfillment instead. Ah, fulfillment! The only thing that can replace that insatiable and self-destructive human desire for happiness and not send a man spiraling into remission or suicidal tendencies. That is what you will possess, and you will never be able to be held down by anything or anyone so long as you live.

"That is when you will hold the key to the door that leads out of your current prison, and that is when you will be equipped to pursue your own perfection at last. That is when you will be given a blank moral canvas on which to inscribe that which is so powerfully relevant and offset at last that which has poisoned you for far too long."

I sat there for a long time and said nothing. At length, he smiled a half-smile and turned around and wrote three words on the chalkboard:

Nil Sine Veritas.

"Class dismissed." He declared. "You've just received a "C+" for the quarter. Feel free to skip Mondays from now on, because I won't be here. If you come anyway, Father Luke will probably enjoy the company." I stood up and thanked him, upon which he assured me that the pleasure was all his. I left in a state I can only describe as euphoric bewilderment.

The Wandering Bedouin
Chapter 2

I walked back up the stairs to the tapestry, called for Father Luke but received no reply. So, with a shrug, I walked out in to the courtyard for a cigarette and saw that the monks were gone. In fact, the grass looked freshly manicured, not a thing like hundreds of feet had been trampling it hours ago.

Yet another puzzling event in an altogether puzzling day.

Then again, maybe it wasn't hours ago. Maybe I'd really been in that classroom for three months. Hmmm. Oh, come on. Don't be stupid.

"Could you please step away from the abbey?"

I looked around for the owner of the voice but could not see him. "Please, sir. For your own safety." said the voice again. I noticed this time that the voice was distorted and very quiet, as if spoken through a phone, so I began looking for some kind of portable radio or walkie-talkie. I did not find it.

"Sir, please do not be difficult. I am trying an experiment."

"Can you hear me?" I replied.

"Yes I can," shot back the voice, which sounded dusty and ancient and like it was growing impatient. "Please look up."

I did, and saw a rope tied to the steeple of the abbey. Not just any rope, but a rope as thick as I am three times over, and which stretched high into the sky and far up the Mountain, disappearing into the fog. It was miles long, and I could not guess where it stopped. "What are you doing?" I asked.

"Trying to lift the abbey. Do be a sport and get the fuck out of the courtyard."

———

When I had traveled about five hundred feet the fuck out of the courtyard, I turned and waited for the "experiment" to happen. At the very least, my curiosity was piqued. The rope, which had little slack to begin with, pulled taut, and I suddenly realized that the whole contraption was a giant pulley.

Sure enough, that entire building lifted off of the ground, about six inches high.

"Archimedes is at it again." came a deep, rich voice from behind me.

I spun and saw a Semite, dressed head (high above me) to toe in brown robes and brandishing a large shepherd's crook, looking down on me with a single eyebrow arched high above his left eye. He sported a grey tonsure and a heavy white beard with a trimmed separation from a Satyric tuft that hovered over a jaw as big as one of the pews in my parents' church. He looked fit for an older guy, his arms were sinewy and his shoulders were broad and wide, like mine, though his torso seemed skinnier and disproportionate in areas. Around his neck was an austere necklace of hemp and wool braided around several multi-colored agates. His skin was brown like tree bark, and he had dark, dark eyes that reminded me of something I could not place. His face was not the age that his hair seemed to suggest. He looked like a robust sixty-year old man, but the corners of his lips looked like a child's and he had the eyes of a…I wasn't sure. I just wasn't sure.

I'd met many men in Mosul that looked like him, but none that looked like him, if you understand me. This gentleman looked more like an African than a classic Arab, I suppose, though it honestly was quite hard to tell sometimes.

"Hi." I said.

"Hello." he countered.

"Who are you?" I asked.

"I am the Wandering Bedouin." A smile slid across his face like a black snake over a flooded Tigris and he put his hand on his heart and bowed a fraction of an inch. I returned the bow (clumsily, I think) and told him my name, but he acted as though he knew it already.

"We are glad you are here, new brother." he said evenly.

"Who is 'we'?" I asked.

"Us."

"Uh. I guess that's probably the best answer I'm going to get, huh?"

"You guess correctly."

"Why the mystery?" I asked.

"Why not?" came the reply.

"Good point. So, uh, why is 'Archimedes' trying to lift the abbey?"

"You ask a lot of questions." The Wandering Bedouin smiled again.

"I'm sorry."

"No, no. Don't apologize. I am loath to refuse inquest. It is good for both the bearer of the inquiry and the answer."

I stopped and looked at the abbey, then the rope that was holding it up. The Wandering Bedouin began again. "Archimedes said once that if he had a pulley long enough and a place to stand, he could move the whole world.

"Archimedes said that about a lever."

"I beg your pardon. A lever, of course. He amended it later, after Mr. O'Malley introduced him to the pulley."

"What are you talking about?" I asked.

"I beg your pardon." The Bedouin cleared his throat and looked amused. "Now, what he said about the lever, that was when he thought the world was flat, but we can forgive him for his mistake, as no one really knew any better until many years after his death…"

"He's dead?" I asked, and I thought of the woman in the white dress.

The Wandering Bedouin put up his hand. "I said nothing of the sort. Please let me continue."

I did, and he did.

"Anyway, this is yet another of his many practice runs. The pulley goes all the way to the top of the Mountain, and he is nearly at ground level on the other side, pulling. It is quite impressive for a man of his slight stature."

"Indeed. Tell me. How is Archimedes pulling that?"

"With his hands and arms and back."

"So I surmised, sir. But Archimedes was stabbed for mouthing off to a Roman soldier millennia ago."

"You must be new here."

I didn't know what to say to *that*, and he didn't say anything else. After the day I had had and the encounter with the woman in the white dress, I was ready to believe that dead people did indeed live on this Mountain (though my companion said nothing of the sort) and did strange, incredible things like erecting miles-long pulleys and lifting whole abbeys out of their foundations. We stood there in silence for a while. Then the Wandering Bedouin looked at me with a twinkle in his eye.

"Four to one he drops it in the next fifteen seconds."

I laughed. "No bet. You sound like you've got insider information. How about a friendly wager with no money?"

The Wandering Bedouin's face suddenly became serious. "If you want to bet that Archimedes will not drop his abbey in the next fifteen, I will take you back to my camp, make you stew and tell you all about this Mountain. I perceive that is something you would think very much of."

"You're on! What happens if I lose?"

"I take you back to my camp and make you a cup of stew and then tell you all about this place later."

"Uh, deal."

"Start timing." he said, and fixed his eyes on the abbey.

I watched my watch until the rope slackened, the great building fell with an incredibly loud crash that shook the earth and shot dust and debris flying into the air in every direction. The Bedouin smiled *en rapport*. Archimedes had dropped his abbey after fourteen and a half seconds.

"Stew, my new brother?"

———

I spent the next hour and half trying to pry answers about this mysterious Mountain and the area surrounding Devine Road from this strange shepherd, but received only cryptically relevant verses from the Qu'ran and lectures on the raising of sheep. And an herbal, peppery stew with subtle vegetable and mushroom flavors and beef so tough I thought I was going to need a serrated anus to pass it out.

In other words, I got from him food and a refusal to elucidate under any conditions. A bet, after all, is a bet.

(His sheep, by the way, numbered nearly seventy-five and stank like nothing I've ever smelt. My respect for this man's profession doubled the minute I met his flock.)

After the sun was setting and the Bedouin had built a campfire at the foot of the western reach of the woods and we had had our fill of the stew, which, for all of the toughness of the beef was surprisingly delicious (I had three bowls,) I lost complete track of time. Our conversation steered away from Devine Road and into other areas, science and philosophy and especially ethics, which he seemed very interested in and where I found him quite a bit more knowledgeable than I would have expected from a pastoral wanderer. Call it prejudice, one of those things I would have to throw out the window tomorrow.

Eventually, our conversation wound back around to the day I had had. I explained everything to him in detail, starting from Archimedes' experiment and advancing in reverse chronological order. The abbey, the class, the tapestry, the woman...I omitted only my near-panic attack. He had smiled broadly and asked if I thought she was beautiful. I had to answer in the affirmative, though I could not tell him that I had seen her face in my nightmares every evening for the last three years.

He looked at me, then, like he knew about her. Like he knew who she was, and how I knew her, and what she had done to me, and I to her. In an embarrassed sort of way he changed the line of conversation quickly, as though he'd suddenly remembered not to broach the previous subject with me. I continued on to the monks, and the Twins of Subtle Oriental Countenance, and then the man in the brown leather coat. He stopped me and got a very concerned look on his face as soon as I mentioned that.

"How many men were there?" he asked. His eyebrows erected a pyramid over the bridge of his nose.

"Uh, I only saw one," I replied, "but I would concede to having missed others. Why is everyone so concerned about men in leather coats? You're obviously not vegans; I saw the beef in that stew. I mean, what's your deal with leather? I have a leather jacket at home."

The Wandering Bedouin looked at me with the same worried look on his face. "Who is 'everyone?'" he asked.

"Uh, you and Father Luke and the twins in the farmhouse all seemed quite perturbed by this dude. Is he a murderer or something?"

"They. They are murderers and liars and cheats and deceivers and tempters and evil, evil creatures. I would not even call them men if they did not display all the outward characteristics. Tell me. You did not make eye contact with him, correct?"

"Incorrect. I looked him right in the eye and ran at him balls to the wall. He shook in his boots for about half a second and took off running."

"Interesting. You tell the truth?"

"Of course. Why would I lie?"

"Interesting." The Bedouin said again, and stroked his chin.

"Say, where is Devine Road from here?" I said, trying to change the subject (yet again.) "I'm still trying to get my bearings as to where we are."

"Ah. Well, this…" he pointed at the woods, "is Teutoberg Forest. Devine Road is west about…three miles from here. I think. I am remiss if I am wrong, but I must convert kilometers to miles for you and it has been many years." He pointed, but I could not see, because our only light was the fire and the stars; it was a new moon. "The farmhouse is southeast, probably a mile or so south of the forest. Twelve miles to the west is a high stone wall; I am sure you have seen it…"

"I have. There's one on the other side, too."

"Yes, they are about thirty miles apart. For now." he said, and smiled wryly to himself.

"For now?"

"'Later.'"

"Come on. Just tell me."

"Allah knoweth the disclosed and that which still is hidden; and we shall ease thy way unto the state of ease." he quoted.

"Ease away." I said. "Are the walls getting moved?"

"Later." he said.

"Okay, so where are we right now?" I asked.

"Why, the Ager Epiphania. At the foot of Teutoberg Woods, in the shadow of the Joyful Plateau. The plateau on the other side of Devine Road, across that little canyon that takes the Road up, you know what I am saying to you?"

I nodded.

"That is the Woeful Plateau."

"What makes that one Woeful and this one Joyful?"

"Later." He said without a hint of impatience. "I go to the Joyful Plateau every so often to graze my sheep, and then move on, either farther up the Mountain or around to the other side." He paused, as if thinking. "So…you *did* make eye contact with the man in the leather coat?"

"Yes."

"And he ran?"

"Yes."

The Bedouin stopped and tucked his knees up to his chin and did not speak for about three minutes. I did not interrupt him, only sat quietly until he spoke again, to himself.

"Perhaps you look more like him to them."

I was trying as hard as I could to suppress the desire to ask what he was talking about (I was sure I'd just get another verse from the Qu'ran) when a bird call came from the hills behind us and the Bedouin spun his head around like he'd somehow zeroed in precisely on the location of the sound, even in the limited light of dusk. "Say nothing, brother." he whispered. I obeyed. He picked up his shepherd crook in both hands as if it were a martial staff and crept silently away from the fire. I sat there, trying not to breathe, when I heard suddenly the cry of a great panther and the terrified cry of a lamb.

Then, a bevy of words in Latin and a scuffle. I heard shouting and more growling, another feline scream and the Bedouin's gruff voice crying out as if in pain. I rose to my feet and ran towards the sound, as fast as I could, but I didn't get there in time. The Bedouin was halfway back to camp. He had a lamb draped around his shoulders, which was crying softly, and the front of

45

his garments was soaked in blood.

"My God!" I whispered as quietly as I could, which was not terribly quiet, given my surprise. "What happened? Is that *your* blood?"

"Some of it, yes." he replied softly. "We no longer have to whisper."

I was panicking. Was he wounded? Could I help him? What could I do? Is whatever hurt him still out there? Should I go break its legs? Or try?

The Bedouin was remaining calm and, I think, wishing I would do the same.

We returned to the camp and he laid the lamb by the fire. I saw that the poor thing had a long cut from its sternum to the bottom of its abdomen, and four long slashes that spanned from one side of its ribcage to the other. Around the four horizontal strokes was a large, perfectly circular cut. Over its brow was another long, precise slash, and there was blood in its eyes. But those marks weren't from a predator cat.

Christ, did someone try to sacrifice the Bedouin's lamb?

The lamb was crying. Bleating in a very high, mournful tone. It broke my heart.

The Bedouin disappeared into his bivouac and returned with a spool of thread, a bowl of water and a needle. From his pouch he produced a leather flask, showed it to me as though I could identify it, and poured a single drop into the bowl of water. The liquid turned gold, the scent was that of the most mysterious Somalian frankincense and it had a retronasal undercurrent of sweet Arabian myrrh.

The Bedouin gave the lamb the bowl to drink, and when it had, it too seemed to calm. After a few tense moments, it stopped crying and lay patiently there while the Bedouin sewed its wounds together.

I exhaled loudly, noticing for the first time that I had been holding my breath.

When the surgery was finally through, the lamb looked at the Bedouin and the man smiled at it, and then it fell asleep. The Wandering Bedouin wrapped it in a blanket and set it by the fire, then stripped himself of his garments. He was bleeding from two stab wounds in both of his shoulders. He unscrewed the top of his flask and, instead of diluting the elixir, took a full drink off of the canteen mouth and threaded a new needle. He reached into the wounds with his fingers, produced two small shreds of what looked like wrought iron from each one, and laid them by the fire. Shrapnel. Like my left hand.

He then stitched his own wounds wearing nothing but the fiercest grimace I have ever seen adorn a man's face.

—

I once met a veteran of the Vietnam War, one night when I was seventeen, before I signed up for that war, before my time in Iraq. This man was homeless, ragged, he smelled of rancid hamburgers and he was nursing a 22 ounce bottle of Schlitz Malt Liquor. I had walked up to offer him a dollar and some change that I had had in my pocket, because it was a cold night and I felt bad for him as soon as I laid eyes on him. I have a soft spot for veterans, being one myself, and I had one then, being the son of a Vietnam veteran.

Vietnam or Iraq, no one should have to go to war. No one should ever experience that.

The homeless man had a cardboard sign that read 'Homeless Vietnam Vet Running for President: Contributions Accepted Here." It looked like he had just scrounged up enough to get a drink, so I offered him the handout, but he had just looked at me and said, "Thanks, no. I got what I need for today."

I'd said, "Okay, stick it in your pocket and put it towards what you need for tomorrow."

"Nope." he said. "I'll make tomorrow's wages when tomorrow happens."

"All right, man." I'd said, not really pausing to consider his words. "You stay warm tonight."

"God bless." He'd said, and taken a pull off of his dinner.

That's what I saw in the Wandering Bedouin's eyes when I met him. Someone who had seen too much tragedy, too much horror, too much pain and suffering for two eyes to see. Someone whose life was being held together by Scotch tape and prayers. Someone on the verge. And yet, here was someone who refused to let others do anything for him. Here was independence, freedom, idealism. Here was someone who refused the free lunch because they knew that, well…There ain't no such thing as a free lunch. I felt very close to him very suddenly. Here was a man like that homeless vet. Here was a man in many ways like myself.

—

"What happened?" I asked him. I was (justifiably) concerned.

"Nothing on this Mountain is just what it appears to be, brother. Of course, everything is what it is, but it is also so much more."

"Is that more mystery for me?"

47

"The men in leather coats are much more than they appear to be. So are the sheep in my flock. And so am I. And so are you."

"The wounds on that lamb weren't made by another animal. They were made with a knife."

"No. That is something I must leave until 'later'." He was clearly tiring.

"Will your lamb be okay?" I asked.

"*Inshallah*. God willing." He yawned. "Can I make you a place to sleep, my new brother?" he asked, and he was smiling again, but he looked much, much older now, as if the stress of the night was just starting to take its toll. His face was sagging beneath his jaw, his shoulders were slumped forward. There were deep circles beneath his eyes.

"Nah, I should really get home." I replied, and cast my eyes downward. I'm not sure why I said that, not sure why I felt that way. I *did* want to stay.

"I should really insist that you not leave the camp." said the Bedouin cheerlessly. "It is late, and this Mountain is dangerous at night, as you doubtlessly have surmised. In camp, I can guarantee your safety."

I thought about this while he waited patiently. "Okay, I'll stay." I decided. "I didn't get to go camping last summer anyway."

The Wandering Bedouin smiled (reflexively, I think) and disappeared into his bivouac, then reemerged with an armful of sheepskin. "Tonight, we will sleep under the stars."

There is no mattress in the world that can compare to the warm, incredible softness of six sheepskins stacked beneath you with three for a blanket and three for a pillow. It's great. The Bedouin and I stayed up for at least another few hours after bedding down. I didn't bring up anything regarding his lamb or Devine Road or the man in the brown leather coat, I just talked, mostly. Talked about myself, not as much because I wanted to but because the Bedouin seemed so interested. He asked question after question after question. Eventually, the topic of conversation slipped into my military service, as any inquest into my history, given enough time, will inevitably do. I told him about my three years of service in the Army, serving in the city of Mosul in Iraq. I was tempted to tell him about *her* because already felt like I could trust him, because I thought he'd understand. But I didn't say a word about it. I couldn't.

"Why did you leave the war early?" he had asked me.

"I was wounded in an explosion." I had half-lied. The injury to my hand was serious enough to have gotten me sent home, but it was *her* that got me locked, loaded and packing to the States with an honorable discharge in my right hand and a tremor in my left.

"Hmmm." he said, and looked at me very seriously. "Perhaps that is something you wish to leave until 'later.'"

I replied in the affirmative, and he smiled a fatherly smile at me. "We should get some sleep." he said.

"I agree."

I slept dreamlessly until I was jolted out of sleep by a sound worse than an alarm clock. A muffled *boom*! Like the sound of artillery fire. I found myself surrounded in faint morning light.

"Archimedes should really get some sleep." said the Wandering Bedouin. He was already up and tending a morning fire.

"I agree. I fully agree. What time is it?" I yawned and rubbed crust from my eye.

"The sun is not yet in the sky, but its fingers are reaching around the Mountain, slowly. What time is your algebra class today?" he asked me. I did not remember mentioning today's algebra class to him.

"Uh…noon."

"It would be good for you to sleep, then. I will wake you when the sun is higher in the sky."

"Uh, that's okay. I have an alarm on my watch. You just go ahead and do what you were going to do today and I'll wake up and walk the rest of the way at seven o'clock. It's not too far back to the college."

"It is a long way back to your car. And I am hesitant to leave you before dawn, but if you ask that I do so, I will. Tell me, you do not want to go back to your residence and bathe and eat before your class?"

"Nah. I'll do that after Algebra. Before Sociology."

"I see. Sleep well, brother."

"I will." I replied, and fell back asleep. I could not see, being in the arms of slumber, but the Bedouin was smiling gently.

———

I am standing on a street corner, watching children running, people bustling, cars honking, a woman gliding. Gliding towards me.

She is beautiful, the most beautiful woman I've ever seen, and a desert rose if ever there was one. Long, dark hair, long, beautiful legs. She wears a white, bulky jacket, one of those big, poofed-out snow coats and a white ankle-length skirt. Odd dress for this climate, I think, and it sets off an alarm in my head. I train my sight on her.

Children laugh, children play. There is a preschool across the street.

Outside of the preschool is a dark, heavy man fidgeting uncomfortably, his eyes darting from side to side, his weight shifting from foot to foot. What is he waiting for? He starts walking towards the woman. I hear an American voice, the voice of Cpl. Daniel Bank, a guy from my old squad, back when my MOS was telecom, like his. Back when I used to guard the radio tower, like he was doing now. Before I made sergeant and went infantry and got stuck with patrolling the streets.

Banks is walking toward the man. I pull my rifle tight against my shoulder, hold it upright, not pointing, just keeping it ready. I keep my eye on him. His eyes flicker over Banks' shoulder.

The woman is now running toward the radio tower. The man is now running away from the radio tower. The children are screaming, people are fleeing the scene, though nothing has yet happened. I try to yell for Banks. He is pulling up his rifle, aiming for the man.

But it's the woman. It's the woman, and everything is suddenly in slow motion.

The woman is running towards the radio tower.

We didn't even see her coming.

The radio tower's shadow eclipses the preschool.

A three-round burst from Banks' rifle rips into the fleeing man's back.

The woman is in my crosshairs.

There is blood in the street.

The preschool is in session.

Banks turns and realizes. He knows, now, too.

It's the woman.

The woman is running towards the radio tower.

The radio tower is right next to the preschool.

My finger tenses on the trigger.

Her eyes lock with mine.

———

I woke breathless and covered in cold sweat to the incessant *bleep bleep bleep* emanating from my watch. I looked around, checked my surroundings, looked for any sign that I might be in Mosul.

I didn't find a single one, because I wasn't there.

Goddamned nightmares.

I stretched, and then surveyed my campsite. The sun hurt my eyes.

The Wandering Bedouin was gone, his whole flock was gone with him, the fire was out and the bivouac was torn down. On a large rock near last night's fire pit were several pieces of unleavened bread and a large bowl of water. I stood up and suddenly realized that the Wandering Bedouin had dug a circle of some kind around me, with all sorts of strange Arabic (?) symbols and a few symbols I recognized as alchemist's letters written in the dust. What was this?

I'm not religious, not superstitious, not worried about things that go bump in the night. But my heart suddenly filled with a boundless gratitude for this man whom I had just met, who would take a half of an hour or more and all of the trouble to carve this intricate protective ward in the ground to dissuade his notion of evil from harming me. Then I recalled his name for me: "New Brother." I went through the same motions that I did in my first moments in History and Moral Philosophy Class. What makes me so special? What do I matter? Me? I'm just *me*. Ridiculous. Preposterous. Etc.

Then I wondered why an Arab, quoting the Qu'ran not twelve hours ago, would do such a thing. A Muslim would *never* draw symbols or magic circles around me like that; it's forbidden by his religion. Was he not a Slave of God, then, but merely an admirer of the Prophet's words? Not too hard to imagine, I suppose. He did describe himself as a Bedouin, and the Bedouins do predate Islam. I wondered what his religion(s?) was (were?) as I scratched myself and returned my pieces of clothing to their correct locations.

When I stepped out of the "magic" circle, it immediately began to rain very hard, though I could have sworn to myself it was brilliantly sunny when I woke. The clouds swamped the sky; armored marshmallows served me a double tall drink of water, straight up.

A flash flood? Or had I not noticed a storm moving in? There was starlight just before dawn, so I know that it was clear not too long ago. How strange!

I walked to the rock where the Wandering Bedouin had left my breakfast. Beneath the bowl of stew he had left was a scrap of parchment, like vellum. On it, in a flowing, beautiful script was written:

"Mankind:"

As promised, I will tell you more about this wonderful Mountain you have found...later. Perhaps a fortnight from today I will be able to bring my flock around and we will again have conversation and stew.

When I mentioned 'We' and 'Us' in our first conversation, I was not deliberately being cryptic. 'We' are the twins, Father Luke, the monks, Archimedes, your instructor, the woman in the white dress...even the men in the leather coats. 'We' are the few privileged to be a part of the First Plateau of this Unnamed Mountain, privileged to walk (or drive, in your case) on Devine Road, on this, the most important of the Plateau's seven partitions. Privileged to be a member of this family. I am in this family. Now that you have seen Devine Road, now that you have stayed here, now that you have attended your class at the abbey, you too are part of this family. You are our brother. Our new brother. You will be able to return here alone whenever you wish, of course, but you must be alone. If you even attempt to bring someone to or tell someone about this place, the Road will be closed to you forever. I can not explain it in any fashion better than that. 'We' sincerely hope you will return to us.

If you ever visit again and would like a truly unique experience, go to the house of the Ecclesiae (that is, the twins of subtle Oriental countenance) and tell them you are hungry. You may not leave happy, but you undoubtedly will leave 'fulfilled.'

Your automobile is still safe at their farmhouse. I checked before I set off for the Fourth Partition. Incidentally, one of the twins noticed that you had a taillight out, so they replaced it for you. Be sure to thank them by sounding the signal horn on your automobile as you pull out of their driveway. That is all they need.

If you see more men in leather coats, do not make eye contact. You are our brother, meaning you possess much power and much strength that you do not know about yet. But until you understand that, you can only rely on your karma to prevent harm from befalling you. Karma is at best as useful as luck, which is at best as useful as prayer.

"May peace be within your ramparts."

Your new brother,
The Wandering Bedouin

P.S. - Never forget Father Luke. You promised that you would go and look at his tapestry with him and then you left before he joined you. Never forget Father Luke.

I read the note three times and pondered over it. What a strange place I had found, what strange people I had met, what a strange time I had had. My head was a maelstrom of confusion, bewilderment, astonishment, elation and a dozen other emotions. But I was calm. Calm and collected. Or trying to be, anyway.

Who was the woman in the white dress?

I turned the piece of paper over in my hand absentmindedly and saw that there was more on the back. Upon further examination I saw, however, that it was not a continuation of the Bedouin's letter. It was three small words imprinted on the bottom right corner of the writing surface. It read:

Nil Sine Familia.

I resolved to learn Latin as I walked to my car. Above me, the rope in the sky pulled taut, like a border on a map of the kingdoms of cloud giants. Archimedes was giving this third effort the old college try.

When I reached the farmhouse, I saw that my taillight had indeed been fixed, which rendered me speechless with humble gratitude anew, because two weeks ago it had been completely destroyed by a vandal, glass and bulb and wiring. Here it was, good as new.

It stopped raining just then, and the sun came out from behind a cloud, as if it was smiling at me. I beamed back at it, got in my car, honked the horn for the Twins of Subtle Oriental Countenance and drove to class. They waved goodbye from the window.

The Dreamlike of Angels (Karthago Delenda Est)
Chapter 3

I am sure I know why I am driving back to Devine Road this same day, right after class, but I feel as though I shouldn't know what is pulling me back. I feel like there should be some mystery, as if that fantastic Mountain needed any more mystique. I feel like it should be some kind of psychic draw, a kind of pressure weighing on my mind, like Frodo's Ring or Ilmarinen's Sampo.

I feel like I should feel like it is the perfect place to throw out all of my old ideas, like the Professor had told me to do.

The place to find myself was there. The place to claim my perspective. To announce that among the newborn millions, I was etc. etc.

But it's just that woman in that white dress.

Strange, the things men do. As if being there, convincing myself that I was there by appointment or coincidence would somehow invest in me the courage to find her. If I could even find her. If she was even there. If I even had the testicular fortitude to look for her. Or at her, if I found her. But I had to know. I had to know if it was her.

—

I drive up and park in the wide, dusty driveway of the farmhouse. One of those twins, the Ecclesiae, looks out the window and waves at me. I wave back and think about going to the door to say "Hello," but I feel awkward. Instead, I grab another packed lunch I'd made at home, light up a Camel and make off for Teutoberg Forest. Three quarters coniferous, the other quarter dead. Autumn, after all. I chuckle to myself at the marginal amount of Zen in admiring the beauty of a season characterized by death and decay.

Hadn't I heard of Teutoberg Forest before? Maybe I heard it from the Professor. He covered a lot of material in that lecture. Ah, how typical of my species. Most important lecture anyone has ever given to me at any one instant in my life and I can't remember half of it.

A handy geographical note: From one end of this partition to the other is roughly thirty miles across. From the edge of the mist-shrouded thoroughfare that leads down the Mountain to the edge of the mist-shrouded thoroughfare that leads up the mountain (the Second Plateau, I guess) the partition is roughly eighteen miles long. The Joyful and Woeful Plateaus are exactly equidistant from both the beginning and end of Devine Road's presence on the First Plateau.

The crescent of woods, Teutoberg, is about a mile from the farmhouse, about five miles length-wise (though it encompasses nearly half of the partition width-wise and reminds me of a smile of trees) and ends on the bank of a babbling little river that I would swim in if I had extra clothes with me.

The strangest thing happened here once, where Devine Road lengthened, the walls moved far apart, the fields stretched wide and clear and the whole partition made room for a hundred thousand tiny feet. When that happened this partition was nearly five times its size. But it's back to normal now, and it was certainly normal when I was making for that forest so long, long ago.

Uh-oh. I'm getting ahead of my narrative. And Father Luke usually gets upset at me if I get ahead of my narrative.

I enter the protective shadow of Teutoberg's canopy and lumber right across the path of a deadly brown recluse as soon as I'm in. We both have the shit scared out of us and we both jump several feet in the air, in the entirely opposite direction from each other. Although this spider is apparently as afraid of humans as humans are of spiders, this spider's fear of me has got nothing on *my* fear of spiders. His is based on an evolutionarily honed drive for survival; mine is not only unreasonable and thoroughly ridiculous, it borders on hysteria. And I have no idea why.

What do angels dream of? I had taken a nap between classes this morning and I had dreamed, for some reason, that I was tiptoeing through a throng of sleeping angels, picking their pockets. So I was thinking about sleeping

55

angels. Do they dream? Do they dream of us? Do they even sleep?

Do they dream of things they've set right on Earth in the Name of God? Do they dream about work, the stresses of saving human souls? Do angels even sleep? Are their names really Hebrew?

Do they talk about each other? Is there a water cooler in Heaven?

Maybe they dream of great historical events. Maybe they dream of that fabled War.

Do angels fall in love, with each other or with humans? Do they walk among us, performing deeds of good and evil in accordance with the inscrutable Will of Heaven? Are they unperceivable by the mortal eye? Could one of my friends be an angel? My last girlfriend? My mom? Could *I* be an angel?

Hmmm…*Is* there an inscrutable Will of Heaven? Is there a Heaven? Throw that out, go back to it.

Do angels love, or just blindly carry out orders? Are they just part of a salvation army wholly at the whim of an omnipotent Father? Is there a God? Throw that out, too. Not that I ever much believed in one. Went through the motions for my parents' sake. It was a labor of love, like Father Luke's tapestry, only a lot less fruitful and much less pretty.

—

The forest is beautiful. Just like all the forests in the movies, with little pillars of light holding up the dark green ceiling and miniature tornadoes of dust and bugs swimming around in those same liquid columns of soft luminescence, like it's all in glass. The floor is covered in dense foliage, the air is thick with the sweet, syrupy smell of cedar and oak and pine sap. Especially pine sap. A cool wind blows across my face; I wish I could caress it back. Searching for some time, I at last locate a path, which makes me happy, because it gives me something to wander off of.

—

What the Hell are angels? What on earth are humans?

Why am I so preoccupied with all of this?

I don't even believe in angels. I've always been of the mind that religion is a nice hand manual for living a good life, and that worrying about what happens in the long hereafter was kind of pointless since I'd find out so soon

anyway. But that dream was vivid. Shouldn't I be working on throwing out
my values? Or something like that? Then again, should I even be approaching
it that way? Shouldn't I be taking charge of my own mind?

Maybe I already knew deep down the name of the Poisoner of my soul.
Maybe I knew exactly what to throw out.

—

You know, in Exodus, verse twenty-two eighteen, when it says "suffer not
a witch to live," the correct translation is actually "suffer not a poisoner to
live." All of that Inquisition and witch hunting and hanging and burning just
because of a scholarly mistake.

I dated a Wiccan once; she was a sweet black girl who was really, really
upset at her parents. She gave it up eventually, when she made up with her
folks and wasn't interested in pissing on their values anymore. She just
became agnostic, the logical end for those intelligent people too lazy to pick
a religion and lacking enough faith to be an atheist. She had really pretty lips,
big full ones. Kissable lips. I kind of miss her. I don't even remember why we
broke up.

—

What is the name of the Poisoner that lives in my soul? My brain takes a
deep breath and wheezes (in a liquid, flatulent sound that you would expect
from a brain) that it is surely canalization. My heart decries faith, that
indoctrination won't let me stop believing in God even when I denounce Him.
My brain logically (it *is* wont to be logical) points out there is hardly a
difference, but my heart thinks it knows better.

—

So I start going through the list of what I'm supposed to throw out as I pick
past thorny branches and variegated ferns. I start with sexual ethics, since that
is sort of on the tip of my brain, being a young man and perpetually
preoccupied with it, and being distracted, also, by the thought of that little
girlfriend of mine so long ago.

What is sex? It's how people show that they love each other.

Oh, come now, dear Protagonist. You've had sex with people whose names are lost forever to you. Names marching around somewhere with the Ninth Hispania and as far removed from you as Atlantis.

Okay, sex is what makes us human. No, because animals do it, too. Why distinguish the two?

Okay, sex feels good. And it's damn good. And it's all we think about. Because it's all we have. Man is the sole inheritor of death and taxes; we've given nothing to the natural world but humor. No mean feat, but is that all? Kissing, too, I suppose.

By God, that's quite a contribution!

But we just live, we work, and then die. Cursed by God to toil for the fruits of our labors all our long years because of Eve's mistake.

Sex is the only thing keeping us going.

But it's also what hurts us. We use it to hurt each other. Sex is as essential to the human mind as creativity, and yet we use that to hurt each other, too. Uh, oh. This is going to turn into a diatribe on how sick and fucked up humanity is. Let's try to stay focused, please.

I pick a flower and smell it. I pick a leaf and smell it. I chip some bark off a tree and smell it. I do love the smell of the forest. There is nothing that smells quite like it. If someone once said that smell is ninety percent of sex, they missed the whole picture. Smell is ninety percent of *everything*.

Or is it sex that's ninety percent of everything?

Nil Sine Familia. Nil is nothing. Sine is…I'm not sure. Familia is probably family. Nil Sine Deo. Nil Sine Veritas. Deo is God.

In Vino Veritas. "In Wine, Truth."

Nothing blank God, Nothing blank Truth, Nothing blank Family.

Without. Sine is Without.

Nothing without God, Nothing without Truth, Nothing without Family.

---

love \ luv \ *n* [**ME**, fr. OE *lufu* akin to OHG *luba* love, **OE** *lëof* dear, **L** *lubere, libere* to please] (bef. 12c) **1 a** (1) : strong affection for another, arising out of kinship or personal ties. (2): attraction based on sexual desire: affection and tenderness felt by lovers. (3): affection based on admiration.

Robert Heinlein once wrote that love is a subjective condition where another's welfare is directly essential to one's own happiness. He also wrote that it is made up of two things: Eros and Agape. According to Merriam-Webster's, his definitions are the same as (1), (2) & (3), only *Time Enough For Love* is considerably better reading than the dictionary.

An official *Devine Road* sticker and lollipop goes to Mr. Heinlein.

Wait a minute. *Ant. hate*? The antonym of love is hatred? There's a thin line between them, sure. Or so we're told. And I've heard that to truly hate someone you must love them in direct proportion. I don't think that's true. I can think of some guys from my youth that I had to share Catholic school with that I'd like to see ruined. I don't love them in the slightest bit.

But then there's her…

No. Isn't love the pursuit of another's happiness? Or at least the betterment of their welfare? And hatred is…what? The pursuit of the detriment of their welfare? Hardly. It's just a seething, festering feeling. Neurons firing.

No good. Totally bunk. Totally unacceptable. A certain professor of History and Moral Philosophy would flunk me. Hatred and love aren't antonyms.

I walk through the forest and think about her. Think about what she did to me. Did to all of us that were there that day. I think about Banks. I try to hate her. But I can't. I can not hate her. Because I saw her eyes. And in her eyes was something that no one could hate.

——

So what is the antonym of love?

Jealousy?

Jealousy, that scourge of the medulla oblongata? Jealousy, that arouser of ire, that perpetrator of crimes of passion? Jealousy, that wedge that drives so many good people apart?

Why do we have room in our hearts to love endless friends but only one lover?

If a man has faith that his wife loves him and desires him and yet she still keeps that old shower massage unit she had from when she was single, is he going to grow red in the face and break dishes and call for a divorce? I think not. I would certainly hope not. Being jealous of a vibrator seems quite silly.

And I'm sure it happens. Because jealousy seems to me one part possessiveness and two parts thoroughly neurotic insecurity about one's self.

Jealousy is us refusing to recognize that among many species of animals on this Earth that *are* monogamous, we are not. We are, by nature, not. Ask my ex-girlfriend, who "cheated" on me Lord *knows* how many times. Ask every friend I've ever had if they've ever "cheated" on somebody. Ask *yourself.*

Everyone understands and yet no one talks about it. There's kind of a trend there, a kind of attitude pervading our whole code of sexual morality. Everything is allowed, nothing is condoned.

If there is insecurity creeping into the makeup of the partners' views of each other, the relationship is flawed anyway. If a relationship is so uneven, unstable and insecure that a splash of semen or a splatter of vaginal juice can wash its love and integrity away, it seems to me like it was a diseased organism to begin with.

And who's to say that two is the perfect number, anyway?

——

If a guardian angel 'guards' a specific soul for decades and then gets reassigned to the front lines and has to have another angel take over the stewardship, would that first angel be jealous? Knowing all of the ins and outs and strengths and weaknesses and lies and cheats and sweets of a person sounds a lot like love to me. Do angels have a medulla oblongata?

———

Let's see, what else are we throwing out the window? Everything. Everything goes. That's it. No God, no sexual ethics, no morals, no nothing. Everything goes. Blue light special on flawed thinking. I'm throwing it all out. I'll pick it up later if it's worth a damn. Everything goes.

———

But what is the "magic" of this place if it is not of some kind of higher power?

———

I come to a large clearing, which relieves me. I light another cigarette, take a piss and pick a few blackberries growing on the east side of my "campsite".

Blackberries. These fucking things have even made it to the Mountain. They stop at nothing. Nothing. They're everywhere. White man's bamboo, they oughta call it.

Clouds roil above me, having moved in fast, and they hang wrong in the sky, wrinkled and creased in funny places. I suddenly visualize the blue sky throwing on a jacket that it has no time to iron and doesn't fit right. I smirk at the thought. When does the sky not have time to do anything it wants?

The clouds, pregnant with possibility and fat with promise, choose to leak water instead of action, tangible liquid instead of intangible force. Not that I can feel many of the raindrops, as the smidgens of pine canopy above me filter out most of the rain that would otherwise kiss my head soaking. I can just hear them coming, tapped beats on a soft, furry drum, beating out measure by measure the natural rhythm of Time. Harmonizing with the clockwork of the forest and the hills and the sky and the fields. Not one per second but several. Completely unaware of the "second" or the "minute" or the "hour." Aware only of Time, in all of its ooey gooey glory. It's infinite, immeasurable, immutable glory.

I keep walking, pulling my coat a little tighter around my shoulders. Not that I'm cold. I just expect to be. After all, it's raining, and I haven't yet learned to turn my face to the cold of the rain and love it like I love the warmth of the sunshine. Two sides of the same coin, right? And how could I appreciate sunshine to its fullest extent if I hadn't been caught in a rainstorm at least once in my life?

I walk out of the clearing and march on for some time, thinking about angels, or, rather, thinking about why I would bother thinking about angels.

Do they like the rain? Do they love it on their cheeks as much as sunshine? Does it rain in Heaven? What is Time like in Heaven? Like Time on Earth, measured only in miniature prisons called attoseconds and half hours and lunar months that don't even synch up with the lunar cycle? Or is Time different there? Inconceivable, moving all directions at once, backwards, forward, side to side? Pregnant with possibility?

According to the Professor, Time is like that here, too, on a quantum level. We just satiate our sensibilities with pocket watches and unfair, inadequate units.

I start thinking I should very much like to ask an angel quite a few things about them. Then I start contriving a scenario where I meet an angel and get only one question to ask them. What would my question be?

What would yours be?

I am not sure I can make up my mind, being torn between so many different questions. I mean, if there's an angel, there's a God. Perhaps I'd ask God's exact nature. Perhaps I'd ask the meaning of life. Then again, the angel might not know. They might know the meaning of their own life, but I harbor the suspicion that deep down *everyone* knows the meaning of their own life.

Ask about this Mountain?

Nah.

I am not sure I know what I would ask an angel.

I am not sure until I see one through the trees. A real-life angel.

Then I know exactly what to ask.

—

Bertrand Russell wrote that he's not a Christian because there were two items essential to being such: A belief in God and immortality, and some kind of belief about Christ, a belief that, at the lowest point, at least acknowledges Him as the best and wisest of men.

Bertrand Russell just couldn't stomach those things. But, then again...I could stomach the first one. I don't have enough faith to be an atheist, as it takes just as much to have no religion as to have a specific one. I think there *could* be a God. If there is one, I'd like to meet Him or Her. I bet He'd be much nicer than Old Testament Yahweh, probably smarter than Zeus or Odin or one of the Old Gods, probably more forgiving than Allah. I bet God would be an interesting Person.

But being Christian…I don't know. I just don't know if I have the stomach for all of the hypocrisy, sensationalism, intolerance, doublethinking and (God save me from your followers) *theology*. Oh, I hate that word.

So what do I believe? I guess I just assume that a higher power is really a higher power. Supreme. Incomprehensible. I don't make God in my image. When I die and if there's a Heaven, I like to think that He or She will understand completely how I came to my conclusions while living and I'll have the whole bit explained to me, then I'll get the stamp on my hand that lets me in those pearly gates.

Because if there's a God, I hope that He's the God of Love, like all the religions say. He just loves everyone. And He knows that "faith" is just about the most retarded concept humanity ever thought up.

———

She stands with her arms at her sides, her hands turned up, as if to show me that she is unarmed. That there is nothing to fear. Her eyes speak volumes. Her lips are full and beautiful; her nose is perfectly formed on her face. Her wings are outstretched to the full of their span. She wears a crown of flowers over fair, curly hair. No, make that red hair. She is definitely a redhead. She wears a long dress that clings to her in all the right places (she has no wrong places) and she kneels, placidly prostrate, staring me right in the eye with a pupil-less gaze.

A raindrop navigates a treacherous maze of crosswinds, changes in barometric pressure, layers of lower clouds, mists, fogs and then branches, needles, twigs and leaves, barreling on a fateful kamikaze flight path all the way from its cloudy cumulonimbus womb to the corner of this beautiful being's left eye. It splashes and rolls down her cheek in perfect facsimile of a tear. Another drop takes the helm of that mad trajectory and succeeds also, hitting her right eye and tumbling down her face. The angel is now weeping.

I make my way through thorns and brambles and goddamned blackberry bushes to get to her, to hold her and comfort her. I find her in full resplendence, kneeling on a Corinthian pillar, staring pleadingly from her hiding place among the ornate acanthus leaves that decorate her pedestal. Silently, she beseeches me to come and kiss her. So I do. Right on the lips.

And you know what happens?

Nothing.

She is, of course, a stone statue. But I feel like she and I have achieved something as I survey the surroundings of her wooded habitat. I am in another, larger break in the trees. To my right is half of the head of Omak. On my left, silent Easter Island statues stand sentry, guarding this beautiful angel. Then I look up and see one of the grandest and largest statues of Buddha I have ever seen. It is thirty feet tall, at least, providing the massive backdrop for this collection of ruined sculpture. *How did I not see that?* Ah, the tunnel vision of the agnostic. We see an angel, see a miracle, see faith and hope and love and yet somehow miss God, looming protectively overhead, a skin of wine in hand and another on His large, naked belly. Smiling ecstatically, crying to be seen.

I apologize to that Infinite Being with an Anglo-Saxon monosyllable for a name if such an Infinite Being even exists. I apologize for being agnostic and taking pleasure in all His works and wonders without giving Him a smidgeon of credit. The agnostic in me then insists that the key words in that sentence are *if such an Infinite Being even exists* and I have crossed Him again.

I take a moment to survey more of my surroundings. Behind the Buddha is a large stone structure with broken walls and no roof. Upon closer inspection, I see that it was the foundation of a tower that once stood there.

K'ung Wu.

That voice again rings through the chambers of my head, echoing off of every wall as if shouted from a parapet.

What the hell is it? What does it mean? I sit on God's toe and think for a while. I've got nothing. What the hell is K'ung Wu?

I walk back around to survey the other side of my angel, crunching twigs and branches and dead leaves below me, leaving indelible prints where it had been many years since anyone had set foot. I see a statue of Saint Francis. Good old Saint Frank. He has a little finch on his shoulder. I see a few smaller statues of Omak and Buddha. I see several Aztec and Mayan sculptures, or at least that's how they look to me. Some African masks carved into rocks, a statue of Anubis. Glyphs adorn his feet.

I look my angel right in the eye and prepare my one question, my one shot. My one chance at touching something diviner (is that a word?) than me.

"What do angels dream of?" I ask aloud.

She says nothing, but I think I know.

She dreams of being the guardian of Cato the censor as he cried *Karthago Delenda Est*! "Carthage must be destroyed!" out into Rome's balmy air, letting the wind carry his cry to every corner of the Boot. She dreams of determination, and of conviction.

She dreams about the Duke of Wellington getting smashed drunk after defeating Napoleon at Waterloo, after his highlanders had decimated the Old Guard and Napoleon's cavalry had unwisely charged thousands-strong squares of infantry. She dreams of fame, of infamy, of battles of epic proportions.

She dreams about the smiles on the souls of every Greek at Thermopylae as they ascended to the Great Hereafter, watching an army of Persians a million strong flee in terror before three hundred Mycenaean warriors. She dreams of triumph in the face of overwhelming odds.

She dreams of V-E Day. Of V-J Day. She dreams of victory.

Victory over that which she and all other angels struggle against. Victory over human suffering, violence, warfare, death. Victory over disease, abuse, depression and famine. She dreams of victory and she dreams of peace, an end to all pain and violence. She dreams of peace, and in doing so dreams of an end to evil.

Poor angel, I think to myself. *Don't you know that nothing ever ends?*

—

I walk to the stone bones of the once mighty tower and look at the moss filling the cracks in the masonry, the bits of rubble and brick that at one point was the pride of a foreman and his crew, a massive stone tower. I wonder if it was just Time or perhaps some other force that destroyed the tower. Then I chuckle. Is there any force but Time? Are not all other forces merely lieutenants to the general Entropy, warrior chieftain of the great destructive army *named* Time?

I kick a piece of rock through a hole in a wall onto the encapsulated stone floor and am very surprised when I hear it *tat brak tat* and fade off, like it is falling down a hole. My curiosity is piqued.

I set to climbing the side of the wall, (perhaps ten or twelve feet high) which isn't easy, but there are footholds and other such byproducts of decay to help me along. When I crest the lip of the uneven, jagged edge, I perceive a room in ruins, a room as big as a basketball court, something that would surprise you if you could see the dimensions of these foundations. These walls look as though they're built to protect from siege weapons. It strikes me as odd.

There, in the center of this small room, is a staircase leading down, down into a cellar of some kind. Around it is drawn a ring of flames. Beneath it, in Sanskrit and its Anglicized translation is the word *Chidambaram*. At least I think it's the same word. Seems to make sense.

I scan the area for a dry piece of wood and some tinder. It is not easy to find, but with my lighter I manage to get a makeshift torch going and I walk right down those stairs.

Of course, I feel a little silly when I find a bin with real torches in it at the foot of the stairs. I light two of them and then douse the MacGuyver torch. Brandishing one in each hand for maximum light and also, you know, just in case…I head into the chamber before me, very warily. There are spiders in places like this.

The cellar doesn't turn out to be too exciting. There are some rusty old weapons of poor quality, a few scimitars and axes. I wonder how old they are, briefly, but my attention is drawn rather suddenly to a detail I had somehow overlooked heretofore. I have done that more than once today.

On the walls, scrawled in blood, are two words. One on the east wall and one on the west wall, for that matter. One reads 'Wrath'. The other reads 'Justice.'

Hand in hand, if You happen to be God.

Hmmm…

One deadly sin, one cardinal virtue. I wondered if there were six more towers with six pairs like this. Maybe Gluttony and Fortitude. Pride and Hope.

Is that human blood?

I suddenly realize that I have found my calling. To move here and just bask in the glory of this place. I need nothing else but this Mountain.

Man, I've gotta go to college. I *can't* quit just to look at ruins on a mountainside.

I sit and brood for a while. What a fantastic place. A life-changing experience. Make that a life-defining experience. I could drop everything and spend the rest of my life in this forest, just living here and delving into every secret on this Mountain. That is a life less ordinary. A life worth living.

Quit my job, quit college, give up my apartment, buy a tent and just live in these woods and explore this place? I don't know if I could get away with that.

Get away with what? It's my life. Mine. My perspective. I'm all that matters. "Get away with…" What? I can get away with whatever I want. I can do anything I want. Free Will. Choice and volition my hammer and hauberk.

No one understands me, no one can. I am mine. I am that is. I am all that matters. If a tree falls in a forest and there are people around to hear it, does it make a noise? Not if *I'm* not there.

What about my parents? Leave them? My ex-girlfriend? Nah, she married my best friend while I was overseas. I don't really have many friends, but I have people who are dear to me…

Okay, there's a solution to all of this. We'll talk later, before we get ahead of our narrative.

I then notice the map.

There is a map encased in a dull, dusty glass frame on the wall, a map of the partition. Everything is there, from the farmhouse to the phone lines to the abbey to the forest. And there are seven towers drawn in. One of them I stand in, presently. Hey, I was right. One for each deadly sin, one for each cardinal virtue. I don't read Latin, which is what the map is written in, but I am able to pick out a few words. *Amor* isn't hard to figure out. It's the same in Italian and French and Spanish and the root of the English word *amorous*. It's love, of course. I deduce that 'Lust' is the deadly sin that accompanies 'Love', just as 'Wrath' is the yang of 'Justice'. Hmmm. Why is the bloody scrawling on the wall in this tower done in English when it seems like so much on this Mountain revolves around Latin? This map, for instance.

Is that…no, it can't be…

Is that just me somehow perceiving the writing on the wall in my own language? How strange and wonderful! How providential!

Shit, I don't believe that for a second.

———

Where is God? Did He make us and then leave, disgusted or bored? Is He around here somewhere, behind the sofa or in the vase? People are always talking about finding Jesus. I'd like to know exactly where they're looking.

—

The writing is on the wall.

That map looks like a battle plan.

"Bene noctis!" comes a voice, heavily accented. Central African from the sound of it. "Ni hao!" the voice says again, switching languages.

Is it nighttime already? Oh, shit. Isn't it dangerous on the Mountain after nightfall? I am suddenly wary of the voice.

"Hello?" comes the voice again, inquisitively, this time in English. Third time's a charm.

"Hello!" I respond. "Who's there?" I raise my torches, trying to be menacing.

"It is I."

I privately wonder why no one on Devine Road but the Professor will answer a fucking question.

"Well I'm down here, so I can't be up there." I say, trying to be cheeky.

"The sun is setting and it is dangerous for you to be out here. Please come with me, so that I may escort you back to safety."

"Who are you?"

"I am who is."

"You're Jesus?"

"No. Please come along."

So I come along, but cautiously. The voice belongs to a tall, lithe black man with an appearance to match his accent. He is a nice, if quiet fellow. I drop my torches, put them out.

"Why won't you tell me your name?" I ask him.

"I do not have one." he tells me. He wears a robe identical to the Bedouin's, but where the Semite's was austere, this man's is colorful and festive. A simple necklace of chimpanzee's bones clatters softly against his collarbones.

"Oh." I shut up, but then open my stupid mouth again. Ninety percent of wisdom is not smell, unfortunately, but keeping your mouth shut. I'm still nailing that down. "Why does everyone here have to present an ontological quandary when I ask them their name?"

"Because a name is serious."

"*I* have a name. And I bet you do, too."

"I do not have a name that you can call me by."

"I think that's a little rude." I frowned.

"I apologize if I have offended you."

"No, you haven't." I sigh. "I'm sorry. I'm the one being rude." I tell him my name and he smiles a big mouthful of perfectly white teeth at me.

"Ah. 'Mankind.' You have a good name."

He says nothing more to me until we are at the farmhouse. After I thank him, he takes his leave.

The night has fallen; the clouds obscure all starlight and the moon is a mere silver sliver, so I have little to see by but the porch light of the farmhouse. I think once again about going into that house and trying to make friends, but I renegotiate with myself and self-justify and just get in my car and go home.

It feels strange to me to say "home." Why, after only two days, should my home no longer feel like home? It feels strange to me that all I want to do is come back to this fantastic place, but natural in the same vein. Perhaps, on some subconscious level, I have made up my mind about this place. Perhaps deep inside my id or perhaps even farther down, in that intangible place where my Great Observer, my "soul" lives, I have already made up my mind. Perhaps I know already that I am meant for this Mountain, as this Mountain is meant for me.

The Man in the Yellow Polo Shirt, Locked Out of His '79 Dodge
Chapter 4

EXT. FIRST TIER OF THE MOUNTAIN WITH NO NAME. DAY.

Fade in from black. Aerial view of a white, fairly non-descript automobile driving up a two-lane thoroughfare, Devine Road, that leads through fields on the right and on the left. The car soon approaches a yellow farmhouse on its left, where it slows, activates its turn signal and pulls into the large, unpaved driveway just north of the house. Close up on driver stepping out of car. He is perhaps 5'11", rugged and fit, with short, dark hair and eyes the color of asphalt. Shot of Man in Yellow Polo Shirt, a short, bald, pudgy Caucasian, leaning against his '79 Dodge pickup truck. Pan from Man in the Yellow Polo Shirt to Protagonist. Protagonist looks at the Man in the Yellow Polo Shirt and addresses him.

Protagonist:
Good afternoon.

Man in the Yellow Polo Shirt:
Howdy.

Protagonist:
Are the Ecclesiae home?

Man in the Yellow Polo Shirt (chuckling)**:**
No, no. They're never around when I need them. Just when I'm passing by on pleasure.

Protagonist:
Oh. Well, I'm _____. *(omitted)*

Man in the Yellow Polo Shirt:
I know. I'm the Man in the Yellow Polo Shirt.

Protagonist:
Indeed You are. Does anyone on Devine Road have a name?

Man in the Yellow Polo Shirt:
Sure. Father Luke does.

Protagonist:
Oh, that's true. I'd forgotten about him.

Man in the Yellow Polo Shirt:
Never wise to forget about Father Luke. Have you seen the tapestry he made? Took him thirty years, and he did a better job on Revelations than I did.

Protagonist:
Oh. Are You an artist, too?

Man in the Yellow Polo Shirt:
So to speak. But I didn't really do anything visually for Revelations. I'm more of a writer.

Protagonist:
Heh. I don't suppose I ever really think of writers as artists.

Man in the Yellow Polo Shirt:
It's because they're not. But I do other things, too. Say, you wouldn't happen to have a wire coat hanger in your car or something?

Protagonist:
Oh, no. I'm sorry. Are You locked out of Your car?

Man in the Yellow Polo Shirt (sarcastically):
No, I just washed it and I want to hang it out to dry.

Protagonist:
Okay, sorry. Stupid question.

Man in the Yellow Polo Shirt (laughing):
No worries. It's how you people work.

Protagonist:
"You people?"

Man in the Yellow Polo Shirt:
Oh, my apologies. I'm God. A God, you get My drift? Yahweh; you may have heard of Me. I made the heavens, the earth and the entire human race. Including you.

Protagonist:
Nice to meet you. I'm Sun Tzu, master strategist. I discovered America and invented the paper clip.

Man in the Yellow Polo Shirt:
Ha ha ha! Good comeback. But I'm being serious. Here, look.

The Man in the Yellow Polo Shirt points to a little nametag he is wearing that says: 'Hello: My Name Is God' in big black letters. The Protagonist chortles.

Protagonist (sarcastically):
Hey, that's pretty convincing. I guess you are God.

Man in the Yellow Polo Shirt:
Your sarcasm is not lost on Me.

Protagonist:
Good to know, as I wasn't being particularly subtle. So, You're completely out of Your mind. You want help getting into Your car, O Maker and Doer of All Things?

Man in the Yellow Polo Shirt:
No, no. I've tried everything I could, and my toolbox is in the cab, so I'll just use the Ecclesiae's phone and call for a ride. You want to come in?

Protagonist:
Uh…are You sure it's okay to just walk into their house?

Man in the Yellow Polo Shirt:
It's okay. I own the house.

INT. FARMHOUSE. DAY.
The Protagonist and the Man in the Yellow Polo Shirt are walking into the Ecclesiae's house.

Man in the Yellow Polo Shirt:
…and the Ecclesiae are just sort of My proxies. Landlords, so to speak. They're kind of like My children, only they're not related to Me. They just sort of moved in and started taking care of things. They didn't do too great, but they didn't do that badly, either, so I let them do what they do and try not to bother them too much. Even if the Basement upsets Me. *Really* upsets Me.

Protagonist:
The Basement?

Man in the Yellow Polo Shirt:
You'll find out, someday. Anyway, I came to visit them today, but I missed them. Obviously. Why were you here?

Protagonist:
Uh, I'm supposed to let them know that I'm hungry.

Man in the Yellow Polo Shirt (smiling)**:**
Of course you are. How silly of me to ask. Hold on, let Me make a call.

The Man in the Yellow Polo Shirt picks up the phone and dials. After a pause, perhaps three or four rings, a distorted male voice answers.

Man in the Yellow Polo Shirt:
Hey, Mikey. I'm locked out again. Yeah. The same place. No. I don't know, maybe. Raphael did *what*?! Incredible. Yes, yes, I know. 'If You knew you were going to lock Yourself out of Your truck, why didn't You prevent it from happening?' What, you think I'm a train on tracks? The concepts of

73

omnipotence, omniscience and omnipresence are omniridiculous. I've told you this a million times and you're still giving Me this predestination trip.

There is a long pause. The Man in the Yellow Polo Shirt appears to be listening intently.

Man in the Yellow Polo Shirt:
Just come pick Me up. No, I don't care; I'm tired of listening to your drivel. Pick Me up. WHAT?! Do you have any idea how *boring* it is here?

The Man the Yellow Polo Shirt cups the mouthpiece, muting it, and looks at our Protagonist.

Man in the Yellow Polo Shirt:
Nothing personal.

Protagonist:
No worries.

He returns to the phone conversation.

Man in the Yellow Polo Shirt:
I'm serious. It's that important. Okay. Come pick Me up. ASAP. Bye, Mike.

He hangs up the phone and opens the cupboards.

Man in the Yellow Polo Shirt:
Coffee? Tea?

Protagonist:
Uh, coffee. Please.

Man in the Yellow Polo Shirt:
I'm a tea drinker, myself. It's milder, you get My drift? Coffee is a vile liquid.

Protagonist:
I protest. Coffee is one of my two vices.

Man in the Yellow Polo Shirt:
Actually, you've got about eight. Smoking, Coffee, Watching the News (I should have made that a deadly sin), Sex, even though you're not getting much right now…Let's see…You curse, but not often, so cursing, though that's not too bad. Yet still a vice. What's that, five? I have a hard time keeping things straight this far down the Mountain. Away from My throne and all. Let's see…Ah, that's why. You haven't developed the other Three. You will, later in life.

Protagonist:
Anything that will put my immortal soul in danger?

Man in the Yellow Polo Shirt:
Ha. Ha ha. Excuse me. No. There's not a whole lot that can put a human being's immortal soul in danger. I go easy on you because I have to. Adam and Eve screwed it all up for you, you get My drift? I'm much tougher on the angels.

Protagonist:
Okay, God. You're a very interesting Person and I'm having a great time playing pretend with You so I'm almost willing to give You the benefit of the doubt and concede for the time being that You're God. But I need some help. Give me a little sign.

Man in the Yellow Polo Shirt:
'I won't believe it until I put my fingers into His hands and my hand into His side.'

Protagonist:
Oh, come on. This is a little different, man.

Man in the Yellow Polo Shirt:
I'm not a man. I was, once. But then you guys killed Me. Quite painfully, I might add.

Protagonist:

I didn't kill anybody. I was going to say that this is a different case from Saint Thomas' because You're locked out of Your car and You refuse to unlock it. With Your magic powers or whatever. So I'm forced, Hobson's choice, to say 'No, You're not God.' You're not even Jewish. But if You want to show me something fancy and miraculous or prove somehow that You are indeed the Almighty, I'll happily do anything You want, as Your loyal subject.

Man in the Yellow Polo Shirt:

Three things. First, I don't refuse to unlock the car. I *can't*. It's the Rules.

Protagonist:

Rules? What do You mean?

Man in the Yellow Polo Shirt (ignoring the question):

Okay. Thing Two: Free Will. If I *prove* I'm God, then you *know* I'm God. Then you don't act the way you would have if you had to go on faith alone.

Protagonist:

I don't go much on faith alone anyway.

Man in the Yellow Polo Shirt:

I know. It's no big deal. I can't establish the religions I like, discriminate against the ones you guys make up and then expect anyone to find the One True Belief by faith alone. That's not just unfair; it's a sloppy way to run things. Especially the salvation system of billions of souls.

Protagonist:

Ah. So which ones did you establish?

Man in the Yellow Polo Shirt:

I can't answer that because it compromises your Free Will.

Protagonist:

I could just say that I don't believe you. Which I don't.

Man in the Yellow Polo Shirt:
Could be. Could be that I'm following the Rules. Tell you what: If My only answer involves something that's going to incriminate Free Will or Myself or anything else, I'll just 'plead the fifth.'

Protagonist:
Deal. What's this third thing?

Man in the Yellow Polo Shirt:
Huh?

Protagonist:
You said there were three things. What's the third thing?

The Man in the Yellow Polo Shirt's voice suddenly sounds exactly like the Protagonist's.

Man in the Yellow Polo Shirt:
'If You want to show me something fancy or prove somehow that You are indeed the Almighty, I'll happily do anything You want, as Your loyal subject.'

Protagonist:
Whoa! That's pretty good.

Man in the Yellow Polo Shirt:
Yeah, I'm pretty good at impressions. You oughta hear my Johnny Cash sometime. It's spot-on.

Protagonist:
Figures. Omnipotence and all.

Man in the Yellow Polo Shirt:
No. I'm not omnipotent. I can't kill myself, I can't sin and I can't microwave a burrito so hot that even I can't eat it. That's at least three exceptions. Should I go on?

Protagonist:
No, no. I believe You. So You're not omniscient, either?

Man in the Yellow Polo Shirt:
Do you believe in fate?

Protagonist:
Does fate exist?

Man in the Yellow Polo Shirt:
Uh, I plead the fifth. No, I don't. Never mind. I don't know everything. I know that if I have an unopened can of Pepsi, there's Pepsi in there, you get My drift? Could be that it's Coke, but I've got long odds against it. Sort of like that.

Protagonist:
Did You know we were going to have this conversation today?

Man in the Yellow Polo Shirt:
Yes and no. I knew I'd be talking to you. I knew I'd be on Devine Road, because I was planning on coming here. I had a few details of this conversation. But it doesn't really work in terms that I can explain to you. Not trying to belittle you, but your comprehension doesn't really work that way, for a good reason.

Protagonist:
What reason?

Man in the Yellow Polo Shirt:
Take Lucifer, for instance. Great kid, lots of potential and a good friend. I miss him; he doesn't come see me very often anymore. Only when Hell is really starting to bum him out, you get My drift?

Protagonist:
Yeah, I get Your drift. You say that a lot.

Man in the Yellow Polo Shirt:

Yeah, I picked it up off of Gabriel. Anyway, I understand Lucifer's depression with being in Hell. I made the place. But I'd forgive all of 'em if they'd just come back and apologize for the whole thousands of years of mischief and the serpent in the garden thing and all that. It's not like the Rebellion in Heaven was any big deal. All the damage was repaired the instant they broke anything, it's just...well, they understand Me, and they can comprehend the way I work. So they don't think that much of Me. You heard the way Saint Michael was speaking to Me on the phone, didn't you? They treat Me like I'm one of the guys instead of 'The Boss'. It's irritating. You want more coffee?

Protagonist:

Yeah, that'd be great.

The Man in the Yellow Polo Shirt gets up and walks into the kitchen.

Protagonist:

You know, you're quite the raconteur.

Man in the Yellow Polo Shirt (from other room):

Doesn't hurt being God. Anyway. Seems like everyone pisses Me off these days.

The Man in the Yellow Polo Shirt re-enters from the kitchen.

Protagonist:

So put Your foot down. Say 'No'. Stick up for Yourself, You know? Or strip the angels of their wings for a while and let 'em know Who holds their life in the palm of Whose hand.

Man in the Yellow Polo Shirt:

Nah. I really love those guys. All of 'em. You guys, too. Humans. Everybody just pisses Me off. I'm the only one who doesn't go around hurting people. Anymore.

Protagonist:

Anymore?

Man in the Yellow Polo Shirt:

Yeah, well...You don't read the Bible often, I suppose?

Protagonist:

I read it, once. When I was a kid. Wasn't much my cup of tea.

Man in the Yellow Polo Shirt:

It's not bad as far as religious scriptures go. Though if I'd had final editing say I'd have left out all the begot, begot, begot and all that. That's just boring.

Protagonist:

Sounds like You've got a short attention span. When did You go around hurting people?

Man in the Yellow Polo Shirt:

Uh...Old Testament Yahweh was kind of a bad guy. In all fairness, I was a sadist, a murderer and a villain. Hell, I'm guilty of genocide and even infanticide. But I *had* to be. Times were tough and I was having to steer the Jews from golden calves every four or five generations. So I hurt people and I had to. But all of those people really got taken care of in the afterlife, you get My drift? I made sure they were really treated special.

Protagonist:

Oh. Well, that's nice. You're telling me that the ends justify the means.

Man in the Yellow Polo Shirt (suddenly very serious)**:**

No. No no no. Pay very, very close attention to what I'm about to tell you. Very close. Because this is very important to your story, your personal tale.

Protagonist:

All righty. Shoot.

Man in the Yellow Polo Shirt:

The ends can not justify the means.

Protagonist:

Elucidate.

Man in the Yellow Polo Shirt:
The means are all that ever gets done. Every event, every reaction to an opposite and equal action, every "end" is just a mean to another end. Which is just another mean. You get My drift?

Protagonist:
You've hardly explained Yourself, but okay. Back to that 'Third Thing.'

Man in a Yellow Polo Shirt:
Right, right. You got me all fired up. I don't want 'loyal subjects.' I'm no fascist, not at all. Sure, I like the power, but angels and humans I made to possess the potential for really great conversation, which is the first great pleasure of life in Heaven and the second one Earth.

Protagonist:
What's the first on Earth?

Man in the Yellow Polo Shirt:
Are you trying to be cute, or do you really not know? It's sex. Of course. I made it that way.

Protagonist (almost accusingly)**:**
Oh, come on! Why restrict it so heavily, then?

Man in the Yellow Polo Shirt:
Hey, I'm not the one who let it get out of control. I knew when I invented it that it could cause problems. For one thing, it's emotional. That's the worst of it. For another thing, it's very unsanitary, which is not as bad but almost. See, if I hadn't made it that way though, conversation would have taken first place on Earth and I didn't want that. I was trying to outdo myself, you get My drift? See if I could come up with something better than intellectual intercourse. So I made physical intercourse. I gave some rough ideas to some prophets and people I liked about how to keep sex safe and happy and friendly and good for everyone, and what happened? They went out of their retarded little minds. Somewhere along the way (I did not do this to your species) humanity developed a need to have a finger in other people's business (no pun intended). Boy, there's little more about your race that bothers Me more. So now there's this hypocritical sexual ethic pervading everything, where

everything is allowed but nothing is condoned and it just turns sex into something dirty and evil. Which is what makes rapists and child molesters out of otherwise decent human beings. The people who derive pleasure from the idea that sex is evil and dirty and not good and wholesome as it was intended.

Protagonist:
Hmmm. What's the Hell policy on those guys?

Man in the Yellow Polo Shirt (thoughtful):
Well…if sex wasn't handled so ridiculously in society, it would be a much less prevalent problem. I wish I could do something about that, but it's the *Rules*. I gotta follow 'em too, or everything goes to Hell. Literally. Anyway, I'm trying to work in some ways, make it a little more acceptable here and there, try to get the statutes of limitations back to my original conception.

Protagonist:
Again. Your ends are justifying Your means. Anyway, there's nothing I could do about all of that. I'm a nobody.

Man in the Yellow Polo Shirt:
You're hardly a nobody. You're on Devine Road.

The Protagonist looks out the window toward the Abbey and thinks he catches, for a passing moment, a glimpse of the Woman in the White Dress that he met in the courtyard last Monday. She is standing in a window on the highest story of the abbey.

Man in the Yellow Polo Shirt:
Boy, she's beautiful, isn't she?

The Protagonist is silent for a while.

Protagonist:
So, if you're God, then you know who she is.

Man in the Yellow Polo Shirt (suddenly compassionate):
Yes.

Protagonist:
"Yes?" Is her name Yes?

Man in the Yellow Polo Shirt:
No. I just think you should ask her if she is who you think she is the next time you see her.

Protagonist:
I don't think I have the gumption for that. You know what happened to me. You know what she did.

Man in the Yellow Polo Shirt:
I repeat: "You're hardly a nobody. You're on Devine Road." You, precisely because you are on this Mountain, precisely because you have the privilege of being on this Mountain, have a right to know.

Protagonist:
So tell me. Is it her?

Man in the Yellow Polo Shirt:
I think we'll keep the story interesting and let you figure it out.

Protagonist (changing the subject)**:**
Yeah, well…I was trying to extract some modicum of the significance of my presence here from the Wandering Bedouin, but he wouldn't hear of it. He'd just quote the Qu'ran.

Man in the Yellow Polo Shirt:
You ever read the Qu'ran?

The Protagonist shakes his head.

Man in the Yellow Polo Shirt:
Wow, you oughta. It's beautiful.

Protagonist:
Better than the Bible?

Man in the Yellow Polo Shirt:
Yes and no. Is the Bible better than the Bhagavad-Gita? Yes and no. Is the Bhagavad-Gita better than the Book of Mormon? Yes and no. You get My drift?

Protagonist:
But You like the Qu'ran?

Man in the Yellow Polo Shirt:
Yeah. It's just poetic, you know? In the original Arabic, of course. The Qu'ran can't be translated, not even close to its original.

Protagonist:
Is that self-praise?

Man in the Yellow Polo Shirt:
I plead the fifth.

Protagonist:
Thanks. You're a wuss.

Man in the Yellow Polo Shirt:
Hardly. It's just the Rules. When you die, I can tell you all about it.

Protagonist:
Ah, so You're telling me I'm going to Heaven, which means I don't have to worry about my behavior or sinning or anything anymore because now I *know* where I'm going to end up, so I can just be a hedonist and not care and still enjoy eternal bliss.

Man in the Yellow Polo Shirt:
Could be. You're a can of Pepsi. But there might be Coke in your can instead. No way to tell until you open it, and we're not going to do that for a while. Besides, I don't send hedonists to Hell. I don't send much of anybody to Hell, really. Actually, you know…I'm not sure there are even any souls there right now.

Protagonist:
What do you mean? Hell is not eternal torture?

Man in the Yellow Polo Shirt:
No. Temporary. They've always got the choice. They can look at Me and say, "Sorry, I know You made me and I'm an asshole for talking bad behind Your back and I'll never do it again…" Or they can cool their heels with Lucifer and Company. Which isn't fun, because those guys get *mean* sometimes.

Protagonist:
So anyone can get out of Hell anytime they want?

Man in the Yellow Polo Shirt:
More or less. I'm the God of love, remember? Oh, wait. That Nietzsche fellow is still hanging out in Hell. He's too proud to come and tell Me he wants out and I'm too proud to go ask him nicely to say he's sorry, so we've got a tacit agreement. He stays down there and I stay up here and we don't get in each other's way. I'm trying to use our relationship as an example for Lucifer and I, but *he's* having so much fun being the Devil, I just can't shake even the tiniest bit of cooperation from him. Oh, well. Ah, and there's a particularly unpleasant corner of Hell I'm saving for a certain writer of religious comics who is incredibly intolerant. He's spreading hate amongst my Christian flock, sowing seeds of dissent among them.

Protagonist:
Who's that?

Man in the Yellow Polo Shirt:
I can't think of his name right now. These 'Rules' are killing me. 'John' or some derivative of it and…for some reason I'm getting a mental image of young birds. Can't stand that guy.

The doorbell rings.

Man in the Yellow Polo Shirt:
I'll get it.

The Man in the Yellow Polo Shirt goes to the door and sees a tall black man standing there. They embrace.

Tall Black Man:
Hi, Dad!

Man in the Yellow Polo Shirt:
Hi, son!

The Protagonist walks over to the two of them.

Protagonist:
Please tell me this is Jesus.

Tall Black Man:
He'll plead the fifth.

Man in the Yellow Polo Shirt:
Jesus was a Jew, dear boy. Now shut up. The adults are talking.

Tall Black Man (introducing himself to the Protagonist):
I'm just the maintenance man. Uh, one of 'em. There's a maintenance woman, too.

Protagonist:
Oh. Well, I'm the Protagonist of the story.

Tall Black Man:
You got that right. The name's Abaddon. I'm one of the good guys. Sort of. A bad guy, too. Well, not really...Aw, you'll see. But anyway, I don't enter the story for a while.

Man in the Yellow Polo Shirt:
Don't give too much away.

Abaddon:
Anyway, I just came by 'cause there was an altercation with Bedhead and the bad guys and I was hoping to catch him 'fore he blew outta here.

Protagonist:
Are you talking about the Wandering Bedouin?

Abaddon:
Yes.

Protagonist:
I was there. It was ugly.

Abaddon:
So I heard.

Man in the Yellow Polo Shirt:
Who's guarding the Abyss while you're here?

Abaddon:
Scholastica.

Man in the Yellow Polo Shirt:
Oh. When's she coming back here? The Tiamat's due out of its cave anytime.

Abaddon:
Yeah, she'll make it. I just wanted to come and thank Bedhead, but he's not here. So, Old Man, when we gonna rumble again?

Man in the Yellow Polo Shirt:
Sometime when I don't have to be in a dumpy human body and I can really whip your ass.

Protagonist (as if to himself):
If we're dumpy it's Your fault.

Man in the Yellow Polo Shirt (to Abaddon):
Hey, it was good to see you, son. You oughta come by the Holy City sometime and we'll rent a movie, chill out or something.

Abaddon:
Well, it sounds like fun, but I'd have to get someone to take over my duties, You get my drift? Not everyone takes up as much space as I do.

Man in the Yellow Polo Shirt:
That's the truth. If you weren't so damn stubborn, I'd put you on the payroll.

Abaddon (grinning)**:**
Nah. It's good being neutral.

Man in the Yellow Polo Shirt:
Yeah, well...next time you see Lucifer tell him that your way is a good option. Not working for Me, just not working against Me.

Abaddon:
I tell him that every time we talk. He doesn't listen. Oh, well. I'll catch y'all later. I'm out of here. *In profundis.*

Abaddon exits.

Protagonist:
So, uh...who was that? One of Lucifer's friends?

Man in the Yellow Polo Shirt:
I'm one of Lucifer's friends, too. I was, anyway. But Abaddon and Lucifer are closer. They were really close before the whole Celestial Schism thing. Oh and sure, they've drifted apart some over eternity, but they're still best friends. That's why Abaddon stays neutral in the conflict but works for Heaven's side. That way he doesn't have to fight if he doesn't want to. Because he refuses to fight Lucifer. Which I understand.

Protagonist:
Wow. You're pretty easy on your mortal enemy, there.

Man in the Yellow Polo Shirt:
Yeah, I guess that the wish to have him back on My good side is softening My words. I really am angry with him, and will be for a few eternities. I mean,

why's that guy got it so bad for Me? All I did was tell him I was making you folks, humans, and he freaked out and stole a third of My friends away and took off for Hell...

Protagonist:
Wait. You didn't banish them there?

Man in the Yellow Polo Shirt:
Well, yes. I suppose I did. Say, I'm getting hungry. You want a sandwich?

Protagonist:
Uh, sure.

Man in the Yellow Polo Shirt:
Feel free to smoke. The Ecclesiae have a HEPA.

Protagonist:
Will do.

Our Protagonist lights a Camel.

Protagonist:
Uh, what are You putting on the sandwiches?

Man in the Yellow Polo Shirt:
Ham, mayonnaise, lettuce, uh...bread, of course...mustard...

Protagonist:
Oh, God! No mustard!

Man in the Yellow Polo Shirt:
How dare you take My name in vain over a sandwich?

Protagonist:
Uh...sorry. I am. Sorry. Uh. I just hate mustard that much.

Man in the Yellow Polo Shirt:

Fair enough. I hate coffee that much. Incidentally, I brewed another cup for you.

Protagonist:

Thank you. So, when do You expect the Ecclesiae home?

Man in the Yellow Polo Shirt:

I know exactly when they're going to be home.

Protagonist:

Okay. When are they going to be home?

Man in the Yellow Polo Shirt:

Soon.

Protagonist:

I see.

The Protagonist looks out the window and sees the man in the brown leather coat leaning on a telephone pole once again. Around him are three others, similarly dressed, trying to act "cool," but they're all scratching themselves mercilessly.

Protagonist:

Hey, if it's not a 'fifth amendment' subject, what's the deal with the men in the leather coats?

Man in the Yellow Polo Shirt:

Who, them? They're the Antagonists. So to speak. For now, get My drift? No, I don't suppose you do. Well, look I'm an Antagonist too, and there's more, but…well, that's much, much later. Let's not get Father Luke upset by overextending our narrative, agreed?

Protagonist:

Agreed. I'll forget what You just said. So I'm the Protagonist, right?

Man in the Yellow Polo Shirt:
  Precisely.

Protagonist:
  So what, do I have to fight them or something?

Man in the Yellow Polo Shirt:
  "Or something." Be patient. That's a virtue, you know.

The Man in the Yellow Polo Shirt looks out the window and sees the man in the brown leather coat.

Man in the Yellow Polo Shirt:
  Stay here. I'll be right back.

Protagonist:
  Like Hell. I want to meet the devil.

Man in the Yellow Polo Shirt:
  No. Sit down or I'll turn you into an insect.

The Protagonist stays where he is and watches them from the couch. After a few minutes, he opens up the window and strains to hear the conversation. The scratching is furious, intense. The Man in the Yellow Polo Shirt's voice raises, as though He's getting angry, and the Protagonist can suddenly hear Him clearly.

Man in the Yellow Polo Shirt:
  …Are you threatening Me? Saint Scholastica is due back anytime. We'll see how well your little bastard does against her.

Man in the Brown Leather Coat:
  I'm done talking to You. We have mischief and mayhem to make while You're here following the Rules.

Man in the Yellow Polo Shirt:
  Yeah? You know what else is in those Rules? The provisions that keep me from smashing Pandemonium City into little bits using your smart ass as a

club. And don't touch My phone towers again or I'll take guard duty for Abaddon and give him a week's vacation. Then we'll see how much trouble you can cause. Or I could just let Michael do it. You all know how overzealous he gets.

The four men walk away indignantly, itching and scratching, and disappear into the fields. The Man in the Yellow Polo Shirt returns to the farmhouse.

Man in the Yellow Polo Shirt:
I hope Mike gets here soon. The sun is setting.

Protagonist:
Wow, dusk already? Time flies when you're having fun.

Man in the Yellow Polo Shirt:
Time flies when you're talking to God.

An engine rumbles as a sleek, 1953 Jaguar Roadster emerges from the mist enshrouding the Second Plateau. It is driving recklessly fast. When it arrives at the farmhouse, out steps from the driver's side a man who strongly resembles the Protagonist Only two feet taller, six kilos of muscle heavier and long, silver hair down to the middle of his back. He wears a long black coat and two pistols in holsters under his arms.

Man in the Yellow Polo Shirt:
Mikey! You're an hour early!

Saint Michael:
Yeah, I made good time. Who's this?

Man in the Yellow Polo Shirt:
This, my friend, is our Protagonist.

Saint Michael:
He looks like me. And him. Just...smaller. And without the hair.

Protagonist:
No car, either. I mean, I have one, it's just not a Jag. Who is 'him'?

Saint Michael (ignoring the question):
Ah, Jags are pieces of shit anyway. Always breaking down. So, Boss. You want me to get you into Your truck?

Man in the Yellow Polo Shirt:
Yeah.

The Man in the Yellow Polo Shirt turns to the Protagonist.

Man in the Yellow Polo Shirt:
Are we still happily agnostic?

Protagonist:
Uh, I think so. I've always viewed religion as more of a good guide for leading a good life than a method of salvation anyway. I don't think that'll change because I met a guy claiming to be God.

Man in the Yellow Polo Shirt:
Good, good. That's what I intended religion for in the first place. You know, I'm an agnostic, too. I mean, I don't know if there's a higher power than Me. I have no idea. So I just keep the ideas I have straight, and try to run this world and treat My people as best I can. Maybe someday that same thing will happen to Me what happens to you and I'll die and be judged and all that, you get My drift?

Protagonist:
Yeah. I definitely get Your drift.

Saint Michael:
Wow, Boss. If somebody gets Your ass under the hot light You better hope the Old Testament doesn't get brought up.

Protagonist (To the Man in the Yellow Polo Shirt):

You know something? Don't worry about my Free Will. You haven't proved anything to me, yet. I've seen crazier things on this Mountain happen than You've been able to show me. Although you do play a pretty convincing God. I like You. We oughta get together for drinks and sandwiches again sometime.

Man in the Yellow Polo Shirt:

Yeah. I'd like that. Okay, Mike. Unlock My doors.

Saint Michael picks up a rock that is right next to the truck and breaks the window out. He then unlocks the door and the Man in the Yellow Polo Shirt lets himself in and starts it up. The Protagonist walks up to the now-broken window as Saint Michael gets back ion his vehicle.

Protagonist:

Why didn't You just do that?

Man in the Yellow Polo Shirt:

Because I don't destroy anything anymore. I made a promise.

Protagonist:

Ah. The Rules?

Man in the Yellow Polo Shirt:

Indeed. Thank you for a nice time, My dear Protagonist. I'll catch you around.

Protagonist:

Hey, God. One more question.

Man in the Yellow Polo Shirt:

Actually, you're about to ask three. Shoot.

Protagonist:

Uh, okay. Is there a point to prayer?

Man in the Yellow Polo Shirt:

You mean, like asking Me for stuff? Sure, I get those. I don't always listen to them. Prayer definitely serves its purpose in religious life, giving people a sort of anchor to the unseen. But they always end it with 'Thy will be done,' so I'm not really sure what to do for them. Are they just sort of praying and hoping that their wishes are aligning with My will at the right time that they'll get what they want? I don't really understand the whole concept. But I like it. It makes Me feel important to people. And what happens when someone makes you feel good about yourself?

Protagonist:

Uh…my will is more inclined to align with theirs?

Man in the Yellow Polo Shirt:

Exactly. So, yes. There's a point to prayer. It's not just blowing smoke up My holy glorious Ass, you get My drift? I answer the prayers if My will, uh…wills it, I guess.

Protagonist:

Oh. Should I pray?

Man in the Yellow Polo Shirt:

Nah. Spend more time believing in yourself than believing in some far off God that has plenty of worshippers. That'll make Me much happier, knowing that you're happier. Help yourself and I'll help you. T'a!

The Jag and the '79 Dodge pull out of the driveway and drive up Devine Road. The Protagonist stands and watches them disappear, then enters his own car and drives down the mountain. Roll credits. Fade to Black.

The Extended Hospitality of the Twins
of Subtle Oriental Countenance
Chapter 5

On Monday of my first week of travels to Devine Road, my life was changed by a German-American professor and a Wandering Bedouin.

On Tuesday I first discovered the Tower of Teutoberg Forest, and understood nothing at the time of what that tower portended for me.

On Wednesday I met a man who claimed to be God, and found Him surprisingly humorous and exactly what I had hoped God, if He existed at all, to be.

But I was upset upon returning home. War still rages between my country and another. I am not sure why, only that it is so, and that there are people killing other people.

Bad memories.

And had I known about the Basement at this time, had I known about what the Basement was, and what it contained…How it facilitated, maybe was indirectly responsible for that war that had just broke out, how it affected the war *I* was forced to fight in…

Well, if I'd have known, I may have done something horrible. But all that is for later. The Basement is for later.

On Thursday I drove my car to my regular parking spot in front of the farmhouse where the Ecclesiae live. I got out of my car, shivered (noticing that it was unusually cold for the season) and walked to the door. Ringing the signal bell, I suddenly felt compelled not to wait for an answer, but to walk inside.

There on small pedestals erected in the middle of the living room floor, sat both of the twins in lotus positions, humming 'Om Mani Padme Hum.' On the couch was a tall man of South American descent, doing the same thing. I stood and said nothing. The twin on the right opened his eyes and smiled, then closed his eyes again. The twin on the left looked at me and smiled in the same way. The South American said in a long, toneless voice, "He whose walk is blameless is kept safe, but he whose ways are perverse will suddenly fall."

I looked at him quizzically. He had the Bedouin's eyes. My eyes.

He said, "You must be hungry."

I replied in the affirmative and the Ecclesiae both nodded. I was ushered into an upstairs bedroom and one drew a hot bath in an adjacent bathroom for me. He motioned for me to get in it, so I waited for him to leave the room, stripped and did so.

I was rejoined almost immediately by the other twin (?), who administered a small drop of the same elixir to the water that the Wandering Bedouin had used to heal his lamb and himself. I felt instantly refreshed and relaxed, and was left to myself for fifteen minutes, then was delivered a large, dry cotton towel and white garments that seemed tailored to my exact size: A white button-up shirt and white three-quarter pants that were airy and incredibly comfortable. Silk, I think.

The bedroom was large and comfortable. There was a fireplace and a large bed; six bookshelves (filled to breaking point with books) lined the western wall. On the eastern wall three small windows poured the light of early afternoon onto everything in the room.

"Is it to your liking?"

I spun on a heel and found the South American and the Ecclesiae standing there, and suddenly realized something I hadn't noticed before: How *tall* the twins were. At least six and a half feet tall each.

I nodded that yes, it was to my liking, and the twins wheeled a cart in. They laid me down in the bed, set a tray over me and served me a loaf of sourdough Ciabatta and a fine red wine. I do not normally like wine, and I did not enjoy the taste of this one. But I found it strangely fulfilling.

The South American spoke to me while I ate, asking me questions, mostly making small talk. At length, though I was hesitant, I asked his name.

"I am the Wandering Venezuelan." He lifted his shirt and I saw a long, stitched-up wound. Around his neck was a silver chain shaped like winding vines. "I am here with the Ecclesiae for the night."

"Oh, great." I said. "Good timing. I think I am, too. How did you get that cut?"

The Wandering Venezuelan looked at me like I was an idiot for about two full seconds and, I think, was about to tell me so when one of the twins shot him a look.

"Uh...that is for 'later.'" he said. I frowned.

When I was finished eating, the Ecclesiae placed a book with one hundred pages in front of me. It was called *Summarium Quaestionis, Volume XXXVI*. I opened to the first page and found that it was written in English, which is (unfortunately) the only language that I read. The twins bowed deeply and took their leave. The Wandering Venezuelan left on their heels.

The first page had thirty questions listed on it. I will list the first five here:

1) The more precise and demanding a compendium of 'moral' standards is, the more strict and agonizing becomes contrition and penance. If one admires a collection of ethics and also the devotion of its followers to the necessary self-infliction of sorrow demanded by their code for acts of transgression, one can just as easily find no admiration for those followers and their refusal to live up to their own standards. Does the fact that atonement would even need to be self-inflicted, no matter how strictly enforced upon the self, reflect as poorly on the fortitude of man as the code of ethics that he has invented would reflect well on him? Our belief, presently, and our commitment to serving justice to those who stray from this preordained path is the material of our moral grit. But can our actions, in rendering 'justice' and 'good' null concepts by eliminating 'injustice' and 'evil', be the true path to a stronger, loving world?

2)Life is the wave of the ocean, from its birth in gravity unto its spectacular end on the shore. Every point, every node, every event is connected, ever-flowing into the other, ever changing, never changing, everything leading up to the crash on the sand and the retreat, and the next crash into the sand again. To discern a single experience and say "What" or "When" is to define every experience leading up to it and every experience following it. Can youth end and old age begin, can virginity give birth to maturity and acumen, can sorrow not blossom into happiness? Naturally. But is it the same in converse? Can blue skies bring tears? Can death bring about life? Are they all not existent at once, flowing into each other, mixing, making love, ever producing until the wave at last crashes and retreats?

3)The ether that is the strength of humanity is possessed in two decanters: Community and individuality. How is this fierce dichotomy, this fearful symmetry resolved into a working union that is the fiber of us all?

4)The ether that is the weakness of humanity is possessed in two decanters: Doubt and fear. It is doubt that begets fear, and conversely fear that begets doubt. Which decanter was the origin, and which the receptacle of its offspring?

5)There was at first the forging of the crudest weapons for warfare: spears of wood and bronze. Shortly thereafter came the sword, a smaller and lighter, less cumbersome weapon. Then an edge of this sword was refined, and made razor sharp. Then both ends were made razor sharp, and the weapon suddenly became as dangerous to the user as to his enemy. Treachery is like this double-edged sword. In one aspect it is a font of evil, a plague on humanity, one of the many evils sprung from fear that preys on doubt. In another aspect it is brandished by the good, the righteous, and the wise for just principles. Do the rare times that treachery is wielded for good justify its existence in light of the uncounted, everyday infidelities and duplicities? Can a thousand evil perfidies be excused so that one may accomplish a noble end? Can the same principle be applied to murder, war, even genocide? A corollary: Do the ends justify the means?

Good God. Those were *ridiculous*. Overwrought, overwritten, overthought. I removed the tray from over my bed and went to search the bookshelves for paper and a pen to start jotting down my thoughts on the first question. One of the twins walked in carrying a desk. Out of the desk he produced a fat notebook and several pens; I took them and thanked him and he left again, leaving the desk in the corner beneath a window.

I am amazed at the small miracles I witness here, but I am no longer paralyzed with awe when they occur, as I was when it seemed like everything on the Mountain operated on the logic of Providence. Like everything was for the Author's convenience, a great collection of *deus ex machinas* all lined up in a row like action figures. I understand them now, understand a little of how they work. They are a deep and beautiful part of that which makes this place up, but they are still a part of the makeup, and though I am learning that they are perhaps the most relevant and substantial stones in that foundation, I know also that they are only what they are: Small miracles.

I jotted down a few notes and doodled a picture of a bird in the top right corner of the page, thinking, picturing, sizing, philosophizing, wrapping my head around, visualizing. I looked at the bookshelf again and there saw Plato's Republic. I opened it, sat down in my bed and began my journey towards an answer to the first question in my new friend's Utopia, the birthplace of moral philosophy.

I was a quarter of the way through the *Republic* by dinner; halfway by the time night fell. I rose from my bed to put on my regular clothes and leave for home, but was again immediately attended by the twins and the Venezuelan.

"I need to go home." I said plaintively.

"Yet you are still hungry." said the Venezuelan.

I admitted that I was. He looked at me and smiled.

"The Man in the Yellow Polo Shirt has provided for you to stay with the Ecclesiae for as long as it takes to answer the whole of the *Summarium Quaestionis*. If you wish to inform your loved ones that you intend to take a vacation, you are encouraged to leave for one day and then return, provided that you make no mention of this place. Do not be concerned about the utilities or rental payment at your dwelling in the city, or your mail or pension from your country's military service. Simply stay here and eat until you are full."

I stated that I wanted to stay the night and return in the morning to tell my parents that I would be gone for some time, and also to withdraw from community college. He remarked that I would find a better education here, then left me to sleep, which I did.

That night I dreamt that I was a baby eagle in a nest full of adult swallows; I was big, ferocious, dangerous to everything around me but utterly unversed and stupid; I was a baby. Sure, the other birds patronized me and tried to make me feel like I belonged, fed me, nuzzled with me, but in my little bird heart I knew that I was different. I knew that with one false movement or one startled reaction or one misjudgment of power I could kill any one of this family of mine at any time. And I didn't know if I could stop myself from accidentally doing it.

I also had my nightmare.

When I woke the next morning I set out for the city, paying as little thought as I could to my dreams, and returned less than three hours later and resumed my place in *The Republic.*

—

Days passed. The Venezuelan left and I did not see him again for some time. How many days passed? Twelve or more. I wrote my observations and thoughts on endless sheets of paper supplied to me by the Ecclesiae. When I needed to talk out loud and get my thoughts sorted, I would walk over to the abbey and converse with Father Luke, whom I found well-educated and extraordinarily intelligent. We would run around the building and lift weights in the rectory, conversing all the while, or we would work in the garden or on repairs to the outer walls (and foundations; Archimedes' experiments took their toll) to get exercise. When I was ready, I would return to my studies. On time, every day, I would receive three hearty, filling meals plus an afternoon meal of bread and wine from the Ecclesiae, and receive a drop of the elixir in my nightly bath.

27)The man from the desert, some say, is shaped by the desert. He is brown and firm, dry and resolute, dangerous without malice. He is warm when pleasant and burning hot when his ire is aroused. He houses thousands of secret oases for those who trouble to look for them. The men from the desert, however, say that it is quite the opposite. That the desert, over time, has come to resemble them. Who is right?

On some day, perhaps the twentieth of October, I answered the thirtieth question on the page and turned it over. There were thirty more.

I found myself strangely pleased.

Around that time, Father Luke gave me an old wooden sword and began teaching me to use it. He was romantic about medieval times, medieval weaponry and medieval philosophy, so I humored him. Besides, it was great exercise. He taught me how to parry, how to counterattack, how to dodge blows. He also bruised me very badly with his own wooden sword whenever we dueled; he was an excellent swordsman. I wasn't bad myself, even if Father Luke said, while pulling on the ends of his mustache, "You will never be good. You will never be the best. If you ever get in a real fight you will be killed. But that is life, *non*? It is shit. Get used to it."

I didn't think I was too bad. Those old combat reflexes they hone in basic don't die easy.

The next page I completed in a week, as the questions were (in my opinion) more theological and less difficult. The next I completed in three days, the next page the next day, the next *two* the next day, and then I completed three pages in one day by having Father Luke read them out loud to me and then type my answers on his typewriter as they came out of my mouth. No correction, no editing, just my stream of consciousness and one Catholic warrior priest working for me.

133)It is said that nothing is impossible, only so improbable that it is *virtually* impossible. If these most improbable events were to occur, they would be called miracles. What is impossibility, then, if nothing is impossible? Is it impossible for something to be impossible?

427)Hatred is a hot flame that burns quickly and dies, but the embers of revenge glow in its ashes forever. Is an act of revenge rooted in hatred, then, or another evil? What, indeed, is revenge? Is it evil at all?

The Ecclesiae set out carved pumpkins on their doorstep in anticipation of Hallowe'en. To my disappointment, however, no trick or treaters alighted on the doorstep. A shame.

The Wandering Bedouin returned with his flock, and I spent the first night of November at the site of our first night on Devine Road, camping with him. He made me stew, but I asked no questions this time, just made pleasant conversation. I knew that when I was ready for a deeper understanding of Devine Road, I would receive it from him, as he had promised. For now, I was just enjoying his company, and I enjoyed it the whole time he was around. We were becoming friends.

1055)The natural passage of events kills all things, from the smallest life to the greatest of stars in the heavens. Nothing lasts forever but God, and that which God has made eternal, the soul. How long is forever? When did eternity begin?

1788)Time, it can be argued, indeed existed before the clock. But before the clock, no entity could perceive it. Did time indeed exist before the clock? Or does relevance define existence?

By the middle of November I found that I had read nearly every book on the bookshelf, and that I had read every major religious scripture and philosophical treatise ever written, from *Leviathan* to the Book of Mormon to *Twilight of the Idols*. I'd read culturally vital works of fiction: The Volsunga Saga and the Nibelunglied, the Kalevela and *One Thousand and One Arabian Nights*, among many. I found also that my body was changing. I was lighter, more athletic, more muscular from my exercise with Father Luke. My body was getting back into the shape I was in not a year ago.

My skin was firming, my complexion had cleared and my teeth had whitened, all as a result of my nightly bath in the unnamed elixir.

I found that I was becoming able to perform complex critical thinking, analyses and mathematical equations in a fraction of the time it would have taken me before. I had defeated Father Luke in four of our seventeen swordsmanship contests in the last week. I thought critically and reasonably. I possessed knowledge and talent very suddenly, and felt as though my intelligence quotient had somehow doubled over the time I'd been here. Father Luke had set to teaching me rudimentary Latin, just some conversational stuff. I was picking it up, I felt, surprisingly quick.

I also found that I had only twelve pages, three hundred and sixty questions left to answer.

I took a break, one whole day to clear my head of questions and to seek peace. I thought it important, and neither the Ecclesiae nor Father Luke protested, so I went for a long walk in an easterly direction, through the fields, and thought about my life before Devine Road. It seemed silly and superfluous to feel superior to others because of my queer invitation to this location, but I couldn't help it. I felt so much different, now. A new man. Like I was finally coming out of my box.

Sunlight cut through billowy white clouds like a river through a landscape, spilling all over my face and body and lifting me high into the upper realms of my consciousness. I lost myself in a grin, a grin so wide and mischievous that a Cheshire Cat somewhere in Wonderland *poofed* into dust. Then I broke out into a run.

I ran through the fields at full speed, running as fast as I could. I ran a mile in six minutes, the next mile in eight. I ran a few minutes longer. A few seconds longer. Then I fell to the ground, my chest heaving, my lungs hurling insults at me. I laughed out loud, and was suddenly attuned to the sound of children laughing with me. I stood up quickly.

Approaching me, running as fast as their short legs could take them and with baskets full of flowers filling their little arms, was a small army of children.

The author exaggerates. I have seen an army of children. This was closer to fifteen or twenty.

They were running and laughing and tumbling and altogether joyful. I grinned another grin, unable to stop it from taking over my face. They paused everywhere they went and at random (as is par with the methods of children) plucked wildflowers from the fields and put them in their baskets, there to cherish and love them. A rainbow inexplicably broke out in the broad, clear sky and arched from the mists that obscured the world below the First Plateau to high into those that shrouded the Second.

The group of children parted around me, picking little flowers, blue and green and red and pink and yellow around my feet. They picked nasturtiums, marigolds, snapdragons and daisies. They even picked dandelions. I have always loved dandelions, and have privately wondered why such a beautiful flower is considered a weed.

I watched them for a time, watched as they sailed by me without paying a bit of attention to my presence. Then, unexpectedly and quite clumsily, a little boy tripped in front of me and went skidding on to the ground. When he rose, I saw that he had cut his face on a rock, and had bloodied his elbow.

The radio tower's shadow eclipses the preschool.

I grimaced at the memory, felt a surge of dull pain in my left hand. The little boy stood up, face scrunched up like a slinky, and examined his wounds. I looked at the blue flower that I thought he was intended for and stooped to pick it up for him, but I stopped at the infinitesimally soft touch of a hand on my forearm.

Standing next to me was the woman in the white dress.

"Not this one." she said.

I nearly burst into tears, so powerful was the anxiety attack I had at that moment. My pulse doubled. My hands clammed up. I felt like I would die, right there.

But her voice was like a thousand choirs. Her eyes were like a sea at peace. I suddenly visualized a soft rain shower on the Saharan sand dunes. I tried to hate her, but I couldn't.

I couldn't think of anything to say, nor could I have said anything I may have thought of. So I just stared at her dumbly, feeling like a caveman.

"It's not time." she said at length, and with all the grace of an angel turned from me and applied pressure to the little boy's wound with her hand. When she lifted it, it had stopped bleeding and looked merely sore. He smiled politely and picked up a daisy right next to the mistaken blue flower, deposited it in his basket and ran off. She looked at me again as if I knew something that she didn't (another talent only women possess), which in turn convinced me that *she* knew something that *I* didn't. I didn't say anything as she turned and followed, with porteuse grace, her children.

I broke off in a run again, in the same direction, wondering if I was still possessed by the wild spirit that had stimulated this journey or if I was trying to get away from, well, her. I ran and ran, breaking only to catch my breath. I don't know how long I ran for.

I finally came to a massive stone wall, probably thirty feet tall, the easternmost of the two partition walls that frame this part of the First Plateau. It looked like it could have been six feet thick, running up the Mountain and down the Mountain, disappearing into the mists that shrouded both ends of the Plateau I had made my temporary home.

I walked and paced and scratched my head, setting to the devising of some plan to get over the wall. Can't jump it, can't climb it, can't walk through it. Can't I? I looked up and down as far as I could see for a door or a window of sort, or some tunnel. Anything.

I don't know how long I looked, but (at last) I came to a hole in the wall, smooth and cylindrical, running from my side to the other side, my partition to the next.

God, the wall *was* six feet thick. At least.

I looked through the wall and saw, to my great surprise, snow falling on an ocean becalmed. No shore, no trees, no clouds, no sun, no wind to disturb the glass surface. Nothing but tiny white flakes of promise alighting on the cheek of the sea. I stood there for a long time, basking in the glorious sight of the placid mirror surface that served as the ceiling of the endless blue depths of the ocean. I smelt the gentle abrasion of the sea's breath, the salty air that called to me, and I heard whispers promised in my ear, promises of serenity, of peace. Of a cold beer on the seashore. A dog playing in water. A beautiful woman in a white swimsuit.

Nothing profound, nothing life-altering. An effortless majesty.

I thought of the Professor.

My eyes filled with the water, my ears filled with the crash of waves, my heart filled with the soul of the ocean. Then, a snowflake. And another. On my cheek. I broke the gaze I had cast out over the sea and looked at the sky in my partition. Stone grey clouds were fast covering the sky.

I took one more look at that ocean view, laughed out loud and ran as fast as I could back to the abbey.

That night I slept at the farmhouse, and the strangest thing I had yet encountered on Devine Road happened to me. I was fast asleep with the door slightly ajar, dreaming of the woman in the white dress. In my dream she was nine months pregnant, walking among the wildflowers that grow among the high grass and wheat in the fields surrounding Devine Road, singing a song I did not recognize. Her eyes were hauntingly beautiful.

I woke when my room suddenly filled with light.

I sat up quickly and looked around, but the rogue luminescence had faded almost instantly. Baffled, I quieted my breathing and listened for a sound.

Nothing. Then I saw a toy, a child's doll with golden hair, propped up against my bed post. I watched the hallway alight with the same brilliance and pass slowly away, as if it were traveling downstairs. I got out of bed and put on a pair of pants, picked up the doll and walked into the hallway. The light disappeared down the stairs, and into the kitchen. I followed.

Once in the kitchen, I saw through the cracks in the door to the living room that this was the place that seemed to be the final destination of the mysterious light.

I walked in and there, standing in the living room in the threshold of the wide open front door, was a beautiful little girl of perhaps five years old, with dark hair and dark eyes, radiating a white light that hurt me to look at her. Tears spilled silently from her eyes. I lowered my face so as not to be blinded by the intense glow, and walked slowly toward her. I was terrified, though I did not know why. I felt as if I was approaching the Muse, or Pallas Athena, or Helen of Troy. I felt as if I was once again looking at the woman in the white dress.

Her light all but faded as I neared, until she was glowing but softly as I stood over her. I stooped to one knee and, as I offered the doll, she locked eyes with mine and seemed to know me. And I suddenly realized that I knew her name.

Not her birth name, or Christian name, or nickname. Not a name she had told me, not a name I had ever heard before.

I felt as though I had suddenly learned God's name for her, the name He held on His lips at her conception. The name He had for her when His heart was still. The name for her that He held in the quiet of His soul. I whispered it and she took the doll from me, then kissed me softly on the lips, and walked out the front door.

I realized then that she was my daughter. And that she was not yet born.

———

I woke up and found myself almost unable to distinguish if it was dream or reality. Can a man dream within a dream? Can a man's dream be so vivid that he mistakes it for reality?

—

The next day, as promised, I returned to the *Summarium Quaestionis*, but found myself unable to concentrate. I was looking out over the snow that had fallen last night and covered the partition, that had dusted the balustrades on the farmhouse, that had crowned the palisades of the abbey. I was looking out over the white landscape, the white ground and the white trees, but I was thinking only of the white dress. Her.

The Man in the Yellow Polo Shirt had instructed me to ask her, but I couldn't even think when I had been near her, much less coordinate guttural vibrations and labial and dental motions into a sentence as incredibly long and complicated as "What's your name?" I'd have better luck dead-lifting a tree trunk. I'd have better luck reciting *War and Peace* backwards in my head. I'd have better luck learning Kiswahili in an afternoon.

I'd have better luck learning to hate her.

So I took another afternoon off and returned to that giant stone wall. I looked around for the "window", realized that my present location must have been some number of feet north or south of the window and wandered the wall until dusk looking for it. When I found it, the sun was almost down. I hurried to it, cupped my hands around the sides and took a deep breath, inviting cool ocean air in, helping myself to a sweet salty mouthful of sea breeze.

What I got was a searing, choking breath of black smoke, brimstone and burnt hair. My chest seized up in a spasm and I fell to my knees, clutching my sternum, trying to force open my diaphragm. I coughed and coughed and coughed, more from shock than anything else, but the burning in my lungs was Hellish as it spread throughout my whole torso. It reminded me of mustard gas, but it more and less painful in a sense that I could not describe to our readers who have not ever breathed mustard gas before.

When I regained enough of my constitution to force some good deep breaths of oxygen in, I wiped my eyes and blew my nose and set my stare through that window. But I did not see the ocean this time. Instead, I saw a long, black, withered heath, a charred plain with dead trees ashy and burnt, like the mountainside of Mount Saint Helens right after it erupted. The sky was sullen and colorless. *Everything* was colorless.

Then a man in a leather coat walked past the window. He had a long aquiline nose, ashen skin and black, black hair. His leather coat was the color of midnight.

He made brief eye contact before passing out of my line of vision and sneered, showing me long, wickedly hooked teeth. I suddenly saw a vision of worms every kind, writhing and squirming, tapeworms as long as my fingernail, night crawlers miles long, ringworms curled into great circles around mounds and mounds of maggots. I felt bile in my mouth. I felt that same creeping violence I had felt my first day here. My old frame of mind kicked in, the frame of mind I had to be in the whole time I was in Mosul. The frame of mind that justified violence. The frame of mind that justified murder. This, I saw, was an antagonist.

Then a frozen perspiration erupted on my forehead. I was chilled to my marrow. My tongue cleaved to the top of my mouth. My teeth felt like they were going to chatter out of my head. My anger and hatred and violence melted into cold, cold fear.

Was it the man in the leather coat doing this to me? Or was it my soul rebelling against my soldier's instincts? Against my frame of mind?

The woman is running towards the radio tower.
The radio tower is right next to the preschool.
My finger tenses on the trigger.
Her eyes lock with mine.

I heard the sound of a thunderclap crescendo behind me, and looked at the sky. It was about to snow, surely, but that was not thunder I was hearing. It was constant and it was growing louder and louder. It sounded like horses.

With furious speed came an army of monks over a hill behind me, hundreds strong, the monks that I had seen in the courtyard on my first visit to The Mountain with No Name. They were all there, every Franciscan, every Buddhist, every one. At their head was Father Luke. I waited for them to come to me, down into the sunken grade between the separate small hills we stood on. I was glad they were here. I needed to tell someone about that leathercoat. Father Luke walked right up to me and shushed me by holding a finger to his mouth, all the while looking around nervously, shifting his weight from one foot to the other. I furrowed my eyebrows.

"Come. We must return to the abbey." he whispered.

"What's the problem?" I whispered back.

"There is a man in a leather coat on the other side of that wall." replied Father Luke. "He will arrive here shortly, and he is not of the quality of character of the men in the leather coats that you have seen until now. He is much, much worse, and much more frightening."

Black claws gripped my heart.

"What is his name?" I asked.

"*Non.* We do not say their names aloud." said Father Luke authoritatively. "To speak someone's name is to give them power over you."

"But I speak your name."

"You do *not* speak my name. I am neither a priest nor a Roman Catholic."

I admit I was a bit stunned.

"Come quickly." he continued. "I have brought the Ecumenics with me for safety and we must return to the abbey, as they have other engagements. The Manichaeans are expected in Florida in twelve hours and the Gnostics will similarly be leaving, up to the Coenobitic Monastery at the north end of the Plateau by nightfall. We depart now."

I walked into the midst of the unlikely throng of theists and returned to the abbey. The moon was winning a duel with Polaris by the time we arrived. Father (?) Luke suggested that I stay the night at the abbey, and that I complete the questions as fast as possible after that. He felt I was being a little free, a little too careless. I reasoned that I could not possibly be careless if I didn't know what to care about. I was merely ignorant, and everyone around me was keeping me ignorant. Father Luke had scratched his mustache and frowned at me. "We do not do so for any other reason than that it is dangerous to know what we know. This is why you must complete the questions and many other courses of learning before all is revealed to you. *Un muet ne trouve pas sa route.*"

"What's that mean?"

"'Dumb folks get no land.'"

"Okay. Be that as it may, I can't avoid what I don't know to avoid." It was my turn to frown. I was being difficult because I wanted so badly to learn just a little about this place.

"In time." was the reply. "For now, stay mostly indoors until we know the business of the men in leather coats, or until either Saint Scholastica or the Wandering Bedouin arrives. By no means should you go out at night. Even with one of them. Just stay with the Ecclesiae or in the abbey and you will be fine."

I frowned a cellist's bow and played a dissonant chord with it. Father Luke bade me goodnight and went to his own room.

The next day I returned to my questions. I answered all but the last three the next day, without Father Luke, because I was still a little angry.

I approached those questions at dusk:

2998) What is God?

2999) What is Truth?

3000) What is Family?

And found that I could not answer them, even though I did not spend long thought on them. Those were not answers I knew at the core of myself. I decided to leave them blank, unanswered, and returned to the Ecclesiae. I found them again on the living room floor, sitting in lotus position, chanting. Behind them was a short, stocky man stroking a heavy mustache and wearing a large fur coat. He identified himself as the Wandering Mongol, pointed conspiratorially to two long, stitched-up gashes on his forearms and also to his necklace, a gaudy gold chain that would have done Mr. T proud. He smiled disconcertingly and instructed me to collect all of the notes that Father Luke and I had compiled and to deliver it to the Ecclesiae. I did so, in four large wooden boxes, and left them on the kitchen table.

That night I dreamed that I was standing on a gigantic man-made obelisk, probably a hundred feet high, protruding from a wide ocean. It was one of seven in a ring of similar obelisks, about five hundred feet off an unrecognizable coast, and in the middle of the seven stones was another obelisk, crowned with a beautiful sculpture of a fantastic city with Greco-Roman architecture and an unrecognizable language scrawled all around the monolith beneath it. It extended all the way down into the sea. In my dream, I dived off the pillar into the ocean below, to see how far the pillars went down, and woke when I hit the water.

The Wandering Mongol came to me the next day and asked why I had not answered the last three questions. I stated that I did not think they could be answered. He assured me that they could, but they had not yet been. Then I suddenly realized that there was an answer, a single answer that could address all three of them. I knew it was not the correct answer (was there a correct answer?) and I knew it was not what he was looking for, but my eyes widened and I smiled triumphantly and stated, very simply:

Nil Sine.

He returned my smile warmly, as if I had just taken my first step as an infant, and left my room. And the house. And the planet, as far as I knew. I did not see him again until the Christmas party. The Ecclesiae, too, were gone. For several days. So I forgave Father Luke and stayed with him at the abbey to pass the time until I saw them again.

Days passed, Thanksgiving came and went and I resumed my daily routine with Father Luke. We exercised, partook in swordplay, and from time to time he would let me into the library to read. I loved nothing better.

Father Luke really grilled me about my history as a soldier. I'm not sure why, it just seemed very important to him. I told him mostly everything.

One night, the Bedouin dropped in and parked his flock around back of the abbey, then came and had dinner with us. It was a dinner of steak, corn on the cob, mashed potatoes, spinach au gratin and black, black beer. The two of them sat at one end of the table and placed me at the other. The conversation was pleasant and small, the smiles were plentiful and then, out of left field, Father Luke fired the opening salvo. "Son, you may have noticed that the two of us are plainly interested in your time spent in Iraq."

"Father, you may have noticed that I am plainly interested in learning more about this Unnamed Mountain." I said, and smiled as convincingly as I could, given the obvious half-joke status of that statement.

The Bedouin sighed. "We are trying to figure out why you are here."

I was taken aback. Did they not want me here? "I, uh…I did like you told me." I said, and cast my eyes down. "I told the Ecclesiae I was hungry."

"No, no. You mistake me. I did not intend it that way." said the Bedouin quickly and diplomatically. "Truly, we are happy you that you *are* here, brother. What we are trying to ascertain is the reason *why* the Man has you here." said the Bedouin.

"I don't know." I said, now suspicious. "I just got the letter and came."

Father Luke stared into the tawny surface of the libation in his stein and said, in a low voice that I'm sure he wanted me to hear, "There's never been a soldier here, it's true. But he's not it."

The Wandering Bedouin's voice was considerably lower, so I could not eavesdrop, but his faced looked disagreeable.

"It's you." said Father Luke to the Bedouin.

I heard the Bedouin this time. "I am not the yin." he whispered, and his voice sounded obstinate. "We are too similar."

"What the hell are you two talking about?" I asked.

They turned their attention back to me. Father Luke had that look in his eyes that he always got when he was about to change the subject. The Bedouin just arched an eyebrow. "You wouldn't be interested even if we told you." he said, and he knew that I knew that he was lying.

"Okay." I said, and ate my steak. The conversation devolved back into small talk, then swung back up into a rather rousing swapping of war stories between the Bedouin and Father Luke. But their tales were so vague that I couldn't place what wars they were talking about or what wars they had participated in. I decided not to ask, figuring I'd just be told at a later time, and rather sat back and tried to enjoy the times. Yes, they were weird, off-the-wall, probably insane and entirely mysterious, but I thought of the both of them as good friends. Better friends than anyone I was missing back home. My old acquaintances were fun, surely, but I just never felt right around them. Never felt like I could trust them. Maybe it was the ex-girlfriend fiasco. Maybe it was because she's Mrs. Him and not Mrs. Me. Maybe that's why I don't keep friends anymore.

And yet, for some reason, I felt like I could trust Father Luke and the Wandering Bedouin, even if they were obtuse and hard-headed and refused to tell me anything about the Mountain. In every other matter they were absolutely honest to the point of bluntness, a trait I both admired and disdained, but at the very least appreciated. Maybe there really were good reasons for not letting me in on things. I couldn't see what they were, as I'd apparently spoken to God (I still didn't totally believe that) not a few months ago and *He'd* seen fit to explain things to me.

At any rate, we passed a pleasant evening in which I drank too much of the beer and got drunk. Really drunk. I threw up on the abbey's steps.

The next morning I emerged terribly hung over, which made Father Luke seem particularly bushy-mustached by contrast, and he informed me that the Ecclesiae would be returning that morning and would I accompany him to the farmhouse? Naturally, I agreed, and we waited there for perhaps an hour, playing chess without a chess board when the Ecclesiae did indeed get back. They entered, disappeared with Father Luke into the kitchen for about ten minutes, then re-emerged with a beautiful, leather-bound book titled *Summarium Explicationis, Volume XXVI.* Inside were all of the questions from the book they had given me and all of my own answers, refined, edited and condensed with no loss of continuity or meaning. It was all inscribed in beautiful, flowing calligraphy performed with a quill and a bottle of India ink. I almost cried as they handed it to me, I was so touched.

Later that day I decided to go back to my home, even though I felt like I *was* home.

The Ecclesiae gave me two more parting gifts: A new book, with the title *Summarium Quaestionis, Volume XXXVII.* I opened it and found that three thousand new questions had been written there, philosophical questions raised by my answers to the conundrums contained in Volume XXXVI. They then opened the trunk of my car and showed me that they had included for me every edition of the *Summarium Quaestionis* preceding volume XXVI, except for the first one.

Father Luke had looked at me and said, "The pursuit of wisdom is in fact the pursuit of a better question."

I understand that now, but did not then.

The three thousand questions in the first volume, Father Luke then told me, are the original questions asked by mankind about the nature of God, the world and the universe, and himself. To learn what those questions were I would have to work backwards through every volume until I understood the nature of the struggle of the accruement of knowledge and of the stimulus of philosophy. When I understood whence flowed the river of wisdom, running throughout all of the history of human wonder and ending in it's hidden destination, I would be able to discern the original three thousand and thus the first volume.

The second gift was a beautifully carved wooden sword with a black leather-wrapped hilt and an iron pummel. On it were inscribed many glyphs of warding and protection, similar to the ones inscribed around me on my first morning on Devine Road, in the magical circle that the Wandering Bedouin had drawn. The wood had a long inscription in Sanskrit across the "blade", as well. According to Father Luke, it read "Prajna Khadga", or "Sword of Prajna." Apparently, it was a graduation present from the Man in the Yellow Polo Shirt, Himself.

I went home and started working my way back, little by little, through each of the volumes. Days passed, and I found that something strange had happened to me. I was no longer enrolled in community college, no longer speaking with my friends or parents, no longer working and receiving any kind of money or anything to sustain me and yet my cupboards were always spilling over with food and my gas tank was always full.

I saw, then, that I was now part of the family that inhabits Devine Road, not the family that inhabits Earth, and that I was not long for the world I lived in.

My heart rejoiced.

Merry Old Yule Log
Chapter 6

I went to Devine Road daily from then on, though I still lived in my apartment. I don't know why I didn't just move there, as I was sure that the Ecclesiae would have gladly taken me in, but I think I was waiting for some kind of catalyst: An invitation or something. Maybe I was being thick-headed, refusing to take the hint. Then again, maybe there really wasn't a hint.

I didn't want to gamble, so I continued on as always, just spending my days there exploring Teutoberg or exercising with Father Luke. It snowed there fairly regularly, which sometimes cut into my exploration, as the terrain was quite uneven in many places, difficult to traverse, and anyway Father Luke warned me away from the north side of the forest without an escort, but it didn't slow down my ingestion of the abbey library. Not one bit.

It was fantastic. There may have been ten thousand books in that library, every one of them a classic or a cultural staple or a religious or philosophical work. Every one of them was by an influential author, a great mind, every one of those books was important to the world in a broad sense. I consumed voraciously.

There was one book case that was locked behind glass panes; it was more of a book cabinet, I suppose. Inside were all of the volumes of the *Summarium Explicationis* though there were none of the *Summarium Quaestionis*. I suppose I'd never really noticed them there before, not while I was writing Volume XXVI. Maybe they hadn't been there, I don't know for sure. I did know that my own authorship was there and that it stroked my ego in the best kind of way.

Of course, I hadn't yet worked my way back to the original Volume I, yet. That was going to take a lot of time, I was sure, and I wanted to spend that time familiarizing myself with the place I would soon make my home. Because make it my home I would surely do.

Other books on the locked bookshelf seemed to all be in Latin, and a good number of them were in longhand, not printed, according to Father Luke. I asked him what the nature of these particular books were and he said that it contained a copy of every book concerning, written about or even containing a reference to the existence of the Mountain with No Name. He said that my copies of the *Summarium* series were the only books having anything to do with Devine Road that were off of the Mountain. When I had replied that I hoped it didn't stay that way, he smiled like I already knew the answer to my question. I didn't, of course.

I really didn't know if I was allowed to move to Devine Road. And I *really* didn't know when I had started accepting the idea of someone *allowing* me to do anything. I've always been hardheaded, I've always struggled with authority, even in the Army. It got me in trouble during boot camp.

I wanted to move here so badly and yet it was more important to me that I have permission to do that before I just packed up and took a room.

The snow fell in great sheets, great blankets, great quilts, great covers. It painted everything white but the wildflowers.

This particular partition is beautiful in the embrace of winter. Not that I have a reference point, as I've never been to another partition, but it is gorgeous here. Everything is white and cold, but the oddest things, the little things, are what make this place so magical.

The birds have not gone anywhere. They still sit on branches and limbs of dead trees, singing soprano gaily as though the cherries were blossoming and the leaves were opening. It is a strange thing to hear birds in winter. You never fully realize that they're gone during the winter until you go somewhere where they haven't left. Winter is so *silent* back home. Maybe that's why it's my least favorite season.

But this partition, all covered in snow, well...It's a great, giant sheet of blank paper to draw on. It's beautiful.

And the wildflowers, the flowers that grow defiantly in the face of winter's chilly grip. Some are lightly frosted, some are untouched. Some are completely buried, but all are alive and well, bursting with color. Have you ever seen fireworks of orange, blue and red exploding against a plain of pure white snow? I recommend it.

I can't say it too many times. It's beautiful.

So I came and I went and I came and I went and I only stayed the night when the Wandering Bedouin was there. We camped in the snow and I helped him manage his flock while he told me little things here and there about the geography and the flora and fauna of the partition. He told me there were seven partitions to a Plateau and Seven Plateaus to the Mountain, then abruptly closed his mouth like he had said something he wasn't supposed to. I saved his grace and changed the subject, which I think he was grateful for, but he didn't slip up again, whatever he was slipping up on. He didn't get that embarrassed look on his face the rest of the time I was acquainted with him.

I didn't go north of the forest, as per Father Luke's instruction, but every day I didn't wander that direction only made it worse. I wanted to go and see what was there very badly, as the Joyful Plateau and the Woeful Plateau (minor counterpoints and mere variations on the First Plateau's arcing theme, according to the Wandering Bedouin) were the borders of the half of the Plateau that I'd never explored.

One day, midway through December, I asked the Bedouin if he knew about the angel. He looked startled for a moment, but softened when I explained that I was talking about the statue.

"Ah, of course. The ruins of the Tower of the Third Foederati. Wrath and Justice." he said carefully.

"Yes, that's the one." I said. "What's with that?"

"The Foederati are… it's really not much, you see? There was a small battle here long ago…"

"Battle?"

"Yes. A battle that eventually led to something we refer historically to as the Diaspora…"

"We're not in America, are we?" I asked rhetorically. Of course I'd have known something about a battle or a Diaspora anywhere in my home country. The Bedouin just smiled vaguely.

"It is a difficult question. This Mountain lies within the borders of America but not within its jurisdiction. You know, surely, that this is not an ordinary Mountain."

"By now? I should certainly hope so." I replied.

"It is…it is open to those who are invited, regardless of their place of residence. So, yes. We are in America. But not at all. So to speak." The Bedouin shrugged and smiled.

"Okay. What was the Diaspora?"

"Have you not read *Diaspora*? In the little windowed bookshelf in the Abbey?"

"Father Luke doesn't let me in there." I said, and felt a little miffed all over again at having had things hidden from me.

"Ah. Well, the Diaspora was a minor event. Perhaps you remember the letter that I wrote you when we first met? The one involving a few rules regarding the conditions on which you would be allowed to return here?"

"Yes, I remember."

"The Diaspora in question is the Diaspora of many of our brothers. My brothers, I should say. They broke the Rules. That is why there are so few now within this partition's walls. Myself, Father Luke, the Ecclesiae, Saint Scholastica on occasion..."

"Which Rules?"

"They are...well, they are not rules which apply to you, so I had better not get too far into detail just yet. But I promise that soon you will know all about the Diaspora, and many other things."

"Will you tell me what wars you've fought in?"

"Uh... You will, of course, learn of every battle and every police action, every skirmish and war..." he broke off and looked at me with a painful strain around his eyes. "You will soon know everything."

I furrowed my brow, noticing that he wasn't telling me that *he* would be telling me.

"Are you leaving?" I asked.

"I will come and go." he stated evasively, and cut eye contact with me to pick at a scab on his ankle.

"No, I'm asking if you're *leaving*." I replied, and I was serious. He was being very cryptic.

"It is possible. Everyone must leave at some point, my brother. Everyone must go."

"What's wrong?" I asked.

"That, unfortunately, is something I must leave until 'later'. Perhaps we will speak again after Christmas. That I am sure I will spend with you and my other friends here."

I left it at that and he left that day, moving his flock on to another partition. I asked him, before he left, exactly how he got to another partition, since there were such high walls and no gates that I knew of, and he told me that though there were routes to the other partitions that went *beneath* the walls, he went up to the Second Plateau and used the gates there.

"What's the Second Plateau like?" I had asked.

"Incomprehensibly beautiful." He had replied.

So I was coming and going, coming and going once again. A night on Devine Road, a few clothes brought here and there and stashed in the abbey for when I was too drunk with Father Luke to drive home, but I was essentially in two homes. I went home to sleep and came to Devine Road to live. To live.

The day before Christmas Eve, Christmas Eve Eve or some such, came rolling around. Father Luke, his mustache, the ever-taciturn Ecclesiae and I put up thousands of little golden lights on all of the trim of the house and on a few small trees here and there around the property. Never mind that the lights lit up on their own without any electrical power at all; I was getting used to the subtle magic of the place already. Father Luke and I fashioned a wire frame of a reindeer (it didn't look very good but it was recognizable) and lit that, too, and the Ecclesiae strung pine boughs collected from Teutoberg Forest in rectangles around every window and door. We wound the Christmas lights around ever pillar, every balustrade, every windowsill.

Many people started showing up, here and there, many at the abbey and many at the now-festive farmhouse. Most I did not recognize. I knew the tall black man, the man who had fetched me from Teutoberg on my second night here. He was the Wandering Kenyan, he said, and had not been informed of how to introduce himself to me when we met the first time. For this he apologized profusely and for this I forgave profusely. He turned out to be a very nice person. I met the Wandering Venezuelan again, of course the Wandering Mongol was there; the Wandering Bedouin came back and was yukking it up with the Wandering Jew and the Wandering Aborigine, and the Wandering Briton and the Wandering Crimean apparently had some years-old feud that had established a mutual silent treatment. I wondered just how old that feud was.

There were many others from many other places, the Wandering Basque, the Wandering Cajun, the Wandering Turk, the Wandering Indian. In short, it was a party of Wanderers, excluding the Ecclesiae, Father Luke and myself. There were dozens of them, coming and going, leaving presents under the tree, exchanging stories, embraces, handshakes, scowls. They were just like a family. Strangers all of them, united by a bond they didn't ask for and couldn't explain.

And they all wore some fashion of jewelry around their necks. Necklaces, pendants, simple chains, simple strings of hemp or wool adorning their throats.

I privately wondered if the woman in the white dress would be coming. I was scared to death. But then, I was trying to resolve to find out, as well. I was trying to screw my courage up to find out if it really was *her*.

And what if it was? What if it was her?

119

The radio tower's shadow eclipses the preschool.
The woman is in my crosshairs.

Well, if it's her, it'll be her. It'll be the woman I killed.

Christmas Eve came and some settled in the house, some in the Abbey. The Abbey was huge, with at least twenty rooms (few of them unfurnished) which led me to presume that it was a regular little Devine Road motel for the Wanderers. At least for Christmas.

Bunked up in the abbey and packed eight to a room in the farmhouse, every Wanderer that was on the First Plateau was there for the Yuletide season. So was every monk from the courtyard, but they said nothing at all, only sang Christmas carols at seemingly random (and often ill-timed) intervals.

The Ecclesiae got to work erecting a tent in the backyard. It was like a circus tent in a way, with an octagonal shape, colored in deep magenta with gold trim and tassels. Beneath it the Ecclesiae assembled several long oak tables procured from *somewhere* (I'd never seen a storage unit handy and I'd never seen them in the house) and a Christmas tree, and moved all of the wrapped gifts out there. Then they started cooking.

Mincemeat and four roasted, sage-stuffed turkeys. A honey-mustard glazed ham with home steak fries and rich coleslaw. Two roasts, six chickens stuffed with herbs and garlic and basted with sweet cream butter. Green beans, corn, summer salad, a heaping platter of baked graylings and smoked salmons, onion kabobs, prime rib, Father Luke's spinach au gratin, the Bedouin's stew, every gravy you could possibly imagine. Apples, cranberries, homemade breads, homemade pies, homemade everything. It put my grandmother's memory to shame. What a feast!

We weren't allowed to touch it until the next day, of course, which made me (and several of the Wanderers) grumble, but we were all politely informed (and reminded) that Christmas dinner has always been *Christmas* dinner and that this year is no different than last year. Christmas Eve wasn't, after all, Christmas.

I tried to pick up some answers about the Mountain and Devine Road from the visiting Wanderers, but they had apparently been severely cautioned against saying anything even moderately informational to me. I'd been ignored, had the subject changed without an iota of tact, been given cryptically relevant verses from various religious scriptures, been given mysterious smiles. I learned very little, only that the Wanderers present were not all from this partition but rather called the First Plateau home, and that there were many, many other Wanderers that no longer lived here. In fact, the Wandering Frenchman, after having imbibed one too many glasses of wine, started talking about his good friend the Wandering Spaniard, who now called Hell his home. Then there was the Wandering Tanzanian and the Wandering Samoan, who lived in a two-bedroom apartment in Ottawa. The Wandering Canadian, on the other hand, was non-existent. There wasn't one. Just like there wasn't a Wandering Estonian, a Wandering Kamchatkan, a Wandering Thai, a Wandering Visigoth (no one likes Visigoths) or a Wandering Babylonian.

I don't know why that last struck me as odd. I'd have thought there would have been a Wandering Babylonian. Perhaps they decided that the Wandering Iraqi, who was present and was having a raucous time dancing and drinking with the Wandering Chilean, was Babylonian enough.

The Frenchman talked and talked and talked, in a voice simultaneously less French than Father Luke's and less harsh and gravelly. He talked about Wandering this and Wandering that, and Wanderers here and Wanderers there until at least, very sadly, he started talking about the Wanderesses. The female Wanderers. Who were all gone.

He didn't get to reveal too much to me. The Wandering Eskimo overheard and, perhaps more astute or less drunk than the Frenchman, roused a rendition of *Have a Holly, Jolly Christmas* that all dozens or hundreds of the monks in the house and in the front yard immediately seized on and sang at the top of their lungs. All conversation was drowned out.

In the middle of the carol, the Eskimo dragged the Frenchman away and I didn't see him the rest of the party.

We partied and drank and danced and sang and got so drunk that the beer and wine and spirits got drunk along with us. Bibamus, moriendum est!

And then we all crashed as hard as Newton's law allowed us to. That is to say, we fell at exactly the same speed without consideration for mass, and the party ended almost exactly at four in the morning. Four a.m. on Christmas morning. I passed out harder than I've ever passed out. Right on the floor.

The woman is in my crosshairs.
The preschool is in session.
My finger tenses on the trigger.

She's trying to blow up the radio tower.
She's not going to make it.
I pull the trigger.
Her eyes lock with mine.
She's just outside the preschool.
The bullet flies, faster and faster, as fast as, well, a bullet. As fast as anything can travel. As fast as the human brain can think. I am the bullet now. I am traveling at the speed of human thought.
I travel at the speed of thought.
I am too late as I crash through her skull and tear through her mind. Her finger was on her trigger. Her finger was tense. She hears the rapport of my rifle and with her last act, her last act of volition, she whispers the name of God and pulls her trigger.
I whisper the name of God as the shrapnel from the suicide bomber's explosion rips into my left hand. I don't cry it out, I don't speak it, I don't say it into a radio, or to anyone. Anyone but Him. I just whisper it.
My God. My God.

—

I wake to the softest glow, the glow of firelight. Why did I kill her? I could have saved the life of every child in that school if she'd just made it to the radio tower.

But, then it would be the blood of soldiers on her hands. My comrades. My friends. My colleagues.

Would it have been better than the blood of children on my hands? No. On our hands. The woman in the white jacket and I. We're murderers by intent and neglect and stupidity. She never wanted to kill the kids. She was attacking a military target. *I* killed her right outside the preschool.

It's my fault.

There is a massive log burning in the fireplace, crackling and spitting and casting it's red luminescence over myriad drunken bodies, passed out in various corners and chairs. or passed out right on the rugs. The Wandering American is snoring softly under his giant cowboy hat, right on top of the piano, dreaming about giant Ford pickup trucks and declaring ketchup the Official Condiment of the World.

The Wandering Bedouin is next to me. I close my eyes again, but I can not fall asleep. I look at the east wall. There is a mouse trap lying outside of a hole in the wall. Fast asleep next to it is a mouse, not caught in it, just safe and sound and dozing lazily.

I hear footsteps on the roof and I panic. What were we doing? A whole collection of enemies for the men in brown leather coats, how ripe a target we were! I stand up quickly but silently. The fire in the fireplace goes out, leaving only the moon for light. I grab the fire poker as I hear a *whoosh!* and the gentle alighting of something, like a piece of paper sliding onto the ground. I look at the mouse. Still asleep. I look in the fireplace and strain my eyes as I raise the wrought-iron utility high above my left shoulder like a baseball bat.

I am halfway through a swing when I see a Yellow Polo Shirt. And a bright red Santa hat.

Halfway is as far as the swing gets.

The Man walks out and smiles at me.

"Not a creature was stirring…" He mouths to me silently. He's got a large sack in one hand and a Coca-Cola in the other. He winks, I smile, and I lie back down and go to sleep.

—

The merry old Yule log was dragged in at midnight, though I do not remember it. It was still burning when I woke, and continued to burn throughout the day, just like a Yule log should.

My first Christmas present was a hangover.

—

No one ate breakfast; no one looked like they could keep it down even if they had attempted it. Except Father Luke, who looked fine. The Ecclesiae, too, I suppose. But they had gone to bed early.

Dinner was at three. We all filed out, me next to the Bedouin, Father Luke and the Wandering Sioux behind us. I looked at the procession and noticed for the first time that the Bedouin, though several inches taller than me, was several inches shorter than all of his brethren. Hell, only Father Luke and I were smaller than him. I smiled privately and wondered if he caught shit from his brothers for it. He was a runt.

Then I smiled outwardly. I was a runt, too. The smallest kid in school until I was suddenly very large, right at the onset of puberty, and the once-bullies were then the prey. Boy, I made payback a bitch. No, scratch that. I brought *karma* down on their heads. And as we've stated previously, well, you know. Karma's bad. Real bad.

We ate and talked and we somehow managed to get drunk again and we ate and ate and ate until we thought we'd split at the seams. It was a merry, merry Christmas.

A very merry Christmas.

That night the revelry continued on, a great celebration of the beloved holiday, and this time the Ecclesiae stayed up with everyone and smiled and looked onward with amusement creeping around the corners of their Mediterranean, no, Middle Eastern, no, Oriental mouths. When the party was winding down, at almost four o'clock exactly, one of the twins walked over and handed me an envelope. It smelled of yak musk and mountain air and peach pie. On the front was my name.

"From the Man?" I asked, and swayed a little, drunk.

They nodded in perfect unison.

I opened it up and there was a little letter inside, written on a yellow Post-it note in handwriting so hasty, so child-like in its sloppiness that it could only be called doctoresque. On it was written:

"Do come and stay with the kids."

-The Man

I smiled at the Ecclesiae. They smiled back.

A Yin for the Horrid King
Chapter 7

I spent four hours at my parents' house one day not long after Christmas. I hadn't been going home at all lately, but I hadn't told my parents anything, either. They still thought I was in college, and I had to lie numerous times to preserve that illusion, including why I spent Christmas and Thanksgiving away from home. I won't replicate here the slew of duplicities that poured out of my lips that day, just know that they weren't as simple as they should have been and that it left them suspicious and thus did I break the Three Rules of How to Lie.

The house was comfortable and warm and my mother cooked shepherd's pie while I watched the news on television with my father and talked with him about the war. We have starkly contrasted views; we don't ever talk politics or anything else for very long before we decide it's better to shut up and just have a happy relationship.

Nothing divides people cleaner and with more vehemence than philosophy.

I confess that I was anxious to leave and return to Devine Road. The Wandering Bedouin had sent a carrier pigeon with news to the Ecclesiae that he would be there on this present day, so I wanted to be there as fast as I could.

I kissed my mother goodbye and shook my father's hand. I haven't hugged him in years.

As I walked out of the living room, I saw a Bible laying tits up on the dining room table. It was open to Proverbs, and someone (my father, presumably) had highlighted, with a yellow pen, Chapter 28 verse 1. I could see that this page was a favorite of my dad's. The binding was extraordinarily worn and the page had dog ears more like a mastiff's than a terrier's.

The wicked flee when no man pursueth: but the righteous are bold as a lion.

Kind of a cool Proverb. When taken out of context, there are lots of great passages in the Bible. Even some are great *in* context. There's a lot of beauty in the Good Book. But there's also a lot of wholesale slaughter and violence and oppression and all manner of wonderful things in the same ballpark. Yuck.

It was snowing as I arrived at the Ecclesiae's house, my house, and I was thinking about a lot of things.

Of course I had not tried to formulate a theory as to *how* I was able to access this strange place, this Mountain with No Name. What I spent most of my time doing was trying to formulate a theory as to *why*. Just like the Wandering Bedouin and Father Luke had asked me. Why?

Why me? What's so good about me? I'm not a unique, individual, beautiful snowflake. If there *is* something special about me, what is it? And why is it that I do not perceive it?

I held out my tongue and caught a unique, individual, beautiful snowflake (and three of its stragg.ing friends) on my tongue, then a few more, and then a few more.

I don't like snow, usually. It's pretty, sure, but I don't like being out in it. Today, however, I was finding it acceptable because I was all bundled up with extra layers of clothing, having expected snow, so I wasn't cold and wet, and there was something really beautiful about the weather itself. The snow was falling from some heavy clouds in the east that had not completely overcome the sun, setting in the west, so the dusk was reflecting off of every snowflake, turning them pink and orange and creating a breathtaking landscape to walk through.

WHAM!

A snowball slammed hard into the back of my head and actually knocked my body over. *That* rather ruined my reflective disposition. I toppled face first into the snow and got a mouth full of bitter, frosty pain.

I stood up and turned around, just in time to watch a second snowball blitzkrieg my nose on a perfect vector, with perfect spin and perfect angle. It even seemed like my assailant had compensated for wind.

As I blew little bits of rock and dirt (conveniently rolled into the frozen missile that had just laid me flat a second time) out of my left nostril, I heard a familiar laugh.

It was the Wandering Bedouin.

I stood up quickly, a massive snowball already formed, primed, cocked, locked and ready to fly in my hand, and let him have it. Right in the face.

—

The Protagonist of *Devine Road* Presents
The Perfect Snowball

Now, I may not like snow. I don't suppose I should say that. I do like snow. It looks beautiful through a window from a big chair next to a warm fireplace. But it's a bitch to drive in, a bitch to walk in, it's frigid and freezing and makes its way into the cracks of your snowsuit no matter what you do and I hate being out in it.

However, sledding is fun. Very fun. Almost worth the cold and discomfort. But not quite. You see, there is only one thing *truly* worth the cold and discomfort of snow in this world and that is a snowball fight with friends. Those readers with us today who are past the prime of their youth and have not been in such an altercation in many years are extended an Officially Sanctioned *Devine Road* Encouragement to partake the next time you get a chance. Dear readers, it is never too late to have that happy childhood you always wanted. And it can start right now, this instant, with a snowball fight.

At any rate, many factors must be considered when packing a snowball. Is your recipient of corrigible health? Of appropriate size? What is their gender? For instance, if you are packing a snowball with which you intend to really fucking knock the shit out of a six-foot-four, two hundred and twenty pound Arabian male, you're going to really want to make that fucker hurt. Because you'll need time to make your escape.

How big is too big for a snowball? A good circumference, not too large and not too small will provide ultimate accuracy and velocity. If too big, the snowball goes wide. If too small, its impact is inconsequential or it breaks in the air. And how much debris is acceptable to pack into a snowball? If the recipient is able to handle it, one may pack a rock or twig or a few of each into a single missile. Not too much, nothing too big. This is a snowball fight, after all. No one gets in rock fights on purpose, because rocks fucking hurt when they hit you. Try it some time. Get in a rock fight. It fucking hurts.

At any rate, the recipient, the size of the snowball and the amount of debris are all important considerations when crafting your snowball.

Of course, if there are participating members of the snowball war that are female and attractive, it is wise to lose the snowball fight very badly to these individuals and demand a chance at avenging your honor in a snow *wrestling* match.

—

Lord, that was priceless. Of course, I didn't make that fucker hurt. Not like I should have. Because I didn't have time to make my escape.

He tackled me and we wrestled for a few moments, but that didn't last long. He was a lot stronger than me. When he had subdued me, he piled snow down the back and front of my jacket and also fashioned a hat out of it for me. Not a terribly aesthetic one, but I suppose it was the best he could do. He was working only with powder snow and a struggling head model.

When he decided to finally let me up, he embraced me and laughed. "How are you, my brother?"

"Fucking cold."

"Yes, you seem to be."

He put his arm around me and I grabbed the Prajna Khadga out of the trunk of my car and we started walking toward the farmhouse, he laughing merrily and chatting gaily and me chattering my teeth. I began to realize at that instant that he really liked me, too. It felt good. It felt good to have a friend.

Then a snowball nailed *him* by surprise, in the back of the head, the same place he got me. I spun on a mirthful heel to see who had instigated this new contest, expecting to see Father Luke or an Ecclesiae or one of the Wanderers stopping by for a visit.

I saw instead a flash of black leather as it disappeared into the encroaching darkness.

Black leather. It was *him*. The leathercoat I saw on the other side of the wall.

I then realized suddenly that my friend the Bedouin had collapsed and the Ecclesiae had burst out of their house and were rushing to his side.

There was blood in the snow.

My fingers tensed around the wooden sword and I began pursuit of the man in the black leather coat who had attacked my friend. The Ecclesiae waved their hands and made horrified faces, as if trying to signal me without speaking, as if trying to communicate telepathically. I could almost hear them say, No, Stop and Come Back.

I paid no heed.

As I ran, the heat of my rage spilled from my mouth and warmed the frozen air around me; steam poured from me like I was a locomotive. My eyes and hands were on fire, perspiration solidified on my brow. I was filled with wrath. My face hurt from the snowflakes, falling however gently that snowflakes fall, because they whipped against me with a fury, one by one, propelled by my own velocity and the force I created by running against the wind. Shortly, I caught sight of my prey making a run for Teutoberg Forest, so I set an intercepting vector and ran as fast as my legs would run. I raised my bludgeon high.

The snowflakes kept stabbing, one by one, as if planned.

I was gaining on him, and he was starting to weave and flail his arms desperately. I mustered my courage, leaned my body forward and ran even faster. Full speed ahead and damn the torpedoes.

There was, at that point, a man on horseback emerging from the threshold of Teutoberg Forest where Devine Road enters it. He was old, very old, with a long white beard and a grey hat, and a grey cloak fastened with a silver brooch. When he saw us running, he suddenly spurred his horse toward the man in the leather coat at full speed, galloping for all the world like a rider in the Kentucky Derby. I thought for a quick moment that the unnamed equestrian was going to assist this devil, but he instead rode up alongside the man in the black leather coat and hit the pursued with a hard kick from his left foot.

One by one, the snow flakes hit my face, but they were no longer slamming into my face. They were falling gently, one by one. The wind had changed direction, and was now at my back, speeding me toward my destiny.

It was at that point, I think, though my memory of this event is somewhat addled, that I noticed a pattern to the snowflakes alighting on my cheeks. I did not have time to stop and ponder it, of course; I was consumed with determination. I was the very picture of fury.

But somewhere, subliminally, I recognized it.

I caught up to my quarry very quickly.

The man in the black leather coat rose from the horseman's attack, bared his teeth and adopted a frightening new speed, on into the forest, into the black, obscuring trees. I pursued, knowing it was stupid, knowing it was suicide. What causes men to do things like this? The Freudian Death Wish? Or the drive to die well, an impulse so strong that we'd die early just to die gloriously? Or is it just plain foolishness?

All three?

Silence slammed into me louder than any crash of any abbey as I entered the forest. The horseman had stopped riding, the Ecclesiae stopped screaming. I was enveloped in a thick wall of darkness. The sun had almost set completely, leaving nothing for me to see by, and there was a demon in the trees. The silence was insufferable.

"Come out!" I cried. I heard a shuffle, a cracking of a twig. I turned, suddenly terrified, in the direction from whence it came. "Coward!" I screamed, as if to project my own fear onto him. I wondered if he was as scared as I.

Another shuffle, another small noise. Oh, fuck. Oh, fuck. Oh, fuck.

My eyes darted in all directions. The corners of my mouth twitched nervously. I had a cramp in my foot and I had to pee. Why the hell did I run into this forest?

I saw a black eyeball in my peripheral vision, lolling, lazy, looking at nothing. As my gaze twisted to lock on the hallucination, the trees seemed in their passing blur to form faces with sharp, crooked teeth and long Roman noses. Their branches constituted in my vision daggers. And then there was no eyeball.

I saw a pile of pale bodies for a brief second, dead and bloated and lying on each other. I was transported suddenly to Auschwitz, forced to look at the ovens, at the piles of bones, at the hate and misery of the camps. Then it was gone.

I blinked and saw a massive, ashen-colored naked body with rippling muscles and scales, writhing and clawing at itself. It was headless, bleeding in fountain-like spurts from its decapitated neck and peeling its own skin off layer by layer. All around the monster and I were burning buildings and human beings, thousands of them, burning, on fire, screaming and running in every direction as I watched the great headless demon thrash about.

I looked down and the demon was gone, but then I felt my legs warm and wet and saw that I was standing in a sea of chum, that disgusting bloody mess they feed sharks. Only there were human remains floating in it. The trees suddenly became worms and snakes of all types and sizes, and they started oozing dirty water from hidden pores. The branches became squirming, slimy tentacles, dripping blood from their hellish tips.

This isn't real. I closed my eyes and thought over and over, like a mantra. When I opened them again it hadn't worked. It wasn't over. I wasn't in the worm forest anymore. I was in the most infinitely terrible, most horrifying place I could think of.

I was back in Mosul. I saw a man, a woman. A woman in a white jacket. Corporal Banks. The radio tower.

I closed my eyes, shut it out. When I forced myself to look again, I was

130

firing my rifle. I closed my eyes again, squeezed them shut, covered them with my hands and then slowly, so slowly, the smell of the burnt flesh of children entered my nose and I could take no more.

"Enough!" I cried. "Enough!" My nostrils cleared, filled with pine sap. I opened my eyes again, saw very little, but knew I was back in the forest.

And for some reason I registered, so subtly, the word "regret" deep within my aural canal. Somehow I got the distinct impression that I was being apologized to.

I heard a growl, a blast of hot breath on my neck. I spun, swung, felt nothing. Another breath, this behind my ear. A low, sustained growl.

He was playing with me. I was in his domain now, the domain of darkness and the unknown. I was on his terms. That's why he took off for the forest. And now he was going to kill me.

All right, you bastard. I thought. *If this is how it ends, then it ends.* My fear left me. I settled into the old frame of mind. The soldier's frame of mind. The Robert Louis Stevenson frame of mind.

With the part of my brain that I don't need to fight I looked back over my life and found that I had more regrets than I had ever planned to have. My failure to complete high school, my tenure in Iraq, my best friend marrying the woman that should have been *my* wife...

My sweet, lovely girlfriend. My best friend of eight years. Traitors. Betrayers.

The ninth circle of Hell is reserved for Satan, Judas, Brutus, Cassius and people who abandon kittens. And those who betray their loved ones.

But there were beautiful things in my life, too. Little experiences, little things. And everything leading up to me being here. On the Mountain. The greatest four months of my life. The four months of my life that redeemed every terrible thing that ever happened to me.

Does everyone get four months on Devine Road?

All right, man in the black leather coat. Let's do it. Glad did I live, glad do I die. And I lay me down with a will.

Ccchrrrrrrrck! My jacket and shirt and the skin on my back ripped into jagged tatters as four sharp swords raked down from my shoulders to my tail bone, shallow cuts in perfect parallel equidistance from my spine. My blood started falling, slithering out of the wound, running hot on the remains of my jacket and dripping onto the ground. I cried out so that it reverberated off of the trees and echoed off of the cliffs on the other side of the forest.

I spun and swung, spun and swung, flailed the Prajna Khadga in every direction, but nothing was there. Almost completely blind, my head pounding, my stomach sick from the pain, I listened intently. A snowflake made its way through the canopy and settled on my cheek. It paused, and there was another.

A light went on somewhere in the attic of my brain and sent an impulse down to my leg to kick, kick for all I was worth as high as I could exactly one hundred and eighty degrees behind me. It caused the skin on my back to tighten and tear at the wounds there and had me howling in pain, but my foot had connected, had smashed into something that felt an awful lot like a face. I heard a growl and footsteps running away from me, so I grabbed a good-sized branch that was lying on the ground and threw it in that direction. There were three *thuds*, a thud from the branch hitting my enemy's head, a thud from the branch hitting the ground, and a thud from *him* hitting the ground.

My eyes were adjusting, slightly. I could see just a little. Just enough to see him getting back up. But my back hurt, so badly.

I charged him, acutely aware of the burning, shredding sensation on my aft side and smashed my stick hard into his back, then kicked him in the face again. He managed to get to his feet and start running again, but it was back into the open, back on the south side of Teutoberg, where the farmhouse and the horseman and the Ecclesiae and the Bedouin were. Where the Bedouin was lying in the snow.

I gave chase again and this time, he could not outrun me, despite the swimming of my perception, the foggy soup sloshing around in my brain.

Just outside of the trees I jumped and tackled him. He tried to bite at my arms, but I grabbed his jaw and the back of his head and smashed it into the pure white snow, over and over again. I twisted, snapped, tried to break his neck five or six times, but it wouldn't work. It was like his vertebrae were made of iron.

A quick wrench of his body and a surprisingly forceful lurch sent me flying off of him. He got up and made eye contact with me for a fateful second, and all of that fear and anxiety and cold, clammy terror I felt that day at the partition wall came flooding back. It took me a half-second to push it down to grip it, to subdue it. It was a half-second too long.

As if he had given up trying to get away and had now adopted the resolve of the cornered animal, he lunged and tore a large chunk flesh from my left leg, right on the back of the thigh. I dropped to the other knee, now in crippling pain. He was snarling and roaring like a tiger. A snowflake hit me. His eyes had assumed an unholy glow and his fingers seemed to have suddenly sharpened to knife points. His eyes turned black as midnight. Veins stood in livid ridges on his temples and throat. I hunched forward, ignoring pain, shoulders at the ready, and smiled. The leathercoat should have bit my knee and not my thigh. Should have severed the tendon, put me out of commission. Should have just bit my fucking leg off.

Yes, he had made a mistake.

Yes, it was possible that he would make another.

I pulled up my "sword," lowered it to the ground, dragged it around in the traditional swordsman's insult of his opponent. His rage seemed to grow, his shoulders started smoking, little wisps of black miasma, like the first beginnings of flame in a bonfire's tinder. His whole form went black to me and I was unable to distinguish details, only the silhouette of the demon, and I abruptly felt as if I was perceiving him through the windshield of a car with the overhead light on. A self-righteousness filled me up from head to toe, a pervading sense of determination rose in my gorge, a battle cry crowded my larynx and tonsils and teeth. A blinding glare bleared out my peripheral vision and made it hard to see.

I blinked hot tears from my eyes and raised my bludgeon.

One by one, the snowflakes fell.

I roared, I projected myself, my anger and my murder and my tragedies and my betrayals and my despairs and I sent them all to the moon, that she might look after them. I didn't need them. I couldn't use them. I was already running at the man in the black leather coat.

He lurched at me and I rolled beneath him, then spun around, swinging the Prajna Khadga in a low, upward arc. A snowflake on my face. I felt his ankle break beneath my blow and a surge of victory filled my heart as he screamed a loud, canal scream and collapsed. I jumped and brought my bludgeon down quickly but, despite his injury, he was already somewhere else. Snowflake, pause. He lunged on one foot from my right, but I evaded his pounce and swung hard, missing his head by a fraction. Snowflake. He lunged again, I missed again, he counterattacked and I dodged, then a lucky swing broke three of the fingers on his left hand. One by one, familiarly, the snowflakes fell.

One by one.

We circled each other, his two left limbs lame and dragging horribly like I had strangled them with a garrote and not bashed them with a wooden sword. They were fast losing color; his ankle was as white as the snow, his hand was as pale if not still as dangerous as a polar bear's paw. Snowflake.

We traded threatening advances, feints, and swipes with bludgeons and claws and teeth and kicks. He was quick and I was quick, he was strong and I was strong. He was deadly, but I was destined to be victorious. Snowflake, pause. Snowflake, snowflake, snowflake.

He jumped at me and connected, pinning me to the ground. He screamed again like a great giant cat and blood burst from his eyes like fountains, spilling all over me and burning into my skin, boring down into my pores and scalding me like his vital fluids were molten rock. The pain was incredible, the worst I've ever felt. Childbirth, kidney stones, migraines are nothing compared with the sheer anguish that is being burnt by the acid lava of leathercoat blood. One by one, the snowflakes hit my face. Fighting the shock my body was going into, fighting the irrefutable impulse to pass out, fighting the will of my soul to leave my body, I grabbed the broken fingers on his left hand and thus solicited an agonized shriek from my enemy, then closed my left hand, the damaged one, into a tight fist and punched him in the jaw, once, twice, three times, more. My hand was working. It wasn't losing its grip. Wasn't losing the fist. Wasn't losing strength. Wasn't trembling. It was working, and it was breaking his fucking jaw.

I felt his face break at the joint so I switched to his nose, which took one blow to split. I grabbed his dangling chin, shoved it as hard as I could away from the break and was rewarded with a loud snapping of his tendons and a tenebrous creak as the force of my hand dislodged his jowl completely. I then counterbalanced myself with a grip on his shoulder, pulled him high enough to get my legs free and kicked him square in the midsection. Snowflake, pause. It sent him reeling over my head with just enough distance to allow me to stand up quickly, too quickly. My head was on my torso now, my legs were flan gelatin, my arms weighed hundreds of pounds. I reeled, almost fell, lost complete vestibular sense and *then* toppled over. I tried to get up, he tried to get up. We both fought death as well as each other.

When he rose to his knees, it seemed to give me the strength to raise myself, as well. I heard the sound of thundering hooves as we lay there, not looking at each other but rendered prostrate before the glory of each other's might. We raised a knee at exactly the same moment, got to one foot at exactly the same moment, stood simultaneously and locked eyes. In that moment we knew each other.

In that moment he saw in me freedom, freedom from Hell, freedom from Heaven, without punishment, without retribution, pure independence. He knew the autonomy of free will, of the human soul.

And I saw that he wasn't evil. I was. I was ending an age-old quest for vengeance for him, a campaign to destroy the works of He that betrayed His own children, of He that was jealous, of He that would accept no democracy, no equality, no prince for His king. Of He that would create new subjects, free people on a hidden plane without so much as sniffing at the pleas for liberty from His most faithful servants.

He knew me thoroughly then, knew me as humanity, as vassal and ambassador for my race, as paradigm of our freedoms and failures and he loved and envied me. He knew for the first time what guardian angels feel about their charges.

And I knew him and I pitied him, feeling for the first time the nascent heat in the blood of guerillas and freedom fighters and revolutionaries. I knew Che Guevara, I knew Frederick Douglas, I knew Zapata. I knew the great freethinkers: Socrates, Thoreau, Bertrand Russell.

We knew each other. We wanted what each of the other had. His eyes welled up with tears and he tried to smile, a horrible and sinister and absolutely genuine gesture that he could not offer for the state of his face but was nonetheless born in the corners of his eyes and died in the height of his cheekbones. I thought of the Bedouin who could be dead and my own eyes moistened.

Hello. I heard in my head, and it was the sound of my own voice.

"Hello, Horrid King." I said out loud, and didn't know why I said that. His eyes twinkled.

Let's have it over with. Send me to Hell.

"I'll make it quick." I promised bewilderedly.

Thanks.

He charged me one final time, howling like a panther, screaming like a cougar, roaring like a tiger. I very nearly missed sidestepping it.

One by one, the snowflakes fell.

A brilliant flash blinded me as my weapon came around on the counterattack, like moonlight, like the shine of my anger and murder and tragedy and betrayal and despair was given back to me all at once, reflecting off of steel. I heard a sound like a great lion roaring from a high mountain, as if it reverberated through every valley, off of every tree, through every river, over every mountain, in the hearts and minds of every human being who ever lived. I swung! And cut his right arm clean off as though I had wielded a sword made of metal. Hot black liquid that was thick as molasses poured from his wound and sizzled on the ground. It stank like sulfur.

Snowflake. Snowflake, snowflake, snowflake, pause.

At that precise moment, my equestrian benefactor, who had come around for a second pass, smashed his horse at full speed into the man in the leather coat. My enemy fell beneath the horse's hooves, I think, because he was left badly broken and bruised and twitching on the ground. Snowflake, pause. I regained my grip on my bludgeon, stood up, and brought the weapon crashing down on the man in the black leather coat's head with all of my strength, the snowflakes caressing me rhythmically all the while.

I love you.

The life left the man in the black leather coat like a frozen wind passing from a black, evil sky to another.

I remember, before collapsing, a boiling hot jet of liquid splashing on me, running up my arm and burning my chest badly, and hearing a choking sob from somewhere outside my body, a sob that was jailed in my throat and let loose in choral unison with the *crack!* that a skull makes when it splits into seven pieces. I lay there for sometime, wheezing as the Ecclesiae ran to the Horrid King and I.

One by one.

His name was Moloch. This I knew, this I knew at the core of me.

Snowflake, snowflake. Snowflake, pause, snowflake, pause, snowflake. Snowflake, snowflake, snowflake, pause.

Something was coming back to me, something from long ago. Five or six years ago. My first job in the Army. Telecommunications. Communications. Before I earned my chevrons.

Those little frozen slivers of ice were spelling something.

S-A-C-R-I-F-I-C-E.

In Morse code.

I woke with that word on my lips. The Bedouin and I were in separate beds at the Ecclesiae's house, placed next to each other in my room, the room where I had answered the bulk of the *Summarium Quaestionis*. Before me was a fresh, hot meal of white, flaky fish, potato pancakes, grilled vegetables and a glass of some kind of white wine. I ate like a man who was starved, and my vulgar manners woke the Bedouin up. "Ah, you are awake!" he cried. He rubbed his eyes, then the back of his head.

"What happened? What did he throw at you?"

"A snowball."

"Yes, I understand that. Why were you bleeding?"

"Ah, that. You may have seen these before." He produced several small iron shards from his bedside table. "I extracted similar materials from the wounds I received on the first night we met."

"I remember." I said fearfully. "What are they?"

"Shards."

"Of what?"

"I'm not sure I should say. If Virgil explains, I will tell you all about them. Otherwise, I will stay quiet."

I frowned, but his face suddenly grew mirthful. "You pursued my attacker, no?"

"I presume that's why I'm here." I said, looking around. "I don't know if he bled on me, or whatever." I examined my chest. There was a long stripe of skin with no pigment running up the left side of it, and dozens of similar little bleached islands in various other places. "I guess that big splash of blood was right along here."

"Indeed. Do you know what it is that you have done?"

I confessed that I did not. He stroked his beard and chuckled, looking wistfully out the window.

Then there was a knock at the door. I gave permission to the unseen inquisitor to enter, and he did so. It was my equestrian benefactor, the one that undoubtedly saved my life. Close behind was Father Luke and Saint Michael. Saint Michael was smiling broadly (incredulously?) at me and so was the horseman, but Father Luke looked very upset. He frowned at me. "Do you know what you've done?"

"I did what I thought was right." I asserted.

Michael coughed/laughed. "Whaddya think, Father? You want me to give him my wings and everything? That *was* impressive."

The priest gave Michael a look that would have chilled a penguin, then turned back to me. "Try to understand. If this person…" he indicated the equestrian, "…hadn't been riding out of the forest at that instant, you'd be dead. I'd appreciate if you did nothing like that ever again. At least until

you're better prepared."

The Wandering Bedouin cleared his throat. "I'm a little flattered, actually."

Father Luke's face softened and his mustache rippled softly in time with a gruff chuckle. "Well, I suppose that makes it all worth it. Are you still hurting?"

"Yes."

"Not for long, you won't be. In the meantime, Uri and Gabe are watching your flock. How are *you* feeling?" He indicated that he was talking to me.

"How should I be feeling?" I asked, and I wasn't being sarcastic. I was obviously out of my league.

"Like shit." said Saint Michael. "But you impressed the hell out of me. And the Boss, too, even though He's not here to say it. You clearly have no idea what you've done, and that's okay. But just you wait, little brother." He winked at me. "Who is like God?" he muttered under his breath as he left the room.

"Be right there." said Father Luke to the archangel. He turned and looked at me. "It's just dangerous. You got lucky. There are other things on this Mountain that you can battle that are not full-fledged fallen cherubim. Granted, that kind of encounter won't happen again, but if it does, it won't have the same outcome. Don't be stupid. Virgil told me about that little backhanded arc you pulled, and it could have just as easily as missed if you'd been a little off as cut that bastard in half if you'd have done it right." Father Luke sighed and looked wistfully out the window. "Now everything's changed."

"What do you mean?" I asked.

"You'll see." replied Father Luke.

"I hate being told that." I muttered. The Bedouin smiled.

Father Luke looked at me again and this time wore a smile of his own, a smile perhaps of resignation, and it hung funny on his face. "That does that. I suppose someone was going to have to do it, but I hadn't thought that the Man was going to put it into motion yet. I'm glad it was you, even if I have no idea what's going to happen to all of us now."

I furrowed my brow. "What's all this? You're speaking mysteriously."

"Don't worry about it. Just be sure and come to the Abbey for practice. Often. You're a terrible swordsman."

"Thanks for the kind words, Father." I said, and he gave me a stern look and closed the door behind him as he left. Which left the equestrian, standing over the Wandering Bedouin and me.

"Well," he said. "I'm Virgil."

"Hi, Virgil." I replied. "I presume you're the *actual* Virgil?

"Could be." he said. "Could be I'm Jules Verne."

"Hmmm. You do look a bit like Jules Verne." I said, and laughed.

Virgil smiled. "Anyway, I wanted to congratulate the soldier here on his first major victory of many to come. I'm heading for the partition wall in half an hour, so I won't be here again for a while. I just wanted to meet the human that killed *the* Leathercoat."

"So it's dead?" I asked. "I didn't know that I could kill it." I noted his use of the word "human." This wasn't *the* Virgil.

Virgil's smile turned to a frown. "Oh, I use 'kill' colloquially. He just won't be coming out of Hell for a while. A millennium or so. At any rate, thank you for doing what you did."

"Thanks for the assist." I said.

"My pleasure." He paused, and scratched his head, as if trying to remember something. "Oh!" he exclaimed.

"What?"

"How do you feel?"

I did a quick mental check. Not too much pain. "Uh, middlin'. I guess."

"Can you walk?"

"Yeah."

Virgil grinned. "Come outside. You should see something."

———

We walked out, the Bedouin and Virgil and I. It was a glorious, clear morning, and as cold as I'd ever felt on the Mountain. Snow lay on the ground, as white as a saint's soul.

"I wanted to show you this," said Virgil. "Because I thought you'd get a kick out of it." He walked over to two sets of footprints leading away from the house. I recognized one of the pair of prints as my own and then noticed that there was no snow where we had tread, the Horrid King and I. The grass was growing and was warm and healthy as if it were summer in my footprints; I looked at the other set, and noticed that the ground was black and charred and still smoking where the man in the leather coat had run away from me.

"He really poured on a lot of effort getting away from you. His footsteps wounded the earth." stated the Bedouin. "You outdid him. The snow fears

139

where he tread, and thus does not fall in his prints, but it is of love and respect for you that it does not fall in your footprints."

I shook my head in disbelief.

"Believe it." said Virgil. "You will encounter many stranger things than this along the Road."

We walked back to the house, where Virgil's horse was waiting. He mounted it and reached down to shake my hand vigorously before clasping the reins. "You did good work, my friend. Good work. I hope that you survive what's next."

"We did good work." I replied, acting like I knew what was "next" was and that I wasn't suddenly chilled by that extrapolation.

The Wandering Bedouin smiled broadly. I smiled even broader. Then Virgil left.

"How strange." I said under my breath as the Bedouin and I returned to our bedroom.

"Hmmm. I should think you would be accustomed to things being out of the ordinary on the Mountain, my brother." said the Bedouin as he crawled between his sheets.

I got into my own bed. "That's what strange." I said. "Being accustomed to it." I fluffed my pillow. "'What's next?'" I asked.

"You'll see." yawned the Wandering Bedouin.

"Christ." I yawned back. "Can't a man just get an explanation around here?"

The next morning, the Bedouin was not in his bed when I woke. I went downstairs and found him taking tea out on the veranda, before the sunrise. I walked out, studied the high, yellow planks of the awning for a moment, cleared my throat.

"Is it safe to be out here before dawn?" I asked, and he jumped.

"Good morning to you, my brother." he said with a sudden, startled smile. Oops. I hadn't meant to sneak up on him. "I thank you for your concern, but I typically spend every night out of doors. Today, especially, we have nothing to fear."

"Why?"

He looked at me as if surprised, as if I should have known. "Because by your action the principal threat has been removed. I presume now that the Tiamat will be set free while our Enemy devises a new means to threaten us, or sends a new general. There is a great amount of commotion in their vile

140

ranks right now, not only from what you have done, but also of some internal strife that has at last come to a head. At any rate, you have bought us a week of time. A week until they free the Tiamat."

"What is the Tiamat?" I asked, and the name sounded heavy and cold on my tongue. I felt a subdued panic. A sudden desire to run from that name.

"It is a fiend from Hell." said the Bedouin grimly. "If you need further explanation I would not know how to present a worse picture. Saint Scholastica will be here, shortly."

I resisted the urge to ask who Saint Scholastica was. I figured (correctly) I'd learn in due time, and if I asked I'd just receive a "You'll see." anyhow.

"I've heard her name." I said.

"It is a powerful name." he said, and that ended our conversation.

The Bedouin and I stood there without talking. I smoked, he drank his tea, and we watched the east together for some time.

I do not remember at what point it was that I noticed that the Ecclesiae were standing directly behind us, but I got the distinct impression that they had been there for some time. They did not look impatient when we at last turned around, but I remember feeling a distinct aura of annoyance emanating from them. And indeed, they seemed to ignore me and motioned for the Bedouin to come inside. I didn't follow (I wasn't invited.) Instead, I lit a new cigarette with the burning embers of the current and put out the smoldering ash on the bottom of my shoe, then pocketed the butt.

What was next? What was going to change?

What the Hell is so special about me?

Vicissitude
Chapter 8

Later that day, the Wandering Bedouin politely informed me that Father Luke was looking for me, so I headed off to the abbey. But I did not walk the road. Rather, I made a new foot tread through the long field, the Ager Epiphania.

I walked and hoped and trembled. But I saw no children, and no woman in the white dress. Maybe I walked the field instead of the road in the hope that I'd see her. See graceful, feminine barefoot prints dancing around the loving depressions in the snow that children's feet make. Maybe not. Maybe I was a little disappointed.

I had decided at last that I would ask her. Maybe then I would be able to sleep peacefully again.

I carefully stepped around wildflowers, bright and alive whenever they came across my path (or did I come across theirs?) so as not to hurt any "before their time", as the woman in the white dress had beseeched me not to do. I was looking at my feet, walking roundabout roses, sidestepping snapdragons, dancing around dandelions.

I arrived at the abbey and saw that the Ecumenics, that prodigious congress of monks, had reconvened for the time being; I hurried through their points, whispers and stares and up the stairs to the door, which did not even creak when I opened it. Not this time.

There was no one in the abbey. I searched the whole place, every quadrant, every section, every hall, every room. Odd. I couldn't imagine why Father Luke would have had to rush off so quickly that he would not have left a note or the like.

I waited in the library for around an hour before deciding to go back to the Ecclesiae's and rest a bit more.

The next morning, I stated to my hosts that I was going home. The Bedouin had left the partition, Father Luke was gone, and the Ecclesiae were giving me the silent treatment, more so than they had ever done. Not that I'd ever heard them utter a single word. They simply refused to acknowledge even my presence.

I was tired, and wanted to take a break. I wanted to see my family. Surely I had no intentions of running away, but I certainly wanted a change of scenery. I thought a little vacation would do me good. As the Ecclesiae had said nothing, only nodded in perfect synchronization, I got in my car and drove away.

K'ung Wu.

I heard that in my head just as I pulled out of the mist that separates Earth and the Mountain, as loud as if a Chinaman had sat in my passenger's seat and screamed it into my ear. I did not ponder it, only waited for fulfillment. I knew that, in time, I'd find out. I could almost hear myself asking the Wandering Bedouin what that meant. I could almost hear him saying "You'll see."

I pulled out of the mist into a crisp January morning. The morning of January seventeenth, to be exact. But I was fast losing track of my concept of the Gregorian calendar; outside of the observation of holidays, there were no months, weeks and days on Devine Road.

I rolled down my window and smelled the frosty air. I caught a whiff of peppermint and hot chocolate. A whiff of pine wreaths and pumpkin pie.

I suddenly realized that I would miss my parents very much. Because I wouldn't be able to see them again.

No. Not *wouldn't*. Couldn't. Oh, God, it would have been too complicated. How does one maintain a double life? The lies would catch up to me. Eventually my mom would just "drop by" the place I "lived" or my father would "drop by" the place I "worked" and then I'd be done for. I'd have no choice but to leave them for good, then and there, in order to preserve the secret of Devine Road.

What was more important to me? Their feelings? Or my life? My new life? I had to make the decision.

What was I doing? I wasn't going home. I was leaving home. I couldn't make my parents understand that I was going to be living in a magical faraway land. I didn't have a choice, only the illusion of one. I couldn't go home. I hadn't been home since right after Christmas. How could I explain that I wouldn't be coming back? How could I look them in the eye? How could I look my mother in the eye? I couldn't go home. I had to be gone. I had to disappear and let them work through it, let them learn to live with it. They were already a few weeks into it, and though it's not the first time I've left for a long period of time, they always knew about it beforehand. Not hearing from me for over a week was unusual. I see them a lot, love them a lot. Spend a lot of time with them. They're kind of my only real friends.

Oh, God. My poor parents. They've at least got a head start on the worry right now, don't they? I couldn't go home. It would be so much more painful for them to tell them that I was leaving them forever and that I'd never see them again *of my own volition*. I should just let them believe that I was abducted, killed, drowned, gone. Let them cope. Let them blame an accident. Not me.

For their sake, not mine. The pain of outliving a child is second only to outloving a child.

I drove by my old apartment and left a note for my landlord stating that I was leaving. I dated it January Third and put it in my apartment.

I left no forwarding address, though I was tempted to leave "100 Devine Road". I was afraid that the Road would be closed to me if I did that.

I grabbed some clothes and a few other things, the *Summarium* series and some other bits of ephemera and got in my car.

I drove by my parents' house and waved goodbye to them, though they did not see me. They weren't home. I hoped they were out catching a movie or doing something fun. I hoped they weren't thinking about me.

A billboard I passed on I-5 extolled a massive New Age convention coming to the city in less than a few weeks. It was even on the front page of a newspaper stand I passed in the parking lot of the McDonald's where I got lunch, right next to a story on a massive new sex scandal spread across various Protestant denominations that mirrored almost exactly the great child-molestation scandal the Catholics had suffered through not too long ago.

Can't say the general populace had been paying a whole lot of attention to the New Age movement for some time; the whole idea of personal salvation, power and responsibility wasn't enough to wrench people from that happy, safe little box that was the Man in the Yellow Polo Shirt. Even though he'd seemed like he would have been fonder of the New Age developments than the older, stuffier religions. I don't know, maybe the scandals were driving people away from their old religions. It's hard to stay in a comfort zone that's not comfortable.

Hmmm. I wasn't much for the New Age either. Sure, it was ecumenical, which promoted tolerance and was important at least to me, but its precepts were just Western and Eastern thought mashed into an unrecognizable mess. Not my style.

I drove to a bar, a broke-down little dive with one pool table and no jukebox that I used to frequent whenever I was low on cash. The drinks here were cheap, renowned for their strength, and made for good prefunk on Saturday nights. Today, I just had a cold beer. Behind me, two couples at a table were breaking established bar etiquette and discussing the Third of the Three Impolite Topics of Conversation. Religion.

One of the women seemed really irate. She was talking about how she'd been reading, about what the Church had done to peace-loving pagan aboriginals the world over. She'd never known, she claimed. Never known about the Inquisition. Or at least never thought about it. Never thought about the chauvinism and violence of the Holy Scriptures. Now she was reading the Bible again, and it was *pissing her off*. So she said. Women were second-class citizens, she says. That's why women are oppressed, she said. Because of ancient, outmoded, patriarchal religions like Christianity and Islam and Judaism. They are the roadblocks to equality, she said. And she was never going to church again. The other woman at the table was nodding her head fiercely, fueling the flames. The men looked slightly uncomfortable.

So I asked the bartender if I could buy the ladies' drinks for the evening, paid for the libations and left. The least I could do was reward that sort of philosophy.

Maybe I was flattering myself.

I left and drove by a movie theater, I think, hoping to see my parents' car there. I don't know why. They don't even go to movies that often.

The marquis, loud and blinking, was announcing the brand new release of yet another remake of *The Last Temptation of Christ*. It was a massive box-office smash. People were looking at the story in a whole new light and an all-female band had composed the soundtrack for it. Their album and the movie's soundtrack had both gone platinum.

I thought about driving by my parents' house again, but thought better of it. They might see me. Don't cause any more trouble than you already have, I thought. Go somewhere safe. Go back.

Safe? Is it safe on the Mountain? I'm cautioned not to go out at night! What the Hell is the Tiamat? Safe? I'm safer, here. I should just go home. Home to my parents. Home to their love and their blissful ignorance.

But I knew that I couldn't. I knew that I couldn't return to my home. I'd be unable to live with myself, and if I cracked and told someone, not only would I be sent to the loony bin, Devine Road would be closed to me forever. I couldn't do it. I couldn't go home.

I couldn't go home. So I went home. To the farmhouse.

—

The sky was the color of a dead television screen. The forest, for some reason, seemed farther away from the farmhouse than it did when I left. The snow was falling again, covering *everything* this time, even the wildflowers. The phone lines were sagging heavily. The wind sang a dirge for the sun, now strangled and decomposing and dying a frozen death buried beneath the dark grey clouds.

There were no birds outside but rooks and magpies, and they spread their angry, squawking choruses from tree to tree. Squirrels were all but gone. I saw a grey one holding a rock in his shivering paws, but he, too, skittered away, and left me with the black birds.

There was not a bit of color to be seen.

The farmhouse came into view.

There was no color in the farmhouse.

It was not bright and yellow, not gaudy and ridiculous, not a great canary with a fat ass plopped down on the side of the Road. Not anymore. Now it was a white house, with slate grey trim. I started to panic. What the Hell was going on?

I got out of my car and power-walked to the porch, my nostrils filling with the smell of primer and paint. The door was fresh and wet; apparently the Ecclesiae had just painted the house. Them or someone else. But Lord, that was a fast job.

I walked in and went upstairs, dropped off the things I had grabbed from my place, looked around for the twins. Not a soul to be found. So I walked to the abbey, solemn and stony grey and without a bit of color and I looked there for someone. Anyone. But there was no one there, either. Hmmm.

I got in my car and drove north. The first time I had driven my car north of the farmhouse. The Road, losing quality and eventually devolving into gravel once I got into Teutoberg, was a fairly straight shot. I drove for a few minutes, fast then slow, not really paying enough attention to worry about my speed, as I didn't think that God had imposed speed limits on the Plateau. I was deep in thought.

No birds but black ones. The house painted. Everything black and white. Hell, at least I had color. I looked at my dashboard clock; it read 6:06 P.M. The sky was losing its light fast.

There was something programmed into me about not going out at night on the Mountain. The Bedouin had told me there was no need to worry about it *now*, after my battle with the leathercoat, but it'd been that way since I got here. Habits of any age die hard.

I crested a small hill and saw the edge of the woods fast approaching. Just beyond that was either a small river or a large creek and no matter what its classification it was completely frozen over. There was a bridge extended over it, a wooden bridge carved to resemble two very large hands shaking each other, as if in accord. I pulled off to the shoulder of the road and got out.

There was quite a crowd assembled on the bridge.

Several Wanderers, several tall men in black suits, several other people of some kind that I didn't recognize. Virgil was there. The Ecclesiae were there. Father Luke was definitely there; he was standing right out in front. They were standing in loose formation, covering the whole of the walkway, as if they were expecting me to rush them and beeline for the Second Plateau. Father Luke had been addressing them until I pulled up. I was totally confused.

But not as confused as I was when I realized that there wasn't a bit of color to any of them. Not their skin, not their eyes, not their clothes, not in the wood they stood on, nothing. Not a bit. That gave me a Hell of a shock. Could this be my fault? Am I killing this place by being here? Am I killing this place by killing leathercoats? I ran scenarios through my head, looking for something to take responsibility for as I got out of my car and approached the bridge. *I* was still in color.

Father Luke had his arms crossed over his chest. Come to think of it, they all had their arms crossed. Now *that* was intimidating. Thirty or so men were already projecting obstinacy to me as I walked onto the first plank, the first "hand."

"Hi, Father." I said.

A few of the Wanderers shifted. One of them cleared his throat. Two of the well-dressed men looked at each other and then back at me. Father Luke was wearing a scowl.

"I asked you not to come north of the forest." he hissed, icily.

"No, you told me not to *explore* north of the forest, and you used it in a context that implied to me that you did not want me exploring as I have been, on foot, because of dangerous terrain, minor avalanches and the like." I countered, and crossed my own arms. "If you are wanting something from me, you have to ask. And there has to be an agreement. I live here too, and you're not my father. I am hardly beholden to your commands."

"No, if I tell you something, you need to listen. Or there could be grave problems. Not problems that are easily remedied, if they're even curable." said Father Luke.

"Or I can just pack my shit up and go home, since we're apparently not being adults anymore." I said. "What the fuck is this? You're blocking me from using the bridge? With a small army? I wasn't even planning on being north of the forest until no one was south of the forest. What the fuck is this?"

"Enough, son. You're being dramatic." put in Virgil.

"No. I want some answers, or I'm going home." I said, in a tired voice. "And I'm not coming back."

"You can't go home." said Virgil. "You tried."

I said, "Watch me." And turned around and started walking.

"Son." said Father Luke.

I kept walking.

"It's important, son. Just go back to the farmhouse." He called after me.

"No, I'm leaving the Mountain." I said over my shoulder.

"Son." said Father Luke again, with a little more volume and a little more authority. I turned back around and faced him.

"Okay, Father Luke. Let's talk." I threw my arms up in frustration. "*Why?* What are all of you doing up here? What makes it so that *you* can be on the other side of the bridge? And why do any of you care? I didn't even have any intention of crossing it. I was just looking for someone to explain to me why there wasn't any color in the place. What the Hell is going on?"

"A vicissitude." said Virgil.

"Great. That's my answer? Two words? Doesn't 'killing' a leathercoat afford a man any respect around this place? Any answers?" I fumed.

"Yes. But not yet." said Father Luke, and he looked sad to be saying it.

"Fantastic. The lot of you go to Hell. This is just crazy."

"We respect you, son. We do." said Virgil in a compelling, quiet voice. "Please listen to Father Luke."

"Okay." I said, and struck my most rebellious, slouching stature, my most defiant face. You'd be pissed, too. All this screaming and all of these orders and no apparent sense to any of it. At least in the military the Will of the Sergeants wasn't inscrutable. Hell, *I* was a sergeant. I didn't need this.

Father Luke took a deep breath. "I understand that you had no intention of crossing the bridge. You were just coming north to look for one of us; The Ecclesiae or myself, or one of your friends. I understand that. But this bridge is closed to you. For a reason."

"What's the reason?" I asked.

"This." Father Luke produced a white envelope. I walked up to him, held out my hand, and as soon as he handed it to me it turned yellow, absolutely instantaneously. My eyes widened.

"Why is there no color, Father Luke?"

"Because the whole of the partition is changing, son. Everything but you. Read the letter."

I opened the envelope and dug out the stationary contained inside. It smelled, well, you know how it smelled. It smelled like a letter from God.

Current Residents of 101 Devine Road:

We regret to inform you that recent changes in the sociopolitical landscape of your Plateau have forced this office to reprioritize your positions. It is important to remember that it is not you or your proxies that are being reprioritized, it is simply your positions.

The Man has requested that you take up your former office on 342 Devine Road on the Third Plateau and resume duties there.

Of course, there is no current time frame for this vicissitude. With the neutralization of Moloch, a.k.a. Hell's Ambassador as Yang of Organized Group Religious Ritual, a.k.a. Prince of the Second Circle, a.k.a. Governor-General of the regions of Strife, Gambling and Politics a.k.a. Commanding Officer of the Infernal Armies of Treachery and Genocide, a.k.a. The Horrid King, your ambassadorship and stewardship of the Yin of Organized Group Religious Ritual is being reprioritized to make way for a new office so that we may best wage, as a unified whole, the everlasting War on Hell.

We thank you for your long, faithful, and continuing service.

> *Eternally Grateful,*
> *Gabriel, Herald of God*
> *Office of Internal Affairs*

Underneath the type was a handwritten note:

Guys:

Sorry about all of this, and sorry about the form letter. You know how this sort of thing goes. Vicissitude and all that. It **should** *happen just like it's happened three times, now. But you know all of this already. You've had the reins since the Romans were sinning it up and Pan was running all of Old*

Europe, when this whole 'Connection' thing got started. The Man is being really firm about all this, and has already dispatched the Spook to rally the Foederati. Make sure your generals are picked and ready. You still have a chance at stopping this bull from fucking up your china shop and getting someone like the Bedouin or the Bony Prince in the farmhouse to keep it happy, healthy and inviting to you. You've already been recorded for participation in the next three Wars, as you know, so get someone in that farmhouse that'll make it easiest for you to win it back after a few millennia.

-Gabe

P.S. Please contain the soldier south of the Flumen Dolere until further notice. His effect on the Plateaus may complicate the early stages of the Vicissitude.

"Father Luke?" I said, and looked up at him from the letter.

"Yes?" he replied.

"What's going on?" I asked with a quivering lip, and felt about five years old.

"The Ecclesiae are leaving."

"Because I killed the leathercoat?"

"Yes."

"Why?"

"Because there are...there are two sides to everything, son. It's the problematic duality of everything. When the line between the yin and the yang becomes blurred, it stops being black and white and everything turns grey. Moloch and the Ecclesiae were yin and yang. The Man in the Yellow Polo Shirt decided, after the duality was fraying at the edges, that he would create a new pair of polar opposites. And now the old duality gives way to the new."

"What is the new? Who is the new?"

"The new is...We should talk. I wanted to talk to you earlier today, but I was busy here, with the Wanderers and the Men in Suits. Do you care to give me a ride back to the abbey?"

"Uh." I said. There was a sick, roiling nausea in my stomach. "Sure."

We drove in silence through Teutoberg, like a Spielbergian burst of color in a *film noir* world. When we emerged, I launched the first question. "So, tell me again. *Why* isn't there any color?"

"Because this partition is being reengineered." said Father Luke.

"For what?"

"The Foederati."

"And what are they?"

"Son?"

"Yes?"

"I'm going to give you the keys to the bookcase."

"Thank you, Father."

"You're welcome. Now that you have that concession, I will have to refrain from making this conversation too long. Not only am I bound by silence by the Professor and the Man in the Yellow Polo Shirt on many subjects, we also must think of our dear readers. Revealing the plot and story through dialogue seems compelling and convincing enough to fool the author, but never the readers. It comes off as cheap, boring and hackneyed. *Trop de paroles noient la vérité.*"

"Okay. Can we get a little out of the way, at least?"

"The bookcase will answer most of your questions, but yes, I think we can get a little out of the way." He slouched a little in his car seat and examined the dashboard intently, obviously lost in the realm of his thoughts.

"Okay...uh, so *why* are the Ecclesiae leaving?" I asked, and grimaced.

"Because you killed Moloch."

"And Moloch was what was keeping them here?"

"Well, look at it this way. It's B-grade philosophy. No good without evil. Two sides of the same coin. Duality. It's in everything, and it's something everyone knows. Like 'wherever you go, there you are.' It's simple stuff that causes teenagers and philosophers into seeing depth that's not really there." Father Luke smiled a small, amused smile and huffed.

"So..." I said almost to myself, and thought back to the letter. "Strife, Gambling, Politics, Treachery, Genocide and Organized Group Religious Ritual are what Moloch represented?"

"Yes, and the Ecclesiae also represent Organized Group Religious Ritual. When they first came into power, they were robust, ideological, passively

151

non-violent in most cases. In every sense Moloch's Yin."

"But now they represent Strife, Gambling, Politics, Treachery and Genocide. The Christians do. Islam does. Judaism does. Even Buddhism used to, if not so much anymore." I said, and it was Father Luke's turn to grimace.

"That is where the problem was. The yin and yang were no longer polar opposites. No more duality. And that's what keeps things alive."

"So God just fired the Ecclesiae?" I asked.

"In a sense. The Man is making them fight to keep Organized Group Religious Ritual the prime form of worship on Earth, making them fight to preserve the position for their ideology, in the event that they would wish to return at the time of the next Vicissitude and take another crack at it. But the new resident must be, by default, free of Moloch's qualities, Strife, Gambling, etc. Because otherwise there isn't enough difference between Religion and its enemies to keep the duality in existence, and thus for Religion to serve a useful purpose. When good and evil become the same thing, the Man wipes the gray area out and gives it a fresh start. Do you understand, now? By 'killing' Moloch you killed the entire embodiment of his qualitative effect on the Mountain, and thus, the spirituality of Earth. Ergo, your neutralization of his qualities reduced the Ecclesiae's influence to nothing, since they had come to represent those qualities as well, and those qualities, *as represented by the Ecclesiae and the Horrid King*, are unable to influence the Mountain any longer."

"I think I understand." I said, but I don't think that I did. In fact, I know I didn't. "So before the Ecclesiae came, what was the prime form of worship?"

"Individual Ritual and Personal Salvation. Before the Church all but eradicated paganism in the West and the Group Ritual advocates of Buddhism and Islam wiped out the heathen beliefs of the East."

"I like the idea of personal salvation better."

"To each his own."

I was silent for a moment, thinking. "Sorry that this is turning into twenty questions, but what happens when they leave?"

"Uh…I suppose that depends. If someone allied with them moves into the farmhouse, takes over, probably not a whole lot. Some change-ups, some flip-flops, some new denominations of the major world religions, some more conservative, some more liberal. Some emergent new religions based on current ones. After a huge period of upheaval, that is. That's already starting."

"On Earth?"

"Yes."

"In what way?"

"I hoped you could tell me. You were there not long ago."

I thought and tried to remember. "There's *another* sex scandal in the Church. There's a new telling of *A Midsummer Night's Dream...*" I trailed off. Those were some pissed-off broads at the bar talking about...Oh, my God. What *was* happening on Earth?

"Yes. And it only gets more chaotic until very suddenly there's order. It'll take fifty years or so."

"Wow. I'm really sorry."

"For what? For carrying out the will of the Man in the Yellow Polo Shirt?"

"Uh...I guess so, yeah."

"Don't be ridiculous. It just means a lot of work, that's all. And it's been a long time since we've had to do any real kind of work. I, for one, am not terribly upset. Just shocked."

"Uh, so what happens if someone *not* allied with them moves into the farmhouse?"

"It will be the figurative death of religion."

Unable to formulate anything intelligent to say to *that*, I lapsed into single-serving sentence-mode. Instant retardation. "I killed the Church?"

Father Luke signaled to me that I was about to drive past the road to the abbey, then scratched his face. I swerved hard and leveled with it. He continued on. "If the farmhouse is not retained through the war? *Oui.* But not *just* the Church. Any and all religions relying on group ceremony as their principle means of worship. That means a lot more than Christianity."

I almost fainted. Had that fateful swing of mine crushed not only the Horrid King but the whole of Christianity? And all other religions involving group ritual? Was that the kind of place this was? Something as simple as that could, if performed within these partitions, drastically alter the world? Did I throw a wrench in the gears of the spiritual clock of the world?

My God.

I got dizzy and my sight started wobbling a little. I pulled into the driveway of the Abbey, threw the transmission into park and just sat and stared at my steering wheel.

"A moment, son. You have to understand, the farmhouse isn't relinquished easily."

"I feel faint."

"Don't do that." he said, and clapped me on the back vigorously. I felt like I should burp or spit up or something, so steady and elongated was his back-patting, but my mind was too fixated on my inner monologue.

Was it the right time for the Ecclesiae to go? Surely, I'd never thought much of Christianity or Judaism or any of the other major religions, but... There were good Christians, good Muslims, good Buddhists, good priests, good ministers, good people. Religion was a source of undying goodness for a lot of people.

Wait a minute. Wait one goddamned minute.

I did what?

I did...what? I killed group ceremony? I killed church? I killed Sunday mornings and Easter and Christmas and Ramadan and Chanukah and people praying for each other and saints and the Virgin Mary and Moses and all of that? I killed temples and churches and cathedrals and basilicas and mosques and the Church of Elvis and...*everything* involving group ritual? What the *fuck*?

But...weren't these religious institutions also drenched in blood? The Christian Church was founded on a dead Jew who had said so many beautiful things and then had those words warped, perverted and fucked so many times that they were lost. I'd read the Bible. The supposed words of the Christ. They weren't anything at all like what the Church taught. The Church had perpetuated war, bloodshed, violence and political takeovers throughout history. The Holy Roman Empire gets to sit up there with Mongolia and Germany and China on the World's Most Historically Evil Nations List. It was a bad thing.

But not anymore, right? Religion had *changed*. It didn't do that sort of thing. If they could go back and do it, they'd make crucifixion the worst that happened to Jesus, not the destruction of his legacy, his message. Right? They'd fix all of the skeletons in Buddha's and Mohammed's closets, right? No more assassinations, no more *ninja*, no more holy wars, no more crusades. No more violence in the Middle East. Kings and presidents not kept as lapdogs anymore. No more Inquisitions. No more Amida Tong. No more Intifada. No more Jihad.

But...

Would the Church(es) continue doing what it (they) had done for millennia if it (they) had the chance to do it again? Wait, scratch that. Would *the twins* perpetuate all that filth again? My roommates? My taciturn *friends*?

I was forced to admit that I did not know. I suppose I also admitted to myself that it was a moot point, now that the Ecclesiae were going the way of the buffalo.

Oh, my God. The twins are leaving. The Church is leaving.

I thought back to the dream I had at the farmhouse. I was a baby eagle amongst swallows. I had taken that dream to mean that I should be silent about Devine Road when at home, so as not to be dangerous to those among my human peers that couldn't handle it. I had taken it to mean I was, when on Devine Road, among eagles. Had I suddenly joined the ranks of sparrows as a bird of prey? Was I so dangerous to everything around me? I swallowed hard, trying to rid my mouth of a horrible taste that had suddenly crept into it.

"When are they leaving?" I asked.

"Not immediately." said Father Luke. "They'll take a while to move. But if the farmhouse is not retained through the war, the decline will happen pretty quickly, within four or five generations. That's what happened to Pan and the Old Religion." Father Luke paused for breath. "See, you're taking it wrong. *If* this happens, *if* the Ecclesiae lose the war, Christianity will still never die. Neither will Islam, or Buddhism, or Judaism, or any of the other group ritual things. Judaism will go first into obscurity, I think, and then Buddhism over time. Christianity will stick it out for a while, and the Muslims are plain stubborn."

"What do you mean?"

"They wouldn't be at the forefront of things. Their worship would be as hidden and 'radical' and as distasteful to the common man as, say, the idea of a coven of witches dancing naked on Midsummer's Eve, each murmuring to their own goddess might seem to the present-day sensible Christian blue-collar worker."

I thought of my father.

"Well, what would be at the forefront?" I asked. My narrow mind was having a tough time wrapping around individual worship. Most religions I knew about involved lots of group ritual. It was easier to herd people that way. That's why I assumed that churches did it. Maybe they were lazy, you know? Kill three hundred birds with one stone, every Sunday.

Oh my God, Oh my God, Oh my God. I killed religion. Lots of it. With one stone. With one stick.

"Probably that naked sabbat. See, humanity likes to worship in groups. It's the *ritual* and the *ceremony* that has started to sever everything so badly. Group Ritual is all about being unable to do anything but the most rudimentary worship by one's self. It's the trivialization of prayer, of personal prayer. 'Wherever two or more are gathered in My name so, too, am I there.' The Man in the Yellow Polo Shirt hasn't thought much of that lately. So if the farmhouse was lost, the landscape would likely flip-flop. All of the worship that counts for anything like salvation and brownie points and Get out of Hell Free cards would be done on one's own. All of the *rudimentary* stuff would be done at, oh, barbecues and other gatherings like Church and covens and the like."

I lowered my eyes, trying to get a grip on an understanding of what was going on. It was like a child trying to palm a basketball.

"Who do they have to fight, Father Luke? The Foederati?"

"No. Well, yes. But no."

"Yes or no?"

"No."

"Who, then?"

"You."

My eyes widened and the breath caught in my throat. I felt like I'd just been shot in the heart and I was waiting to fall over. Like a corpse in a six-foot depression as the first shovelful of dirt hit my coffin. "That's impossible."

"Is it? You're a soldier. You were asked to come here by the Man in the Yellow Polo Shirt. You were educated, trained with that bludgeon and then dispatched to defeat Moloch. There's no difference, son. None. No difference between Moloch and the Ecclesiae now. You started the job, you finish it."

"So…" I took a deep breath. "The Ecclesiae are evil?"

"Come, now. You know better than that. Is anyone evil? Doesn't everyone have a cause? Good intentions? Doesn't everyone self-justify, isn't everyone self-righteous?" He sighed. "I am going to go inside. I am very tired."

I looked out my window and grimaced fiercely. The hills looked like they were stretching after a long sleep, the Ager Epiphania seemed to be moving, out and away, growing larger. The flowers were burying their heads in the dirt. The trees were lumbering slowly away from each other, widening the forest. The whole partition was getting bigger. Miles and miles bigger.

"I'll never fight again, Father Luke." I whispered.

"You fought Moloch." He replied.

"I understand that. But that came from somewhere else. A reaction, not proaction. I won't settle myself in to fight, won't consciously choose that. No more wars. I can't live through another one."

"We shall see." he said, and no more. He got out of the car and went into the abbey. I followed, feeling woozy, anxious, dizzy, panicky, sad, angry, frustrated and helpless. I felt like my back was made of iron and I was wearing shoes made of ice.

I followed him through the courtyard, where the monks had gathered, the Ecumenics. They didn't have any color to them either, and they looked kind of grainy and low-quality, like they had just stepped out of a flick made in the forties. They were singing softly, singing a low, throaty hymn that was at once hauntingly melodic and unsettling. Like something out of a movie. Made in the forties. I didn't understand the words, just felt the music dramatically.

I followed Father Luke into the great hall, and he walked to the center of the tapestry and looked at it sadly with his colorless eyes.

"This place, this Mountain…" he said, and I wasn't sure if he was talking to me or himself for a moment. "This wasn't created." He turned and looked at me. "It's a kind of…side effect of Creation. The Man in the Yellow Polo Shirt didn't make Devine Road or the Mountain with No Name. When he made the Earth, it just sort of rose up to meet Him. That's why He's agnostic. Figures someone else made this place to test him. Because Earth doesn't give him any trouble at all."

"None?" I asked.

"None. All of the trouble comes from this Mountain, and this Plateau, especially."

"Father Luke?"

"Yes, son?"

"Why do I have to fight the Ecclesiae?"

"I do not know why you were chosen."

"I'll leave the Mountain."

"I do not think that you will. I think you will stay and fight, and see the new resident, or residents, take the farmhouse or lose it. I believe you will see the war's end."

Everything caught up with me at once. The entire gravity of my strange battle with the man in the black leather coat. The entire gravity of my actions. All of everything, the Church and my dumb ass killing it or at least threatening it and, oh, my God. My God, my God.

My eyes hurt, so badly, like a great pressure behind them was starting to bleed all of my horror and neoteny and acumen and immaturity, all of my pain, all of my disgust, all of my bewilderment. Starting to bleed a deep ache, a deep Truth, a rawness. To bleed the bleeding heart of the moon. My nose was leaking the tears of the sun. My mouth had forged a hammer from love and regret and shattered my face.

My soul cried out in utter despair. Unable to bear being in the abbey any longer, I slinked off to the courtyard, feeling lower than a snake, eating dust and striking at woman's heel, and just cried and cried to the music of the Ecumenics.

I cried myself to sleep, and slept until morning.

———

When I woke, the sky looked like a rumpled bed sheet. No sun got through, only filtered light, and that light hurt my eyes. I lay there on the abbey's doorstep, alone. The Ecumenics had gone to wherever they go. I was alone. So I started to cry again.

I wanted to go and hug the Ecclesiae and cry on them and tell them how much I appreciated them and how sorry I was. But I couldn't. I just went back inside. I walked through the Great Hall, walked around the tapestry, not wishing to sully it with my feet for some reason. I walked in, went to my 'room', the place I slept when I stayed at the Abbey. After freshening up, I went to the dining room to rustle up some leftovers or something. I wanted to be alone, wanted to think, wanted to catch up with all of this stuff.

Well, that's a lie. I didn't really want to catch up with anything. I wanted to run away and forget any of this ever happened. I wanted to just slink back to earth and throw myself a pity party and move to New Zealand and learn to surf and just be a beach bum the rest of my days. I wanted to get the fuck out.

Father Luke walked out of the kitchen with a plate of black-and-white breakfast for me, bacon and eggs and a half stack of pancakes with peanut butter and a carafe of orange juice all to myself to wash it down. Whenever I speared a piece of food with my fork, it instantly gained color.

You have no idea how weird that is. But I ate like a starved man.

Father Luke looked at me. "Have you been crying?" His voice was less like a French wine and more like a French cigarette. It was harsh.

Wow. I still looked like I'd been crying, after a shave and a change of clothes. I must have really poured on the tears.

"I'm sorry. For destroying organized religion." I said with my mouth full, not even looking up from my pancakes.

"Why?"

"Because it means that everything's going to change and that there's going to be a war and all of this change and I'm just so, so sorry."

"My son, this is *change*! Change the world has needed for so long. This Mountain has needed it for so long. That yearning in the human spirit that whistles freedom between the clenched teeth of conformity has been repressed for so long, oppressed for so long that it was almost forgotten. You are healing the world of her heartsickness, giving religion a good shake-up. This sea change, this vicissitude, no…you! You are the Vicissitude. You are like the coming of rain after drought. There is no one unhappy about it. Dry your eyes." He disappeared into the kitchen, emerged with his own breakfast, twice as large as mine though I knew he wouldn't eat half of what I was going to. He always served himself ridiculously large portions and then picked at them.

Father Luke sat down, looked at me concernedly and started fiddling with a piece of sausage he would never ingest. "Actually, the Bedouin wanted to tell you all of this, but he wasn't sure exactly where to start. How to just lay all of this out for you in a way that wouldn't shock you too badly. So he asked me to do it."

"A real bang-up job, Father."

"Well, and am I supposed to read your mind? *Merde*."

"Funny to hear a priest curse."

"I told you already that I'm not a priest."

"What are you?"

"We'll get to that." Father Luke's brow cemented over his forehead and his face set in a stern statuette. "Look, son. It was the Ecclesiae that empowered the Horrid King, do you understand? And vice versa. The Ecclesiae made him into what he was, and he kept them in business. Because their jobs were to destroy the other, to get rid of the other, and the only way to get rid of each other was to employ each other's methods. Every victory against the Horrid King drenched the Church's hands in blood, every victory against The Ecclesiae bound Moloch tighter to religion. Listen to me, talking about him in the past tense for your sake. Another problem. You're going to have to learn to think like us. Like a true resident of the Mountain, a true constituent of the Road. You're going to have to learn to fight like us. You're going to have to learn to question us, you're going to have to learn how to take orders from us. Then you're going to have to learn how to kill us. Because we are the appointed guardians of Islam, Christianity and the other major world religions. *We are those religions*, as much as the Ecclesiae. You're going to have to learn to find beauty in Group Ritual, understand it, love it, but you're going to have to be the most fiercely individualistic thing to ever happen to Devine Road, because that's what the Man in the Yellow Polo Shirt is clearly intending for you. You're going to be the champion of Pan."

I was thoroughly baffled. "The champion of Pan? What? Why me? I just had a class here! One class through community college!"

I'm not a beautiful, individual snowflake, etc.

"You looked God right in His eye and told Him that you didn't care what He thought, that you were going to be you. Period. Nametag, no nametag, conversation, no conversation. You got His drift and said, 'Nope. I'm still me and You're still You and I'll do it my way anyway, thank You.' Do you think that His 'conversation' with the leather coats was for nothing? A coincidence? Lucifer's not even in Hell!"

"He's not?"

"No. He left and plays piano in a little bar in New York City now."

"Incredible."

"He was done. He didn't want to fight anymore. Gave the reins over to Beelzebub, one of his Princes of Hell, and stopped making trouble."

"When did this happen?"

"This summer. May I continue?"

"Uh, yes. Please do."

"Anyway, the Man in the Yellow Polo Shirt came to this Plateau and contacted the men in leather coats to let them know that the Horrid King, Moloch, devil of strife, greed, politics, power, treachery, gambling, genocide and group ritual was not only invited to come to this partition, this most important partition of the first Plateau of the Mountain With No Name, he was welcome. Because the Man in the Yellow Polo Shirt had finally found his counterpart. His antithesis. A new yin. And He told them all of that without speaking a word aloud that would clue you in."

"What? I'm just a human being! I'm not a devil, or like you and the Bedouin, whatever you are. An angel or…"

"Angel." said Father Luke. "I am called a throne. But we're outlaws. We refuse to work against God, but will not operate under his jurisdiction, either. Thus, we fight our own war. And the Bedouin is another story."

"Another story?"

"Forget that for now."

"Okay. So you're outlaws. Like Abaddon." I said.

"Precisely. Abaddon is perhaps the most celebrated of us."

"So what the Hell am I?"

"I do not know." said Father Luke. His face did not crack. "None of us know. I thought the Man in the Yellow Polo Shirt meant the Bedouin as the opposite to Moloch. The Bedouin is fiercely independent, you know. I thought that perhaps the Man in the Yellow Polo Shirt was honoring his faithful, if unattached, service by giving him a chance at Moloch. The Bedouin did not think so. He thought it was you, or someone soon to come. Moloch, on the other hand, thought like I did, so he threw the snowball at the Bedouin and not you. Had he thrown it at you, you would surely have suffered much less injury than your friend."

"What are the shards?"

"They are pieces of the tower of Babel, the pieces of Babylon. Pieces of the capital city of Hell. Pieces of Pandemonium. They are all shards of the Divine Brilliance, a piece of which Lucifer stole from the Man in the Yellow Polo Shirt when the Revolution happened. They are pieces of God, twisted and evil and perverted by Hell to destroy those beings that are bound to Him. Some angels and thrones and beings like the Bedouin are bound to the Man in the Yellow Polo Shirt. Most humans are. I suspect that you are not, however, because of the nature of your soul. You are too rebellious, too independent. You looked God in the eye and said, 'No. I don't believe in You.' Even though you did. You knew from the moment you met Him who He was. That is why He likes you. That is why He chose you. That is why this is happening the way it is. Like a thief in the night."

I was silent. So was Father Luke. We stood there for some minutes until he spoke again.

"You are the spitting image of Lucifer, my son. You look exactly like him. And you came to us on the day he left Hell. That is not to say that we believe you are Lucifer. We just believe that is a sign of portent, an omen from the Man in the Yellow Polo Shirt."

My face wrinkled up. "Like Lucifer? I thought I looked like Michael."

"They are twin brothers."

"Oh."

"Indeed. The only one who knows more about that subject is the Man in the Yellow Polo Shirt. And possibly Michael and Lucifer as well, but I do not think so. Michael doesn't think that the two of you are related, but he's been wrong before and he'll be wrong again. We know you're a human being. We think you're a human being. The Man in the Yellow Polo Shirt is very mysterious, and sometimes seems to enjoy keeping us as ignorant as possible." He sighed a heavy, wet sigh. "We did not even know about the

'History and Moral Philosophy' Class until two days before it was to happen. And we certainly did not know the purpose."

"Why doesn't He just come talk to you?" I asked.

"I have not spoken to Him since the Revolution. Only three Thrones have spoken to him since. They are the only ones whom He has enfolded, even partially, in His forgiveness. You are the only being within this partition's walls with the exception of the Ecclesiae that He has spoken to since the War in Heaven."

That shocked the hell out of me. "You mean…"

"Yes. You are the only human being, if that is what you are, since before Christ to ever speak face to face with the Father aspect of the One True God."

I broke down into tears again.

"Soon you will choose. To stay or to leave."

"I'll leave." I sobbed.

"Don't say that until you know. It may be the plan of the Man in Yellow for you to stay. It may be your only option. Only know this: You will never have to fight me, regardless of what you choose. I understand now that I have been wrong for many years. Son, I will be your ally until the end of this. I will forsake the Church, the Wanderers, to assist you. As a Throne, I thought for many years that the best indirect way to champion Goodness was to safeguard Religion as it is, Religion with a capital *R*. That is, the phone lines. The Connection of humanity to God. I see now that I was in error. The Connection is poisoned, the farmhouse is corrupt. The best part I can play is in assisting you and what you will be to this Mountain. The reshaping of the Connection, the rebuilding of the farmhouse."

"Th-thank you. Father."

He got up and picked up our plates, mine empty and his barely touched. He brought them into the kitchen, motioned for me to come and walk with him to the Great Hall, so I got up and followed him there.

"You *will* have to fight others who you regard highly, perhaps even those you love, regardless of what you choose." he said, and sighed.

I tried to imagine myself fighting the woman in the white dress. I tried to imagine killing her again.

"Nevertheless, you will have to choose whether or not to stay." We got to the Great Hall and he walked over to a small stone in the east wall, removed it and pulled out a key ring. "When that time comes, when you choose, we will speak again, but not until then. I am forbidden to influence you in this way."

Father Luke handed me the keys to the bookcase, left the room and went downstairs. I simply kept crying. It was the only logical thing to do. When a human being is faced with something that makes no sense, he laughs or he cries. Both are excellent indicators of a panic attack or a nervous breakdown. I had both at once, right there in the Great Hall, right over the beautiful tapestry portraying Revelations, and suddenly saw through the eyes of the Virgin, alone and cold in the desert and staring into the maws of the seven-headed Dragon. I then gained the Dragon's perspective, poised over goodness, poised over righteousness, dealer of the death of Innocence.

I fell to the ground and wailed and gnashed my teeth.

Who would be my Deliverer?

Answers
Chapter 9

Well, let's make this quick. I had my nervous breakdown, it lasted for the rest of the day, I fell asleep again and slept all the way until the next morning. And you know what? I got over it. Fast. These episodes happen more often than I care to admit, something Dr. Schreiber doesn't even know the full extent of. So they're not as exhausting as they used to be.

Maybe I'm coloring this poorly. A nervous breakdown is not an easy thing. It is a very difficult thing, a horrible experience, one I wish on no one, not even if they're wearing a leather coat. But I've got some practice in. And I know a few tricks. And they're just easier for me then they used to be. Oh, I could have described the whole messy ordeal but *why*? Do *you* care? Do you care more about something so insignificant as an emotional upheaval than the advancement of the plot, and the beginning of Chapter 9?

For that matter, should we really start Chapter 9 on such a depressing note? True, there is little joy in the preceding pages, but I *am* obliged to inform you that the times from here on out got rough, got violent and didn't play nicely. That's what's coming up, dear readers. Violence and adventure and blood and death. Sex, politics, religion and other things not suited for conversation at the dinner table. Let's gloss over the unpleasant episodes while we still can.

Agreed? Good. Let's carry on.

On to the color. Of the partition. It all came back. Just a minor, oh, default mode the partition went into while the format was reset. I was never intended to have to see it without color, certainly not the whole thing, anyway; they thought I'd stay off the Mountain for a little less than a week, for some reason. It was Father Luke's guess: He'd thought I was so upset about the Moloch thing that I would wilt, shy away, stay home until I couldn't bear not being in my real home. Little did they guess I'd be gone only a few hours.

I recuperated at the abbey without seeing or speaking to Father Luke, which was better than the alternative, as I was unable to bring myself to go back to my room at the farmhouse. In my spare time, I perused the recently accessible bookshelf, read the titles, read summaries, read whole books and before setting about to consume it in its entirety, established a set of questions, a *Summarium Quaestionis* of what I needed to ask, and what I needed to know.

1) What was the Diaspora?
2) What are the Wanderers?
3) What is this Mountain?
4) What more do I need to know about this "Connection?"
5) What is the Vicissitude?
6) How do I undo what I did?

1) The Diaspora was a battle that took place when half of the Wanderers on the First Plateau of the Mountain with No Name were expelled by the other half for trying to force a "sea change" back to Individual Worship and Personal Salvation. That is, to virtually strip the Connection to bare nothing, to create Disorganized Religion. They lost, as you may have surmised, and the errant Wanderers went to many places, some to remote areas on the Mountain, some to Hell, most to Earth to eek out "normal" existences. None are allowed back on this particular partition ever again, by edict of the Ecclesiae.

2) The Wanderers are cops. Immortal super cops, I should say. They battle, on behalf of the Man in the Yellow Polo Shirt but not directly under His authority, the men in the leather coats. Which begs another question: What, truly, are the men in leather coats? Demons, surely, but are they really the way we imagine them? Cloven hooves and tails and pitchforks and all the horrible imagery the Christian Church used to associate their Devil with the Old Religion's Pan in order to continue the destruction of paganism?

We'll get to that, eventually.

The Wanderers, and others like them that come along with every "sea change," or "vicissitude," are in actuality what causes the death of religions, the blurring of dualities, the need for Vicissitude in the exact same fashion that authority of any kind destroys earthly societies, in the exact same way.

"What?" the reader asks. "How?"

Well, I'll tell you.

"*Quis custodiet ipsos custodet?*" asked Juvenal. "Who watches the watchmen?" You have a criminal problem until you have a police problem. It's simple. The Wanderers go around and clean disorder and evil and strife and pain all of these things off of the spiritual consciousness as best as they can and don't understand that those negativities are the other side of the coin. The yin, so to speak.

Not doing bad, doing good. Fighting evil. Very noble.

Stipulated. So, what would happen if the cops got rid of all of the criminals? With no criminals, there are no cops, right? Everything is fine and dandy, but the cops don't have a job anymore. Except on the Mountain, that means they don't *exist* anymore. Which, in the sense of the 'duality' present in all things, especially on this Mountain, means that *good* doesn't exist anymore, either. So you see, the cops work as fervently as possible to get rid of their own jobs, here as on Earth, but in doing so they destroy themselves and everything they work for, as well, because with less and less evil to define what 'good' actually is, 'good' takes on its own independent meaning, becomes 'good' for the sake of 'good', is taken for granted. Then its actions are 'good' because they are done by the 'good' side, not because they're specifically *not* evil, simply because they're committed by the side that doesn't *champion* evil. As you clearly have deduced, the last few sentences are (and an official *Devine Road* congratulations to you for deducing so well!) existentialist nonsensical bullshit. Bullshit.

Here's a little more, and then we'll shut this bitch down and get back to the story.

Good and evil don't exist without each other. When evil starts going away, good does, too, and everything just becomes gray and indistinguishable, and then the concept of 'duality' is shot to complete fucking Hell.

The cops *have* to do it, of course. Have to destroy themselves. They can't let evil just stain everything without *representing* good, or everything would collapse faster than a blink of the Man in the Yellow Polo Shirt's eye.

But the denial of a whole half of existence, minus the cracks of filth and slime and pain and agony and despair that ooze out from time to time, that really takes its toll. Then the ball unravels and there's a revolution, like what we'll supposedly be seeing soon. A war.

That's what this really boils down to. B-Grade philosophy. No good without evil. No evil without good. Evil is just a moral compass, blah, blah, blah. It's another chicken and egg syndrome, only we don't attribute good characteristics to one and a black mustache to another. The cops bring down humanity's Connection to God much harder than the criminals do, but that's only because the criminals are kept at bay. If they weren't, the Connection might even be severed. Which, if you have not deduced by now, is their whole goal. Which, if you have not deduced by now, involves the phone lines that run the length of Devine Road. Which, if you have not deduced by now, is Religion itself. The farmhouse, nestled between those two towers, is the boss chair, the dais, the Oval Office, the Buckingham Palace, the shot-caller's ball. It not only guards the connection, but indeed affects the nature of the connections running through those lines so profoundly that everything that happens here has an opposite and equal reaction on the spirituality of every human being on Earth. So profoundly that a war is fought over the Connection every five hundred years or so.

Everything done on this Plateau and in this partition particularly, from the smallest flight of the smallest bird to the most horrendously huge occurrence you can think of, *everything* indirectly affects the earth. Bring a few guns to the Plateau? Somebody, somewhere, gets violent. Make love to someone on the Plateau? The world feels a little more at ease, a little more playful, a little happier. A little more in love. Kill someone? A nation goes to war or a dictator starts a "cleansing" pogrom. Run the length of it from one end to the other, taking in everything as you go, smelling the Ager Epiphania and the sunlight and the fresh wind on your face? Everybody everywhere all over the world subliminally registers the sound of laughter.

Everything affects the Earth, from the presence of a new earthworm to the presence of a new Vicissitude. Me. I don't know *what* changed when I got here. But I know what changed when I killed Moloch. Another scandal was unearthed in the Church and thousands, if not hundreds of thousands or even millions of Catholics, Lutherans, Presbyterians, Methodists, Christian Scientists, Episcopalians and all manner of other Christians lost faith. Lost faith and left the Faith. A mass exodus. Because I killed one of God's enemies.

It's weird, I know.

So what happens when the war comes? Well, that's different, I guess. God takes over the Connection and the Mountain's chopped off from affecting the Earth. Not too big a deal. Why doesn't God just always have control of the Connection? Free Will, of course. You can't have belief without non-belief, can't have theism without atheism...you get the point. Shall I vomit more of this ridiculous semi-philosophical dross all over your shoes? No? Then we'll continue.

The Ecclesiae have made war and been victorious through more than one attempt to wrest the farmhouse away from them. They took it in Roman times, right after Christ, they retained it through the seventh century, Mohammed's time, they survived the attack on them right after Martin Luther nailed his complaints to the cathedral though it caused the Diaspora (we've covered that) and have been sitting pretty until *now*. Now, as the New Age creeps into every corner of spirituality, now, as Christian housewives align their chakras in weekly yoga class, now, as occultists and Scientologists exert their influence over the entertainment world, making principles into ideas and ideas into cultural mores. Just like the Christian Church did to Europe. Just like the Buddhists and Hindus did to Asia.

The time was right for another Vicissitude, the fruit was ripe for the picking. For me to pick. Surely the Ecclesiae saw it coming. Perhaps, in their arrogance, they didn't care and took me into their home anyway. Perhaps they fought it and held out until the order came down from the Man Himself. Perhaps they sought to dissuade the sea change by showing me kindness, as if I had any choice whether or not to trigger it. I mean, I didn't know the Horrid King was what he was.

I haven't found an answer in any one of these books as to who, exactly, is attacking the farmhouse. What other parties are trying to gain control. I have guesses, of course. But no idea. I know that the men in leather coats inevitably end up attacking the farmhouse during the "wars", but they never seem to have put two and two together to try and *control* it. So the Ecclesiae have fought Wanderers in one war, "Foederati" in some of the other wars and the men in leather coats in all of them. But who is planning on controlling the farmhouse if the Ecclesiae are ever defeated?

3) The Mountain is steeped in mystery. Open only to those invited, it is, in a sort of SAT way, the _____ : the world as soul : body. If you fill in the blank with "The Mountain with No Name", you get the answer correct. Everything that affects the world in a spiritual sense manifests physically on the Mountain. That is where the magic of this place comes from. The connection between the Diaspora and Martin Luther and so on. The change that happened in only a few generations on Earth that saw the meteoric rise of Christianity and the swift decline of paganism was the last "war" where the "Foederati" were used. The "war" that caused Islam to go beyond Mecca and Medina and engulf Africa and Arabia was fought on a different Plateau, by the Ecclesiae and for the farmhouse, though I am not sure why. Perhaps it wasn't the big catalyst, the great sea change for the whole of universal thought, so it was handled differently. Who knows? Not me, not these books.

4) The Connection. Organized Religion. Religion as a whole. The way that man can come to God. At first, I assumed that perhaps it was a "checks and balances" system. I don't know why, perhaps growing up in a democratic society impregnated me with such notions, that it was the best of all possible ways to govern and thus the Best of All Possible Governors, the Man Himself, would also use this system.

I was not entirely wrong.

But the Man didn't just want to outsource some of his power, to put it in the hands of someone else in order to keep *Himself* in check, no. Not entirely. The real motivation for creating religion, that is, the phone lines, that is, the Connection, was quite benevolent. Does that sound strange? Knowing all of the evils and alienation and bloodshed that religion has caused through the years, that it still causes? Does it sound strange that *God* actually did think it up and it wasn't just man and his perversions that made it that way?

Of course, God had no intentions of it *being* as disgusting as it was. That took a lot of help from mankind and certainly a good push from the Ecclesiae and others who have occupied the farmhouse.

So why? Why did God allow someone to come between Him and His people?

Free Will.

God, if you've ever read a religious text of almost any variety, used to be around. Used to hang around. Used to talk to people directly, or send angels to talk to people directly, or walk with people in gardens, or expose himself to Jews, or defeat monsters in Asia, or send Revelations to merchants living in caves and criminals living on islands. He used to do all of that miraculous shit because he liked it. But it violated one principal Rule.

Free Will.

How? It's much like the Man tried to explain to me when we had drinks and sandwiches at the farmhouse that day. If you *know* God exists, you don't act the same way as you acted the day before, when you *didn't* know. Dear readers, if God had walked through my front door one day before the Mountain and showed I.D. (real proof) and then told me, "Hey, I just dropped by to let you know that your soul is getting a little dirty. You should probably clean up that act before you die," well, I would have joined a monastery. And you would, too.

So that's not Free Will. In the same vein, if God came and told you that nothing you could do would prevent you from going to Heaven, you'd be a hedonist within a week. Hands down. And that's not Free Will.

Free Will is choosing what you're going to choose because you choose to choose it. Choice. Choice, choice, choice. It's all about us, all about us being in control of things, in control of destiny. We are in control of everything, dearies. God sometimes handles details, God always handles our affairs when we die but God rarely intervenes on earth on any level but the smallest one. God usually peddles in hope and nothing else.

And why not? It's *our* lives. Most of us would resent having anything extra *given* to us. 'There Ain't No Such Thing As A Free Lunch" is ingrained into us by now. Our *pride* wouldn't allow it. We'd show antipathy towards any of that kind of benevolence. And he knows it. The world has always resisted being saved, and in fact actively works against those who would save it, and in fact gets very angry if it *is* saved and told about it later.

So God just tries to do a little here, a little there, and save the world whenever we're not looking. Everything else is religion's job.

Yes, the farmhouse. The farmhouse nestled between those phone towers. The farmhouse determines the nature of the Connection, the theme of the Connection. But that's not to say that the Pope or the Dalai Lama are somehow puppets of the Ecclesiae, no. They're human beings and they go through life with just as much foreknowledge and faith and everything else we all have to have, too. No preferential treatment. That would rather have defeated the purpose of God having outsourced control of the Connection, wouldn't it?

No, the Ecclesiae determine the nature of things, purely by merit of the kind of beings that they are. What are the Ecclesiae? Angels? Demons? I don't know. I'm not sure that I care.

They are what they are, and they embody what they embody, and their preferences are what shape the over-arcing theme of the Connection. Everything they do, everything they are, everyone they allow on this partition and particularly in the farmhouse have a subtle effect on the farmhouse. When the Wandering American brought me that gun, it changed things slightly, made things a little more violent, a little more disposed to violence. Because when you have a gun you can use a gun. If there's no gun to shoot someone with, you won't shoot anyone, and a peaceful resolution to a problem is a little more likely. When people are armed, more violence happens. When *anything* is armed, more violence is more likely.

Whoops. I'm ahead of my narrative again. The Wandering American won't give me that gun until next chapter. Forget that last paragraph.

I know we just went over all of this, but I can't stress it enough. *Every little thing* that enters the partition changes things very subtly on earth because it puts a small amount of some kind of psychic pressure on the phone lines, exerts some magical or miraculous influence on the Connection. Which is why cops are bad for this place. Which is why guns and weapons are bad for this place, why Father Luke and I carry *wooden* swords. Why most of the Wanderers live somewhere else. Why men in leather coats are so vehemently expelled whenever they turn up.

People don't realize it, but there is an undercurrent of violence, a hint of murder in their everyday religion. And thus, their everyday lives. It is the violence that happens on this Plateau, I have learned, that directly correlates to wars on earth. No one means for them to happen, they just do. It's sad, but true. That's the Connection. It exists so that people may come to God, but it also keeps them down, in a way. Because water flows downhill.

Not to mention that the organization and rules and everything else is very stifling. Not good for the soul.

A lesser evil than stripping Free Will away? God thinks so. I think I do, too.

5)The Vicissitude is me. And the Vicissitude is what is going to happen to this partition. Same word, different things. I'll try to keep things straight for the readers.

The Vicissitude is the challenger, the upstart warrior who is historically vying for control of the farmhouse during, well, Vicissitudes. The Vicissitude is also what happens to the Plateau, a great geographical shifting, of sorts. Things are apparently going to be getting a lot bigger around here.

Why do Vicissitudes happen? Why do these 'wars' or whatever happen? Why doesn't God just appoint someone, or make people play a game of football, or whatever?

When the Man in the Yellow Polo Shirt insured that mankind could have true Free Will by establishing the phone lines, He understood, necessarily, that the Connection was an immediate liability. Why?

He was in the middle of a war with Hell. And the Connection was a juicy military target.

So He picked four contenders, equipped them with armies and weapons and told them to fight it out on the partition. Who ever won got the farmhouse, and all of the responsibility of protecting it.

171

The winners were the Ecclesiae.

They have survived other Vicissitudes since that day, and have become potent, perhaps more so than the Man ever imagined or intended. Perhaps that is why He overstepped the Rules He had in place and removed the twins personally. Or maybe he was just retiring them as champions and giving someone else a shot. Dynasties are interesting if you're a member, no fun at all if you're on the outside looking in.

In the interest of fair play, the Man is removing the twins. That is my theory.

And that apparently is *supposed* to count for something. I am the Vicissitude. I am not only the catalyst for this sea change, I am not only the Ché Guevara of modern religion, I am also intended to be the Champion of the opposition. The Lord General of the armies. I'm supposed to be the Big Boss, Tai-Pan, Shogun, King, Brahma, Shaka Zulu, Emperor, Leader, Manager, *The Guy in Charge*, you know? I'm supposed to be running a whole fucking show, here. That is, if I were staying.

I don't know. I think I want to leave sometimes because I feel like if I were to leave it would set things right (see question 6) but somewhere deep down I know that the war would just go on without me.

And maybe that's okay, too. Maybe I just want to leave because I don't want to fight anymore. I'm not scared of dying, not scared of being killed in battle. Hell, no. If I'm going to die, that's how I want to die. I just don't want to have to hurt anyone ever again. I don't want to have to kill people again.

6)How do I undo what I did? I still didn't know. I suspect that I won't be able to change it, now that it's been done, though I'm trying not to act on that. I'm not a fatalistic person by nature, nor am I a pessimist. I'm just…well, I don't know. I guess I just have a sinking feeling in my gut that I really fucked things up bad and that now I don't have any choice but to roll with the punches. Will I be able to leave, and thus make it okay? No one has told me yes or no, no one will talk to me about it. It's apparently my decision.

We'll see. We'll see if I stay. We'll see if I *can*.

Well, and there I had it, I suppose. Five out of six ain't bad. But those questions raised so many others that by the time I was finished jotting down everything I wanted to know, I had filled up half of a notebook full of questions and was going to have to read a whole *library* about Devine Road and the Mountain, never mind this little bookshelf.

So I started with the bookshelf. Or rather, I tried.

I began with *Diaspora*, finished it, went onto the next one on the shelf. Three hundred pages went by without a mention of the Mountain. I put it down, frustrated. Every book that even mentions this place *in passing* is on the bookshelf. How many of them *only* mention it in passing? Where are the hard facts?

I wish the Professor was here.

I read and read and read and read and, well, read. Read and read. And overdosed. Way too much reading. And only got halfway through the shelf before I burned out, because I'd only come across, at most, two or three references in any given work, outside of *Diaspora* and another little book concerning flora and fauna in Teutoberg Forest. Way too much reading. Way too much drivel. Didn't want needles in haystacks, wanted concrete, solid answers to tough questions. And wasn't getting them.

So I went for a drive, over the Ager Epiphania (the wildflowers were all but gone) and out to the wall.

I went to the window in the wall, checked it cautiously, prepared to jerk my head back if I saw that awful vision again. There was the sea again, the mighty sea, only it was no longer becalmed, but roiling and churning and crashing and the sky was storming rainlessly, slamming the ocean against the wall.

I looked down and found that I was standing in mud. Then I looked behind me. The snow was melting, if it wasn't already doing so on my way here and I had simply failed to notice. Melting into half-frozen sludge for a solid quarter mile.

Was this the Vicissitude, then? Was the sea going to creep in under this wall? There was certainly room for it, now. The partition had almost doubled in size, and it grew a little larger everyday. But why the war? Why not just fight with smaller armies, make the war simpler and shorter, with less killing? Why make the damned thing so big? It all seemed so romantic and antiquated and silly. Why a war? Why not a chess game, or something else? That seemed so much more preferable.

It's not like the Man couldn't just institute anything He wanted.

Or could He? What, exactly, were the extent of those Rules?

Am I making God up in my mind, assuming things, basing things on canalized conceptions? Does He even have any magic powers? Or is His will done solely through proxies? Proxies like the angels and Wanderers, and, well, me? Was this how the Will of God was executed?

I confess I know roughly as much about operations on the God level as a turtle knows about six-dimensional geometry.

I wish the Professor was here. He'd have a thing or two to say. And he'd give me some goddamned answers.

The Tale of Brave Saint Scholastica
and the One Hundredth Death of the Tiamat
Chapter 10

Time passed and Father Luke never said a word if he saw the Protagonist at all. Feeling a bit unwanted, feeling a bit like an outsider, feeling rather disillusioned and more than a little depressed, our Hero returned to his room at the Ecclesiae's. They showed no signs of blaming him for their demise; he showed no signs of being responsible for it. They did, however, continue to refuse to say a word in any language. Maybe they knew all along that he was their murderer, but they sure weren't taking it that well. They were treating the revolutionary that would topple their empires not *poorly*, per se, but not *well*, either.

And understandably so. Imagine that you had a house, that you bought a house and protected it and loved it and paid your mortgage on time every month and then, one day, God sent some kid to live with you and he burned your house down. You'd be pissed at God. Don't say you wouldn't.

A man calling himself Dionysus came in from time to time and took a few prints with a daguerreotype (The Protagonist hadn't the foggiest idea where Dionysus laid his hands on one of those) and then left. He dropped the silver prints by not too long after that; the Protagonist looked them over and they looked like the house, all right, only there were changes. The piano was gone. So was a lot of the furniture. The windows in the living room were gone and there was a door in the kitchen leading…somewhere. The Protagonist guessed that this was Dionysus' vision for the farmhouse, but he wasn't sure. All he really had in the world at that time were his guesses, and that didn't suit him. He was sinking lower and lower everyday.

One day it was snowing again. Very lightly. So the Protagonist got out of bed and went outside and arched his cheek, feeling for a pattern. Nothing.

He took a lot of walks, taking in the changes that were happening on the Plateau. Everything was miles bigger now, filled in mostly with wide, flowerless grass, even if it was covered in snow as fast as it appeared. The ocean had started, as he had guessed (damn those guesses to Hell), to flood in beneath the wall.

Most of the hills were leveled to a solid elevation, so that the lower partition looked more like a flat, flat ring encircling the Woeful and Joyful Plateaus. Flat, because it was easier to fight on even ground.

There was going to be a war. Another war. Damned if the Protagonist was going to fight in it, either.

Then again, he didn't know about the Basement, yet.

Our Hero walked in to the farmhouse one cold January afternoon feeling temperamental and mean, being frustrated with the changes and the silent treatment and perhaps stressed from the thought of the coming troubles, and found there in the living room a cowboy. There was a loud *Cling! Clang! Cling! Clang!* emanating from the kitchen. The Protagonist's eyebrows furrowed a half-inch.

"Howdy." he said, because the cowboy's huge, ten-gallon hat had hypnotized him. Implanted that in his brain. Psychic suggestion and the whatnot. That had to be the explanation. The Protagonist didn't think he'd ever said 'Howdy' before in his life.

"Howdy." said the familiar cowboy. "Have we met?"

"No, but I saw you at the Christmas party. You're the Wandering American."

"So I am. Who are you?"

"Me." said the Protagonist.

"Not trying to learn the meaning of meaning, podner. Just yer name." The cowboy tried his best and most disarming *faux bonhomme* smile.

"I *am* trying to learn the meaning of meaning. I don't tell people my name." asserted the Protagonist, and it was true, if a little rude. Father Luke's admonishing that names equaled power had stuck with him.

"Then yer name's Slim to me. And you can call me Tex. I'm the shirriff of the partition 'round the other side of the Mountain.

Quis custodiet ipsos custodet?

"Say, why are the areas *between* the walls called partitions? Shouldn't the walls be the partitions? Since they're *actual* partitions?" inquired the Protagonist.

"*Cling! Clang!*" said the kitchen.

"The walls are the Palisades. And the Partitions separate the Palisades from each other."

"Oh. So the partitions are actually partitions."

"Yeah."

"Separating the walls from each other."

"Yes."

"I'm confused."

"Ya wouldn't be confused if you knew what the Palisades were all about."

The Protagonist, befuddled, didn't bother asking what the Palisades were all about, remembering the Official Wanderer Policy on revealing anything. Nobody told him nothing.

"So you're a sheriff? Elucidate." said the Protagonist instead, and the cowboy did, but not before he took a deep breath.

"See, the cops watch over things. Some of them watch over tracts of land, some over forests, some over the walls, some over the river up north of here. Some of us operate on the other partitions, like me, and some of us, like the Finno-Ugric and the Kenyan, operate only on this particular one."

"I've never seen the…how do you say it? Finno…Ugric? But I've met the Kenyan." interrupted our Hero.

"The Kenyan's only out at sunrise and sunset. Him and the Bony Prince make sure it happens, both ways. The Finno-Ugric watches Teutoberg Forest. He's Virgil's friend. You ever meet Virgil?"

"*Cling! Clang!*" interrupted the kitchen.

"Yeah, I've met Virgil."

"He's a good one, that Virgil. Nice guy, but too smart fer his own good."

"Hmmm. I disagree. So, what brings you to the farmhouse?"

"I was gonna ask you the same damn question, son. What a coincidence."

"I live here. What brings you to my home?"

"Oh, so you're the sonofa that got Moloch. Shoulda known, you look just like *him.* That shoulda been my first clue. Uh, well, I brought something for you."

He pulled a six-gun from his holster, a silver revolver with a pearl handle and spun it around his finger, over his head and behind his back and at one point launched it off his finger and caught it on the other one, gun still spinning. The Protagonist was impressed (rightfully so), but still in that bad mood. Woke up on the wrong side of the bed and it all went downhill from there, evidently. He just couldn't shake the cloud over his head.

"Did you bring me the gun or the buffoonery?" the Protagonist asked, and there was a puddle of disdain at his feet where it had dripped off of his tone of voice.

The Wandering American stood up lazily and took a flask from within his suit. He unscrewed the top and took a pull off it, teeth clenched, jaw flexing as he swallowed, like he was trying to break it in two. "I brought you the gun.

But I don't like yer attitude."

"*Cling! Clang!*" said the kitchen. What exactly was going on in there? Were the Ecclesiae building a railroad in the kitchen? A Subtly Oriental Express?

"Look, I'm sorry." said the Protagonist. "It's been a rough day. Just leave it for me and thank you, if you're giving it to me, or extend my thanks to whoever is giving it to me. I just need to go up to my room."

"You got no manners. They told me you was real polite."

"I am, usually. Just a shitty day. Surely you've had shitty days."

The Wandering American took another drink, put the flask away, and punched the Protagonist square in the mouth. Hard. Dizzyingly hard.

"Damn, what a punch!" bellowed the punchee reverently. "What a hell of a punch!" His head swam. His temples throbbed. His teeth ached. His tongue was being fried on the burning slabs of Hell (he had bit it) and bleeding, too. His lips felt three times as large but they were, in fact, only twice as large as normal.

The American was shaking his hand out, all the while chuckling and licking his lips, as if our Hero's praise of the pugilistic externalization of his irritation was just what he was looking for.

"You gotta show me how to punch like that." said the young man.

"*Cling Clang* " said the kitchen.

———

So the cowboy did. Not on the Protagonist's face, thankfully, but on a saddle, which he stuck on a branch pointing straight out of the ground in the front yard of the farmhouse. He'd unsaddled his horse and made this contraption while our Hero iced his mouth. When the Wandering American was ready, he showed the Protagonist how to do it. He wound up, clenched his teeth, made his fist into a brick fucking wall and knocked the saddle seven feet back. He replaced the saddle, did the same thing, offered the Protagonist a shot at it. So our Hero punched and punched and punched, with less spectacular results, and that's to be expected. Not that he was weak, not that he didn't know how to punch. He had been in enough schoolyard brawls; He also remembered the hand-to-hand stuff in boot camp. But this saddle was heavier than he'd expected, and the wind was wrong. So he told himself. In all actuality, the Protagonist's problem was that it takes more than two attempts to learn to punch the way an immortal super cop punches. Ask anyone and they'll tell you the same thing.

He tried a few more times. The cowboy corrected his form. He tried more. And was corrected further.

On the eighteenth punch he knocked it clear to Wandering American distances.

"See?" smiled the cowboy through two fistfuls of teeth.

"I do." said the Protagonist, and knocked four American teeth out of the Wanderer's head with a fistful of fist.

They brawled for probably three minutes, there in the front yard, kicking and scratching and throwing each other into the ground. Our Hero stomped, the cowboy stamped, our Hero biffed, the cowboy boffed. The Protagonist stomped some more, the Wandering American stamped some more. One whammed, the other whammered, then cracked and it was the other's turn to clock. Finally, the Protagonist slammed and the cowboy said: "Slim."

Our Hero said, "Yes, Tex?"

"Enough. You gon' kill me."

The Protagonist laughed, relieved beyond relief. "Okay."

He helped the cowboy up and they went in and got ice for their swelling, a refill for his bag and an extra helping for the Wanderer. The Protagonist had two black eyes and a busted lip. The cowboy had a dislocated jaw and four missing teeth. He shoved the missing masticators that he'd collected from the yard back into his gums, then the Ecclesiae helped him set his jaw and gave both of them each a glass of water with a drop of the golden elixir in it. The first sip was like the tallest glass of the coldest iced tea on the hottest day Death Valley had ever seen. The Protagonist was cool and free of pain almost immediately.

And so was the Wandering American. His teeth were back in place and his jaw looked okay. On that note, the Protagonist's eyes felt much better. He could actually see out of the left one, an improvement over five seconds ago.

They clinked glasses and drained them. Then they passed the Wanderer's flask, full of strong, damned strong rye whiskey, back and forth until it was gone and they were approaching drunk.

Then the cowboy stood up like he had to go, and our Hero noticed that the Wandering American, for some inexplicable reason, was sporting an erection. "You *are* polite." Said the cowboy. "You musta just been havin' a shitty day, huh?" He smiled broadly. "Here's that shooter." said the Wandering American, and he threw the gun to the Protagonist.

"CLING! CLANG!" cried the kitchen.

Our Hero opened the chamber. "No bullets?" he said.

"Go see what yer gooky friends are makin' in there. I'll see ya around, Slim."

"Later, Tex."

The Protagonist went into the kitchen and saw that the dining table had been replaced by an anvil. Standing around the anvil were the Ecclesiae, clinging and clanging on a piece of molten iron. On one of the chairs near the back corner was Virgil.

"Hi, Virgil. When did you come in?"

"Not long ago. Right after the fight. Nice job."

"Thanks. What are you doing?"

Our Hero looked over at the counter where all the smithing materials lay and saw a hammer and tongs and various other tools. He also saw the black shards they had pulled out of the Wandering Bedouin's head.

"Are those the..."

"Yes." said Virgil. "Some of them. Some of them they just extracted from the Wandering American. That's why he was here."

The Protagonist pulled the gun out from his belt. "He said he was here to give me this."

"Well, I think that he got that idea while he was here. The Ecclesiae offered to melt down the shards and get rid of the taint on the alloy, then make bullets that worked the other way...you do know how the shards work, don't you?"

The Protagonist nodded in the affirmative.

"They offered to make bullets for the gun that would work the other way. Against the men in leather coats. From what I've gathered, it sounds like he wanted to give one of his guns to you, sort of as tribute to the man who bested Moloch. There's a lot of respect for you among the Wanderers, you know that? They all feel indebted to you for avenging the Bedouin."

"Wow." said our Hero. "I don't know what to say."

"Then go practice your shooting." said Virgil. One of the Ecclesiae took off his apron, went upstairs and returned with a box of garden variety lead bullets for the Protagonist's newly acquired six-gun, but he never said a word.

———

The Ecclesiae continued with their work and Virgil helped the Protagonist set up a small shooting range. Bottles and cans on sticks implanted in the soil of the Ager Epiphania. Our Hero tried to hit the closest one and it took him three shots to do it. Out of practice, of course, and he was never much good with a pistol. Virgil motioned for him to lower the gun and walked out to the can. Our Soldier had only grazed it.

Virgil walked back, took the gun, took a shot, and missed. It took him *ten* shots to hit it.

"Hmmm. I guess I'm no good, either. Anyway, keep practicing. I'll be staying the night here."

"Okay." said the Protagonist. "What's the occasion?"

"Saint Scholastica is coming tomorrow." Virgil stated. "I need to speak with her."

Our Hero shivered. What Virgil didn't say was that the Tiamat was coming tomorrow. He still had no idea what it looked like, only that the mere thought of the name collected cold beads of fearful sweat on the tips of his fingers. He turned and kept shooting.

Shooting a gun is really quite natural once you have the hang of it, according to the Protagonist. Not exactly like riding a bike, he says, but once that gun is in the hand long enough, it *is* the hand.

One of the twins came out and refreshed, wordlessly, the Protagonist on how to shoot while running (wildly inaccurate, but necessary sometimes) and how to fire after exhaling to get the steadiest shot. All the while, the Protagonist wished for a rifle. He was so much better with a rifle.

So he spent most of the day practicing his shooting. And did okay. Focus and grit and determination got him to a level where he felt okay about turning in for the night, and when he did, he slept beautifully.

———

He woke to a feminine voice, the first he'd heard since the woman in the white dress had asked him not to pick a flower. It was deep and throaty and smoky, a whisky-voice. A deep contralto. The perfect pitch for a woman's voice, the perfect texture.

The Protagonist looked out the window, at the snow on the ground, on everything. At least everything had its color back, but there wasn't much to be said for that, since everything was basically white and black and gray, anyway.

The wildflowers were completely gone.

He came downstairs and walked into the living room, and saw there a redheaded woman, not pretty but beautiful, not stern but determined. She cocked an eyebrow at him.

"Congratulations."

"Sure. Thanks."

She was speaking business with the Ecclesiae (who weren't actually speaking at all) and Virgil, who was spitting rapid fire bursts of Latin too quickly for the Protagonist to catch anything but the redhead's name. *This* was Saint Scholastica.

Dressed head to toe in dazzlingly white full plate armor, with a pale gold chain mail hauberk lurking beneath the broad swaths of tempered, snow-colored steel. There was a wide white shield on her back that bore the same insignia she bore on the chest plate of her armor: A golden Celtic cross. At her hip hung a short broadsword, like the ones that Father Luke liked, and it hung in a jeweled scabbard. No helmet. That struck the Protagonist as odd. She should really have had a helmet.

She looked a little scary, he mused, just before the earthquake hit.

He was thrown to the ground. Outside, the earth's teeth chattered. The quake shook a flurry of snowflakes loose from the clouds. And the Protagonist panicked.

It's a funny thing about earthquakes and hurricanes and tornadoes and other disasters. A man can run around screaming his damned head off about *absolutely nothing at all* and everyone will forgive him when he's done. He could recite Absurdist Theater and it would make perfect sense to everyone, scream that the mice are not chauvinists and that his pubic hair was graying and that Chicago may indeed hold the secret to whether the chicken or the egg crossed the road first and not a person alive would think a thing less of him after the earthquake, nor even mention it. This is not a free lunch, a coupon that promises the freedom to do whatever one pleases in a disaster, mind you. It is simply a truism, as anyone who has ever been in an earthquake will attest to. People say the dumbest things in times of trouble.

The Protagonist screamed none of these things, of course, but he did break out into a sweat and tried to get outdoors as fast as he could.

A small (but surprisingly powerful) hand yanked him back into the house. The tremor had ended. He was alive and had, in fact, never been in danger of foreign alteration of that abstract condition.

"Don't go out there." Scholastica whispered into his ear.

"Why?" he asked. Even though he knew. An image of a dead child was hovering in the front of his mind, like it had been burned behind his eyes by the sun.

"You know why." Virgil said to the young man. "Go get your gun."

He ran up to his room and got his six-gun and the box of bullets, then loaded up. Once downstairs again, the Ecclesiae looked at each other and left the room. One came back with our Soldier's wooden sword, the Prajna Khadga, and six bullets in his hand. He took the Protagonist's revolver, emptied the chamber and put the new bullets in, then attached the bludgeon to his side with a leather strap. The other came back with two Korean War-era vintage 60. anti-aircraft sniper rifles. They parked at the windows and opened them, then took up positions. One was crouched on one knee, the other on top of cushions, prone. Our Hero looked at Saint Scholastica.

"Where is it?" he asked.

"In a cave on a ridge on the cliff face of the Woeful Plateau. Miles away." she said.

"I presume it's responsible for the earthquake?" He looked around the room and saw that nothing was wrong, nothing had fallen off the shelf, then suddenly remembered that neither Virgil nor the Ecclesiae nor Saint Scholastica were thrown to the ground, either.

"Good job. You're not terribly bright, huh?" she asked.

"No, but I'm good-looking." He grinned a stupid grin.

"You're not that, either. Come on. We've got a ways to hike to its cave."

"Wait, wait. I'm going with you?"

"Of course. Safety in numbers." said Virgil.

"Uh...cave?" he asked. The Protagonist phrases questions in such utter proportions as to be called even Neanderthalesque in times of distress and trouble. It boggles *his* mind, too.

"Not in the classic sense. That's where it emerges. We've got four hours." Said Saint Scholastica.

"Then why pull me back, earlier?"

"If I have a can of Pepsi, I got good odds there's Pepsi in there. But it might be Coke. I know what I know. I've fought this thing dozens of times, get my drift? But I always prepare for the worst." She smiled at him like she was a patient older sister and he six years old.

"Uh, thanks. I get it, sort of."

Virgil handed the Protagonist a vigorous shake. "Good luck." he said. "I'll be here."

The Protagonist tightened his belt (He hadn't eaten breakfast) and headed out the door, Scholastica leading the way, her callused hand holding his callused hand. They ran as far as they could, rested, ran as fast as they could, rested, and repeated until they were half the distance to the Woeful Plateau. *Making good time*, the Protagonist mused. Thirty miles to cross in four hours. On foot. No easy task, but then, our Hero and Heroine aren't just any old runners. They jogged intermittently to conserve energy and once stopped just before Teutoberg Forest because Scholastica looked faint.

"What's wrong?" asked the Protagonist breathlessly.

"Sorry. It's tough on me." She pointed at a dead, black spot on the ground, where no grass would ever grow again. The place Moloch was defeated.

"Oh. Uh, I guess I'm sorry, too."

"Don't worry about it. Let's just get out of here."

—

If this seems completely wacky, as if the geography of the Plateau has been completely forgotten by the author and he is just making things up now, keep in mind that the Vicissitude is still in progress. Thirty miles was really the distance from the farmhouse to Moloch's resting place, compared to perhaps two miles when our Soldier performed the task of "killing" the Horrid King.

—

They crested along the southern side of the forest, heading east until the trees veered north again.

"On the other side of this is…well, you know." said Scholastica.

The Protagonist shook his head. "Actually, I don't. I haven't explored any more than the north end of this forest, near the tower."

"Hmmm. You'll see enough before your time here is through. On the other side of this is a giant wall of brambles. The vines are a foot thick, they span probably thirteen feet into the air. Like a giant barbed-wire fence. One hundred and thirty-seven, no, make that one hundred and thirty-nine steps east of here is a stairway, an Eightfold Path that leads up to a small ridge halfway up the Woeful Plateau. I will climb it and the Tiamat will emerge from its cave. That's your time to shine."

"What should I do?"

"Well what do you think I brought you along for?"

The Protagonist's brain froze. "Oh, shit."

"Don't worry about it. The Tiamat's too big to miss."

That didn't reassure him. It made his heart quail in its little ribcage cottage. Too big to miss? Did she *know* how poor his aim was? Or was the Tiamat actually that fucking big?

He tried to count the steps they took eastward along the briars but was interrupted at sixty-seven by another earthquake. This time, before he could be thrown down again, Scholastica grabbed his hand and suddenly he was standing on a rock in a turbulent sea. The ground shook and vibrated and lurched and threw up and screamed and cried all around him but there he was, untouched. Unhurt. Standing on firm ground. The earthquake didn't even faze him. To this day he's still not sure if it was some power that Scholastica had or if it was the fact that he was holding a woman's hand for the first time in months.

The deep, cloudy sky, high above him dropped a single snowflake on his cheek.

"Focus." Scholastica whispered.

K'ung Wu.

He shook off the sudden resounding in his head and focused, as per Saint Scholastica's directions.

They walked as the earth shook. Try as it might, it could not derail them. Scholastica finally got to the stairway and motioned for him to take out his gun. He did so.

She walked up the Eightfold Path, which was not eight steps at all but rather hundreds. There were, indeed, eight huge steps, like they had been carved for giants, but there was a single staircase that had been hacked into each of the larger "steps", a single staircase that went up, all the way up to the top of the Woeful Plateau. She murmured something at every one of the large steps, one by one, stopped and murmured, climbed the next set, stopped and murmured. Praying? It seemed unlikely to the Protagonist. Perhaps she was calling the thing out.

When she crested the eighth step and finished murmuring, a small ridge east of the stairs, below Scholastica and above the Protagonist suddenly cracked as wide open as you've ever seen and a *thing*, a hydra, a giant dragon/worm/lizard with six, maybe seven heads and no arms and no legs, just a round ball of sickly grey-green flesh and six, maybe seven necks as long in yards as pine trees, levitating four feet in the air, crashed out of the opening. It had pieces of stone and black tar and human bones embedded in its skin, like it slept in a molten graveyard. Its teeth were yellow, its eyes were the color of whitewashed cement and its pupils did not exist. Its cubist snouts looked like they'd been molded by Picasso. Its nostrils poured forth black smoke. Carved into the brow of each head was an upside down pentagram, and from that oozed a sickly, pale, off-white pus that dripped off of its head in little globules that made a sound like a human scream whenever one hit the ground.

It roared, and there was another earthquake. A big one. Nothing seemed to be affected by it but the Protagonist, of course, and it certainly affected him. It threw him to the ground and he hit his head on a rock. He saw stars for the second time in two days. Then blacked out.

Now, he probably wouldn't have blacked out from the blow alone; it was the shock of seeing that thing that did it to him. Dear readers, at the risk of being repetitive, I entreat you to remember that you are reading this and not living it, so you can suspend that wonderful sense of disbelief of yours and visualize this thing without fearing for your very survival. Wherever you are, at home or work, or standing in that bookstore aisle (still?) you don't ever have to see something like this in your life. Bless the Lord.

The Protagonist woke not ten seconds later to Scholastica screaming his name. He stood up, sick to his stomach, sweating profusely, cold as ice. His fear and shock was too great for him to do anything at all but gape. He was utterly bowled over by the sick, horrible, evil sight before his eyes. He vomited, violently, and kept vomiting all over the ground.

Then the lurches slowed, the spasms in his stomach spaced out and he suddenly had a vision. Like the ones he got when he saw the first man in a leather coat he ever saw on this Mountain. Like the one he had at the farmhouse earlier. But it wasn't an atrocity he saw, not this time.

It looked like a motion picture, like 8mm film. It was night, but well-lit; the woman in the white dress stood solemnly on a rock amidst a rushing river, only she wasn't in her white dress. She was nude; the moonlight shone on her skin, on her breasts, on her black hair. She was looking at the Protagonist, standing on an identical rock twenty feet away. Looking at him with apologetic eyes. The same eyes he looked into just before she pushed the trigger outside of that preschool.

Cold, cold water lapped around his feet. He looked, and saw that the water was flowing over a waterfall not ten yards from where they stood.

They stood there and stared at each other, and though the Protagonist's pulse was racing and his hands were wet with perspiration and the hairs on the back of his neck were saluting the moon, all of them at once, he did not fear. The Protagonist looked at his hands, realized he was holding his pistol, and threw it into the river. She turned entreating eyes on him, smiled slightly, and herself took a step into the water. Instantly, she was swept away by the raging current. Horrified, he dove in after her and managed to grab a hold of her body just as the two of them went over the falls together.

Weightlessness. Even with the water slamming against the two of them he felt weightless in that fall. His eyes were squeezed tightly, his grasp of her even tighter. He could feel her breasts pressed against his body, warm even through cold water and wet clothing. He realized that when they hit the water below, they would die, together and in each other's arms.

And that was okay.

She raised her head and kissed him, ever so softly, and then his eyes were open.

—

He was lying on the ground at the foot of the Woeful Plateau, in the shadow of giant, thorny vines, in the shadow of the Tiamat. Miraculously, he was suddenly able to focus, to grasp, to suppress his black fear of this monster. Slightly concussed, he stood up on wobbling legs and fired a fateful bullet from the fateful barrel of his fateful pistol.

He was at last able to forgive the woman in the white dress. This he did. And he forgave himself, too. He was, finally, able to free himself of his burden. At that exact moment where it counted most.

Somewhere far, far up the Mountain, a Man in a faded, pastel Yellow Polo Shirt sat and watched. Watched the Protagonist become what he became, realize what he realized, forgive who it was that he forgave.

And He smiled a rich, meaty, glorious Smile.

—

The bullet went right into one of the Tiamat's twelve or fourteen eyebrows. It ripped through its hide, through its scales, through its bone and passed completely out the back. The head erupted into flame and began splashing geysers of molten blood all over itself. Where the blood landed it burned the skin away, exposing tender flesh and charred yellow bones. This caused it to bleed even more, which only expedited the chain reaction. The

Tiamat's blood was burning itself up.

Scholastica wasted no time. She screamed a single word: *Desinere!* "Cease!" and the blood did. The Tiamat kept thrashing. One of its heads dipped low and grabbed her in its monstrous maw, closing around her armor. She hacked into the head with her broad sword repeatedly, over and over until the maw dropped her onto the body of the dragon. She ran over scales and skulls on the Tiamat's "torso", all the way to the burned part, a great gaping hole in the Tiamat's body (ball?) and chopped into the bone of the thing. It almost threw her off in its agonized spasms.

The Protagonist wondered why she had stopped the bleeding. It seemed like the lava/blood would have burned up the whole thing if she had just let it. Then again, she knew better, he was sure. She was the one who fought it every time it came out.

"Are you planning on fucking shooting?" She screamed at the Protagonist.

He raised his gun and fired another shot. It went into the meat of the thing, the body, if it can be called that. Another fountain of lava. It burned a giant hole into it and a colossal globule of lava blood splashed onto the (already hacked) head closest to it, burning it almost to the skull.

Two heads down, four or five to go.

Make that six to go. The Tiamat had *eight* heads.

"*Desinere!*"

Scholastica was busily poking a third head in the eye, so the Protagonist aimed at the sixth (?) head and fired. He missed. So he pulled back the hammer, re-aimed and... missed again. Pulled back the hammer again, aimed for the body and tensed his finger on the trigger just as Scholastica fell off of its third head and landed on a jutting bone that had thrust up through the ball of the Tiamat's body and given the creature the look of a three-dimensional sundial. The neck that Scholastica had just jumped off of was now dangling horribly, dragging on the ground. That head was clearly neutralized.

Three down, five to go.

"*Desinere!*" came her cry just as the Protagonist fired off his shot.

The bullet connected with the body. Or, rather, *a* body. Scholastica's. It knocked her right off the Tiamat and all the way down to the ground below, just as another head was swooping through the air in a deadly vector towards her.

The Hero had just killed Saint Scholastica.

His face hardened. At least he'd spared the Tiamat the victory. At least she wasn't defeated by this thing. At least her death came at the hands of a friend, or a fellow warrior, or whatever. That's how he'd have wanted to go, right?

He continued trying to justify the ill-placed shot because he didn't have any room in his emotional chambers for grief at that moment. Determination was crowding everything else out.

The Tiamat lumbered in its graceless hover toward the Protagonist, down to his level, roaring another earthquake as it came, a seismic calamity that threw the Protagonist down yet again. It raised two of its heads in the air and came right for him just as he got to his feet. The heads snaked down with the speed of a cobra's strike and thrust into the earth, sending a plume of debris high into the air that showered down on the Protagonist's head.

Our Hero fired, then, his final bullet, his last chance at victory, at triumph, at *survival* and it went (by luck) into another head.

Four down, four to go. And there was never much of a chance, dear readers. One bullet for five heads? Nearly impossible. Our Hero was down to his bludgeon. He saluted Caesar, he who was about to die, then consigned his soul to the Man in the Yellow Polo Shirt and ran at the Tiamat, wooden sword held high. A single head of the beast, boring at him with all of the speed of a freight train, crashed into him with its abstract snout, breaking all of his ribs on the left side and sending him airborne, farther than even the Wandering American's punch had sent that saddle. The Tiamat positioned itself in front of our Hero so that it's shadow fell on him, raised all of it's heads into the air as if crying it's victory in defiance to the Mountaintop and then looked at him with eight eyes, the four heads grouped together in a perfect cross. Right next to each other. The Protagonist's head filled with anger and frustration and regret. He wished for one more bullet. Just one more bullet and a little better aim. Just to shoot the one head above the other three, to send a waterfall of burning molten dragon demon blood cascading that smoldering death atop the whole thing. He visualized it, then, laying *in media crucis*, in the shadow of that hideous cross. He visualized one bullet. And prepared to die.

Crack! Crack! Crack! Crack! The powerful blasts of four gunshots reverberated off the trees just west of my soon-to-be grave. *Four* bullets stuck right into the head at the top of the cross formation. Blood leaped out, burning molten dragon demon blood cascading smoldering death onto the other three heads. Just like the Protagonist imagined in that extrapolative near-death fantasy.

The Tiamat twitched and screamed and gargled and lolled horribly. Then our Hero saw something extraordinarily strange. A glint of sunlight on steel, or rather, several of them, in a succession of bright flashes. A sword was spinning through the air. That sword went up into the sky and then straight down into the middle of the Tiamat.

The great beast roared a final earthquake and it was so fierce, so loud, that the Protagonist's skull split inside his head, fractured clean down the middle.

The Tiamat fell to the ground with an earth-shattering crash not unlike Archimedes' abbey. And that was when the Protagonist suddenly heard the cry. The cry of victory, of true victory. A redhead with a gritty contralto climbed to the top of the horizontal beast and screamed her own voice to Heaven. The clouds parted, the snow stopped. The sun shone on her for just a moment.

She wasn't dead.

Karthago Delenda Est.

Then the snow started back up again. There still wasn't any message in the flakes. No Morse code. Just snow falling on a coniferous forest, a crowing redhead who should be dead, a fractured skull of a Protagonist that should be dead. Snow falling on a dragon's corpse. Snow falling on the Mountain with No Name.

Snow falling on Virgil. Snow falling on twins whose faces looked Mediterranean sometimes, Oriental other times. Snow falling on twins walking toward Scholastica with smoking rifles in their hands.

Virgil broke and off and came toward the Protagonist, lying with his broken ribs and broken skull and (possibly) broken arm. Virgil smelled of the elixir.

"I...I shot Scholastica." said the Protagonist to wise old gray-cloaked equestrian.. Virgil smiled at him and said nothing.

Scholastica eventually made her way over to the Protagonist's side, as well. She was beaming. "Wow, kid. I'd be dead if it weren't for you. Thanks for the save."

"But...I shot you." he said. The twins arrived and helped Virgil and Scholastica hoist the injured young man up onto a stretcher.

"I know. If you hadn't knocked me off the body, the head would have gotten me sure." gushed Scholastica. She kissed him right on the lips, sweetly and thoroughly. "And you said you weren't much of a shot. Men are so modest." She kissed him again.

Naturally, our Hero was bewildered. "Uh, you're welcome." he said, and passed out from the pain. They wheeled him home straight away and began tending to his wounds.

The Last Good Day of the Year
Chapter 11

I woke to Father Luke's gritty French voice resounding solidly off of every corner in my small bedroom. He was speaking in Latin to one of the twins, who was standing next to his brother and Virgil. I clenched my eyes closed again and listened.

"The wounds are not as bad as the ones he received from Moloch. He'll be fine. But don't tell him about the Tooth. As much as he's entitled to it, he's not ready. Let him wait, perhaps until after the Foederati have come. Perhaps until spring."

The Ecclesiae nodded and I pretended like I was still asleep. Father Luke left the room with Virgil, and the Ecclesiae just stood there and looked at me. In a kind of creepy way.

Unnerving stares notwithstanding, I mused a while in fake slumber. Father Luke and I couldn't speak, I guess, but he was still watching over me.

So many father figures on Devine Road. Father figures almost ruined Earth, almost ruin Earth everyday. And yet I felt comforted.

K'ung Wu.

There was that voice again. Those words. I sat up in bed, feigned a yawn and took a very real stretch. The twins looked at me curiously, perhaps wondering if I had been awake during the conversation. "My friends," I said to the Ecclesiae. "How do you say K'ung Wu in English?"

They looked at each other as parents look at each other when they notice their firstborn son has discovered the difference between boys and girls. One of them left and got me a book. He handed it to me and then left with his brother.

The book was entitled *Shu Ching*. I opened it and there was Chinese on the left half of the page, Latin on the right. I got out my Latin dictionary and began translating.

When I got to K'ung Wu, or the first mention of it, I proceeded with my translation extra carefully.

191

The K'ung Wu was a magical knife given to the Shang Dynasty by a magician who lived in the White Mountains of China, west of the inland sea. It could cut jade like wax, the book said. Thus, the sacred Sky Ring of Shang was created from blue jade sent from Heaven, and was passed from father to firstborn son, a totem that symbolized the harmony between Heaven and Earth. The Shang Dynasty was blessed because of this ring.

That was it? A knife, mentioned in passing, that could cut jade like wax? What was that doing reverberating around inside my skull?

Oh, my skull. That reminded me. My skull was pounding. Jesus, that's pain. A skull fracture. Fuck.

—

Outside, birds burst into song. The tender twittering of a thrush, the staccato chirps of a swallow and the gut-wrenching squawks of a blue jay all in one, a single virtuoso performance that served absolutely no purpose and could thus be called art.

Oscar Wilde once said that we can forgive an artist for making something useful as long as he does not admire it. According to the English playwright, the only excuse for making a useless thing was to admire it.

"All art is quite useless."
-Oscar Wilde

I looked outside to see what a thrush, a swallow and a blue jay were doing in the same tree. I was surprised by little on the Mountain with No Name.

But for all that useless, beautiful art they were only singing. I saw, far away, several Wanderers were pulling apart the corpse of the Tiamat, wheeling it away in chunks heaped high on large wheelbarrows, off to the abbey.

Then I saw the woman in the white dress, up and away, on a hill overlooking Teutoberg Forest.

Ah. The birds were singing for her.

I didn't hear the door open behind me.

Saint Scholastica walked into the room and looked out the window with me, though I didn't notice her there. She watched the woman with me for a few seconds. I don't know what she was thinking. I know that I was thinking that I had to figure something out concerning that creature. I had to figure out if she was the woman in the white jacket. And I had to figure out whether or not I was in love with her.

"She's beautiful, isn't she?" said Saint Scholastica.

I was startled so badly that I fell out of my bed, knocking Scholastica over and sending both of us toppling to the ground, my arms and neck tangled in her legs.

She cracked up laughing.

I stood up, ribs smarting. They had been broken and, elixir or no, they really hurt. I offered my hand to her and she took it, helping herself up. Then I crawled back into bed.

"Jesus. You scared the shit out of me."

Her guffaws atrophied to giggles. They made her shake beautifully in the sarong she was wearing.

"Wow." I said. "You look better without the armor."

She smiled mischievously. "Yeah? You look better without the clothes."

I suddenly realized I was naked. I hadn't been around anyone but men (and the woman in the white dress, but not often) since Scholastica showed up and I was in my bedroom, anyway. I never wear clothes in bed. Shit, I hadn't even considered whether I was wearing something or not.

At least I was back under the blankets.

"Thanks." I blushed.

"Don't be shy." she said. "I just came up to check on you. And to thank you again for all of the assistance." She sat on the bed next to me.

"Uh, no problem. I just sort of acted instead of thinking about it. Tried to turn the brain off and just *go*, you know?"

"Uh-huh. I totally understand. A little girl fighting some giant demon and no way she was going to win by her little old self." She smiled demurely.

"No, no. Not like that. I have absolute faith in everyone on this Mountain. On this Plateau, anyway. I knew you were here specifically to kill that thing. So I didn't think twice."

"How did you know? Virgil?"

"Uh, I believe the first time I heard your name was from Abaddon."

"You met Abaddon?"

"Yes. And then there was the Man in the Yellow Polo Shirt."

"W*hat*?!" Saint Scholastica looked at me like I'd just told her that He was dead.

"He, uh, mentioned you by name..."

She started to cry. That baffled me thoroughly. Then she was shedding tears uncontrollably. She shook and wept. That's a very uncomfortable thing, you know. Sitting naked next to a sobbing woman.

Forgetting my clothesless condition, I put my hand on her shoulder in a protective gesture. As if she needed anybody, much less me, to protect her.

"H-He...He said my *name?*" she stuttered.

"Yes. One of the men in leather coats was saying something about the Tiamat, and the Man in the Yellow Polo Shirt said, 'Are you threatening Me? Saint Scholastica is due back anytime. We'll see how well your little bastard does against her.'"

Scholastica cried hard for about two solid minutes. Need the gesture or not, she wriggled onto my lap, sunk her face into my shoulder and just cried. I sat and tried to be still.

When she seemed like she was a little better under control, I ruffled her hair and smiled at her.

"Why are you so upset?" I asked.

"He hasn't said my name since the Revolution. He's refused to speak it out loud because I don't work specifically under His standard, even though He speaks to Abaddon. He talks to me sometimes, sure, but always without saying my name. He refuses to utter it. He's upset. I mean, understandably, I refused to take a side in the War, you know? But..." She made a very unattractive sound with her nasal cavity. "But now you tell me He said it again. While I was in the Abyss, right? Thank you. Thank you, thank you, thank you."

She peppered my face with kisses and, mortified, I suddenly realized that my manhood was fully erect.

Either women's tears are the most powerful aphrodisiac known to humankind or something about switching my brain over to "protect" mode just gets the old boy excited. It's not even that I was particularly aroused; the tears just had the corporal standing at attention before I had any idea what was going on.

I blushed again, but she (thankfully) didn't seem to notice the warmth in my face or the hammerhead trying to break through her right leg. Maybe she just expected it and knew that it's something that happens to men in times like this and didn't think anything of it. I hoped so. She kissed me again and stood up, smoothed out her sarong and sniffled her last sniffle, then sat back down. On the bed, not my lap.

"So, anyway," she started, looking a bit embarrassed, either about her outburst or the condition of my penis; I couldn't tell which. "How are you feeling?"

"Uh, I'm okay. My head hurts, and my ribs smart a little, but I feel good. A few days and I should be right as rain."

"That's good." She looked at the tent I was pitching but didn't say anything.

"Uh, sorry." I managed sheepishly.

"It's okay."

"Uh…" Change the subject. Quick. "Uh, what's this Tooth? Or whatever? Some Tooth I'm entitled to, right?"

Scholastica snapped to attention. "Where did you hear about the Tooth?"

"I heard Father Luke in here talking to the Ecclesiae while they thought I was asleep. He said to wait until spring to tell me about the Tooth. But I heard him. So tell me about it."

"It's nothing, really."

"I suppose you have some nice oceanside property in Colorado to sell me?"

"What?"

"Nothing." I frowned solemnly. "Just tell me."

"If Father Luke thought it was a good idea to wait, you should wait. Don't you trust him?"

"No, I don't," I said, and suddenly realized that I didn't think much of his judgment. "The people here, or beings or whatever, have been keeping me ignorant since I first got my tires on Devine Road. I don't even know why I'm here. All I know is my ignorance caused the death of something very important to the world and that it's the fault of Father Luke and the Wandering Bedouin and the Ecclesiae and even the Man in the Yellow Polo Shirt for keeping me in the dark about it."

"How do you know it wasn't the time for it? How do you know that events weren't working up to your arrival, and that everything didn't go according to plan?" she said, and frowned.

"What?"

"How do you know that everything that has happened since your arrival here wasn't planned meticulously? How do you know that even your next response is not thoroughly anticipated and prepared for? How do you know who you're even working for?"

"What?"

"Is this the new word of the day? 'What?' Listen to me. You're being obtuse. How do you know anything? You've been making assumptions since the first day you got here." She sighed. "You, of all entities on this plateau,

195

should be careful about making assumptions here. Because you're not accustomed to how things work on the Road. So don't assume anything anymore. Just go with the flow. Not against it, go with it. I mean, be independent, question the answers, do all those things. But if something happens, it happens for a reason. Understand? Everything's connected. Everything happens for a reason."

I grimaced. That didn't make me feel better. Then she looked at me like what I had said earlier had just sunk in with her. Maybe she just had a piece to say before weighing my whole paragraph.

"What do you mean, 'I don't know why I'm here?'"

"Exactly that. I don't know why I'm here."

"Are you serious? You're..." She stopped and looked embarrassed.

"I'm what?" I asked, Hell bent on this answer if I could get none to any other question. Hell bent on this answer if there was no answer to any question I ever asked again. Hell bent on this answer if no other question existed.

She took a deep breath. "The Tiamat's Tooth is deep in the cave that the Tiamat emerges from every winter. It is not, in fact, a tooth. It is a stalactite, stories high, upon which is written the name of every Saint who has fought the Tiamat over the years. Every person, everybody.

"Everyone who did it on Earth, fighting unseen against overwhelming odds, trying to hold the world on their shoulders, trying to bear the sins of their loved ones. Every father who worked the steel mill unrelenting every day with cancer eating his intestines. Every waitress who worked nine to five at one restaurant and then ten to six at another, every day, just to support her small children, spending most of her pay on day care just so she could provide macaroni and cheese and meager lodging. Every widower. Every widow. Every single father that raised a baby without a mother. Every single mother. Every man who silently suffered the infidelity of his wife to preserve an illusion for his family, and for his neighbors. Joseph, stepfather of Christ. His name is there. Judy Jenson's name is there. Rodin's name is there for capturing the spirit of the battle against the Tiamat, even if he never fought it himself. The top of the Tooth is actually perfectly reproduced to every detail to resemble his sculpture of the Fallen Caryatid. It symbolizes the battle so many fight, without thanks or foot rubs or a warm body to curl up next to every night. It symbolizes the human aspect of it.

"And everyone who fought it on this Mountain is there, too. You, me, The Wandering Bedouin, the Ecclesiae, Father Luke, all of our true names are

196

there. Don't you see? You can't learn their names, not yet."

"You didn't answer my question." I said.

She took another deep breath. "You are an eagle among swallows."

"I know that. I had the dream."

"Then what are you asking me for?"

"Because I don't know what that *means*!"

"Well, I guess things are tough all over, huh?"

"What the Hell? Why can't anyone just answer a fucking question?"

"Hey. Patience. No one is afraid of telling you answers. We're afraid of your impatience. Be cool. If I told you everything you wanted to know, what would you do?"

"I'd be happy, that's what." I crossed my arms.

"No, you'd curl up and have another nervous breakdown."

"How do you know about that?"

"Father Luke told me. You freaked out. That's why everyone waits. They let you come to your own conclusions. That serves two purposes: One, you don't have panic attacks if you figure it out yourself. Not as bad, anyways. You're a very nervous fellow."

"I know." I said, and cast my eyes downward.

"Two: It sticks to this whole 'individuality' theme they're trying to smash into your head. You make your own truth. Everything exists in your perception, and you can change that perception. What you think of things is what they are until you're corrected. Even then, you have to accept the correction for yourself. So *this* way you're better prepared to be your own man when it really counts."

She looked back at the blanket. The corporal apparently had heard none of the conversation, and was still eagerly awaiting…something. Like a dog on his hind legs, uncomfortable but nonetheless anticipating a cookie. Or at least an "Atta boy."

"At ease, soldier." said Saint Scholastica, and she grinned coquettishly. Maybe the best he was going to get. He wasn't satisfied.

I laughed, embarrassed but strangely relieved. As much as I wanted answers, Scholastica was right. I was scared to death of them.

Scholastica was paying quite a lot of attention to my penis. "Well, talking to it ain't gonna help." I laughed uncomfortably. "Just ignore it and it goes away."

"Is that how that works?" she asked. She was laughing and blushing a little, too. "You know, uh…" she looked at the door and it shut itself, propelled by a sudden breeze that found its way in through the window. "You know."

"Uh, no. I don't know."

She leaned in very close to me, very suddenly, like she had been opened up and filled with confidence so quickly that I couldn't notice. Her breath was sweet, her tiny nose brushed against mine. Perhaps she had been galvanized by the fortitude and duration of the priapic display, but I thought it just as likely that she was reading my mind. I don't think I was guarding my thoughts too closely, either. She was incredibly attractive.

"Maybe I don't want it to go away." she purred.

"Maybe I don't either." I said.

"You know, I didn't mean it when I said you weren't good looking. You are. Really handsome. And brave, too. And you saved my 'life.'"

I didn't bother bringing up the fact that I'd shot her *accidentally*, which by some freakish act of the Man had knocked her off of the Tiamat's body onto a ridge on the cliff face of the Woeful Plateau of nearly the same height. The bullet was stuck in the breast plate of her armor and she had suffered no other wounds to speak of. So, yeah, I'd saved her "life," whatever a "life" is for an angel. But it was totally accidental. Totally retarded. I thought I'd *killed* her.

No, I didn't bring that up. And why would I? If I was not mistaken, I was seriously on the verge of getting laid.

She smiled again, with half of her beautiful, round mouth. "I've never, you know...with someone like...with a..." She looked at me, suddenly all business but for a glint in her eye. Her breath was hot on my face, and she was so close to my face that I could smell the inside of her mouth, like butterscotch and cloves, like a hot, heavy sauna, like Heaven.

"What? With a man? A human?" I asked. Yes siree, I was most *certainly* getting laid. The corporal got his reinforcements. The blood that crimsoned my face in blush was draining away and fortifying his front lines. He was getting air support. Ammunition. The troops were ready to invade. God, it'd been years. I hadn't been with a woman since my ex-girlfriend, the one who scarred me bad enough to render me totally celibate since I'd left from and then arrived home from Iraq.

And then Devine Road threw a wrench into my only partially existent social life, so I don't think I'd even seriously *talked* with a chick for years.

God, it'd been too long. The boys were swelling up, puffing out their chests, ready, eager and every other adjective implying "horny to the point of desperation."

"Uh, yeah. A man, I should say." She set her hand on Mount Protagonist, on the support beam of the bed sheet pergola I hid my lower half beneath, on my overeager, over stimulated, overexcited member. "Always wanted to, though." she said, half-whispering, gently and confidentially. "I mean, if you wanted to… with a…you know…"

I nodded.

"Are you sure?" she asked, and smiled evilly. "I bite."

"Yes."

"Hard."

"You couldn't bite hard enough."

"You want to sleep with an angel?"

"Hell, yes."

———

So we did. It.

A ménage à trois with the tail end of a rainbow. The aurora borealis painted across the ceiling. Fireworks between the sheets. Sunshine reflecting off of snowflakes. Moonlight on red, red hair. Magic, magic, magic. Etc. *ad nauseam.*

We made love until midnight, pausing only to catch our breath. And for short intervals between my…releases.

"I *am* only human." I'd said to her.

She'd giggled. "I know."

———

I'd stopped smoking a few weeks ago. Not of my own volition, just because I'd quit. I don't know how it happened. Sort of when I wasn't thinking about it. Tonight (this morning?) Scholastica and I opened the window and had three Camels each. I still had a pack in the room. Come to think of it, there was always a pack in the room. I hadn't bought cigarettes since November. That made me chuckle.

"What's so funny?" she said lazily.

"Oh, just little things."

"Hmmm? What little things?"

"The cigarettes. There's a full pack here, and I haven't bought them since November."

"Oh. Ha ha. Yeah, that's cool, huh?"

"Yeah. The Ecclesiae provide everything. *Everything*. It's a trip."

"They're nice." she said.

"So, uh…I'm curious. You're not actually Saint Scholastica, *the* Saint Scholastica. Right?"

"Sure I am."

"But Saint Scholastica was human."

"Oh, her. No, no. She was named after me. I'm the real deal."

"Seems that way." I replied. With a chuckle, I pinched one of her nipples.

"I thought you couldn't go anymore." she said.

"I'm not sure I can."

"Then don't *tease*."

Clop, clop, clop. The sound of footsteps crept through the floor from downstairs.

"Oh, shit." she said, and groaned. "I totally forgot. I was supposed to meet with Virgil and the Ecclesiae right after I checked on you."

"I'd say you're not quite finished checking on me."

"Stipulated." She cocked her ear, listening to voices I could not hear. "They're talking about me right now. They think I left." She strained a little. "They think I'm with the Bedouin. Oh, but we were *noisy*!"

I sat up in bed. "The Bedouin's back?" I asked.

"Yes. Up near the forest, from the look of it."

I smiled, and looked out the window, where Scholastica's gaze lay. I didn't see a thing.

"I gotta go. I shouldn't be caught in bed with you." she said.

"Oh, come on. We've been quiet. You…uh, you weren't quiet, not by a long shot. Besides, where's your sense of adventure?" I dipped my pointed finger beneath the sheets and between her legs, and made a beckoning motion with my finger tip. The jewel in her lotus saluted smartly.

"You better be careful, or you'll have my sense of adventure all over the sheets." She said, then relaxed her shoulders, smiling. "Okay, you're right. One more time." She smiled. "Even though you said the old boy couldn't handle anymore."

The corporal had perked back up. "See?" I grinned. "He just needed a breather."

So we did it again, and the details are for me and Scholastica and no one else. So don't be nosy.

An hour or so later of cuddling and nipple pinching, she decided she had to leave, so as not to get caught.

"What, are there rules against us doing this?" I asked.

"No, silly. Of course not." She was so full of sex that she *squish*ed as she stood up. "It's just that you're supposed to be recovering. No strenuous activity."

"Strenuous? Don't flatter yourself."

"Oh! Damn you to Hell!" She punched me so hard in the ribs (the ones the Tiamat didn't break) that I thought I was just going to have to be a ribless mass of flesh forever and ever.

"Peace, woman." I wheezed. "I'm teasing. I haven't had this much fun since, uh….ever. I've never had that much fun."

She kissed me. "I know, darling. I was just teasing, too. If I'd wanted, I could have punched straight through your torso."

"I don't doubt it." I laughed. And I didn't doubt it. "Hey."

"What?"

"Why did you stop the bleeding? Not just let the Tiamat burn itself up?"

"More fun to give it a fighting chance against me." She said, matter-of-factly.

"Bullshit." I crossed my arms over my chest.

"No, I'm serious."

"What?!"

"Listen to me. It's a boring goddamned thing to fight that fiend every time it comes crashing out of the Woeful Plateau, understand me?" Now she had her arms crossed. "Same old thing, time after time. So I think up ways to make it harder for me. It never really is hard, of course, but I've been spicing it up for I don't know how long, now."

"But, you almost got me killed!"

"No, I didn't. The Ecclesiae were there."

"Did you know that?" I asked, incredulous.

"Sure I did."

"That's fucking great. Wow. Just fucking great."

"Hey, it's not like you're dead, right?" She sounded irritated with me.

"Sorry. Ja. Da. Oui. Sí. You're right. This is your pigeon. I'll shut up."

"Okay by me." she said, but her tone was playful again. "I'm going to get dressed now. Before I get in any trouble."

"But we're celebrating!" I cried, mock-offended. "The death of the Tiamat."

"Oh, I wish it was the death of the Tiamat!" she said, and laughed haughtily. "If this was a death, it was its one-hundredth death. Your damned brothers and sisters keep hurting each other. Then a new one is born. A new Tiamat. Then I kill it again." She struck the air with her fist, effectively punctuating her sentence, and then walked to her sarong, laying in a crumpled mess on the floor.

"But it looks good there." I said, and she smiled and picked it up anyway. "So... what exactly does it mean to get in trouble? I mean, for you." I asked.

"I don't take your meaning."

"What's it mean to you? When you get in trouble on the Mountain, that is." I cocked my head and must have looked thoughtful, because she did the same thing.

"Uh, I don't know. Trouble is...feeling like people are disappointed in me. That's the worst of it, I guess."

"That *is* the worst of it."

"It never gets easy." She said, and she wrinkled her little nose.

"I believe you." I said, and exhaled. "So tell me again why it's against the rules to sleep with me?"

"Oh, no, no, no." she said. "No, no. There are no *rules* against trysts like this. It's not condoned, but it's not condemned, either. Besides, I'm a Throne. Rules are sort of mine to break." She paused, as if thinking. "Haven't you ever read the Bible? About the Nephilim, those children of humans and angels born before the Flood?" she asked.

"Actually, I always wondered about the Nephilim. How's it go in Genesis? 'The sons of God went to the daughter of men and had children by them. They were the heroes of old, men of great renown.'" I frowned. "Did they die in the Flood?"

"God in Heaven! Of course not! They came here!"

"What do you mean, 'here'?"

"Here. The Mountain. This Plateau." Scholastica looked at me incredulously. "What else haven't they told you?" Seeing its chance, perhaps, with her distracted and me baffled, some of my semen started making its Great Escape down her leg.

"How should I know? No one tells me anything! I don't know anything about anything!" I exclaimed, in a particularly vituperous tone of voice, waving my hands to accentuate my frustration with the "Let's Not Tell the Protagonist Shit" policy that was so prevalent amongst my friends and teachers on Devine Road.

"The Wanderers." she said.

"What?" I cocked an eyebrow.

"The Wanderers are the Nephilim."

———

"My friends " cried the Wandering Bedouin as Scholastica and I approached his camp at the foot of Teutoberg Forest. We had snuck out of my bedroom window; no small task as it was on the second story. She had grabbed onto the windowsill with her little hands and had me shimmy down her until I was holding on to her ankles. It was a short drop from there, and she just jumped down and landed on her feet once I was safely dirtside.

Angels.

You shouldn't be wondering why we were "sneaking" out, but if Virgil or Father Luke knew I was out of bed they'd have flipped their respective fucking lids. Never mind Scholastica, there wasn't Anyone or anything that she answered to. Rules were subjective to her. Me, I could get "in trouble" *real* easy.

Then again, I did defeat the Horrid King. Although that apparently bought nothing in the way of much respect on Devine Road except from strangers, and I guess that had to suit me. I just wish it bought me some answers to my questions.

I embraced the Wandering Bedouin heartily. He smiled broadly at me, asked how I was, how I felt, if I had had an adventure, etc. Normal Bedouin questions. I answered like I always do, I'm great, I feel great, I've had tons of adventures. He smiled and nodded vigorously. Then he asked me to turn around.

I'm no fool. Two people, or angels or Nephilim or whatever don't kiss like that because they're friends. I had to remind myself that I was the first *human* Scholastica had slept with, not the first anything else. Given her obvious talent and gusto in the area, I knew I couldn't have been her first lay. But it was funny, anyway. All that jealousy I despise and I get a tiny twinge of it.

Christ, that was a long kiss. Noisy, too. Then again, you don't kiss Scholastica. You experience her mouth.

I turned around and, no, there wasn't even any "inappropriate" touching going on. No hands in bathing suit areas. Just a sweet, long, beautiful kiss.

"Your beard is too damned scratchy, Bedhead." Saint Scholastica teased. "I like kissing him better." She motioned towards me.

The Bedouin laughed. "I just like kissing, Redhead. But you're right, I've kissed many better than you. Usually, I'm too busy counting your wrinkles to focus on anything even resembling coition."

"You brute!" screamed Redhead.

"You hag!" cried Bedhead.

They went back and forth like this for about another minute or so before remembering I was there. Then the Bedouin coughed, smoothed out his robes, attempted to regain some of his composure.

Too late for me, I thought. That old lecher.

I grinned. "So, what have you been doing?"

"Grazing my flock, making them strong." he replied.

"Good, good." I said. "You've been gone a while."

"Well, and I do not come here often." stated the Bedouin. "It was chance, or the will of the Man that I was here the day we met. I have been returning here on account of you."

I was flattered.

We sat for a while and chatted while the Bedouin made stew. Sex is hungry work and *I* was famished, but I had a sneaking suspicion that Scholastica didn't have to eat if she didn't want to.

On another note, the Bedouin was being much quieter than usual. Not any less cryptic, just less talkative.

"What's on your mind?" I asked him.

"Well, many things." he said, with a long pause between "Well..." and "...many things." It came out more like this: "Well..............many things."

I'd never seen him hesitate like that.

Scholastica piped up. "So, uh...Bedhead...what's going on with the, uh...you know?"

The Bedouin's weathered face scrunched up, his tufted eyebrows forming a thick black railing over his eyes. "The Foederati. It is necessary to explain to our Protagonist what the conflict of his tale will consist of."

"The war." I said.

"Yes, the war. It is upon us."

"How soon?" asked Scholastica.

"Soon." he said. "My brother, listen. I will be brief. There are seven armies that will soon inhabit this Plateau. Armies that are thousands strong. They will raise their towers…"

"Yeah, we talked a little about this before." I interrupted.

"Indeed." replied the Bedouin. "There are six other towers, as we have discussed. They will come here, and the characters in your story, ones that you have met and ones that are to come will take sides with these Foederati. Rather, the Foederati will be as arrows in our quivers. Swords at our sides. In no uncertain terms, we will use the Foederati, the Seven Armies of the Second Plateau to fight this war. It is how a change like what is to come is accomplished."

"Well, good luck to you."

"What do you mean?"

"I'm leaving." I said. "Before the war starts."

"My brother, you will find that you will not. Not that you can't. That you won't."

"Are you sure?"

"Yes." he said flatly, as if to say, "End of discussion."

"Okay. Let's pretend you're right. Who are we fighting?" I said, and sighed.

"That is unclear now. Most certainly the men in brown leather coats, though they have no access to the Foederati. They fight with their own army, because they are not a contender for the farmhouse. Beyond that, I do not know for sure." The Bedouin looked sad. "The Ecclesiae will fight with the Foederati of Hope and Avarice, as they have ever done. I do not know yet what I will choose, but I will fight for the Ecclesiae. I will fight to see that their influence remains constant, though the landscape is shifting."

I shuddered, remembering Father Luke's words. *And then you'll have to kill us.*

"So, in the hypothetical situation that I'm staying, which I'm not, who would I fight for?" I asked.

The Bedouin thought on this for a moment. "I am not sure, my brother. You should know that we will stay friends, though. No matter the choices we make regarding our allegiances."

"Agreed." I said, and then paused for a long time. "I won't fight you."

He was quiet for a moment before he replied. "I think that this will be a difficult time for us all. I *will* fight. For my God. I will fight for him by way of the defense of the Connection."

"But…I defeated Moloch. Isn't religion already done for?"

"Of course not. It is going to change, and drastically. But the world's religions, Christianity and Islam and the like, those I must safeguard and I must see to the other side. Through the change. So that the Ecclesiae may reclaim the farmhouse when another Vicissitude comes."

"So nothing's really going to change that much?"

"Not if the Ecclesiae and I and our allies win the war. You see, it is not a matter of philosophy. It is a matter of...well...while I draw breath, so will the Church. Not of my volition. It is what I have become. It is what my flock is. It is what the Ecclesiae are. It is very simple, my dear little brother. The change can not happen in my lifetime. Nor in the lifetime of the Wanderers. We are the Church."

"So who are you fighting, then?" I asked, hoping his answer would differ from Father Luke's.

"Those who would usher in a new connection to God. Those who would change the phone lines, those who would replace them."

"The men in leather coats?"

"No, they seek to *destroy* the phone lines, though I will fight many of them. My true opponent is he who champions the change."

"Who's that?"

"Do you not know?" he asked.

"No." I said.

Scholastica, quiet until now, spoke up. "Yes you do. You are the eagle among the swallows."

"What the fuck does that *mean*?" I shouted.

Neither of them spoke. They just looked at each other. The Bedouin hung his head and whispered, "You tell him."

"Tell me what?" I asked, but I knew it already. I knew it before she said it. I'd known since I killed Moloch.

I knew it deep within me and I hated it. I hated myself. Because I knew it.

Scholastica looked like she was going to cry. "*You* are the Vicissitude. Didn't you know?"

"I...I knew. But...why?"

"That is not a question I can answer." said the Bedouin. " But we will always be friends."

"I won't fight you." I choked out.

"You must. For we are also enemies." he countered softly.

"No. You're wrong. Why would you say that? That's bullshit!"

"Listen..." started the Bedouin gently. Always gently.

"No. That's…No. How dare you? We're friends! You're…you're more important to me than my family. My family!"

"We are family."

"Yes! *Nil Sine Familia*. I won't fight you! How can you say something like that?"

The Bedouin was very quiet. "Because you have to."

"No, I don't. Not if I leave, I don't."

"That remains your choice." he said, "but I wish you would understand what we mean when we tell you that everything happens for a reason. You remember, of course, when Father Luke and I were trying to ascertain the meaning of your presence on this partition? There *is* a reason you are here. I have found the answer."

"Why am I here?" I asked.

"You are here so that you may choose to stay." he said, and *that* was the end of our discussion.

————

The fog that hung over Devine Road, the fog that obscured the way to the Second Glorious Plateau of the Mountain with No Name, that fog that obscured the whole Second Plateau from our sight and perspective, the fog that hung over the Joyful Plateau now like a cloud, that fog began to illumine, softly. So softly. It started so quietly. Beautiful in its subtlety, rich in its color, the fog turned from the dull silver of the bright reflection of filtered moonlight to a warm, golden yellow. It only took an hour before the whole of the fog was as golden as if Midas himself had given it a hug. None of us spoke, none of us said a word. I had no idea what was happening, but I was too embroiled in my mess of emotions to think anything of it but another small miracle of Devine Road. At last, when we had sat there in silence for so long, and the silence had become so thick between us that I thought I would suffocate, the first of tens of thousands of tiny yellow and red blinking will o' wisps began descending slowly from the fog and pouring onto this, the most important partition of the First Glorious Plateau of the Mountain with No Name.

"It begins." whispered the Bedouin, and his soft voice thundered through the silence as though he had proclaimed it from a mountaintop.

The Foederati were coming, and nothing would ever be the same.

Book 2
A New Partition

Sentient beings are numberless; I vow to save them.

-The First of the Four Vows of the Bodhisattva

Whispers of heavenly death murmur'd I hear, labial gossip of night, sibilant chorals, footsteps gently ascending, mystical breezes wafted soft and low, ripples of unseen rivers, tides of a current flowing, forever flowing. (Or is it the splashing of tears? The measureless waters of human tears?)

-Walt Whitman, *Leaves of Grass*

Ah, Love! Could you and I with Him conspire
To grasp this sorry Scheme of Things entire
Would we not shatter it to bits - and then
Re-mould it nearer to the Heart's desire?

-The Rubáiyát of Omar Khayyám

Reengineerings Engineered, Decisions Delayed, Friendships Affirmed and Foederati Loosed
Chapter 12

Well, and happy April to all of our readers who are joining us for Book Two. It is the morning of April the Seventh, and it is a sad morning, as most mornings within the partition's walls are sad, now. We of the Mountain live in a black, ominous shadow, a shroud of threat, an odious cloud of portent. We live in a fog of war. It is not *the* fog of war, but it is a fog, and it smells of blood, battle, bone and steel.

Yes, we've skipped, oh, two months of the narrative or so, but for good reason. Our space in which to recount this story is limited, lest this work be judged 'meandering' or 'lacking focus' by literary critics, and the author considers, also, the stewardship of the readers' interest in this book (if there indeed remains any of that) somewhere in his top five priorities. At least in the top five. Somewhere.

We'll get to everything that's happened around here, but we'll have to summarize, I fear. Let us hope that the soul of wit serves us well as these last chapters of Volume 1 begin to wind themselves up.

Here goes:

You would not believe the changes that have been made to this place.

You might, possessing that wonderful neutrality and that delicious ambivalence through which you are able to enjoy this story, believe in the abstract of the thought, the very fact that it has happened but that it is not there, before your eyes, and thus you may believe that changes *have* happened. But you would not believe the changes that have been made to this place if you were here. Not if you saw through my eyes, or with your own.

Of course, you'll remember that the Vicissitude had been taking place before the Last Good Day of the Year, but it kicked into full speed when the Foederati got here. The earthquakes were tremendous, the climate fluctuated unbearably, the weather was random and intense. The color shifted in and out on various personalities and landmarks, sometimes partially and sometimes fully. One of the Ecclesiae would be cooking dinner and would suddenly be black-and-white, then in color again. Then the wallpaper would suddenly become black and white, then in color, and then the twin would blank out again. When Virgil went out riding he was sometimes a colorless rider on a brown horse or a colorful rider on a grayscale horse. It was the strangest thing in the world.

It did this for days, weeks, almost a full month before settling into a constant, when it did not lose its color again. And that's when the disasters started. The eighteenth day of February saw a tornado touch down on the Mountain. Granted, it was a small one that did nothing but blow a few branches and pine needles off a few conifers, but it was a full-on spinning, blowing, cycloning tornado. I'd never seen one before, and it was kind of neat, if frightening. The nineteenth, the very next day, saw a blizzard in the morning that dropped a foot and a half of snow and then typhoon-force gales in the afternoon blew it around in great sheets, casting these huge walls of snow in every direction including up and down. It was a bizarre thing to look out a storm window and hear the Supreme Winds doing their work without being able to see anything but a constant blur of pure, virgin white rushing past your eyes. On the twentieth day the mercury on the thermometer on the porch at the farmhouse read one hundred and seventeen degrees, and it melted almost all of the snow in one day.

One hundred and seventeen degrees according to the thermometer. That instrument was in the *shade*.

Good God in Heaven, but it's been weird around here. I try to just tough it out at the abbey, wait through it, spend a lot of time in the library reading and rereading. The Bedouin hasn't left and doesn't plan on leaving, so we spend a lot of time together, as well, bittersweet time, with the knowledge that it won't last. The knowledge that soon I will either choose to leave and never see him or the Mountain again, or that I will choose to stay and we will become enemies.

We stay indoors, mostly because of the fluctuations in conditions outdoors. Out of boredom, perhaps, we have both picked up a habit of pipe smoking, sneaking up to the attic when Father Luke is busy to sneak a few puffs before throwing open a window (weather permitting) and venting it all out. We have raided the wine cellar on several occasions, drained a good amount of ale and beer from the casks, imbibed a few gallons full of distilled grain spirits and I think the better bulk of the whiskey just figured, "Fuck it, what is there to lose?" and jumped down our throats when we weren't looking. We got in trouble (Correction: The *Bedouin* got in trouble. Father Luke is not speaking to me yet) when we drank up a full keg of good vintage champagne that Father Luke had been saving for some years for some special occurrence or party or something.

Not that the event in question matters a whole lot now, I suppose. That supply of alcohol, like the supply of joyous occasions around here, is going the way of the buffalo. And Father Luke is *pissed*. So angry that he's taken to locking the cellar, to keep us "hoodlums" out.

I don't how long it took him to build up that much booze, but it's half-gone, now, and since it's under lock-and-key, the Bedouin and I have had to devise grand strategies to sneak in. Let me tell you, the implementations of these designs have proved, many times, to be epic adventures in their own right. Just for a little goddamned beer. But it's worth it.

Liquor of any kind tastes so much better when you have to work for it.

Anyway, getting drunk is the only sensible thing to do when faced with shitty weather and the constant reminder of the impending war: Shouts, grinding, hammering and other various sounds of construction coming from outside (we'll get to that.)

But the Bedouin and I have been having a great time within the confines of the Abbey walls. Mostly, we talk a lot about him, about his life, his history, the Nephilim, the Wanderers. And the Wanderesses. They exist, as surely as I do, but they refuse to show themselves if they're ever off of the top of the Mountain. Apparently, there's not a female Wanderer alive (whatever that means) that has not sworn utter fealty to the Man in the Yellow Polo Shirt, and thus they all dwell in Heaven. The Wandering Bedouin's wife, called the Wandering Hittite, disowned and divorced him when the Bedouin decided to move to the first Plateau and enlist with the Thrones and the Church, not God Himself, to fight the war against Hell.

I feel bad for my friend. It must be a lonely thing, being a Wanderer.

And I still don't understand it. Why this has to end, why I have to be his enemy if I want to be his friend. I don't understand why it's *me*. Why did it have to be me? I'm not that independent. I'm not that agnostic. I'm not the pillar of autonomy the Man made me out to be. Hardly material for an avatar-spearhead of religious revolution. Just a regular old guy.

Can God be wrong?

Well, and I guess He moves in His own damned mysterious ways, so who am I to question that, right? Who am I to question God?

The Vicissitude, that's who. I'm here to question the answers. I'm here to fight for a new Connection, a new identity for the phone lines. I'm here to make God in my own image.

I'm here to choose to stay. But I haven't even chosen, yet.

Sigh, sigh, sigh. So many questions, and so few that anyone is able to answer. No one really refrains from answering me anymore, of course, now that the plot has been revealed to me. I realize now that the better part of my present questions *can't* be answered by them. Sigh, sigh, sigh.

Father Luke is still tight-lipped, as I may have mentioned before. I did get a giant grin out of him one morning by surprising him with a mock-attack with the Prajna Khadga, one he was totally unprepared for (even though he had his own wooden sword on his belt) and that resulted in a forty-five second duel that he lost. But he still didn't say anything to me. Just grinned that crazy fucking grin and wore a black eye for a week.

It served him right for beating me fair and square all those times.

So let's get down to business, then. I'll tell you all about what makes this place so weird now, so different now, some things to look out for so that we don't lose you.

We'll start with the parameters, the mileage, acreage, hectarage or whatever. The sheer *size* of the place, now. It stretches out, rolling and flying in every direction, six or seven times as big as it was last September. The partition is now about half of the area of the state of Washington. About ninety miles of Devine Road now, end to end and about one hundred and seventy-five miles from wall to wall.

Devine Road is filled with a constant line of Foederati moving up and down with wheelbarrows, horse-drawn carts and elephant caravans, carrying building materials back and forth from the Second Plateau to their construction sites. We'll get to that. And them.

The place is much, much bigger. Everything's bigger. And there's so many changes to the terrain, the makeup, the geography. Like the brand spanking new desert in the southwest corner of the partition.

God's blood! A fucking desert!

A desert perhaps fifteen square miles in size, it is like a microcosm of the Sahara. Wildly scorching temperatures during daylight hours and corpse-cold weather at night. Sun-bleached bones of giant animals litter the sands, though what these animals were or are remains a mystery to me. One of the maps I found in another old shell of a tower up on the Woeful Plateau (I'm allowed up there now, and the tower was under new construction, but we'll get to all that) named it the Yari Desert, so it's stuck in my head that way.

The desert winds are nearly unbearable and the sandstorms are incredibly destructive. In the middle of this desert is the unfinished Tower of Hope and

Avarice (it's being built right now), the tower called *Virtutus Crucem,* or the Rampart of the Cross. One of the Ecclesiae has chosen this as his base of operations, one we shall refer to as Twin One, and he, like his brother (Twin Two) and the Bedouin and Father Luke and myself and others, is waiting for its completion.

(That old tower I found in Teutoberg was one of seven, as you may remember, and now all seven are being rebuilt, then doled out to the "Kings", those who will be fighting this war.)

On to the sea.

Yes, about half of the partition on the lower east side (south of the Woeful Plateau) is now a lapping, salty ocean. The water crept in slowly at first and then, as though it had dug the trench itself with it's own mighty shovel, started pouring in, carving a depression in the grade of the partition for it to sit in. This Plateau, this mountain plateau is now at sea level, bizarre as that sounds.

The smell of the sea is beautiful, even if its very existence serves as a reminder of the Vicissitude (with the big V), and the Vicissitude serves as a reminder of the war.

There is an island out there in the middle of the ocean, the Mar del Prisca Tempora, or Sea of Good Days, an island that sees no bad weather, nothing but blue skies and sunshine. The weather never changes, and the reason for this is because the island is in the middle of a tiny, spiraling hurricane perhaps two miles across that never moves, never passes on, never terrorizes other parts of the sea, only sits with its brilliant, clear eye fixed on the island at all times.

A fantastic natural defense, and one I've given much thought as to how to assail if I decide to take the helm of an army. Because it is a defense that will have to be thwarted if I choose to stay.

The island houses the tower of Prudence and Sloth, called the *Castellum Orientus*, the Eastern Fortress, and this is what Twin Two has claimed for his own in the coming war. The island is not much larger than a good-sized apartment complex, so there is a huge floating system of wood docks and bridges that surrounds the island and moors six galleons with white sails, which Twin Two's personal band of Foederati are manning. The ships are docked directly on the border of the eye of the storm, so that the occasional raindrop propelled by a raging wind might moisten their masts, but they are never disturbed by the furious waves not six inches from their bows.

There is something "magical" or "miraculous" about that storm, of course, and I have been hard pressed to think of ideas to exploit weaknesses, to penetrate defenses, to figure a way to get an army through that storm. But I do have an idea. Or two. We'll get to those.

And we'll get to the Foederati in a moment. Promise.

Everything else is comparable to what it was before, only bigger. The Ager Epiphania is four times its size and I have not seen a wildflower growing there since the whole place went fucking ballistic with its color.

Teutoberg is twice as big, now. The Foederati came and used the foundations of the old tower in the forest, the Tower of Wrath and Justice, to start constructing a new one. The Wandering Bedouin has claimed this and renamed it *Turris Crescentus et Astra*, the Tower of the Crescent and Star.

There is a tower that is being constructed with the foundations and within the walls of the abbey, as well. You may have surmised that Father Luke appropriated this tower. I may award you a sticker and a lollipop if you continue to guess so smart. The building is the Tower of Faith and Pride, and Father Luke has named it *Turris Babel*. Not terribly inventive of Father, but it works. And it's fun to live inside the Tower of Babel, even if it's not finished.

Hey, the *real* one wasn't finished, either.

Father Luke chose that name, I think, because of the arrogance implied with it. The first tower of Babel was built to try and reach Heaven. To flout God's laws and to take something for humanity, something mankind obviously believed it deserved. I think that Father Luke is insinuating with the title of his fortress that he believes the same thing will happen to us (or rather, his armies and my own if I choose to stay) that happened to the builders of the original Tower of Babel. I think that he thinks we'll be swatted and sent to bed with no dinner like so many misbehaving children. I don't *know* because he doesn't talk. But I have my theories.

The first thing that was built, before anything else, was an extension of the wall, and a massive complex of stables just within that. Able to house two hundred or so horses (cavalry, I take it) the Foederati filled it up fast with beasts they led down from the Second Plateau.

These *are* horses, but I doubt I would call them ordinary. There's an intelligence in their eyes and a kind of pureness to their appearance that sets them apart from every other horse I've ever seen. It's really kind of unnerving, in a way.

The Wanderers keep their horses here, now, when they come to the partition, unless they need them or they'll be spending a protracted period at the farmhouse. Many, including the Wandering American and the

Wandering Kamchatkan, leave their horses with us at the abbey and have me drive them around in my automobile, weather permitting. Just for the love of it.

I suppose driving is commonplace to me, but to some of these Wanderers you'd think it was better than sex.

Up on the Plateaus, the Woeful and Joyful, there simply isn't much to see. A forest I named Sherwood rests on the lip of the cliff face, overlooking the Tiamat's Ridge (where the fiend explodes out of, when it explodes at all) and the Eightfold Path that Scholastica climbs to defeat the monster.

North of Sherwood Forest is a complex of crestfallen stone temples called Cassandra's Ruins. Athenian architecture, pre-Roman looking stuff, a lot of those pillars like the one my angel sits on. She is still there, and I have discovered several other collections of abandoned, decaying statues all around the newly reengineered partition.

As a side note and if you hadn't connected the two, my stone angel is Saint Scholastica. I just hadn't realized it until I went back and looked at the statue again after she left. She's no less beautiful in stone than in person, and not a smidgeon different, except that in stone she has wings.

Just east of Devine Road as you're pulling up onto the Woeful and Joyful is a road that leads back through some blackberry bushes into the driveway of a modest, pretty little house with simple American architecture, a house that is inhabited but whose residents are as yet a mystery to me. The Bedouin insists that I'll meet them when the time is correct, and that everything happens for a reason, so that I should just wait until I'm supposed to meet them. Naturally, I threw it in his face by insisting that if I were to go meet them *now*, it would happen for a reason, so why shouldn't I do as I please and let the reasons sort themselves out later? The Bedouin smiled and told me I'd meet them when I was ready. I don't know why, but I haven't found time to go and say hello, not yet.

On the Joyful Plateau, there are two towers being constructed. The Tower of Love and Lust is a beautiful mahogany and oak pagoda painted blood-red and dark brown and is surrounded by cherry and olive trees transplanted from the Second Plateau. The Tower is not complete, not yet, but the landscaping around it is. There are fountains, little rock gardens, moss gardens, an incredible work of art that is a bed of sand with intricate, sprawling curves and lines that form an endless knot, right in the tower's backyard. There is a pool, rows and rows of hedges, high fencing and paper walls that frame a small courtyard, as well. I have dibs on it if I stay and I have temporarily named it the *Shirivasta*, in case I do decide to stick around.

But I may not. Not after I saw what they decorated the front lawn with. The Foederati erected the most God-awful, disgusting, pretentious, ridiculous thing I have *ever* seen. Right next to a weather-beaten stone statue of some Spanish-looking swordsman that was lying in ruins (not unlike my angel but away from the protection of the woods) that they have now restored, they have also fashioned a twelve-foot statue of *me*.

My likeness. My ugly mug. My stupid, disproportionate body.

My silly haircut, my damned nose and eyes and ears and mouth, everything. I'm wearing an absurdly ornate set of armor and holding a mace, a war mace, with a handle and a head, just a simple weapon. In my other hand is a shield and on my head is a circlet and I'm depicted as looking up to Heaven with this obscenely and preposterously wise and embattled expression on my face. I would swear with my hand on any given religious scripture that I have never made a face like that. I hope I never make a face like that. God in Heaven, it's just *pompous*. And gaudy. Like too much perfume, like a three carat diamond ring, like a giant pearl necklace, like a mink coat, like a swan-down hat. It's exaggerated and ostentatious and I hate it.

But it's flattering as Hell.

Have you ever had a statue of your likeness built? I recommend it, once, but tear it down as soon as it is completed, lest you learn to like it.

The *Shirivasta* is being built next to the Coenobitic Monastery, just off Devine Road at the foot of the incline that goes to the Second Plateau. The Coenobitic Monastery is another abbey, just like the Abbey, only it's a Germanic castle with high walls and high towers. The Bony Prince will explain to me later in the story that it is the home of the Ecumenics, the crazy singing monks that congregate arbitrarily at the other Abbey. He'll also tell me more about the Ecumenics. In the meantime, it is the castle of the Bony Prince, whom I have not met at this point in the story, so we will save that for later. On to the next tower.

The Tower of Gluttony and Fortitude, which is as yet unclaimed but is already named *Turris Venti Mola*, is the other tower up top. I named that one, too, but I haven't an idea who will reside in it. Well, maybe I do have an idea. And they might live in a little house with American architecture.

The *Turris Venti Mola* is a windmill-tower, a complex thing with all sorts of Renaissance clockworks and levers and pulleys inside. Beneath it is an underground barracks where the Foederati will stay, when whomever will come just comes and claims them for his or her own army. It is the smallest tower, speaking strictly in terms of height, but its walls are *fourteen feet thick* and I'm just hoping that whoever gets it is on my side. If I choose to stay.

The last tower is back down on the Ager Epiphania, about a mile northwest of the farmhouse, and is, with the *Turris Babel*, one of the two towers furthest along in its construction progress. This is probably due to the ease of the terrain they're building it on and the proximity to Devine Road, which is used to transport everything that is required of building towers. Then again, there might be some other crazy, supernatural reason I haven't descried that's causing those two to get built faster than the others. I don't make assumptions anymore. Well, I try not to, anyway.

Virgil's getting that one, and refusing to take sides yet. Or at all, if it suits him. He's the wild card. There's always one, I'm told, and Virgil swiped it up as fast as he could, although in my mind it's not terribly fair, considering his closeness to the Ecclesiae. He has named it the *Saxum Salus,* Salvation Rock. Whose salvation, I wonder?

On to *them.* Or, perhaps, *they. They* are building the towers. *They* are transporting the goods. *They* will be the armies.

The Foederati. What are *they*? More fitting, perhaps, is asking *who* are *they*? Because they are, indeed, people.

Little people.

Children.

My God, the bewilderment I experienced when I first laid eyes on them. They all look eight years old, little boys and girls, prepubescent bundles of life and joy and carelessness and they're all armored and armed to the teeth and they work like nothing I've ever seen, without resting but for an hour a night and taking only a small break in the middle of the day. They don't smile, don't laugh, don't drink water, they don't have job-site accidents, they just build their towers and train all day and all night for the coming war. Children. Fucking kids. They're building towers that should take years to complete in so many *months*.

I have thought many times that these are boys and girls who ought to be concentrating on candy and video games and what they want to grow up to be. Not war. Not fighting. Not working like slaves to build fortresses that would house them and protect them and subject their existences wholly to the masters of those very same towers. I'd almost made up my mind then and there, as soon as I laid eyes on them, to leave. This was ridiculous. Out of control. Children? What the fuck was the Man doing?

And why? Why a war? Why were we marionettes, why were we just dancing to His absurd tune, beholden to a game that served *absolutely* no purpose at all? Why children? Why not just *appoint* residents and have it be done with? Or if has to be a contest, why not a fucking *football* game?

Is this His system of checks and balances? His temperance? Or is it some macabre coliseum for him? What is the Goddamned point?

Fucking ludicrous.

Why kids?

Jesus, if I fight in this war I'll have to kill kids.

And I can't kill any more kids. I've killed enough. And that wasn't on purpose.

I can't knowingly, willingly murder a child. Choice my hammer, volition my hauberk. I can't do it on purpose.

But they're *not* kids, argues the Bedouin, and he's right. They're spirits, angels of a sort, not children at all. Merely childlike in appearance because of their inferior grasp of their sentience. Much like human children. Doesn't make them any less capable warriors, as they are apparently quite well-trained and extremely deadly and that's all that really matters. When kids are fighting kids, nothing's really unfair, is it? A sword is just as sharp in the hands of an eight year old as it is in the hands of an eighty year old. Or anywhere in between. They're not any less dangerous physically. But they're a lot more dangerous psychologically. To me.

I constantly feel on the edge, on the verge of a breakdown. I sometimes get a whiff of an explosion or a nostril full of the scent of sand, the smell of Mosul. Sometimes I hear the *wheet!* of a bullet fly past my ear and I sometimes flash back to Corporal Banks' face, sometimes transpose it onto that statue of me that they built. The expression on his face is as terrified and desperate as the actual countenance of the statue is judicious and regal. My hand hurts all the time, now.

And the worst of it? My nightmares are back.

But I haven't seen the woman in the white dress since the Last Good Day of the Year, nor her children, nor the wildflowers they picked together. No, the only females on this partition are the little girl Foederati, if they are indeed female and not just feminine (there is apparently a world of difference, if the Bedouin is to be considered reliable.) Scholastica left the day after the Foederati came (I don't know where she went but I was disappointed) and I haven't seen *her*. Which is also disappointing. After that episode I had right at the feet of the Tiamat, well…I'd really like to see her and tell her everything. Tell her all about the nightmares and everything else. Just talk to her.

The funny thing of all this is that I think I've already had a long conversation with her. She was, according to my hypothesis, the Man.

The Man. It had to be the Man, making me come to grips with what I had to come to grips with. The woman is here to heal me, to force me to heal myself. That's the only explanation. Not a logical one, as logic is tantamount to a hill of beans when dealing with the goings-on of Devine Road, but it remains an explanation, and the best I have.

Is this arbitrary notion ruthlessly solipsistic? Egotistic? Even *narcissistic*? Maybe. Okay, definitely. There's certainly an inflated sense of self-importance implied with a hypothesis of that orientation. But if I have a big head it's because I was given one. I came here humble and was made a Vicissitude. I came here an ex-soldier and was christened "Warrior King" of a stories-tall pagoda, Lord General of an army thousands strong. Tell me you wouldn't feel important if you were personally selected by the Glorious Goof Himself. You would. And you know it.

So the place has changed. Drastically. A single partition is now Seven Kingdoms. And a question remains, in margins. Will I stay? I think you know that answer already, but Father Luke beseeches me to stay with my narrative, so we'll trudge on with ample suspense toward that decision like we're in the dark. Like we're not privy. Our little secret.

In the meantime, so begins Book Two. I thank those readers that have made it this far and salute those who fell along the way. I love you anyway.

On to Chapter 13, dear readers!

The Basement
Chapter 13

On the morning of April thirteenth the sun was shining. No, not shining. It was beaming, radiating, blindingly white, hell, anything but shining. To say that it was shining would imply an ordinary old day, an ordinary old sunshine that shines on ordinary anywhere, and that was not what the sun was doing. The sun, on the morning of April thirteenth, was whitewashing the whole plateau, treating it with solar Spray n' Wash and then bleaching the shit out of it, casting it in the most brilliant light the Protagonist had ever seen. The Plateau almost looked like it had when it lost all of its color, only there was a definite green and brown to the tendrils of the Ager Epiphania quietly stealing a kiss from a warm spring breeze that promised rain, there was a definite blue to the sky that stretched so far it might have made Montana greener than it already is with envy and there was a definite sun-drenched hue to the vines and grasses slowly climbing the Abbey walls, solemn and dark though they usually were.

Our Hero sat in his bed and squinted, tried to see Teutoberg Forest but could not, whether for the glare of the sun or the new distance between his second-story bedroom in the Abbey's dormitory and the great woods that lay in the shadow of the Woeful and Joyful Plateaus. Perhaps it was the crusted green stuff he was now rubbing from his eyes, the little smidgeons of unwanted grossness that had hardened in the corner of his eyes into little chips like bark dust, a sliver of which was now poised threateningly at his cornea, then plastered to his interceding finger, then falling and landing with an inaudible thud on the stone floor of his bedroom. He squinted again, his eyes free of this minor menace, this insignificant (if a little grotesque) byproduct of sleep, but no. He couldn't see anything but the rolls and rolls and grassy knolls of the Ager Epiphania.

He yawned. And then noticed his headache.

Well, shit. he thought to himself. *Another hangover.*

The night before, he and his friend the Bedouin had tricked Father Luke into "meeting" them at the farmhouse with a little note taped to his study, reading:

It is of the gravest importance that you meet the soldier and myself at the farmhouse exactly at dusk. Be punctual, or there will be unsolvable problems inflicted on this area of the partition that can only be prevented by our swift action.

-The Wandering Bedouin

Most of it was conceived of by the Protagonist and written by the hand of the Bedouin, and the part about "unsolvable problems" had similarly been our Hero's idea. The Bedouin had gone along with the correction gladly, commenting that it added a dramatic weight and a sense of urgency that was otherwise lacking in the note's original incarnation, authored by the Wanderer:

Meet us at the farmhouse for drinks at six?

-Bedhead

Of course, they had no intention of being at the farmhouse.

They had involved the Wandering Japanese, who was a guest at the abbey, asking him to visit Father Luke around lunchtime and announce the arrival of the note, inconspicuously. The Wandering Japanese had no natural talent for lying, and the schemers knew this, but they knew also that Father Luke was privy to the fact that the Wandering Japanese rarely told falsities, and thus the typically taciturn Oriental man made an all the more credible (and devious) conspiratorial addition to the plot. The plot, you ask? Why, the plot was to steal brandy.

Father Luke left the Abbey for the farmhouse just as the pale rays of the sun began to disappear over the horizon, and fully expected to meet his friends and roommates at his destination. He was armed with a longsword, so he may have been expecting danger of sorts, and he had taken a horse, so he may have expected to have had to travel a long distance. In short, he joined the ranks of those who, in the words of the wise Mr. P.T. Bailey, are born every minute. He got suckered.

Of course, the three plotters had gone nowhere and had only hid in the attic until the clueless priest left, and had then crawled into the cellar through an underground passage the Protagonist had discovered (Father Luke,

225

displaying characteristic foresight, had locked the door) and "liberated" a gallon of fine brandy. They returned to the Great Hall, poured themselves a glass each and a glass for Father Luke, who would no doubt return in quite an unpleasant mood, and then had had three more each and were feeling rather inebriated when the priest indeed returned. He threw open the doors, and the squeaking of the doors joined in unison with the bell (it tolled on it's own, when it felt like it) and had created a major chord stunning and precise, which had sent an army of monks assembled in the courtyard to singing a loud and powerful version of *Cantate Dominus*. Under such dramatic circumstances, the Bedouin felt he had only one choice: He raised his glass to Father Luke and the three mischievous individuals responsible for the acquisition of the spirits simultaneously shouted and then drank a toast to the quality of Father Luke's brandy. Much to the priest's chagrin.

The Wandering Japanese had, quite naturally, offered Father Luke a glass (it *was* his brandy, after all) which the old Throne had knocked out of his hand with a growl and a disdainful look. He was quite upset at being constantly outwitted by the Protagonist and the Wandering Bedouin in matters regarding the alcohol supply, even though he bested both of them at chess regularly. He seemed especially angry today as he stomped off upstairs.

The Protagonist, already drunk enough to do something so silly, had gotten down on his hands and knees and started supping the puddle of burnt whiskey off of the ground, with his hands cupped around it, like he was drinking from a sweet, brown river. This set the Japanese and the Bedouin to roars of laughter, naturally, and their high spirits caused that gallon to disappear faster than any of them had initially anticipated.

Thus, the hangover for this present day.

The Protagonist squinted and squinted and strained his eyes, but could see nothing, so he got up, hit the showers (the Abbey, for all of its medieval charm, also featured modern amenities in the restroom facilities) and got dressed. He walked down to the kitchen from his room on the second floor, grabbed a bite to eat, swung by the library and then returned to his room with a copy of a book he had read three times already (something called *Eros and Civilization* by Herbert Marcuse) and sat and read it all the way through, start to finish. Many times as he sat and read, the Ecumenics, the monks who convened in the abbey courtyard, did just that and got together and trampled the grass without leaving footprints and pointed accusatorily at each other and whispered and then from time to time suddenly burst into song, individually or in a few groups or all at once. They ran the gamut of religious tunes, everything from the seemingly toneless chants of aboriginal religions to the most melodic Indian tunes ever composed for the Amida Buddha.

Upon finishing his book for the fourth time (…*the revisionists yield to the negative features of the very reality principle which they so eloquently criticize)* our Hero headed downstairs and had for dinner what he had had for breakfast: Another ham sandwich on sourdough with extra mayo, and hold the tomatoes. He went back upstairs, sat for a while and sang a few bars of *Georgia on My Mind*, though he didn't know all of the words, and then noticed that the sun would set in, oh, a half hour, and started preparing to hit the sack early. Another boring day, another eventless day, another of the precious few days he had left before a decision had to be reached.

He wasn't sure why, but he suddenly thought back to the Wandering Kenyan, and who he was. *He and the Bony Prince make sure it happens, both ways.* The sunrise and sunset happen because of the Wandering Kenyan and the Bony Prince, whoever the Bony Prince was supposed to be.

The Protagonist suddenly wished for more time in the day, that he might go and find the Wandering Kenyan at sunset and ask exactly what that meant, that he and the Bony Prince make it happen both ways. Then he saw three black figures silhouetted against the Ager Epiphania, far away, walking north.

He reflected on his day, remembered that no one had been at the Abbey all day, and realized that his friends were off doing something. Something without him. On purpose.

Bastards!

The Protagonist was starving for an adventure. He hadn't had one for God knows how long, but it was way too much time since he'd had any heat in his blood. Way too much time since he'd felt any pain, felt any soreness, run for a mile or two without stopping. It'd been way too long since he'd spent any significant time outside. He'd explored most of the Plateau, sure, but that was in February, before the wild weather started and had virtually confined him within the Abbey, which was now half of a tower, but was nonetheless the Abbey all the same. Now that the crazy weather was through the Protagonist had become a homebody, and it was catching up to him. He was flabby, stiff. He really wanted out. Bad. So he changed clothes from his silky, white pajamas he normally wore everywhere and threw on a black ribbed sweater with inlaid leather pauldrons that the Ecclesiae had made for him and an old pair of black corduroy cargo pants he had moved to the Mountain from his apartment and ran downstairs, almost forgetting his bludgeon in his haste.

Almost is our key word, because the Protagonist did indeed requisition his weapon, remembering that there was very possibly an adventure in progress, and that a wooden sword, wooden though it may be and sword though it might not be, was better than nothing against whatever danger might be lurking out there. Hell, this wasn't any wooden sword, dear readers. You'll do well to remember that this was the wooden sword that put to rest the Horrid King himself.

Prajna Khadga in faithful tow, he ran silently, something he learned from the Wandering Bedouin, and kept low, as close to the tall grasses of the Ager Epiphania as possible, trying to remain unseen and unheard but also trying to gain on his quarry: Three Wanderers he could see, now that he was closer. The Bedouin, the Japanese, and the Kenyan.

Fortuitous, thought the Protagonist. *If I don't get sent home, I can ask what all that stuff about the sunset means.*

After a mile or so of padding along, the destination of the Nephilim became apparent: Three horses were grazing quietly on the south side of a knoll, saddled and bearing large packs and also medieval weapons strapped to their inventories, weapons that the Wanderers used, and holding also for the Bedouin and the Kenyan automatic assault rifles, AR-15s from the look of them, black and wicked and situated snugly near the stirrups. The Wandering Japanese had two flint-lock pistols, the only firearm he allowed in his possession, and these were next to his massive, red-sashed *odachi*, a pummel-less *samurai* sword with an arched, four-foot blade (legendarily forged from a meteorite that crashed into the Fifth Glorious Plateau two centuries ago this August. The Protagonist didn't think this was true, and the Wanderers always smiled wryly when they said it. so he had good reason to be skeptical.) On the Bedouin's horse was his staff, now lined on all four sides with small steel wires the diameter of a thumb that ran the length of the weapon, which made it not much heavier but twice as destructive. The Wandering Kenyan's horse bore a long spear with an ornate ivory head.

"What are you doing way out here?" cried the Kenyan, and the Protagonist almost shouted from surprise and dropped to his stomach, lying flat on the grass. He winced as he realized that he'd been careless and had been spotted. The Kenyan laughed. "You were supposed to stay near the Abbey!" came the black man's rich, African tones, filling the air. And you're over here doing *what?*"

"Easy on him. Easy." came the soft rumble of the Bedouin's voice. "Come here!" he cried.

The Protagonist stood up and hung his head and started walking toward them, ashamed of having been caught, feeling quite stupid for following the way he did and not just speaking up and gotten himself sent home like always. He prepared a few apologies for the inevitable reprehensions and looked up, preparing to meet the disapproving gaze of the Bedouin.

The Wanderers were, indeed, gazing disapprovingly, but not at him. They had their backs to him.

They were talking to their horses.

His cover not blown after all, he dropped back to the ground with a soft crash, a crash that went unnoticed in the ears of at least two of the Wanderers.

—

The Wandering Japanese, on the other hand, heard the crash like it was a full-sized Abbey being lifted out of its foundations by a giant pulley and then dropped. Fully outfitted in his most regal red armor and his most frightful mask, the Japanese had seen the Protagonist leave his bedroom and watched the young human trail behind, running with an admirable lack of noise of any kind and making very good progress on overtaking them. The presence of the young soldier was unnoticed still by the Kenyan and the Bedouin, and that made the half-angel, half Japanese man smile, smile with his whole face, and this caused his almond-shaped eyes to narrow sinisterly. It was a disconcerting thing to be smiled at by the Wandering Japanese, because even those who considered him a good friend feared him greatly, and feared his *odachi*, and were always on their guard around him. But not the Protagonist, not the young soldier with bright eyes, not the little American human who became the Vicissitude. There was no fear in the Protagonist's eyes when he looked at the Japanese, and this the Wanderer respected above all else.

No, he wouldn't tell the other Wanderers about the presence of the Vicissitude in their midst, not yet. And that was not just deferring to the Protagonist, who would almost certainly be sent back to the Abbey by the Bedouin if discovered. The Wandering Japanese was also plotting as to how he and his friends were going to survive. You see, where the Wanderers were going, this destination that they would be trudging toward with heavy hearts, this place was a place where it might have been a true boon to have a secret ally covering their flank.

They were walking into mortal peril.

The Wandering Japanese suddenly felt compelled to try to communicate to our Hero that they were indeed journeying to the Tunnel, the Tunnel that led to the Tooth, the Tunnel that led to the next partition over, the Tunnel that so recently led…there. Wanted to at least give the poor young man a heads-up as to what they were heading into.

Not an hour ago, the Bedouin and the Japanese had been enjoying grits and eggs and sausage for supper with the Twins of Subtle Oriental Countenance (they ate what was generally considered breakfast fare in the evening sometimes) when the Wandering Kenyan had arrived breathlessly and announced the terrible news: That the Tunnel up on the Woeful Plateau had been changed somehow during the Vicissitude and that the way to That Evil Place had been opened again, and that at least two men in leather coats were, at this moment, emerging from the Tunnel and entering the partition unmonitored, unchaperoned, unchecked. This was a most unfortunate thing; before the Vicissitude, men in leather coats had to brave hordes of dangers in crossing over the Abyss onto the Second Plateau, and then had to come down by way of Devine Road. That thoroughfare was hateful to them because it burned their feet and shined with a light that the Wanderers could not see but nonetheless blinded the demons and scalded their faces and caused legions and black sores to break out on their skin. It did not stop the Enemies, no, but it deterred them, and that was the best the Wanderers could ask for. Now the men in leather coats had no deterrent. The hated Antagonists had a Get Into The First Glorious Plateau VIP Pass, now, and the three Wanderers, the only cops within the partition at present, had had to do something.

So they set off to find and engage the men in leather coats, to defeat them and to find a way to plug up that hole before all of Hell amassed and invaded. The Wanderers did not want to see the progress that the Ecclesiae and many of the Thrones and that they, themselves had worked so hard for be destroyed by men in leather coats, no. There was a steady, if unstable connection to the Man established for Earth, even if it had its flaws (The Wandering Japanese did hate its flaws) and the Wanderers would be damned if some vengeful little fallen seraphim were going to come and fuck it up. Not today, thank you. Not ever.

But there were only *three* of them available to take action. And, almost, insultingly, their horses had wandered off to graze while they had plotted with the Kenyan, further delaying them. They were just now catching up with their beasts, just now ready to start. And the men in leather coats could number in dozens by now.

What could three do against so many, if they were indeed already accruing at the mouth of the Tunnel?

Kill as many as possible, thought the Wandering Japanese. *Kill as many as possible, and earn as much glory as is attainable before we are defeated and our souls move up the Mountain and this Plateau is lost to us.*

The Japanese had been unhappy with the prewar state of security on the Plateau, which was why he had come early. All of the other Wanderers except for the Bedouin were tidying up their old homes, wrapping up unfinished business before setting out on the migration, to participate in the coming war. None of the Wanderers but the Kenyan made permanent dwelling within the most important partition (excepting of course the Finno-Ugric, who had retired in spring and gone up the Mountain) where the farmhouse and the phone lines were, because they did not want to have undue effect on the Connection. Noble, and perhaps necessary, but now the partition and perhaps the whole of the First Plateau was threatened because there weren't enough Wanderers here.

Virgil was due next week, and thus no help. Father Luke was picked up that morning in a noisy Jaguar by Saint Raphael and brought to a committee meeting on the Second Plateau concerning the reprioritization of the Twins and also the status of the soldier's decision. Was the Protagonist leaning toward staying? They'd never had a Vicissitude threaten to leave before. This could be disastrous if there was no catalyst for change, no Champion to take over the farmhouse were the Foederati of O'Malley and Father Luke to be defeated.

The Ecclesiae couldn't help, either. They were busy with packing their things up, collecting all of their belongings and preparing to shuttle themselves to their respective Towers, and anyway, if one of the Twins were injured before the War, when the partition was going to be fully protected, well, that would spell catastrophe for the Connection. Utter chaos. If they got hurt *during* the War, things would be fine, because the phone lines would be different then. The angels would be running the Connection from Upstairs, and the Ecclesiae would have already officially lost their positions as the Stewards of the Farmhouse, so it was okay, in a way, as long as it happened as it was supposed to. *This* was not okay. *This* would not be all right. The men in the leather coats had to be stopped. Because if they were not stopped there could be no war; the whole of the partition would be devoted to stopping the invasion. And if the invasion could not be stopped, the soul of the earth could be indelibly stained.

The Japanese smiled again, grimly. No, the war had to happen. It had to happen, and quickly. For glory? Certainly. For the heat of battle, the thrill of violence, the transcendent bliss of warfare? Naturally. All of those things had to happen, and had to happen through the war. It was what the Japanese was, what he was born to do. To fight, to kill, to be a warrior. And he was the greatest warrior that the Nephilim knew, the equal, perhaps, of even Saint Gabriel the Steadfast, though that was only hypothesized and never tested.

And there was another reason: The Ecclesiae desperately needed to be supplanted. Their mismanagement of the phone lines had been so grievous since the Diaspora that the Connection... No. Not the Connection. God Himself was dying in the hearts of humanity. And the Wandering Japanese could not let that happen, anymore than he could allow some puppet of the Ecclesiae to occupy their former position, to be operated by remote from wherever the Twins ended up, until the Ecclesiae came back around at the next Vicissitude and took it again. Organized Group Religious Ritual had run its course. And the Japanese knew it. So did the Frenchman and the Ottoman and the Maori and many other Wanderers. They had discussed it, briefly, just after the "death" of the Horrid King, and they knew that the Ecclesiae had to go.

That also meant that the Bedouin could not be allowed to occupy the farmhouse.

Which meant defecting.

Allying with Father Luke and the young soldier, if he chose to stay, the naïve human Vicissitude, so clueless and innocent and yet so devastatingly dangerous, if he would ever figure out what he's good for. If he ever figured out what the Vicissitude really was, and what he was in possession of as the Vicissitude.

Of course he'll find out, mused the Japanese. *The Vicissitudes always figure it out, not a moment too soon, not a moment too late. The eagle among sparrows. He'll get his talons just when he needs them.*

The Wandering Japanese whistled for his horse and it came with no delay. He smiled again, this time at the Kenyan and the Bedouin, who were watching his eyes move rapidly, watching him as he stood there lost in his thoughts. They were silent, and patient, but he could tell that they were mystified by his sudden withdrawal, given the urgency of the situation. He reproached himself for his weakness, allowing himself to be seen plotting, even if they did not know that. An unnecessary risk, and he was now suspect if word of the planned defection of so many Wanderers were to reach the contemplation of the farmhouse before fruition.

"I have settled the matter regarding my *jisei*." said the Japanese flatly to them, and their faces suddenly registered understanding and compassion. The Japanese people had composed *haikus* before their deaths for many centuries; it was a tradition when the Wandering Japanese had been born in the seventeenth century and it continued to be a tradition today. "If we go to our deaths with this battle, I would want my *jisei* to be with the earth of this Mountain, that the spirits of the land might forever remember me."

The Wandering Bedouin nodded and mounted his horse. The Kenyan did likewise, and they turned their mounts north. "We will progress as slowly as can be allowed, given our circumstances. When you have done what must be done, ride swiftly. We will meet you at the bridge." The Bedouin's eyes were shining as he spoke thus, and the Japanese thought suddenly of how much he admired that great Wanderer, the Bedouin, the greatest and most esteemed of the Wanderers, and how much he regretted that the Nephilim had become such pawns of the Ecclesiae. He regretted very deeply that the Bedouin was foremost among the pieces being played by the Twins' conspiratorial hands.

They galloped away, swiftly, and the Wandering Japanese produced a piece of parchment and a quill pen from a haversack tied to his horse's saddle. He had not settled the matter just then, the matter of his death poem. No, he had settled it long ago. So what he said was not a falsehood. He had never told a lie, in its most base sense, and he never would. He flattened the piece of paper and dipped the pen into a small pot of ink. On the parchment he wrote:

And had my days been longer, still the darkness would not leave this world. Along death's path, among the hills, I shall behold the moon.

They were not his words, they were the words of a woman, Oroku, an ancestor of his sister, who had lived and died long after he himself had come to the Mountain. But it was a great honor to give glory to another by adopting their *jisei*, and this he did gladly. He raised the poem, lowered it, brought it to his face and laid it on the ground. He then produced a strip of magnesium and a strip of aluminum and caused a spark to ignite the paper, but before the poem was fully engulfed in flame, he added with his pen, on the top right corner of the parchment:

Wait until sunrise, and come to the American house. There you will find my horse. Mount it, and it will lead you to me. Do not come until morning.

The small fire caught the rest of the parchment, setting it ablaze, and the Wanderer raised the flaming paper, lowered it, brought to his face a second time and laid it on the ground. He smiled and retreated into his thoughts. *My dear soldier, young Protagonist, beautiful little human being, fully what I am half of. You have my sword and my life. This I give, and thus do I embark upon death's path. Together may we expel the darkness from this world.* He unsheathed his sword, pressed it to his chest, and sheathed it again. Then he motioned for the Protagonist, still laying in the grass, still believing himself hidden, to stand up and show himself.

———

The Protagonist had watched the two walk away, the Bedouin and the Kenyan, then watched the remaining Nephilim, the Japanese, perform the strange motions with the piece of paper, then burn it and repeat the motions. Then he saw the Wanderer motion to him.

Shit. He *had* been caught.

He stood up again and repeated a few actions of his own: Hung his head, started walking, felt ashamed of having been caught, felt quite stupid, prepared an apology for the inevitable reprehension.

The Wandering Japanese then spoke. "Walk, you, to where I stand, and kneel when you have reached this place. I take my leave."

The Protagonist, more than a little confused at the directions (only compounding the sense of disorientation he always got when he heard the Wandering Japanese's slightly antiquated form of speaking,) walked toward the designated place as the Nephilim mounted his horse and rode away like a chill winter breeze in spring time. When he reached the spot, he knelt, as he was commanded to, and saw there some scattered ashes. Then, the grass moved aside and showed bare earth, as though it had just scooted to either side, picked up its roots and shimmied, like some small Moses of the grass had just parted its stalks. His eyebrows shot up a little, involuntarily, and then the earth began to glow. No, not the earth. Letters scrawled in the earth. He immediately recognized it as a *jisei*. And that meant there was trouble, the Protagonist knew, if the greatest warrior of all the Wanderers feared enough for his life that he would at last compose his death poem. He read it, thought it sounded familiar, pushed it from his mind. The letters faded, and he suddenly realized that he had to get to his car and overtake the three of them, that he had to go grab a sword and shield out of the thousands that the Foederati were just starting to transport in and catch up to them, to help them fight whatever they would be fighting.

A sword and shield? He shook his head, surprised at having some kind of medieval reaction to a sudden sense of danger. Was he not a modern man? *You idiot. You're going to get your revolver. And a whole box of bullets.* Then he smiled grimly, unaware of the grim smiles that had passed the lips of the Wandering Japanese standing there just minutes ago. *No, you're going to stop by the farmhouse and see if they've got anything heavier there. You're going to get a shotgun and whatever else they have there and go fight with your friends. And die with them, if you must.* He started to get up, then saw more letters glowing there in the earth.

Sunrise, huh? At the American house. The Japanese's horse. But did the Protagonist remember how to ride a horse? It had been years since he'd ridden one, on a beach in Oregon, during a romantic getaway with his ex-girlfriend, Mrs. Him. They'd been really happy that weekend. It was one of the last times he saw her before he went to war. Before he went to war and she married his best friend.

Fucking bitch.

Yeah, he could ride a horse. He could ride a fucking duck-billed platypus if he had to. He was going, going to fight alongside them, and with the blessing of the Wandering Japanese. Finally, some fucking respect.

Respect.

He walked back to the Abbey, slowly, and got in around ten o'clock. He brushed his teeth, washed his face, then walked downstairs to Father Luke's study, where the old priest was reading. The Protagonist leaned against the doorway and looked at Father Luke. Father Luke returned his stare expectantly, almost eagerly, hoping that the young man had made up his mind. He was tired of waiting, he really needed to know the answer, he had to make plans for the future. There was pressure on him from Up the Mountain to get an answer fast, even though the edict passed down from the Man Himself preventing him, a Cherubim of the Highest Order second only to the Archangels, from influencing the soldier in his choice whether or not to stay was still being enforced. He desperately wanted an answer.

And, strangely, his biggest motivation for getting the answer was that he missed the little guy. He missed the good times, the meals together, the drinking, the long philosophical discussions. They were friends, and it pained him to give a friend the silent treatment. He smiled inwardly, smiled at how the soldier had managed to best him, a Warrior Angel, one of the most fearsome of the Father's Creations, in even *one* duel. No, the Protagonist had bested him in multiple duels. Of course, the young man wasn't ever going to be as good as he could have been had Father Luke trained him earlier in life, but in the name of the Man in the Yellow Polo Shirt, the kid was a genius at everything he applied himself to.

Everything but writing a novel.

That's enough out of you!

The Protagonist looked at Father Luke a long time. Then he spoke. "Father, the Bedouin and the Kenyan and the Japanese are in trouble."

Father Luke cleared his throat but said nothing. The Protagonist went on. "They're going somewhere, fully armed, on horseback. And the Wandering Japanese composed his *jisei.*"

Father Luke looked very interested very suddenly. "His death poem?" he asked, and the Protagonist barely choked a sob back, so glad to hear that ton of gravel being shoveled out of the old priest's throat was he. "Where are they going?" asked Father Luke.

"Haven't you talked to the Ecclesiae?" replied the Protagonist.

"I just returned from the meeting Up the Mountain. We must go, then. Quickly. To the farmhouse."

"We will. In the morning." said the Protagonist.

Father Luke looked at him bewilderedly. "In the morning?"

"The Japanese left me a note. Wait until sunrise, go to the American house, and his horse will lead me to where they went."

"Do you have the note?"

"No, he used some...miracle or magic or something to make it appear in the earth."

"He commissioned his *jisei* to the Mountain. He may truly be afraid for his life."

"We'll drop by the farmhouse in my car tomorrow and pick up guns and maybe a heavy coat for me. "I haven't got all of my stuff moved out of there, yet."

Father Luke's eyebrows furrowed. "I know. But they're leaving soon, so you should get that taken care of."

The Protagonist's eyes dropped to the floor and his voice became very quiet. "I really missed hearing you, Father Luke."

"I missed speaking, *mon ami*. I missed speaking with you. Have you made up your mind?" His face was earnestly searching the Protagonist's.

"I don't know." sighed the young man. "Sometimes I'm absolutely sure I'm going to stay, sometimes I'm absolutely sure there's no way in hell I can stick around. So I don't know. Yes. I've made up my mind. And it's to do both, leave and stay. So until I settle, I can't say anything. But please, don't give me the silent treatment again!" He said this last with a childlike burst, not befitting him at all. Father Luke was almost amused.

"I must." the priest said heavily. "It is the will of the Man." Then he sighed. "But I have broken it now, and it feels good. It feels good to have broken it. I am a Throne, after all. So…"

"So what?"

"So I will speak to you now. It is not worth it to me any longer to hurt our friendship. *Il ne faut pas laisser croître l'herbe sur le chemin de l'amitié.* But our words will be sparing, and they will not concern the Vicissitude in the slightest manner, do you understand me?"

"I do."

"Go to bed, then. Tomorrow we'll go raid the Ecclesiae's cache."

"Their what?"

"Their cache. We shall be armed to the teeth if the Wanderers are expecting an encounter. And besides, the cache needs to get used up, because anything invented or involving technology not known to medieval Europe and China is going to be outlawed during the war."

"There's a cache of weapons directly below the Connection? Doesn't that affect things, you know…doesn't that cause problems?" The Protagonist looked simultaneously stunned and suspicious.

"We can't talk about it right now." said Father Luke hastily. Uh-oh. He had forgotten about the Basement. And he had sworn to never, never, never forget about the Basement. Now he would have to show the Protagonist, the young soldier, and explain all about the Basement. *Merde, merde, merde.* This could be very, very bad come the morrow. "Uh, the guns must go, and quickly. No guns in the war. You won't be able to use your automobile, either. Not in battle."

"Uh, I thought we weren't talking about the war."

"We're not."

"Oh." The Protagonist's shocked expression faded and he smiled faintly.

"I was starting to piece that no-guns business together, anyway. Not one of those kids has a gun, but they're all starting to carry swords."

"They're not kids. And we can speak of this no further. Go to bed."

"Goodnight, Father. I missed you."

The priest said nothing, only huffed a little, and the Protagonist marched up to his room and slept peacefully, more peacefully than any night he had slept since the Last Good Day of the Year.

———

In pitch dark, I go walking in your landscape
Broken branches trip me as I speak
Just because you feel it doesn't mean it's there
There's always a siren singing you to shipwreck
Steer away from these rocks, we'd be a walking disaster
Just because you feel it doesn't mean it's there.

———

The Protagonist woke from a strange dream, panting as though afraid. He could remember nothing vividly from it, only a Radiohead song playing over and over again, like a soundtrack on repeat.

He looked out the window and saw that the sun had yet another hour before it rose. Good enough. He went downstairs to Father Luke's rectory and threw a book (it was, in fact, *Eros and Civilization*) at the priest's feet to wake him, then went to the kitchen and started packing various contents of the cupboards into a spare backpack. They'd eat their breakfasts in the car, he decided, to preserve as much time as possible, so that wherever the Wanderers were going, they wouldn't have to go in alone.

Why hadn't the Bedouin or the Kenyan left a note asking Father Luke to join them in wherever they were going? Father Luke was pretty badass in his own right, definitely someone the Protagonist wanted on his side in a fight. So why hadn't they wanted the backup? Hell, why hadn't they called up the Mountain and gotten some help from the Man? Did it work that way? Did he have a foreign legion that helped out when partitions were in danger? And what the hell kind of danger were they all in, anyway?

Maybe they just hadn't factored in the automobile, that great smoke-breathing mechanical abomination that could blow past a horse in no time, that Father Luke could have taken to meet them wherever they needed to go, whatever they needed to do.

Why hadn't *they* just taken the automobile?

Maybe none of them knew how to drive. The Protagonist smirked a little. He hadn't thought of that.

How cute.

Or maybe they'd just wanted to exclude the Protagonist that badly. Afraid of him discovering their plot, they'd considered a message for Father Luke too much of a liability and put their own lives in more danger, without backup, just to prevent him from coming to where they were going. They hadn't done something like that in a long time, left him out of an adventure or purposely dodged one of his questions or anything that used to upset him so badly. They'd treated him like one of them. So maybe this wasn't some silly protocol, some notion that they had, some idea that he shouldn't be learning too fast, or whatever the reason they had hidden things from him before. Maybe where they were going really was too dangerous for him.

Well, and the Wandering Japanese didn't think it was too dangerous, and that stroked our Hero's ego quite nicely. He was going to back them up. And he was bringing his own backup with him.

He walked outside into the courtyard and produced a cigarette for the first time since the Last Good Day of the Year, lit it, then thought better of it and dropped it and put it out with his foot. The sounds of early construction rose into the air, a few sounds of sawing, more of hammering, the creaks of pulleys as laborers and materials were hoisted to temporary scaffolding on the sides of the half-finished towers. The sun was rising, and the Foederati were working. One of those small beings, heavily armored, scuttled up and picked up the Protagonist's litter and deposited it in a burlap sack, then scurried back to wherever he was going to. One of the Foederati, who generally remained out of sight unless actively building or transporting goods. Where did they hide, all thousands and thousands of them when you weren't looking for them? He whistled for the little being, the child, and when he got it's attention he beckoned for it to come to him.

"Hey." said the Protagonist. The child said nothing. It was a little "boy", blond with a generous smattering of freckles across his face, which was half-hidden by a giant iron helmet. "Can you talk?" asked our Hero.

The child again said nothing. The Protagonist wondered what the hell these things were, how he was supposed to utilize them if he was going to stay and command an army of them. But he wasn't allowed to know anything about the war unless he chose to stay.

Idiot angels and their stupid Rules. If he had enough information, he'd have made a decision a long time ago. That's what he told himself, anyway. He sighed, and the child just looked at him.

"Go away."

The little angel did nothing of the sort.

"It's all right. Shoo." The Protagonist pointed away, toward a wooden horse that was being transported by two little "girls," and the "boy" ran and helped them carry it to wherever they were carrying it. The Protagonist shook his head. What the hell were those things? And why this stupid goddamned war?

Why couldn't he just leave it all behind? It'd be so easy. Why couldn't he just forget the Mountain, forget Devine Road, forget his friends? Why couldn't he just go? He asked himself these questions six times, sometimes seven times a day. But he knew he couldn't. He couldn't physically leave, because he didn't feel like he knew how to get home again. How to be a regular old guy again. How to not be a denizen of the Mountain.

What he really wanted was to stay and not fight. But he couldn't do that either. The only thing he could really do was stay. Stay and fight. He knew he couldn't leave. He knew he couldn't be peaceful, and he knew that if he was pushed he could stay, and if he was pushed especially hard he could stay and fight.

Could he? Really? Maybe.

Does that count as making your mind up? Knowing that you have only one option? What an illusion of choice he'd created for himself! He'd never had a choice. He knew he had to stay.

Or did he?

He, well…he still didn't know. He'd never wanted to fight again. And here he was contemplating going to war. He just didn't know. He didn't know anything.

Father Luke opened the door and came out alongside the Protagonist, rubbed his hands together and breathed into them. The Protagonist shifted the backpack on his shoulders, yawned, and exhaled loudly. Then the Protagonist started walking and Father Luke followed, out of the Abbey walls, to the small, unpaved thoroughfare that connected to Devine Road. The young soldier's car was sitting in the tall grass just off to the side. He walked around, got in the driver's seat, unlocked the passenger door so Father Luke could crawl in, and then he started the car up. As he sat there, waiting for the engine to warm, he turned his head and looked at the old priest.

"Father Luke?"

"*Oui?*"

"I wish we knew what we were getting into."

"We will, when we reach the farmhouse."

"Father?"

"*Oui?*"

"What happens to Thrones when they die?"

"They don't die."

"What if you don't make it back? Or fall in battle, or whatever? Where do you go?"

"Hell."

The Protagonist paused, affected by the gravity of that one-word admission, then put the car into gear and did a three-point turn, setting them in motion toward the Ecclesiae's dwelling.

Father Luke scratched his mustache and reached forward and turned up the heater. "I'm a Throne. I'm not allowed into Heaven, not until the Man forgives me. If He ever forgives me. So I would go to Hell until I was strong enough to return to the Mountain."

"Into the middle of all those demons? All those enemies?"

"It is not pleasant, I am told. But I have never been there. I hope never to go."

"Don't they try to prevent you from returning?"

"Abaddon helps to ferry the righteous angels out of Hell, back to the Mountain. When they have strength enough to cross the Abyss, that is."

"Oh. I think I see. What about the Wanderers?"

"I do not know. I have never seen one of the Nephilim return to the Mountain after falling in battle."

They drove in a thick, somber silence for several minutes, until the lights from the farmhouse windows became visible, nine shining squares of yellow luminescence, like firefly combatants practicing military formations. The Ecclesiae were already up and at it, had already started their day. When did they wake? Hell, when did they sleep? The Protagonist had lived with them for months and had never gained even an inkling regarding their schedule. Did they even sleep at all?

Father Luke interrupted his thoughts. "We'll break fast here." he said, and nodded in a direction up the road, indicating the farmhouse.

"No, I packed food." said the Protagonist, reaching behind his seat and rummaging around before producing breakfast for the two of them. "We're going to eat on the road, to make as much progress as possible. It's a forty minute drive, at least, to the American house. The sun, incidentally, is about forty minutes from dawning. So I want to make it quick at the farmhouse and be at the American house *fast*." He threw the meals, two sandwiches and two apples, on the dashboard.

Father Luke nodded solemnly.

The Protagonist pulled the car into the driveway, got out and walked hurriedly into the house. Father Luke followed closely behind.

"Where's the cache?"

Father Luke's breath caught in his throat. "In the basement."

"There's a basement?"

"*Oui.*"

They walked in, through the living room, into the kitchen, into a door that the Protagonist, in all of his months living at the farmhouse, had never seen. Or maybe it hadn't been there.

"It wasn't available to you." said Father Luke, who had apparently just read our Hero's mind. The priest swung the door open, and it led to a staircase that wound down, down a very long way, at least four or five stories below ground. "After you." said Father Luke, and the soldier started down. And down. And down.

The Protagonist was breathing a little heavily when he finally reached the bottom. Everything was pitch black, but the floor seemed even and his feet weren't registering anymore steps, so he assumed that they had at last reached the basement.

Three things happened in quick succession: Father Luke reached the bottom just after the Protagonist had, Father Luke flipped on the lights where the Protagonist had failed to, and the Protagonist's jaw hit the floor.

K'ung Wu.

The "Basement" was an underground complex as loaded with weapons, ammunition, grenades, rockets and mines as any silo of any Army base he had ever been stationed at. It was thousands of square feet in area, the ceiling was high, stories high, and the walls were aluminum or steel or some such, faintly illuminated by harsh fluorescent lights. It was packed to full with high shelves loaded with crates bearing such labels as "HE ROCKETS" and "HIGHLY FLAMMABLE", shelves containing dozens of different guns

from different eras, with unnecessarily large amounts of ammunition for all
of the weapons held in the stores.

They walked into the corridors framed by the packed weapons, took
innumerable lefts and rights, turns and more turns, a left and then straight two
intersections and then right and straight on until morning and then another
left and marched on until they arrived at a shelf painted black, which stood
out conspicuously against the mahogany color that all of the other wood
shelves were stained.

"This is my personal store." said Father Luke. "*Les belles plumes font les
beaux oiseaux.*" He reached out, took a ten-round shotgun and six or seven
clips and handed them to the Protagonist, trying not to notice that the young
soldier's face was reddening, filling with blood and heat. He knew why, too.
But he tried to ignore it, to stay on task, and to try to think of a quick excuse,
something, anything. Something to explain away the Basement. Something
to explain why there was a giant silo of violence festering beneath the
Connection. Something to assuage the Protagonist's rightful anger over it.

He produced two belts, handed one to the Protagonist, who took it with a
shaking left hand, fastened the other on to himself, then put two more belts
around his midsection and chest. He attached six leather holsters to his belts,
and these he filled with huge 50. caliber pistols, of the Desert Eagle variety,
chrome plated, each of them bearing an engraving, *Job 30:20.* He strapped an
automatic rifle, an AK-47 to his back, and put on a blue helmet with a spike
on top, an old WWI-era Kaiser helmet. He then held out a Kevlar vest to the
Protagonist, and looked up only when he had been offering it for several
seconds and the Protagonist had not yet taken it from his hands. His gaze
searched upwards, met the red-eyed, irate look of our Hero, and Father Luke
saw that the young ex-soldier was now filled with wrath, and that there would
be no excuse.

He knew what our Hero's problem was, of course. He knew exactly the
problem. Because it had driven he, himself to such helpless rage on occasions
previous that he had sometimes had to leave the partition itself, stay
somewhere else until his fury had subsided. He knew it would happen. He had
simply hoped that the Protagonist would take it a little better than he was
clearly about to.

"*What the hell are all of these weapons doing here?!*" roared the
Protagonist.

"Son…"

"*Answer me!*"

"*Let* me answer you." said Father Luke quietly, and that seemed to temper the Protagonist, if only slightly. "It's the same old problem. We can't fight off the men in leather coats without weapons."

"And so you fill the soul of the world with tons and tons of killing machines?" yelled the Protagonist. His eyes filled with tears. "Do you realize what this is? There is a *stockpile of weapons* directly below the phone lines, directly below the farmhouse, directly below this, the most important of the partitions of the First Glorious Plateau! You know what the partition is to the world! You know everything here influences everything on earth!"

Father Luke looked down. "The Foederati have been bringing many weapons here…"

"Nothing we can do about that! A temporary problem, and there's going to be a *war* here! But you've had *this* fucking war machine sitting beneath the Connection for *how* long?! *What the fuck do you think this is doing to the earth, Father Luke?!*"

Father Luke could not have spoken quieter. "I understand. We all understand. But we have had no choice."

"So the ends justify the means? The best way to save the village is to destroy it?!"

"It was the only way to keep peace."

"'One can not simultaneously prepare for war and prepare for peace!' Oh, my God. I… I can't even think of anything to say. I'm totally fucking speechless. Do you know what this is?!"

"I am familiar with that quote. Albert Einstein, *non*?" whispered Father Luke.

"*Don't change the subject*! How long has this been here?"

"Since the fall of the Holy Roman Empire. Before, it was much, much less."

"So that's what has been happening to world, huh? That's why *I* went to war. Because the soul of the earth is armed to the teeth. The soul of the world is so fucking dangerous, so able to make war that it does. Because it has to. Because that's what it's geared for, packed to bursting point with artillery, filled to the brim with ferocity…"

"Son…"

"…only it doesn't make war *here*, on the Mountain, does it Father Luke? Where do you think the influence of all this shit goes?" The Protagonist bared his teeth and raised his gun, and Father Luke suddenly felt in his heart a feeling, an emotion, a *phenomenon* he had not felt since the War in Heaven.

He suddenly found himself filled with fear.

He was afraid of the young soldier. And afraid of the gun now pointed at his chest. Shit. Why had he armed the Protagonist? Why hadn't he waited?

Did it matter? They were surrounded by guns. The soldier could have armed himself.

Yes, it mattered. The Throne was *fast*. Not as fast as a bullet, no, but *damned* fast. Fast enough to subdue the Protagonist had he gone for a weapon.

He shouldn't have given the Protagonist a weapon.

"The influence is on the earth." the priest whispered hoarsely.

"Probably is, isn't it?! That's probably where it goes! What do *you* think? 'Cause that's where *I* think it goes!" The Protagonist's chest was rising and falling, his breath coming in gasps. "That's why *I* killed the woman in the white dress, why *I* accidentally killed all those fucking kids? Because you people have been destroying the peace by stockpiling all of these weapons and just letting them shit all over the phone lines? Jesus *fucking* Christ. All of these are going. All of these are going, and never coming back." The Protagonist pumped the shotgun once, and Father Luke realized that it was loaded. It was loaded and pointed at him. He started quailing. Could he move quick enough to stop that gun, disarm the soldier? Could he prevent his own "death?"

Did he deserve to prevent it? The guns *were* horrible, the stockpile was causing havoc on earth. Many wars and evil events in the last century were caused in part by these guns, because of this "preparedness," this arsenal. World War I, Korea, the Russo-Japanese War, the Maoist takeover of China, the various wars and revolutions of South America, 9/11... The war that the young Protagonist fought in was caused indirectly by the Basement's influence on the Connection. The thick undercurrent of violence and fundamentalism that pervaded the world's religions, the intolerance and impulsiveness and refusal of change of any kind, it was all in league with the farmhouse. How many wars could have been circumvented had the Basement not been?

And countless wars before that?

Surely, the Basement committed nothing, fought nothing, did nothing. It just sat here. It took men, after all, with all of their sins and need for gain and their vanity and their *consumption*, their never-ending consumption...

It took men to turn the influence of the Basement into a real-life war on Earth.

And would you blame an infant for blowing himself up with a stick of dynamite if you *handed* it to him?

Hadn't he handed a child a gun when he let the Basement come into existence? Hadn't he just handed humanity a noose to hang itself by? You can't blame mankind, not fully. All of these inquisitions, pogroms, holocausts, wars…all because the Connection was being influenced by the proximity of killing instruments. No, not just killing instruments. Tons and tons upon tons and tons of guns, missiles, bombs, hell, even nuclear weapons stored just below the farmhouse, which was the *very nexus* of the whole Connection.

And Father Luke had allowed it! He had allowed the Ecclesiae to do this. Did he *really* deserve not to be "killed?" Did he really deserve not to be sent to Hell, right here and now? Didn't he go along with it? Didn't he decide it a necessary evil? Yes! What would the men in leather coats have done to the partition? Would the Wanderers and he and the Ecclesiae have been able to fight them off without all of the weapons?

No, they wouldn't have been able to. And the men in leather coats would have blown up the phone lines, and thus Religion.

But Father Luke was as adamantly against the current Connection as anyone! He hated the misdeeds and the mistakes, the seemingly purposeful, willful ignorance of progress.

What would have been worse? Letting religion die and leaving the world in the hands of people like Bertrand Russell and the other freethinkers? That would have been terrible. But was it worse than justifying the means by keeping the Connection around and allowing all of these wars to happen?

What was the right decision? Had he made it? Was he really justified in keeping the guns here, allowing the whole arsenal to be here? Was all of the suffering and horror on earth worth it just to keep Christianity and Islam and Buddhism and Hinduism and all of the other religions alive? Was God that important? Did God really matter that much?

Well, did He?

Father Luke's face scrunched up, his eyebrows tripped over his eyelashes. He felt like his stomach was struck by lightning. He felt like his entire body would burst into flame, right here and now.

No.

No, God didn't matter. He wasn't that important. It was Him that outsourced the Connection. Him that gave control of the Connection to others, all out of guilt over what His need for control did to Lucifer and the rebels. He was the one who did this, who let it get out of control.

And Father Luke had been complicit in the worst atrocity ever committed by God against His children on Earth. He had helped that Deadbeat Dad abandon the Connection to unqualified individuals. Helped the Man in the Yellow Polo Shirt create organized religion.

He had helped Him write the scenario where only the strong could force their way in on the head of it, so that religion *would* become organized, and become central and powerful. This so the Connection would always be guarded by strong entities, beings or individuals that could protect it from the men in leather coats. Because the Connection, once established in the hands of proxies, became the focal point of the Valde Bellum, the war between Hell and Heaven.

The Connection wasn't worth it. Wasn't worth the death, and the terror, and the war.

God wasn't worth it.

Father Luke saw that, now.

He decided that if the Protagonist was going to shoot him, he would be shot. He would not try to fight. He would simply go to Hell. He knew then the atrocity he had committed, and knew that he deserved what was coming to him.

He knew that he deserved it, and yet his heart was breaking all over again. He started to cry, softly.

The Protagonist's face hardened, then softened as he realized that Father Luke was weeping. Our Hero lowered the gun, and his face hardened again. *And the old bastard would deserve every bit of suffering coming to him if I were to just blow his fucking head off, right here.* He raised the gun again, lowered it again, as if he couldn't make up his mind.

"Are you going to shoot me?" asked Father Luke.

"I don't know. Should I?"

"Yes."

"I think so, too." He raised the gun, his finger tensed on the trigger. He held it there for a very long time. Then he lowered the gun again.

"But I'm not going to, Father Luke." The priest looked into the Protagonist's eyes and saw there a coldness, a deep and indescribable coldness. In the silence he could hear their heartbeats, both pumping wildly, together tapping out the ancient rhythm of conflict. He could feel the heat from the Protagonist's face, and could feel a nauseous heat in his own. He watched the light glint off a single beaded tear falling from the Protagonist's eye.

The Protagonist gritted his teeth. "Instead, I'm going to stay. I'm staying, and I'm fighting, and I'm going to win the war and take over the farmhouse and then I'm going to expel every weapon from this fucking partition. I'm going to fight the war. You tell your friends that, you hear me? I'm *fucking staying*. And I'm going to set it all right, once and for all. Gimme that fucking Kevlar. And give me four more clips for this shotgun. A helmet, too. I need a helmet. We're going to go back up the Wanderers, help them fight whatever they're fighting Then we're gonna get this war rolling."

Father Luke filled every request, and the Protagonist equipped himself summarily. "Let's go." said the young man, between still-clenched teeth. "I don't want to look at this place anymore."

The Protagonist spun on his heel and marched back towards the stairs. Father Luke waited for his heart to stop racing before he followed.

So the Vicissitude is going to stay, and Father Luke is still kicking. thought the old priest, and he adjusted his own helmet as he hurried to catch up. What a terrible way to have to convince him to stay. He then had a thought, and chastised himself immediately for thinking it. But he couldn't help but feel he was right.

He should have shown the Protagonist the stockpile earlier. Then the war could already be underway.

What better proof would the young soldier need that the Ecclesiae had to go? It had become proof enough for Father Luke all those long years ago, right after the Diaspora, and had been the reason he was joining with the Vicissitude for the war and had not chosen to defend the farmhouse against the sea change. It had been *his* reason.

Yes, he should have let the Protagonist know about the weapons, about their destructive influence on the Connection as soon as the question of the Vicissitude's presence here had come up. But he hadn't, and perhaps that *was* for the better. He didn't know. All he knew was that the Vicissitude had decided to stay, that the war was going to happen after all, and that, God willing, the farmhouse was now able to be taken. Now the reign of the Ecclesiae could be ended. Maybe the Connection could be deconstructed, stripped to its barest functions. Maybe religion could stop plaguing mankind, because it could be a choice again. It could be a choice, not a way of life, a choice, not canalization. Free Will, not something indoctrinated into every human being at birth. Maybe then the focus of the War could be shifted. Away from the Connection.

Maybe then the guns could go, and the soul of the world could be healed.

The Endless Stair
Chapter 14

I stomped up the stairs and didn't wait for Father Luke. I couldn't wait. I needed to get out of there as fast as I could.

Fucking bastards.

The Basement was at fault. Religion was at fault. This stupid fucking Connection was at fault. Maybe the men in the leather coats were the good guys, after all. Maybe destroying Religion was the best thing for the world. Maybe then the horror could stop.

But then what stopped the men in leather coats from turning the earth into something sick and horrible?

What *was* worse?

God, or the Devil? Who was the worse of them, really? Who was the real bad guy, here? Who was the Antagonist to my Protagonist?

Which one was my Yin?

Fucking bastards.

Fucking *bastards*.

I kicked open the door to the kitchen and saw, sitting there at the dining room table and enjoying a cup of coffee, one of the Ecclesiae. One of the perpetrators. One of the generals of this madhouse, one of the architects of all this fucking evil. He pointed at the coffee pot, onomatopoeically indicating that I was welcome to the brew if I wanted it. I detached a calendar off the wall and threw it at his head, which connected with an unsatisfying *thwip*! and I marched out with my middle fingers flying high, like flagpoles, like banners of *le resistance*, like obelisks of defiance. The twin's eyes narrowed as I exited the room, but I detected an understanding in his face. As unhappy as he was about being disrespected, he was at least as unhappy about the Basement as I was. Maybe.

Maybe it was a necessary evil after all. I almost felt bad about throwing a calendar at him.

A necessary evil?

When is evil ever necessary? It's not. Never is. There's always a better way. The ends don't justify the means. Because the ends are just a means to another end.

Fucking bastards. They know that.

I bumped into the other twin as I backed out of the kitchen, birds in the air and not looking where I was going. I shoved him against the stairs, good and hard, and raised my fist like I would hit him. His flinching was reward enough. I lowered my hand and stomped to the front door, threw it open, almost ran to my car.

Fucking bastards. I started up the engine, flipped the heater on high, its highest setting, as high as it would go and just sat there, armed to the teeth and brooding in the driver's seat of my stupid, non-descript, white sedan.

Father Luke emerged from the house a few minutes later, head held high, wearing an indignant grin on his face. What the hell did he have to smirk about? He sauntered over to the passenger door and let himself in.

"What the hell are you smiling for?" I asked rudely.

"I just gave those fuckers what-for." said the priest, and it made him smile even broader.

"Hopefully you did so after remembering to find out where the Wanderers went."

"*Oui.* I remembered. They went to the Tunnel. Apparently this geographical Vicissitude we have experienced has caused the Threshold of Leviticus, the door at the Endless Stair to open."

"What's that supposed to mean?" I growled.

"It means that the door to Hell is open."

"Maybe that's not such a bad thing."

"Maybe you're just upset. There *are* varying degrees of evil, young man."

"And I suppose they're worse than you?"

"Ouch." Father Luke winced. "Yes, I would say that they are worse than me." He reached into my glove compartment, pulled out a pack of cigarettes I didn't know was there and lit it with a match he produced from within his body armor.

"I wonder what *they* would say." I backed the car up, turned around, started driving north on Devine Road. The sun was peeking out now, rosy fingers and all (thanks Homer) and the partition was pink. I wasn't much in the mood to enjoy the dawn, however. We rode mostly in silence, until we reached Teutoberg.

"Gimme one of those cigarettes." I said.

Father Luke pulled one out, lit it in his mouth, put it in mine. "I understand that you would be filled with anger and reproach, even sorrow for the existence of the Basement." he said evenly.

"Do you, now?" I asked sarcastically.

"I do. Because I, too, am similarly afflicted."

"Shoulda stuck to your guns, not let them build it. Oh, wait. You *did* stick to your guns, didn't you? You stuck to *the* guns."

"Unfair. We saw no other option."

"I got an option. Tell God to go to Hell. Tell Him that the Connection's not worth it. Tell Him to leave humanity alone. Tell Him that He's only making it worse."

"I am of that inclination."

"Really?" I asked, a little surprised.

"Yes. I don't think it was ever real to me until I saw its effect on you. On you, a denizen of the affected sphere. That is, the earth. I saw what the war on Hell was really doing to all of you. And I changed my mind. I'm not only backing you up in the war, son, I'm renouncing Religion itself. We'll think long and hard about the Connection once we control it. We'll think long and hard about how we can undermine it."

"That might not even be necessary." I said.

"Eh?" inquired Father Luke thoughtfully.

"Depends on who we move into the farmhouse, you know? Depends on what kind of personality we're dealing with. We might be able to rethink it, remake it, keep it around. In a reengineered incarnation, get my drift? Or we could just blow the fucker up and let humanity deal with it."

"I get your drift. On all but one point. *You*, upon attainment of the farmhouse, will be the new resident."

"The hell I will."

"But you must!"

"Why?"

"It's the Rules."

"Fuck the Rules!"

Father Luke was quiet for a moment, as if trying to decide whether he agreed with that sudden, explosive statement. "Who did you have in mind?" he asked, at last.

"You."

"*Non.* Absolutely not. Out of the question."

"Why?"

"I don't trust myself." he sighed. "I've been complicit with Organized Group Religious Ritual for so long. I'm afraid it's all I know."

"Well, all right, then. But there's no way I'm taking it."

251

"What do you mean?"

"I mean I don't want all that blood on my hands. I don't want the responsibility of all the world's religions. I wouldn't even make a good bishop, never mind a pope, never mind a farmhouse resident! I'm a fucking high-school dropout veteran with anxiety disorders and bipolar manic depressive syndrome. Not some Pontificus Maximus."

"And who did you have in mind?"

"Don't care. We get a third person on our team, right? A third army?"

"Possibly even a fourth, if Virgil joins us."

"Well, and there you have it. We'll talk to Virgil. He might know someone."

"Virgil will pick himself. And there's no guessing what Virgil would do. He's unpredictable, unfathomable. If you think that the Ecclesiae have done a bad job, Virgil would be worse, ten times worse, the worst. We can't go to him."

"Well then, we'll figure it out after we win, huh?"

"That's a little unorthodox, I think, but not against the Rules."

"I repeat: Fuck the Rules."

"How, exactly, do you intend to break the Rules and get away with it?"

"What's God going to do?"

"He is God, young man. *God.*"

"Okay. And He's a smart God, I'm sure. But everything happens for a reason, right?"

"*Oui.*"

"So fuck Him and fuck His Rules. That's why he brought me here. So I could choose to stay. So I could choose to stay and break the fucking Rules."

"You'd better be right."

"Goddamned right I'd better be right. You still on my side?"

"*A jeune chasseur, il faut vieux chien.*"

"What?"

"With a young hunter, one needs an old dog." he said, and grinned his best crocodile smile.

"That's a *oui*?"

"*Oui.*"

"Father Luke?"

"Eh?" he said.

"Where are all the angels?"

"In Heaven."

"All of them?"

"All but they who fight on Earth."

"Why don't angels guard the Mountain?" I asked.

"There's not enough. They're busy on Earth."

"I thought the farmhouse was the focus."

"It is. And it's our problem. Thus, the Basement. But we can't fight demons with guns on Earth. So the choice is to sustain the Basement and thus our defense on the Mountain, or relocate angels from the Earth front and let the men in leather coats run amok. You see our predicament."

"Why won't God just make more angels?"

"The Rules."

"Fucking Rules!" I cried in exasperation.

We started up the incline that would lead us to the Woeful and Joyful, having just crossed the handshaking bridge or whatever that spanned the Flumen Dolere, the river between Teutoberg and the faces of the Plateaus. The hill wasn't much taller than it used to be, because the Plateaus didn't get much higher during the Vicissitude. Before we knew it we were on top of the Woeful Plateau, cruising Devine Road, then taking a right into the driveway of the house with American architecture.

"Who lives here, Father Luke?" I asked as we got out of the car. There was a horse whinnying in the backyard.

"The O'Malleys. Inventors. World-Famous Inventors and Alchemists, to be exact."

"Why haven't I ever met them before?"

"The time wasn't right."

"Why not?"

"They're our third ally in the war, and you hadn't made up your mind."

"Oh." I grimaced at the house. "Well, is it a family?"

"Yes."

"Nuclear?"

"One husband, four wives."

"Are they Mormon?"

"I do not think so, but it is possible." Father Luke leaned on his arms, crossed and folded on the top of the car.

"Who runs things?"

"I do not understand your question."

"Come on. More than three people can't decide on what to eat, much less run a family. Families are necessary dictatorships. Who's the big woman?"

"Uh, well, Mr. O'Malley... I suppose he runs the show, though he would tell you it was his wives that really ran things."

"Then we *are* talking about a woman for our Champion."

"*Non.* I have spoken with them. He is adamantly opposed to putting women in harm's way if there are men to go first."

I smiled. "How do the wives feel about that?"

"They think it's sexist and horrible."

"They think that it's sexist and horrible because it probably is. And why does Mr. O'Malley feel that way?"

"Mr. O'Malley's reasoning is that it takes twenty-eight days for a woman to create an ovum, while a man produces hundreds of thousands of spermatozoon an *hour*. So men are cheaper, more expendable. Says that men are good at what's *wrong* with the world, government and fighting and controlling and *authority*..." he shuddered. "...And physical labor and so forth. Says women are good at everything that's right with the world, nurturing, caring, thinking, healing, birthing, dancing, taking joy in life and the like. So a few less men around might do the place some good."

"Mr. O'Malley said that, huh?"

"*Oui.*"

"I think maybe that makes sense to me, too. He's our champion."

"Not necessarily a bad choice. But all decisions we are to make should be given careful deliberation before they are declared and set in stone."

"Wasn't that just a careful deliberation?"

"Mr. O'Malley was hardly present."

"*Touché.* We'll talk about it later. Let's go find that horse."

We walked behind the house and found, sure enough, the Wandering Japanese's horse, stripped of most of its pack, including the weapons. It stamped and made that *pppphhhh* sound with its lips.

"Can you ride a horse?" Father Luke asked me.

"I think so." I stuck a foot in the stirrup, swung my leg over to the other side. Patted the beast's long, brown mane. What a fine, fine horse the Wandering Japanese rode.

Father Luke jumped on the saddle behind me, kicked the horse, and we were off.

We were *off.* O-F-F. OFF. Like a torpedo launched from a submarine. I've never ridden in a *car* going that fast, much less a horse. I'd never imagined something that could run like this. Everything was a blur going by us, moving too fast for me to see. I just shut my eyes and held on for dear life.

Father Luke, naturally, seemed like he was enjoying himself.

Angels.

We were going incredibly fast until were suddenly not. We were suddenly galloping, then trotting, then walking, then shimmying, then slow, slow, slow. I opened my eyes and the horse stopped.

There, yawning before me, was the maw of a great opening in a huge stone cairn that rose up from the ground. We were near Cassandra's Ruins, that much I could tell, but I don't think I'd ever explored *this*.

"Is this the Tunnel?" I asked Father Luke, who was getting off of the horse. He didn't reply.

The sun wasn't very high in the sky, so I had missed something I should not have missed on our approach. Then again, my eyes were clenched tight for most of the ride. Even with better light I may not have seen what Father Luke saw. The priest walked around to the other side of the giant rock with the cave carved into it and fell to his knees.

There, on the ground, lay the Wandering Kenyan. In a pool of blood. The gentle black man who had escorted me home from the Tower of Wrath and Justice my second night here. His big smile and his perfect white teeth, now forever gone.

His eyes were closed, had been closed by someone. He lay separate from a pile of six bodies, all sporting leather coats. Father Luke kneeled and kissed his head, stood up and looked at me. I had nothing to say.

We sort of stood there together for a moment in a daze. Is it more of a tragedy when a Wanderer dies, since a Wanderer does not have the guarantee of Heaven the way that a human being does? Is it a real tragedy the way humanity, unaware of their great boon and afraid always of eternal damnation, never realizing that they're in like Flint, well, is it as big a tragedy as it is for humans? Because Wanderers *really* don't know where they're going.

I suddenly found myself praying that the Man in the Yellow Polo Shirt would forgive the Kenyan. He was a good guy, even if I never got to know him very well. He was a nice guy. And a brother.

They make it happen, both ways.

"Father Luke?"

"Yes?"

"Who will make the sun set, now?"

"The sun will set."

"Oh." I was silent for a moment. "Do you think he made it? To Heaven?"

255

"I hope so."

"Me, too."

The Bedouin and Kenyan's horses were dead, too, riddled with small-arms bullets, lying in pools of blood. I wished suddenly that we had time to bury the Kenyan and these two noble animals.

We collected ourselves and headed into the Tunnel. There was a fine trail of blood leading down the stairs, which were well-lit by some light emanating from wherever the steps ended at.

We walked and walked, more stairs by ten or twenty times the amount that led to the Basement, and still we were not at the end. We were surrounded on all sides by walls, sort of haphazardly constructed, with little patches here and there of brickwork and stonemasonry complementing the raw stone and occasional stalagmite that the natural cave offered. Water dripped here and there, not much of it, but enough to make the creepy, echoing *drip-drip-drip* that's so unnerving in caves. Well, *I* find it unnerving.

I put what little there was of fear in the back of my mind, trudged on as fast as I could. It didn't take me as long as Father Luke to get a little tired, but I did. And tried not to show it. I kept my gun at the ready, guarded the rear, looked over Father Luke's shoulder for him, as he was on point. I tried not to talk, but I did have questions. A few slipped out when I wasn't thinking about it.

"So the Vicissitude opened the…"

"Threshold of Leviticus. The Gate of Hell. Rather, the Gate to the Abyss, which is accessible from Hell. Please be quiet."

"Not yet. Where does the Tunnel go if the Gate of Hell is not open? What's its purpose?"

"It goes to two places."

"Those are?"

"The Tooth and the Sepulchers."

The Tooth. The Tiamat's Tooth. Where everyone's real names were inscribed. Including mine.

"What are the Sepulchers?"

"Enough. We must be silent."

You remember that light that was emanating from way below, that seemed to illuminate everything from the bottom of the stairs? It turned out to be a constant light, like it was always just a little ways ahead of you, but we never did find the source of it. Another funny little miracle. I wondered if Father Luke was making it happen with some sort of angel power or something.

I was silent, as long as I could be. Which turned out to be long enough, because we did get to the "bottom," eventually. It was a lit room of some kind carved out of stone, like a man-made cave, but there were no lights in it. It was simply illumined, and that was that.

On the floor in this room lay four more men in leather coats, again slung in a pile on top of each other.

"Another fight, here." said Father Luke.

"Very astute, Watson." I said, searching for signs of injury to either of the surviving Wanderers. I found nothing but Father Luke's dirty look, which I deserved for my sarcasm. I searched the whole of the room, found another set of stairs leading farther down. "The blood trail ends here, so maybe whichever one of the Wanderers was bleeding bandaged themselves up after the battle."

"Perhaps it was a man in a leather coat who was bleeding, and was pursued here by the Bedouin and the Japanese."

"The trail isn't consistent with that scenario. Back on the other stairwell, the drops are on every fifth or sixth step. If someone was running, it would seem it would be a lot less frequent, because they'd be covering more ground. Anyway, don't the men in leather coats have black blood?"

"Only the cherubim."

"Oh."

"It could be that a Wanderer with a quickened pulse would cause their heart to beat faster, and thus cause a heavier loss of blood. With respect to the frequency of the bloodstains."

"Do angels work just like humans? Angels and demons, that is?"

"Much the same. We're tougher, I think, than I'd expect from an ordinary human being. We're a lot faster, too. Stronger, smarter, and generally better-looking…"

"No contest."

"But not really much *different*, in most things. We do bleed. And when we're in our element we can utilize some miracles, grow wings and do other things. But anyone can do that."

"Humans too?"

"I don't know about *wings* for human beings, *per se*, but humans have all sorts of powers that we as angels can only dream of having." Father Luke gestured down the staircase and I took point this time. We started tramping down at a hurried pace, continuing the conversation. "Humans can, for instance, live with a broken heart." rasped Father Luke. "Their soul can all but wither and die from emotional distress and yet their bodies keep going."

"It ain't easy."

"Neither is growing wings."

"Hmmm. I think I see your point."

"Do you? Anyway, humanity's got all sorts of oddities I love and admire."

"Really? Angelkind fascinates me, too. We'll really get into it sometime when the circumstances are less dire and there's maybe some beer. No beer down here, as far as I can tell, and I don't think I'd touch a drop right now, anyway. My stomach's twisted and my balls are all shriveled up."

"You're nervous."

"No shit."

We went down, down, down. And down. And then down. And then down. Down. Then down.

The stairs went on for almost a quarter-mile, by my reckoning. At some point our source of illumination had switched from being below us to above us, and then it had twinkled out entirely and left us only the light of a thousand little green, phosphorescent, bioluminescent mushrooms that seemed to cover the cavernous rock walls. I started to smell a lot of water, started to feel cold. It had been almost pleasant farther up toward the surface, kind of warm, the air was fresh. But it was really getting murky and scary, now. Even Father Luke seemed a little claustrophobic.

We stopped twice for a breather, me breathing and him encouraging me to hurry it up and get back on the road. After the second such break from the action, the steps had started to get mossy and soft. And slick. I'd almost fallen once, and Father Luke had had to catch me, lest I'd gone sliding down and cracked my head open, or worse.

What an ignominious end that would have been! Breaking my neck or my head open on some fucking stairs while my friends were at war with demons. Very anticlimactic, and very unfair to the readers, too. I, personally, would have thrown this book out the window if it had turned out like that.

"And then the Protagonist slipped and broke his neck. The End."

I wouldn't do that to you, friends. Regardless of your opinion of this novel, no book deserves an ending like that.

All though it might be kind of comedic, in its own black way.

Back to the story. The softness of the stairs muffled our steps, which I was glad for, because I was worried about the *stamp! stamp! stamp!* of our footsteps coming down, worried that we'd alert any hidden enemy lying in wait, give them time to set up an ambush. I took solace only in Father Luke's silence, trusting that he'd notify me if there were any precautions we needed to take. Apparently the only thing we needed right now was haste, so we were running, flying down those stairs as fast as we could, given the aforementioned slipperiness. Very tiring work. I was almost ready for a third break when we at last heard a voice.

Speaking a cracked form of some Semitic language I didn't understand. Aramaic, it sounded like. I couldn't pick out very many words, because I didn't speak it, although I'd encountered some in the Abbey library.

It was harsh, and gravelly, and whomever was the origin of it was spitting, not speaking. Father Luke and I advanced cautiously after that, slowly but deliberately, until we were just near the foot of the stairs and could peek in on what was going on.

There, at the bottom, were my friends. Being held up by a lone man in a leather coat. A man in a *black* leather coat, holding a big fucking rifle. The Wanderers had apparently been forced to lay down their weapons.

Black leather coat. Which meant it was a bigwig. A fallen cherubim, not a fallen seraphim, a demon like the Horrid King, like Moloch. My hand suddenly hurt, and I just as suddenly smelled Teutoberg Forest. That was a big fucking gun he was holding. I peeked my head down a little farther, caught the Wandering Bedouin's eye, winked at him. I looked up at Father Luke, grinned, saluted, and jumped down headfirst, shotgun extended out in front of me, and blew a hole in the man in the black leather coat before he even knew what was happening. Luckily, the two Wanderers had seen me a split second before I fired, had seen my trajectory and where I was aiming, and they knew where *not* to be. They knew *not* to be on the other side of the demon when I fired. Because I sent that fucking bullet right through him.

Father Luke rushed downstairs after me, knocked the man in the leather coat over (he had not fallen, even from the violent removal of a good chunk of his sternum and its reorientation in a splatter all over the wall in front of him) and drew two of his six handheld firearms. The old priest unloaded both clips into the leathercoat's head, saw that he or it or whatever was still twitching, unloaded two more pistols worth of shots into its face.

If you think that's not a strange thing, watching a Catholic priest unload four pistols worth of ammunition into a demon, well, you've never seen it.

Okay, granted. Maybe he's not a priest, but it's no less weird. If he'd just ditch the vestments and the little Roman collar, I'd be a lot happier. And so would he, I think.

Finally, the man in the black leather coat stopped moving, stopped writhing. It was "dead," or on it's way back to Hell, or whatever. It wasn't a threat anymore. We were safe for a moment.

The Wandering Bedouin looked at Father Luke, then me. The Wandering Japanese smiled. Then the Bedouin embraced me.

"First you avenge me, then you save me. I owe you *two* now. But what are you doing here? It is dangerous!"

"I'll say it is. You two were just about done for." I said.

The Wandering Japanese then detached a false arm he was wearing and revealed a small flintlock pistol that would have been pointed right at the man in the leather coat.

"We had a Plan B." said the Wandering Bedouin "But your help is still greatly appreciated, and sorely needed." His eyes lowered slightly. "The Kenyan fell."

"Yes, we saw him outside. May God forgive him and all Wanderers and enfold him in loving arms." said Father Luke.

"Inshallah." said the Wandering Bedouin. "Amen."

We stood there for a moment, silent and deferential, for the Kenyan. Then the Wandering Japanese spoke.

"They opened it. Themselves."

"The Gate?" asked Father Luke. "How?"

"We do not know. Abaddon may have been distracted." said the Wandering Japanese solemnly, and he stroked his chin. "It is open, however. And we can not close it."

I looked around the room, saw two staircases going down. Then I looked back at my party.

"Are you sure there's nothing you can do? Big rocks, or anything?" I said.

"Not even with all four of us could we block it. The gate is two stories high." said the Wandering Bedouin.

Father Luke unbuttoned the coat he was wearing under his pistols and revealed, in addition to a bandolier, three belts of dynamite, ten sticks to a belt.

"Maybe we don't need to block it. Maybe we can just blow it up." said Father Luke.

"Destroy the Threshold of Leviticus?" cried the Bedouin, disbelievingly.

"Why not?" asked Father Luke.

"Because it is God's creation! An ancient gate, older than the earth itself!"

I think I was a bit more iconoclastic, a bit more like Father Luke, because I didn't see the big goddamned deal, either. If it was preventing the demons from getting through, then it had to be done. The end. No more. Done for. No matter how fancy or significant it was. I spoke up.

"Big fucking deal. Better it go than us. Better the Threshold of Leviathan or whatever than the Abbey."

The Wandering Japanese cleared his throat. "Unfortunately, I am in accord with the soldier and the honorable Throne in this matter. It must be done."

The Bedouin was silent for a moment, then nodded, slowly and carefully. "Yes. It is the lesser of two evils."

"It's not evil." I said, and Father Luke looked at me suddenly. "It's not. It's necessary, sure, but not evil. It's only a minor inconvenience. Seriously. Look at this in God's perspective. How long would it take for Him to make another one of those gates?"

"No time at all." said the Wandering Japanese, nodding.

"So it's not evil. That's an important distinction, Bedhead, and I know you're wondering why I'm being so obtuse about this, but it *is* important. Evil is seldom necessary."

The Wandering Bedouin blinked, then looked at Father Luke. Father Luke sighed. He saw the Basement this morning."

"Allah!" cried the Wandering Bedouin. "I am sorry, brother!"

"Don't fucking get me started." I seethed.

They all nodded, I got mad all over again, then I just clenched my fists and counted to ten and then to ten again. I *was* mad. Damned mad. I fought to control the tone of my voice. "So are we going to blow this thing up, or what?"

They kept nodding. "Fucking fantastic." I growled. "We're all agreed. Which one of these staircases leads to Hell?"

"That one." said the Japanese, and pointed.

"And where's the other one go?"

"The Sepulchers."

"What's in the Sepulchers?" I asked. "Who?"

There was suddenly a noise from that staircase, the staircase leading to the Sepulchers. A noise that sounded like a creak and then a pop! like a door had just been opened and then pulled off of its hinges. We all looked at each other.

"*Merde*." said Father Luke. We all went flying down the staircase to the Sepulchers, mindful of the slippery moss but moving with as much haste as we could muster. I didn't know why, didn't know who, but I followed. Gun at the ready. It scared my friends, so it scared me too.

We arrived at the bottom and found a lagoon, flanked on both sides by large oak coffins bathed in the same weird light of those crazy neon fungi. A small waterfall trickled down from a hole in the wall and fell into the pool noiselessly.

Really. Without hyperbole or linguistic license of any sort, it made no sound when it hit the water. The room was completely silent.

Then I stopped and *really* listened. I couldn't hear breathing. My own or any of my companions'. I tried to speak aloud, tried to say, "Hey, guys…" but I couldn't. I could, I did, I felt the vibration in my throat and the buzzing in my chest but I registered nothing in my ears. Then I shouted, then I screamed. No sound whatsoever.

Holy shit, that's weird.

I looked at Father Luke and he winked at me. The Wandering Bedouin had his hands on his hips and the Wandering Japanese was picking up a stone. He held it, seemed to consider its weight for a moment, rejected it, picked up another, seemed satisfied. He dropped into the pool and fell with a *splash!* and I was suddenly surrounded by the sounds of air moving, of breaths being taken and expelled, of the Wandering Bedouin talking.

"…seems Nepenthe's Sepulcher has been opened."

"Yet Lethe's remains intact." Father Luke finished his thought.

"'Curiouser and curiouser,' said Alice." remarked the Wandering Bedouin.

"At least they are dead, *nee?*" asked the Wandering Japanese, and Father Luke looked at him.

"Not dead. Sleeping. We need to seal this back off, and quickly."

I was a little bewildered. "What's all this?"

"These are the Muses." said the Wandering Bedouin. "They served their purpose at the Creation of the World and at other various times but they were deemed too destructive for further use. Thus, they sleep."

"Oh. Shouldn't we be quiet, so we don't wake them up?" I asked.

"A novel idea." said Father Luke. "Let us seal this place."

"We can't." said the Wandering Bedouin. "We'd need Virgil, or Scholastica. Or Abaddon. We couldn't handle something like this."

"I am aware that I am not of Virgil's constitution or standing, naturally. I did not intend to seal it in the fashion that he would seal it." Father Luke produced a stick of dynamite and held it high. "This is what I meant."

"Ah." said the Wandering Bedouin. "But it will wake them up. And any obstacle that is created will not hold them long."

"Can even Virgil seal it once they are awake?" asked the Wandering Japanese.

"It is possible." said Father Luke. "The top of one of the coffins are already open. The men in leather coats must have intended to wake them."

"How can you fail at waking someone up?" I whispered.

"There are many ways to fail when attempting to wake the Muses. Dynamite, however, is not one of them." Father Luke grinned insanely and held up a match.

"Wait." I said. I looked at the room I was in, took it all in. It was a cave, lit by the mushrooms like normal, but there was something inscribed just over the little waterfall. "What is that, there?"

"What is what?" asked Father Luke.

"There. That inscription." I got a little closer to the water, felt a firm hand on my shoulder preventing me from getting closer. The Bedouin was behind me.

"It says, *Awake I thirst never for these waters, but as all men must sleep, all men must drink, and thus do I wound the world.*" said the Bedouin gently.

"What is that supposed to mean?"

"Look below the inscription."

Beneath the words was inscribed *Font Dolere*. "How do you say *Dolere* in English?" I asked no one in particular.

The Bedouin answered. "Oblivion."

"This is the 'Fountain of Oblivion' then? And the river up above us, or rather, at the foot of the plateaus, that's the 'River of Oblivion?'"

"Yes."

"Kind of hackneyed. Like something an eleven year-old Metallica fan would come up with." I chuckled.

"It is not oblivion, as in nothingness. It is oblivion as in being unaware. There is an important reason that these waters are named Oblivion."

"Uh…Elucidate."

"Of course. You see, when we are oblivious, not paying attention, taking refuge in ourselves, being unaware of the great systems of people, nature, society, family and so many more that are around us, we cheapen those systems."

"Okay."

"We cheapen them, we fail to see their significance, and thus they become to us as air and we think nothing of them. Taken for granted. But they *are* beautiful sculptures, immensely and richly complicated works of art that we should never grow tired of looking at. When we take them for granted, we flaunt the systems, disrupt the equipoise, unravel the tight balance. And then great evil is done, though we have done but a small evil in being near-sighted."

"So what's the deal with the lagoon? And the river?"

"In a complicated way, these waters are linked. As this lagoon rests near the graves of the Muses, it casts its essence out on surrounding waters, which turns the river at the base of the cliffs into a River Oblivion. Never swim in the river, never drink from the river, be absolutely sure that you never touch the waters of the Flumen Dolere. They are oblivion, and they cause great change on earth when a denizen of Devine Road touches them."

"To what end?" I asked.

"I do not take your meaning." he replied.

"Well, change isn't always bad." I reasoned, and scratched my head.

"Let me say, then, avoid the narrow occasion of sin, so that changes on Earth may happen according to the will of the Man in the Yellow Polo Shirt."

"Well, and I don't suppose I think much of the will of the Man in the Yellow Polo Shirt, to be perfectly honest with you."

The Bedouin was silent, but the Wandering Japanese was not. He was running. Fast. As fast as he could up the stairs. I heard a hissing, noticed a small light behind me.

Jesus Christ. Father Luke had lit the dynamite at the foot of the stairs.

Me and the Bedouin ran for it. Ran for our goddamned lives. Stupid, crazy Father Luke, already ahead a full flight of stairs, was laughing manically.

At least he had used a *long* fuse. A couple of feet long, judging from the time we had to get away. We were already at the top of the stairs, back at the corpse of the man in the black leather coat when we heard the BOOM! from the dynamite come slamming back and forth on all the walls, surrounding us. It was almost deafening, and almost as loud as Father Luke's laughter. When the ringing died down, he was still laughing.

"Ha ha ha! You little shits! You should have seen your faces! Ha ha ha! I have avenged my brandy at last! Ha ha ha!" He doubled over, his face swelled with blood. "Oh, it hurts! My stomach!"

The Bedouin and I looked at each other, then at Father Luke. Then we tackled him and started punching him in the ribs.

"Ouch! Aaaooowww! No! No!" he sputtered, half-laughing, half-pleading. "No more! I'm sorry! No I'm not! I'm not sorry! Fucking bastards!"

We kept assailing his midsection until he couldn't fight back anymore, then punched some more. At last, out of breath, we stopped. Father Luke lay on the ground heaving and gasping. "Revenge." he whispered, and then started coughing. It was the Bedouin's turn to laugh. Mine, too. We helped him up, having temporarily forgotten the Threshold, and brushed each other off. The Wandering Japanese, who had escaped the fray, just stood there and looked impatient, and when we finally all noticed him and remembered ourselves, there was a moment of brief embarrassment.

That passed quickly.

Father Luke belted me hard in the back of the head and then bull-rushed the Wandering Japanese. The Japanese, due to being caught off-guard, was exactly a third of a second slow in his reprisal, if no less successful: He dodged the charge, flipped Father Luke's foot up with one hand, sending the old man into the air, and then sent the priest's body meteoring back to the ground his other hand. He pulled out his sword, took a few hairs of Father Luke's mustache in his hand and swiped them off with the weapon, then stuck them in a pocket on his undergarment (beneath his armor) and patted his chest. "Spoils." he said glibly, and everyone laughed.

"That's what I get for attacking *him*." said Father Luke as the Bedouin helped him up.

"That's what you get for wasting so much time." said the Wandering Japanese, and he motioned toward the stairs.

I cleared my throat, picked my gun up and took point down the tunnel that lead to the Tooth, followed closely behind by my companions.

The Abyss Gazes Also
Chapter 15

Zach Davidson. Josef Al-Mu'min. Abu Bakr. Mary Magdalene. Mary, Queen of Scots. Tristan Keeler. Mary, Mother of Jesus Christ. Jesus Christ. Joseph his stepfather. Saint Francis. Pope John Paul I. Anne Frank. Frederick Douglas. Ezrahel. Izrail. Ibrahim. Virgil. Scholastica. Mother Theresa. Michael, Gabriel, Raphael, Metatron, Lucifer (The Devil's name is on the Tiamat's Tooth?) and many other angel names. Thomas Aquinas. Kinsey. Russell. Socrates.

Copernicus. Galileo. Saint Peter. Basho.

Anyone who ever fought suffering while suffering. Anyone who ever stood up for what was right at great personal cost. Anyone who led in the name of goodness, whatever Good is.

My name is on that tooth. So is the Bedouin's, and Father Luke's, and the Japanese's and Virgil's and of course Saint Scholastica's, among many, many others. There are millions of names on that Tooth that I can't even pronounce, without mentioning the millions I *could*.

Millions and millions of names.

The Tooth is as big as you can imagine it. Try to visualize a stalactite, a great craggy cone reaching up toward an impossibly high cavernous ceiling and etched with millions of names. Make it as big as you have to make it in your imagination to fit *millions*, here. Thousands of thousands. This page has a few hundred words on it. Multiply the size of this page by hundreds of thousands. That'll give you an idea.

It's quite even and quite easy to climb. Plenty of easy footholds and handholds, not too rugged or sharp, not so dangerous that you can't climb right to the top.

I did climb to the top, the first time I saw the Tooth. I climbed right up, all the way, a feat that took me no less than ten minutes. I ascended and looked right in the eye of Rodin's Fallen Caryatid, crushed beneath her burden. Poor thing. The world was just so big. So, so big. I reached out and touched her cheek. So many people forced to fight so hard.

Why did God make the world?

Why did God create it if there has to be so much suffering? Why did God make a world where so much suffering is possible? Aren't there limits? Fail safes? Some kind of system to prevent things from getting as bad as they have gotten?

Why doesn't He do something about it?

Why don't *we* do something about it?

What the hell is wrong with us? We don't deserve existence. We don't deserve *life*. Look at what we do. So much wrong with the world. And everyone knows it, yet nothing changes. Why is that?

Oblivion? Like that fountain, like the river? We sleepwalk, oblivious to the pain and suffering in our fellow man's lives? Is it our refusal to see it, or are we just self-absorbed? Are we too busy fixing our own problems?

Do we fix our own problems? Or do we fan the flames? Are we making it worse? Does the world just get worse and worse because there's more and more humans to add problems to it? Every unique, individual, beautiful little snowflake with his own psychosis and his own hates and desires and duplicities and loves and unrequited loves, every new set of problems, are they adding up? Are they multiplying exponentially and affecting the Earth in some back-ass New Age way? Is there some great "negativity" wafting up into the atmosphere and falling all over us all of the time?

Why is it that everyone I've ever known has stabbed me in the back?

My best friend and my old girlfriend? What makes people do that sort of thing? What makes them have to inflict that suffering on me? Why can't people just *wait*? *Jesus.* They knew me! For years and years! Isn't a friend important above all things? Aren't *real* friends unique and rare? Why would my best friend move in on her?

Or did she move in on him?

Were they really thinking about hurting me? Intending to? Is knowing the consequences of your action considered intent? Is it manslaughter or murder? It's just obliviousness. Knowing but letting the passions get the best of you, and then you've done something you can't reverse, and even if you *could* reverse it, it's just easier to go on being oblivious.

I wouldn't have done it to them. I didn't do it to them.

I've never *really* hurt someone in my life. I've been mean, I've been really mean, I've left women without a word of explanation if I didn't feel it merited one. I've hurt people physically and emotionally, I've killed people with an M-16. I killed a whole preschool full of children.

But I never betrayed someone I loved, and I never truly, deeply hurt someone who loved me. At worst, I've been an asshole. Never a villain.

Because evil is always a last resort for me. And maybe that's what makes me different. Maybe that's why I'm here on the Mountain. Because I pay attention. I pay attention and I love, love, love. Just love everyone. I'm not oblivious.

Am I a rare breed? Is there really so much oblivion in the world that I, as someone who has always tried to be a good person, a person who is *attentive*, have been marginalized? Am I really a minority? So drastic of a minority? Why do human beings do this to each other? Why do families do this to each other? Friends? Girlfriends and boyfriends, husbands and wives? Why do we do this?

The late, great Einstenian physicist/postal clerk Albert once informed authoritatively the world before his timely death that space is love. He may have been the only man since he said that who understood what in the jiminygeeGodfuck he was talking about. He might also have been babbling. But it has always intrigued me.

Is love space, then, Mr. Einstein? Does it work in converse? Is the concave of space also the seeming convex of love? Is love, being space, a division? A divider? A space between objects, even self-aware hairless apes? Is that why we hurt the ones we love? Because we are separated by our loving connection?

Is love space, then, Mr. Einstein?

Were he resurrected for just this purpose (and yes, it *is* unfair to ask him questions when he's not here to answer) I suspect he would refrain from an election of clarification, even a coy one. He was mysterious, a little crazy, and had a right to both. Both are requisites for genius.

Albert Einstein, where have you gone? So many questions that we need your help with. Never mind the bomb, Mr. Einstein. Burning questions, not burning cities.

How do we make love stay?
Why does familiarity breed contempt?
What makes war so great a pastime that we start one every week?
Why can't everyone see how short (and sweet) life is?
Why did Joe DiMaggio take all of the magic with him?
Where did all the magic go?
What's it all about, Alfie?
Where, for that matter, did Joe DiMaggio go?
How did our medulla oblongatas get so damned oversized?

Why do we hurt the ones we love?

Why *do* we always hurt the ones we love? We do! It's a time-honored truth, which is a nice way of saying that it's a cliché. We always hurt the ones we love, when the ones we love should *never* be hurt. Why do we take out our aggressions, our hurts, our depressions and our pain on those we are close to? Is it just another cliché? Is it 'familiarity breeds contempt?' Does that apply to everything? The closer you get, the worse you treat someone?

And why were Scholastica and Father Luke so worried about the Tooth? It's not like I know these names, like I can correlate these names with my friends. *I* don't know. There's *millions* here. I'd never be able to discern a Wanderer's name just by looking at it, so what the hell was the big deal?

Why is this place so damned confusing?

I climbed down the Tooth and rejoined my party, patiently waiting for me at the bottom.

And as I looked at them, one by one, I found that I *did* know their names. Searching their faces, I could see that it was written in their brows, inscribed in their jaw lines, etched in their lips. I could see their names shining in their eyes.

Father Luke's name was actually Hebrew. How funny. Angels (or at least *this* angel) have Hebrew names. The Bedouin's name was Arabic, which leads me to believe that he was born after Mohammed's revelation, but I do not know. I supposed I could ask him, sometime.

The Wandering Japanese's name was Bushi Chiaki.

The Wandering Kenyan was not Kenyan. He was Og, King of Bashan.

I opened my mouth to speak but was interrupted. "Shhh." said Father Luke, and put a finger to his lips. "Are we any different now? Is there any reason to change the way you address us? Come. I am Father Luke, these are the Wanderers. And you are our brother. Let us go."

———

As we descended, I noticed the air warming around us. I touched the rock on the walls surrounding us, felt them at room temperature. It was, indeed, gaining warmth. Or losing coldness. I am not sure. We were traveling deep, deep into the Mountain, if we were not already far below it.

"I never meant to…" came a murmur from down below.

I snapped to attention, saw my party carrying on. "Who said that?" I asked. None of them replied, and only the Wandering Japanese looked back at me, with sad eyes.

"I was only trying to…"

"Father Luke?" I asked. He motioned for me to be silent.

"If I'd have known…" came that voice again.

"Who the hell is talking?"

"No one." said the Wandering Bedouin, who was at the front of the procession and who had now stopped it . "No one is talking. What you hear is what you are hearing. We hear what we are hearing. But know that we *are* descending the stairs to the Abyss that separates this Mountain from Hell. We are, in essence, walking to Hell. Prepare yourself for some occurrences that you may not be able to explain."

"Yes." added Father Luke. "And please be silent."

"What I was trying to do…" I heard, and I strained my ears. All of the sentences kept getting chopped off. I then realized another thing.

It was the sound of my own voice.

You don't hear your own voice, usually. You hear some echo, some distorted version of it in your head. Ever recorded an answering machine message? Doesn't it sound weird when you play it back? That's why it didn't register with me at first. I didn't recognize it.

I probably should have recognized the American accent. None of my companions have American accents. Stupid of me.

But then, why would that occur to me? I don't think I'll ever get used to the miraculousness of this place. I won't ever get used to how out-of-the-ordinary the place is.

What is the proper word for out-of-the-ordinary when weird happenings are ordinary?

"Look, if I knew it was going to go so wrong I wouldn't have…"

There it was again. We descended down and down.

"I had good intentions…" I heard myself say as I walked the road to Hell.

—

These stairs we walked were not so long. The Endless Stair was approaching its end. At last, I saw the Bedouin enter another chamber, then Father Luke, then the Wandering Japanese. They all broke into a run the minute they alighted on level ground.

I reached the bottom and saw a large cavern, mysteriously lit, sourceless light illuminating the craggy walls, casting wicked shadows on the rocky, uneven floor. The ceiling was tall and domed. It loomed mute over the cause of the commotion: There were dozens of men in leather coats in a semicircle standing below a stories-tall golden gate, engraved with thousands of scripts and embedded with thousands of jewels. On either side of the gate sat two ten-foot tall statues of angels, and on either side of the statues were men in leather coats. Facing Abaddon. Standing all alone, then beside the Bedouin and the Japanese and Father Luke, who had rushed to his side. I, too, ran to stand alongside him.

"Parley?" said one of the men in leather coats in a high, rich voice I could almost describe as sing-song. It was a beautiful voice, a complex and disturbingly pleasant sound. A natural, smooth tenor. He smiled innocently at Abaddon.

Abaddon's deep, black baritone voice shook the room. "There will be no compromise. You may not pass."

Five men in black leather coats emerged from the throng and stood casually at the front, making their presences known but not making any overt statements. The man with the beautiful voice went on. "You're outnumbered."

"I'm always outnumbered." was Abaddon's reply. "There's not enough of you here to get past me."

"Are you sure? It would only take one, slipping away unnoticed." said the man.

"Better send someone that can actually fight." I said, peering over the man in the leather coat's shoulder. The Abyss, just past the Threshold, was incredible. A starless field of black, black velvet going on into pure nothingness.

K'ung Wu.

I went on, ignored the voice in my head. "Not some small fry like that last little bastard you sent. What was his name? Moloch? Short work."

I stared into the Abyss until I got the uncomfortable feeling that it was looking right back at me. Then I focused on the man in the brown leather coat. He looked surprised. "You hear it."

"What?"

"You know what I mean. And now I know that it *was* you that defeated Moloch."

"Indeed."

"He had much kinder words about you."

"Big fucking deal." I said, trying to appear tough and uncaring, trying not to look scared. "One of you gets through, you've still got to go up against the Ecclesiae."

The man with the beautiful voice shuddered and winced, like the mention of their name hurt him. I went on. "Better make sure whoever slips through has a black coat on. And better make sure that there's all five of them." I started backing up, toward the door. The men in leather coats started murmuring, started pressing forward. Abaddon discouraged them by drawing his sword, and this caused a great unsheathing of guns, cudgels, chains, blades and various other weapons. It also put the attention back on the great Throne. I stood in front of the door and pulled out my shotgun, loaded it to brim, brandished it menacingly. Then Father Luke started to glow.

Not blindingly, not dramatically. Just...his skin started to fill up with light, with luminescence, until he was radiating gently, casting a soft glow on all the walls. He was revealed to the men in leather coats as a Throne, himself. The Wanderers bared their teeth. A fight looked inevitable.

It was, indeed, inevitable.

Bang! A blast from a rifle hit Abaddon directly in the chest. He didn't even move. Just focused on the shooter, sneered, and in a blink of an eye the great angel had taken off the demon's head and had dismembered the three men in leather coats closest to that initial and most unlucky assailant. The men in leather coats ganged up, paying no heed to the Wanderers. Three of the men in black leather coats rushed Father Luke, another made his way towards me, standing in the doorway. The other disappeared.

I fired, missed. He raised a pistol, a SIG .40 from the look of it, and fired twice. Both ricocheted off the sides of the door with sharp *pings!* I fired again and caught him in the leg. He kept coming, seemingly unhampered. So I rushed him.

He fired again, right at my head, and suddenly everything went silent.

I initially thought I had been deafened. Then I thought that, perhaps, just perhaps, I had been hit by the bullet and that I was dead, and was now looking through a ghost's eyes. Everything had slowed down, like I was watching everything in two frame-per-second slow motion. I watched the bright flash of the muzzle, the small gasp of smoke escape from the pistol's mouth, watched the bullet flying toward my head, slowly, slowly. I tried to move, found I could not.

Or could I? I was, indeed, slowly drifting to the right, ever so slowly. I was moving, at a speed so slowly it was disorienting.

Was I going to *dodge that bullet?*

I was beating it! My head was almost out of its trajectory!

What the hell is going on?

The bullet passed over my left collarbone with a half of a millimeter of clearance. It lacerated the top layer of fabric on my Kevlar, sent a rush of scaldingly hot air sweeping across the surface of my neck, then bounced off the wall behind me and embedded itself in the floor. Then a rush of air, of commotion, of gunshots and metal meeting flesh. Time ran at its normal rate again, sound was working again. The man in the black leather coat was staring at me incredulously.

So I fired. And blew his head off. And everything went silent again.

I felt a strange feeling, when time slowed for me again. I felt like a mix between a foul odor, a red light and a dissonant chord were registering with me from the direction of Father Luke, and when I turned my head, slowly, so slowly to see what was going on, I watched, in slow motion, a sword rushing downward to strike my friend, mentor, priest and favorite all-around angel I'd ever met. A man in a black leather coat, a fallen Warrior Cherubim of God, was about to administer the old priest's execution. The sword was falling, now, so slowly. Then it was connecting, and Father Luke was screaming. I could not hear the scream in my ears, but I could hear it in my heart. Because I was screaming, too. I roared and roared, and tears sprang up in my eyes and a burning vengeance possessed me. A helpless rage was spreading like a chemical fire through my whole being as time went back to normal, and as sound met my aural canals once more.

Father Luke was there, still with a head, still fighting three men in black leather coats.

But one of the archdemons was behind him, out of his field of vision, and the old priest was too distracted to realize that there was a sword poised dangerously above his head. I raised my shotgun, fired at the would-be decapitator, and suddenly felt a rushing wind on my face, a whistling in my ears, a searing heat all around my body. I was flying toward a massive throat, pulsating and full of pores. But I was off by a few fractions of an inch, and I would fly directly past that throat and that jugular, fly right into the shoulder of a hapless Wandering Bedouin.

I was the slug, the bullet I fired from my shotgun, and my shot was going to miss.

I gritted what mental thought of teeth I had and leaned left, left, LEFT! With everything I had, and I'll admit that what I had was a complete mystery to me. I just leaned and leaned.

And felt a warm splatter of liquid on my face, felt flesh and veins tearing beneath the onslaught of my rapidly decelerating tip, felt myself imbed in a spine.

I opened my eyes and gasped. I was back in my body and Father Luke was alive. His would-be decapitator was dead.

My God. I had seen the future. And then I had become a bullet and changed it.

Right after dodging a bullet. What the fuck?

What kind of goddamned whacked-out comic book had I fallen into?

One where you're in the middle of a battle with demons, so get your ass in gear, soldier!

I straightened up, raised my shotgun and ran into the fray where the Wanderers and Abaddon were struggling against dozens of men in leather coats wielding wicked-looking weapons.

A rifle butt to one head ended in a satisfying crack that informed me I had broken the demon's head open. A well-timed and well-aimed shot put a slug through one man in a leather coat's midsection and went straight through to lodge in a second man's stomach. The weird light/odor/sound came again. I turned and fired without thinking about it, ended up blowing the jaw off of a man in a leather coat poised to smash my head with a nasty looking flail. I checked on Father Luke, saw that he had dispatched another of his three attackers.

I'm too close. Too close for a shotgun.

Too close for a shotgun? Can you ever be too close for a shotgun?

Yes. I'm too close, and there's too many. I breathed hard, ditched the shotgun, unveiled the Prajna Khadga. I remember thinking, *This would be so much easier if I could just slow down time again.*

And then I did.

I was in that strange world, painfully silent, everything so ultra-slow.

What was happening when this was happening? I, apparently, was much faster in this time-sense. Was everyone really slower? Or was this just my perception?

And why wasn't this freaking me out?

Shit. Why analyze it?

I swept in, slowly, ever so slowly to me...

But I killed six men in leather coats in the time it took the Wandering Japanese to blink. I know. I timed it. I stretched and stretched, maintaining this strange power, exerting it over everything in the room, laying waste to everything wearing leather. A crack of bones here, a smash of skulls there, and then rinse and repeat.

It seemed like an hour to me, but when every last demon had fallen and I readjusted myself, felt the whoosh of air and the sound trickling back into my perception, I found that the Wandering Bedouin had only been able to manage a one-hundred and eighty degree pivot on his right foot in the time it took me to kill forty-one men in leather coats. Abaddon had finished a two-handed baseball swing that chopped a man in a leather coat in half. The Wandering Japanese had begun to raise his massive odachi just before I started the massacre, and had nearly finished getting it over his head.

Father Luke had been able to take a knife in his gut.

I ran to Father Luke and smashed with everything I had on his remaining assailant's ribcage. The man in the black leather coat's torso crumpled like paper beneath my blow, and he howled in tortured, traumatic anguish.

Then the Wandering Bedouin was upon Father Luke checking the wound, producing elixir, preparing for surgery.

And I couldn't see straight.

The demon was on his side, was screaming, and he screamed and he screamed and the scream never went away, even after he stopped screaming. It bounced around, soared left and right, up and down and long after it was audible, long after its issuer had choked and gargled on black acidic blood that had filled his lungs, it traveled into the Abyss, there to exist as energy for all of sonic eternity.

A sad fact, a single morose truism among myriad morose truisms about violence is that the sounds it produces never die. Clinks, clangs, bangs, grunts, screams, war cries, gurgles, the breaking of bones, the smashing of skulls, the sizzle of flesh all live on forever and ever. Floating somewhere in the cosmos or absorbed by some surface, some facet, some piece of the earth in whatever fabricated or organic incarnation it exists. They bear ceaselessly their macabre signature, fly unendingly their murderous bar sinister. It is a sad thing that there are not as many pleasing noises we humans make to balance it all out. It is a sad thing that the horrible racket is winning by a landslide.

The cave turned on its side, the Abyss flip-flopped and grabbed the Threshold, spun it 'round, dosey-do.

Abaddon was at my side in an instant, caught me as I wobbled and lost balance and almost fell to the ground. He spoke in my ear, a whisper, a rich whisper filled with words I couldn't understand but nonetheless sounded like a children's choir, like trees soaked in April rain. Like a blue, blue sky. Words that smelled like autumn. I smelled autumn, and it thrilled me.

He laid my newly good-for-nothing body on the ground, and I remember hearing, just before I lost consciousness, the Japanese talking about the men in leather coats.

"They're not all here." he said to Abaddon. "Two browns and a black are missing."

Everything was suddenly nothing, and my vision was a field of stars.

One Goth, One Dog
(The O'Malleys, World-Famous Family
of Alchemists and Inventors)
Chapter 16

I woke up two weeks later. I didn't know that when I woke, but it was. Two weeks.

A man and four women and Father Luke stood over me.

The man wore a mustache like the men of the American Industrial Revolution wore their mustaches: It was giant and full and ostensibly black, black as the devil's heart (not actually true, the part about the devil's heart. See *Volume II* for more on this) and twisted up slightly at the edges. He wore a tweed suit with an American 1930s cut, khaki and maroon and white. He wore no hat. His hair was as black as his mustache, parted neatly on the side and well-oiled. He smiled, and his mustache smiled with him. I correctly assumed that this was Mr. O'Malley.

I looked at the women, next. The Mrs. O'Malleys. All four of them. Lord, it's a good thing he showed some good restraint, some good humility by stopping at four. Because *five* wives might just have been ostentatious.

One was Indian, probably Hindi, beautiful. Wrapped in a blue traditional dress of some kind unfamiliar to me. Another was black African, equally beautiful, with a long and irresistibly graceful neck and full, pouty lips. She wore an elaborate red and ivory wrap and a silver headpiece that looked vaguely Byzantine. The third in line was Caucasian, golden haired, fair-skinned, emerald-eyed, with a perfectly formed nose that whispered *retroussé* just audibly. She wore a sarong tied at her waist and nothing else, and I'll confess that I may have gawked at her bare, indescribably perfect breasts longer than Ms. Manners would have recommend in such a situation. As she seemed a little flattered, I didn't sweat it. The last was some variety of the thousands of varieties of Native Americans. I couldn't guess at what, exactly, her ancestry was, but her face had an air of the placidity of a lake that has never been seen by human eyes. Her eyes spoke in volumes of ancient clarity.

"Mr. O'Malley, I presume?" I said, as I looked at the sixth person, or, if you like, angel, in my room, Father Luke. He nodded.

"Our dear Vicissitude, I presume?" asked Mr. O'Malley in a deep, throaty American accent.

How wonderful! I hadn't heard an American accent on the Mountain since the Wandering American, and his was a sturdy New York variety, virtually unlike my flatter, West Coast speech. Mr. O'Malley's voice was rich and pleasant, if a little bit antiquated. Like an educated man of the first half of the century. Twentieth century, that is.

"In the flesh, speaking *ex cathedra*. I'm the Protagonist of the story, too." I said.

"Speaking *ex lectus*." interrupted the bare-breasted blonde. (Christ, but her voice was incredible! A low alto, not quite contralto, not as deep as Scholastica's, making up for lack of whiskey with ample melodiousness.)

"My Latin isn't perfect, sure. But I was making a joke." I said.

"It was funny, dear." said the Indian wife in a thickly accented voice through a thickly accented smile. She *was* Hindi.

"I *am* Mr. O'Malley. This is Vinaya. That shameless Caucasian is Braunwyn…"

I reflected that her breasts were, indeed, white.

"…and the darkie over there…"

"Indeed!" huffed his African wife in a soft South African accent.

"Quiet, woman! I'm orating. This beautiful woman of ebony countenance is Linda, and she's my favorite. Ask the others."

The others nodded. I laughed.

"And that little thing with the gentle eyes is Niwetúkame. Looks unassuming now, but she's about as calm as a hurricane if you upset her."

"The Divine Mother?" I asked.

"Might be. She refuses to say."

Niwetúkame smiled mysteriously.

"And you're…some kind of priest?" I asked Father Luke.

"It would have been nice if Saint Gabriel, when he was scheduling your class and the ensuing masquerade, had decided on any other vocation for me but a *priest*. For *your* benefit, you little bastard. Now I'm confined to this fucking collar and I can't even *breathe* half of the time."

"Look however you want to look. Dress however you want to dress. I could care less. And, speaking in strictly solipsistic terms, here…I'm sorry, as a figment of your imagination, that you imagine me looking the way I do, or I could be a penguin. I always liked penguins." I said.

"You mock me."

I winked at him. "So, uh, did you get hurt, or whatever? From the knife?"

"Merely a flesh wound."

"Sure it was. Are you okay?"

"Fine, now."

"And what about me? Did I get hurt?"

Father Luke suddenly looked very uncomfortable. "Uh, no…"

"Then what happened?"

"Uh, you…made short work of the men in leather coats…"

"I don't even know how I *did* that."

"Well, neither do we."

"*No one* can do that, Father Luke! *No one* moves that fast."

"Not true." he said, and for some reason I thought I detected a hint of a waver in his voice. "*I* can not, surely. But others can."

I looked at him quizzically, expectant that he would elaborate. Father Luke just scowled.

"Who can?"

"'Later.'"

"I haven't heard that in a while."

"I am sorry. We will discuss it another time." He indicated the other five people standing around the bed and I suddenly got the hint.

"Oh, of course. Tactless of me." I apologized, and got a resounding nod of forgiveness from all around the bedside. "Could I have done all that on earth?" I imagined myself slowing down time on the football field, winning every game, enjoying a lucrative NFL career. Maybe after the war was over?

Oh, shit.

Was I going back to earth after the war was over? I hadn't even thought about it. What happens when all of this is over?

"Ha ha ha!" he snorted/laughed. "Of course not! This is the Mountain with No Name and you live on Devine Road. Your greatness, whatever it might be, is not of this Mountain, it's true. But neither is it free of it."

"That doesn't make sense, but all right. I'll take your word for it." There went that dream. No agent, no Hall of Fame, no thousands of adoring fans. Geez, like I would have accepted it over the Mountain, anyway.

"What happens after the war is over, Father Luke?"

"One step at a time."

"No, I mean…can I stay here? Do I stay here? Or do I go back to…you know…" my voice trailed off. The thought scared the shit out of me. I didn't want to go back, really. Not even to play crazy mutant football with crazy mutant powers.

Mr. O'Malley cleared his throat noisily. "I do believe you were the intended recipient of the farmhouse upon victory."

"Yeah, I meant to talk to you about that." I said to him. Father Luke smiled.

"I already have." said the old priest. "He's graciously accepted, if a little baffled. I waited to explain until you woke up."

"When did he accept?"

"Two weeks ago."

"Christ! I've been asleep that long?!"

"*Oui.*"

"And I'm not dehydrated?"

"*Non.*"

"Or starving, or whatever?"

"Magic." said Father Luke, and I got a famous grin.

"Oh." I leaned hard against my bed. No bedsores, as far as I could tell. But two weeks? I guess those altogether inexplicable powers of mine wore me out. Wore me out enough to put me in a coma.

"Father Luke? Did we bury the Kenyan?"

"*Oui.*"

"Where?"

"In the Moslem cemetery north of the Abbey. You have not seen it? It is where all Wanderers who perish go, and where the Wandering Japanese committed his *jisei* to the earth."

"Where the horses were? That was a cemetery?"

"It is unmarked, since the winter."

"Oh."

"Ahem, of course I don't mean to be rude, but…" said Braunwyn, her clear voice cutting through the thickness that crept into the room. "Can you tell us why our husband is Champion? And why the Vicissitude is not?"

"I don't want it."

"That's rather against the grain of historical precedent." she said.

"I'm rather against most historical precedents." I said. "They're bad for the liver."

"He's cute." said Niwetúkame.

"Can we take him home?" asked Linda.

"Not now." said Mr. O'Malley." You tarts make me jealous enough as it is. Listen, son…" he said, turning his attention to me. "If the Vicissitude asks me to do something, I do it. It's an honor to be in your presence, truly, but…"

"Dreck." I said, and blanched. "I'm a high-school dropout and only made E-5 in the Army. The most repulsive and, for that matter, *dangerous* thing I can think of is a title. In anyone's hands. So just call me by my name. Or just say 'Protagonist.' Or call me son, like Father Luke. You already have. Don't pay any attention to anything else. I'm only human."

"So am I. And so are the girls. With the possible exception of Niwetúkame. She's not saying. Did I say that before?" asked Mr. O'Malley.

Niwetúkame smiled mysteriously.

"What I'm getting at…" continued Mr. O'Malley, "is that I don't know *why* you want me to have this honor."

"I already said so. *I don't want it.* I'd rather see the farmhouse destroyed. I'd rather see God do His own damned dirty laundry."

Mr. O'Malley seemed to consider this. "I do not think that He would allow that."

"I don't give a shit. If we win, we should be destroying. If we are forced to instate anything at all, it will be the most minimalist Connection we can establish."

"The very principles of the idea of Individual Worship and Personal Salvation are minimalist. So you're on the right side." said Vinaya. "We're all working toward the same thing. But destroy the farmhouse?"

"Destroy the Basement, at least."

"And then how will we fight if Hell mounts a full-scale invasion?" asked Mr. O'Malley.

"I haven't figured that part out, yet. Strike a bargain with the Devil, maybe."

"Not funny." said Niwetúkame.

"Really? I thought it was. I thought it was funny because I think it's the only way we're going to work this out. We're going to have to simultaneously fight a war and stop one. Or at least figure something out regarding a truce or cease-fire with Hell. The Basement is worse than *Hell* running things." That last sentence struck with me a funny thought, but I filed it away for future contemplation.

"Not true." said Mr. O'Malley.

"Hmmm. We'll cross that bridge when we get there." I said. "Look, Mr. O'Malley, I don't want the job. Too big for me. Too much work, to be honest. I don't have the taste for power, I find. I want to get done what I gotta get done and then maybe go find a wife on earth and bring her back, live here until my time to go on up the Mountain comes."

"First, no one comes here without invitation." said Father Luke softly. "So no wife from earth. Second, your 'time to go on up the Mountain' won't happen naturally. Not here. Surely you've noticed that you've not had a sniffle or a flu or so much as a cough since you got here? Haven't gained a pound of fat, despite the way *you* eat...?"

"Yeah, I'm kind of a pig, huh?" I agreed.

"...suffered no worse than a hangover? You won't age, either. Look at Mr. O'Malley. Came here in 1936 at the age of forty-three. Niwetúkame came down from the Second Plateau, we don't know when she got here. The other three were invited for various reasons, ranging from their accomplishments to their intellects."

"You look good for a centenarian." I told Mr. O'Malley, a little incredulously. He grinned. "Okay, scratch all that. I'll find a wife on the Mountain." I conceded.

"Good choice." said all four women, almost at once.

"There we have it." I said. "Women are right ninety-nine percent of the time. I'll vote with them."

"Women are right *all* of the time, scoundrel." said Braunwyn.

"Except when we're not." said Linda. "Then we're *really, really* wrong. Doesn't happen often."

"Pax." I said. "Look, what matters is that I don't want it. So consider that my first official edict as Vicissitude and consider this my second: I won't make any more official edict as Vicissitude. You're the Champion. I'm fighting for *you.*"

"Uh..." Mr. O'Malley looked at Father Luke, then at his wives. "I suppose I've already agreed. Not that I would change my mind. I'm honored."

"That's that." I said, and tried to muster an air of finality to attach to my words, though it didn't come off well. I am of the impression that the weight of my words command all of the presence of the baboon, the linguistic equivalent of standing up too quickly and knocking one's head on a dangling lamp. Things just sound weird coming out of my mouth, and they never really come off as great as they sound in my head. I'm not stupid, I just prefer to communicate through the written word. Less thought on the fly, more time to pick what to say.

Hell, I'm not much good at that, either. Father Luke was sniggering.

I pointed at him and cried in mock anger, "And that's enough out of you, prick! I'm no good at saying anything important, and you know it. Where's my goddamned breakfast?"

"Downstairs. In the fridge. And it's leftovers. We ate grandly last night."

"Fuck you, too. What was it?"

"Ham and etc. The works. It's good cold."

"I bet." I sighed. "Anyway...I suppose now that it's all locked in, Champion chosen... the war will be under way soon, huh?"

"In a manner of speaking. The Foederati received some unlooked-for assistance from the men in suits, rather, the Seraphim, and got the towers nearly finished. The *Shirivasta* or whatever you're calling your tower nowadays...that's done. So you can move out, you shitty roommate. Eat your own food."

I stuck my tongue out at him. He went on. "So is the *Castellum Orientus* and the *Virtutus Crucem.* The Abbey's almost finished. Virgil's is almost done. The Bedouin's Tower is done. The Tower in the Desert is taking longest. Call it another few weeks."

"I'd better go see the Bedouin, then."

"Indeed. He has been quite busy, though. All of the Wanderers are being assembled. They will make up the generals for their side, which Braunwyn has recently been referring to as 'The Farmhouse Boys...'"

"Yup. And we're the Abbey Gang." added Vinaya. She smiled.

"'We?'" I asked.

"No choice." said Mr. O'Malley. "They're as capable as you or I of fighting, and we're short of competent help. Without my wives, we'd have no one but ourselves and our Foederati. Better in some ways, not so good in others."

"I see."

"I should have introduced them as 'generals' although they, too, are disdainful of titles." said Mr. O'Malley. He wasn't kidding. All four of their faces were wrinkled in displeasure. "At any rate, they will work under us, as will my two oldest sons, to whom you will be introduced later today."

"When?"

"At dinner."

"Dinner sounds great." I said.

"You were focusing on breakfast not a few moments ago." teased Father Luke.

"Take a hint." I shot back with a smile. He put on his best offended face. "I'm hungry. Uh, what time is it?"

"Ten a.m., in your terms. You can eat and not spoil dinner." said Niwetúkame.

"Fantastic. Let's relocate."

"To the kitchen, then?" asked Mr. O'Malley.

"To the kitchen." I agreed heartily, and my stomach rumbled its appreciation of our consideration for it.

—

We sat and talked for an hour, me wolfing down food as though I hadn't eaten in two weeks, the women looking at me like I was some kind of savage cartoon caveman yanked right out of the cartoon Pleistocene and transplanted in the real-world Abbey dining room. We talked about everything but the Farmhouse and the Wanderers and their part in the war. When we finally got around to that, I received a real whopper. In fact, when I heard it, I choked on a small, cold kernel of corn that had, at that precise moment, transformed from unassuming morsel of goodness to an unrelenting vegetable particle assassin hell bent on murdering me. Vinaya had to apply the Heimlich.

"He's what?!" I sputtered, once the offending matter had successfully been expelled and launched across the table and had landed square in the middle of the little white square in Father Luke's Roman collar.

Father Luke had calmly removed the kernel with a napkin before he repeated himself. "The Wandering Bedouin is the selected champion of the farmhouse. So long as he lives the war can not end."

"Oh, Jesus." I said, and cast my head into my hands. "What the fuck? What the FUCK? Goddamn, Goddamn, Goddamn…" I repeated, over and over, into my hands. My friend. My good, good friend. My first friend on this Mountain. Oh, how I loved the Bedouin so. That stupid bastard. Doesn't he *see*? Doesn't he see how fucked up the farmhouse and the Twins are? Doesn't he *see*? Christ. I looked up, crossed my arms over my chest, tried to keep two tears that had rudely barged in on my vision from moistening my face. "I don't suppose that stupid fuck had this same reaction about fighting me, huh? Motherfucker. Why did I trust him?"

Father Luke said gently, "Actually, before accepting the nomination for Champion from his colleagues, he came and sat by your bedside for about an hour. He apologized to you, oh, thirty times in that hour, son. You didn't hear, you didn't know. But he shed at least two more tears than you have. This anger of yours is an odd reaction to such news, even for you."

The tears had had enough. They were there, then they were leaving. Down my face. Down to my chin. "Coast is clear!" They called to their comrades. My eyes turned on the old lubricator. There went my tears. Ducts in overdrive. They eschewed proudly my pride. God, I was crying in front of women!

Oh, God. I thought…I mean, I knew that the Bedouin and I would be enemies. I've known that a long time and I even had it told right to my face on the Last Good Day of the Year. But I thought…I don't know. I don't know what I thought. I thought he'd be faceless, another body in an army, and that after I won I could just forgive and pardon him and we could be cool.

I don't know why I thought something like that. Of course he'd end up their Champion. He is the foremost of the Wanderers.

But goddamn. Goddamn. Why the Bedouin? Why my friend?

Linda and Niwetúkame came to my chair and Linda draped her arms around my neck and Niwetúkame knelt and placed her head on my arm and cried with me. I sniffled, then sniffled loud, then sobbed. The others waited patiently for me to get myself under control. When I was able to, I did. "Thank you, ladies." I said shakily. "I'll be fine, in a minute."

Mr. O'Malley's eyebrows had the capability of looking more worried than any other set of eyebrows I'd seen in my life. His expression was so pained, so sympathetic, I almost started crying again. But I didn't. I just sniffled again. And held it together.

"Okay." I said. "Okay. That's how it is, I get it. So we're it? We're the war council."

"My sons, as well." said Mr. O'Malley. "William and Patrick."

"And do not discount Virgil." added Father Luke. "He may yet join our side, although I believe that we will be well into the war before he chooses. It is in his nature to support the underdog. He will wait to see how things shape up."

"Let's play on that." I said.

"I don't take your meaning." said Father Luke.

"Capitalize on that. What if we…"

"Let us save strategy for dinner, son." interrupted Mr. O'Malley without a hint of rudeness. "There are many things to talk about before we establish anything in the way of strategy. Many things you should see."

"Okay." I said blandly. "That's fair." I wiped my eyes again and snorted. "Okay." I took another bite of breakfast but found that my appetite was lacking. "So it starts…when? Tomorrow?"

"Possibly," said Father Luke.

That was it, I supposed. The war could start any old time, as soon as everyone was ready. We seemed ready. They were probably close or near to ready. It would be any day before I was once again dragged into armed conflict. It would be any day, now that I was promoted from "Sar'nt" to "Lord General" and that I would be killing children by the dozens. Any day. Jesus.

I excused myself, stood up, stated that I was tired already, that I'd be glad to see the O'Malleys again when I was showered and shaved and rested and properly clothed. "Would seven p.m. be acceptable for dinner? Excellent. Father Luke, I beg your pardon. I'm going upstairs."

I went upstairs and cried, cried, cried.

—

Father Luke woke me at six. I fulfilled all of my preparatory obligations, dressed in my best slacks, took my car. Smoked about fourteen cigarettes on the way. Got to the top of the Woeful and crawled along the driveway, through thistles and thorns and blackberry bushes and high grass and the occasional tree. I got out of my car, noticed for the first time a lonely, plaintive poplar in the O'Malleys' backyard and forced metaphorical meaning on it in my mind. Standing alone, sad, symbolic, but true. I almost retched when I realized what I was doing.

I rang the doorbell and was greeted by two handsome boys not much younger than me, dressed in fine, turn-of-the-century black suits. The older, Caucasian and fair-haired looked twenty, the younger was Caucasian and black-haired and looked eighteen. They led me through an anteroom to a living room, then left after making sure I was comfortable.

The living room was exceedingly large and exceptionally cozy, mostly blue and white and charcoal, with four couches and three loveseats, five coffee tables and about a dozen bookshelves. Two fireplaces, one on each wall. Three busts, the same busts that the Professor had in his classroom, sat on his mantle. Whitman, Emerson and Thoreau stared at me disapprovingly. I stuck my tongue out at them.

I perused the bookshelves, found that most of the books were in Italian. Couldn't read the titles, even though my Latin is almost fluent. (Italian didn't fall too far from the Romantic tree, you know.) There was one that I recognized: Boccaccio's Decameron. I flipped it open, found it was written in Italian too, and though I couldn't read it, I knew the contents, so I flipped through the pages and the small pictures that accompanied the short stories. Great stuff, the Decameron. Full of happy, happy endings.

That made me sad, all of the sudden. Sometimes even blue skies bring tears.

I replaced the book as Braunwyn entered, dressed in a form-fitting black dress, adorned with pearls, looking like an angel. Her hair was pulled back tightly, and her earrings sparkled in the dim lighting of the living room. She beckoned for me to follow her through a door, and I did, floating on a cloud of her intoxicating fragrance, lecherously watching her lower half undulate as I went, through a hall, an anteroom, and at last into a dining hall, where a great oak table set for seventeen was filled with Mr. O'Malley, his wives, and his children. *Thou shalt not covet thy neighbor's wife* my ass.

Mr. O'Malley had twelve kids. There was a place for me at the head of the table, and Linda sat at the other head. At her right was Mr. O'Malley, at her left was where Braunwyn took her place. Next to her was Niwetúkame, and the oldest son who had brought me into the house. On Mr. O'Malley's left was Linda, and the second oldest son. In order of age went the other ten children, on down the row, to the youngest, a precious little girl of maybe four. She looked like she had started eating early and had been caught; there was a conspicuous ring of color around her mouth, and she was smiling gaily.

I got the introductions, one by one, as the children stood up and said their names, youngest to oldest. Ceana, the youngest, the little girl, introduced herself through the gaps in her baby teeth and was clearly Braunwyn's daughter. Then it was Dorjan, the youngest boy, perhaps five and of Vinaya, and then two girls, twins by Linda of about eight. Sauda and Kamaria were their names. Next was another girl, Umay, from Niwetúkame, and then a boy, Casimir, by Vinaya, ten and twelve years old, I thought, and then Almira, the oldest girl, about fifteen and an exact clone of her mother, Braunwyn. Almira was at that tender period in girlhood when she was just starting to push out her dress in front, and she was beautiful. The next were two boys of sixteen, born of Vinaya and Niwetúkame, it seemed, respectively, and their names were Gunnar and Yasuo. Then another boy, of Linda, named Augustus, seventeen, and then the two boys I had met earlier, both sons of Braunwyn. William and Patrick. Those were my other two generals. Their voices were deep and full, the eldest wore a thin wisp of a beard on his face. They all had solemn looks on their faces, all but Ceana and Dorjan, who seemingly were not privy to the fact that half of their family was headed off to war.

I sat down uncomfortably, acutely aware that my defeat of Moloch forced this war on the Plateau, and thus upon the children.

"Greetings." said Linda. "Welcome to our home."

"Thank you all." I said. "I am happy to be here."

"Do you have any dining customs? Prayer, or the like?"

"Uh, no. I'm, uh, a bit savage in that department."

The children stifled giggles. Linda smiled, too. "Good. So are we."

Dinner was delicious!

Heaps and heaps of smoked salmon, spinach and mushroom-stuffed chicken breasts, basil-and-oregano pesto spread over sun-dried tomatoes ate on top of wrapped slices of baguette and jugs and jugs of white wine that only the adults and the three oldest were allowed to partake of. There were thick curds of goat cheese soaked in a light vinaigrette, a salad comprised of exotic greens that was drenched in the same, a great giant heaping bowl of some unidentified pasta that I had four helpings of and every vegetable you've ever thought of plus about thirty you never thought were edible. There was more there, I just can't remember all of it. My memory was quite cloudy when I was finished. I don't even remember talking much, I just remember laughing, remember Mr. O'Malley getting slightly drunk and that I was a little tipsy, too, and that it was a wonderful evening.

Casimir, Gunnar, Yasuo and Almira had gone to the trouble of learning a song "from Earth" to sing for me, and it ended up being a rousing rendition of *Hurricane Eye* by Paul Simon, one of my favorites (Father Luke must have told them, because I taught it to him and the Wandering Bedouin on one of those boring nights during the crazy weather changes.)

Tell us all a story/About how it used to be/Make it up and write it down/ Just like history

About Goldilocks and the three bears/Nature in the cross hairs/And how we all ascended

from the deep green sea/When it's not too hot/Not too cold/Not too meek/ Not too bold

Where it's just right and you have sunlight/Then we're home/Finally home/Home in the land of the homeless

Finally home

Soon I was singing along, and Almira was dancing on the table, and the children who knew it and I were all laughing and screaming the lyrics at the top of our lungs and it was fantastic.

Oh what are we going to do/I never did a thing to you/Time peaceful as a hurricane eye
Peaceful as a hurricane eye

I think we sang it three times, and by that last revolution, everyone at the table had caught on (mostly) and we were all alternating between repeating it as loud as we could and yelling, trying to drown each other out. Everyone was dancing with everyone else, two tentative harmony parts were established (the baritones were outnumbered, though), some of us were singing badly (me and Mr. O'Malley) some were singing beautifully (everybody else) and all of us had a ball. Then we ate some more, and laughed some more, and the children sung some songs they had made up, and we tried to sing along where we could, and clapped along where we couldn't, and it was just what I needed to pick up my spirits.

Finally home/Home in the land of the homeless
Finally home

At length, the festivities drew to a close and the younger children were sent to bed. Almira had elected to put them all down, had said goodnight herself, had kissed me firmly on the lips on the way out the door, drawing reproachful looks from every older brother, mother and the lone father in the room.

"I'm, uh, sorry about that." I apologized feebly. I *had* been taken by surprise, and she was only fifteen. I certainly wouldn't have kissed her.

"No worries. There's not a lot of traffic on the Mountain, you take my meaning? The kids fall in love with everyone they meet." said Mr. O'Malley. He glanced around him. "Well, we, too, have a Basement, of sorts, and I suppose we should show you that, now."

My eyebrows furrowed immediately and my posture must have shot straight up into rigidity, because Niwetúkame had said, immediately, "Not *that* kind of Basement. Wait and see."

We left the massive dining hall and traveled through another hall filled with reproductions of famous sculpture on pedestals, then on into a full-fledged library, then an anteroom, then a second living room, a "den." In the den was a door leading to the basement.

The O'Malley basement was not a Basement. Niwetúkame had not lied to me.

It was a fucking hangar.

The first thing you noticed was the massive aircraft, the giant six-mast galleass with the sloped lateen sails and huge helicopter rotaries. The second you noticed was the accompanying xebecs, styled exactly the same way, with three masts and half the rotary wings, but impressive in their own rights.

The ships were a pearl-color, with high sterns and blood-red sails. The figureheads of mythological female angels, bare-breasted, wings and arms outstretched to their full spans, adorned them. On the galleass, named the *Autumnal*, the angel held a spear in one hand and an olive branch in the other. On the two xebecs, named the *Sovereign* and the *Steadfast*, the angels held swords and oblong tower shields.

Mr. O'Malley took me, appropriately speechless, on a tour. We stood on the forecastle (he said it fo'cs'le) and looked over the whole of the deck. There were fifteen ballistas armed with harpoons on either side, a massive old maritime steering wheel on the poop, netting, gaskets, halliards, a hawse, futlock shrouds, pawlpitts and even a giant, useless iron anchor, just like any old ship you can imagine. I suddenly saw, in my mind's eye, the O'Malley children crawling all over deck, using words like 'lubber' and 'cockswain.'

"This *flies*?" I asked, incredulous.

Mr. O'Malley nodded and grinned.

"How?"

"Magic."

"Oh." I didn't need to know how, I supposed, just needed to know that it did. Yes, this quite changed the dynamic of things. I understood why we put off any talk of strategy until I had seen these ships.

"These are fantastic."

"Took me long enough to make them so, but yes, I agree. I could never have achieved the engineering possible had I not been invited to the Mountain."

"How did you get *your* invitation?"

"For inventing things. I was, according to St. Gabriel, a 'visionary' engineer and he wanted me to team up with a few others he knew and create some art, some working inventions that might please the Man in the Yellow Polo Shirt. I guess He was down, regretting making mankind, and the boys were trying to perk Him up by reminding Him that humans are good for *something*. They let me bring my wife, Braunwyn, and I met the other three, here."

"And Braunwyn didn't mind?"

"Not after we'd been here for goddamned fifty years, she didn't. She was ready for something new, and then we met Niwetúkame, and it was wonderful. Father Luke married us."

"Oh, that's cool."

"Yes, I think so. We met Linda and then Vinaya, she's the newest, only about twenty-two years, and then all four of the women ganged up on me and started demanding children. Braunwyn! After eighty years of marriage, she finally wants a child! Anyway, we tried and tried, and it's not easy to conceive on the Mountain, let me tell you. I don't know why, but it just takes careful persistence and a lot of years, and I think that the children just arrive when the Man is ready for more residents. Otherwise there's no reason that Almira should have been born when she was."

"Why?"

"Well, we traced back the night of conception to a week that I was visiting the Fourth Plateau, teaming with Archimedes on some pulley or another (he's quite obsessed with those) and we all know that spit doesn't make babies, so I think that here on the Mountain children just come when they come."

"Oh." I blushed. Seems weird, I know, but I had been assuming that Mr. O'Malley had had the audacity to think he could please four women. I realized then that his wives shouldered some of the burden, too. "So, uh, I see why the girls aren't fighting over you." I said.

"Well, rarely. There's only one of me in the house, and they've talked for years about finding a second husband…Of course, to help *me* out with everyday things. Company for *me*. Another male, balance out the estrogen, easier for *me*. Hmmph! Thinly veiled thoughtfulness. I don't need any of that. The boys are old enough now for company and help and they're both shaping up to be excellent engineers. Patrick's smarter than William, but William's bigger and stronger, and I think the ratio's going to stay that way. And Will is turning out to be an excellent swordsman. Father Luke started training him when he was about four years old. He *almost beat* Father Luke in a duel. Once. A human nearly defeating an angel in combat doesn't happen often."

I was quiet about my victories over Father Luke, and I think that my silence ended up being more conspicuous than had I mentioned it. "Well, and you're the Vicissitude." said Mr. O'Malley. "A different case. Anyway, on the subject of having a co-husband, well, the wives are just looking for another penis, I think." He looked amused. "The idea of novelty is always alluring. They'll either forget it, or they'll get it. And if they do I'll have to put another room on the place. Damned if whoever he is won't help, though."

"You'd be ckay with it?"

"Oh, I don't have any more use for jealousy than anyone else on the Mountain. It's the antonym of love."

I smiled inwardly. Mr. O'Malley continued: "Besides, I never argue with women, not unless they're wrong. Which is very, very rarely."

I smiled embarrassedly, tried to change the subject. "Uh, how is it that your children have aged on the Mountain when, uh, you haven't? I mean, none of us age, right?"

"An excellent question. I wondered about it myself. It is Niwetúkame's hypothesis that when they reach an age they are happy with and that they can be happy with, they just freeze, stop aging. Kind of an innate thing, I think. When you can stop, you do stop. I don't ever argue with Niwetúkame in matters regarding the Mountain." Mr. O'Malley looked wistful. "I don't know if she's some Divine Mother or not, but she's certainly not like any of the rest of us."

I inhaled deeply of the basement air, which was surprisingly clean and not stuffy, and looked over at the rest of our party, who had boarded the ship behind us and found places to sit on the poop deck. Niwetúkame was looking right at me.

"Come on, I'll show you some other things that the kids and I have been working on." said Mr. O'Malley, and led me off of the ship. He led me deeper into the hangar, where there were more flying contraptions, about one hundred and twenty-five, by my count. They were made of iron, painted gold, the size of motorcycles and they employed an engine on the back to make bat wings on either side flap and lift it up in the air. They were preposterous, physically guaranteed not to work, technologically impossible and Patrick gave me quite an impressive display of their speed and in-flight maneuverability by turning loop-de-loops around the foremost sail of the *Steadfast.*

"They're called *sephirah*, plural and singular, and I invented them." Patrick had told me proudly. I was amazed. The sephirah looked almost comical, with their flapping wings, but they behaved just like birds, utilizing their flight appendages to pick up speed or elevation and otherwise gliding most of the time. All of them had large, steel-mesh nets that they carried in a drop box beneath the engine, and they were similarly equipped with grenades of a kind I had never seen before: Greek fire grenades.

"These are *my* inventions." William said as he showed the incendiaries to me. They were little brass globes with a wind-up key on them. Inside, there were four compartments, the first filled with sulfur, pitch and a foam-like substance mashed out of corn husks, the second compartment filled with quicklime, the third filled with magnesium powder and the last with water and fragments of iron, brass and bronze. When the wound-up key returned to its original position, it would click a gear to the left and the compartments would shift slightly, so that the quicklime was released into the pitch mix and the magnesium opened into the water, which caused the fire, and then after one half-second's delay, the gear would click again and the two would mix, igniting the Greek Fire. The resulting hydrogen buildup, caused by the magnesium and water interaction, would cause the grenade to break apart in explosion, propelling wicked, crumpled metal shrapnel in all directions and splashing primitive napalm all over everything.

Probably the most disgusting and least humanitarian grenade I could think of, but it was brilliant-and was going to be a major asset. Especially for Teutoberg-clearing, if it came to that. The Bedouin's Tower was going to be difficult to assail with all those trees; if we just burned a path to it, we could march an army through with much less trouble…

I tried to imagine lobbing one of these at the Bedouin, but had to push the thought as far away from my head as possible. I put down the grenade I was holding and walked over to where Mr. O'Malley was fiddling with a giant, wheeled contraption beneath a huge purple and gold velvet drape. My hand was hurting, thinking about shrapnel.

The contraption, it turned out, was called the Arbalest. A giant spool covered in twenty-five rows of twenty-five crossbow-like contraptions was encased in a twelve-foot tall, wheeled, hollowed-out oak rectangle with a long, horizontal slit carved in the front. The spool was turned by gears, powered by a steam engine, lining up twenty-five "crossbows" at a time with the horizontal opening in the wooden armor. When the bolts could safely fly out, they did, with startling speed. The spool would then turn and line up a new row of "crossbows" with the chink in the oak, and fire those. The spool moved *fast*, too. It completed a one twenty-fifth revolution in just under a half of a second, so all in all, it would be firing six hundred and twenty five bolts every ten seconds.

A long "tail" of sorts, like a bridal veil that hung off the back of it and was similarly wheeled, housed a system of gears that propelled conveyor belts carrying bolts, so that the Arbalest could ammo up without stopping its fire. Atop the veil was a silo capable of holding three thousand, one hundred and thirteen projectiles, which were belt fed into the "veil," which were then used to arm the "crossbows" firing through the slit, which never stopped raining a flurry of death into the sky, or straight into an advancing army, or wherever it was pointed until it ran out of bolts.

If you add up the math, that's enough ammunition for just a little less than a full minute of an almost fully automatic hail of sharpened, feathered wooden stakes flying right into whatever it needed to fly into. If you can think of any manner of anti-personnel artillery that would be more destructive and could be fabricated using only medieval technology, you are a smarter man than Mr. O'Malley.

Next were the Bolapults. Not cleverly named (they had been christened by Casimir two years ago, when he was ten) they were nonetheless spectacular for the fact that they were invented by Almira when she was only thirteen. They worked just like miniature catapults, perhaps six feet in length, and in the bowl were dozens of small triggers that flipped up and sent a mess of bolas, which are three iron balls connected by barbed razor wire and which spin as they propel to create a kind of chopping wheel upon impact, in the direction of whatever needed to be utterly decimated.

Another excellent anti-personnel weapon, not as effective as a line of archers but it was *faster* and probably scarier. I know it scared *me* to think of having one of those bolas take off my head.

We walked back by the sephirah, Patrick asked if he could show me some more stunts, Mr. O'Malley vetoed on the premise that it was getting late.

It was, indeed, getting late. I knelt by the sephirah and saw, on the nose of each cylinder, a small etching of the Kabala and around it, three drawings of three jewels.

"What are the jewels? Just design?" I asked Mr. O'Malley.

"Well, no. The Kabala, of course, you recognize. Each of the ten interconnected circles called a sephirah, thus the name of the craft. But the jewels represent the three jewels embedded in the Mace of Turéada."

"I'm afraid I'm unfamiliar with that."

"Turéada was the first Champion that fought for the Ecclesiae. The one that won them the farmhouse. A noble, proud giant. One of the Anakim. Perhaps you know them as Nephilim. The Wanderers."

"Yes, I got that."

"He was a fantastic warrior, the equal of which has never been seen, the mere shadow of which can still be seen in the line of the Repha'im, that is…"

"I got it."

"...only in the Wandering Japanese. The last of the original biblical Wanderers died with Og. Oh, I beg your pardon. You knew him as the Wandering Kenyan."

"I knew his name." I said.

"Is that so? You must have seen the Tooth, then."

"I have."

"The exploits of Turéada, which of course was not his name but a *nom de guerre*, the exploits of Turéada are a long and storied collection. He won the farmhouse for the Ecclesiae shortly after Christ's appearance, defended it against the Bedouin during the Second War..."

"The Bedouin fought against the Ecclesiae?"

"Yes. On the Second Plateau. He rose up on behalf of the teachings of Mohammed, but did not fight long. He was assuaged by diplomacy. Seeing that Islam was complicit with Organized Group Ritual and, indeed, the Ecclesiae's vision of the Connection, he chose instead to combine his forces with them. When he did so, he insured most or all of the Wanderers' alliance with the farmhouse. He is well-respected, you understand."

"Yes, I suppose that he is." I said, and furrowed my eyebrows.

"The Diaspora would follow, and half of the Wanderers would leave, including Turéada."

"What about those Wanderers, Mr. O'Malley? Can we enlist their help somehow? Give them a second chance at taking the farmhouse for our cause?"

"I do not believe that we can find them. They are on Earth, in most cases, or farther up the Mountain. And the ones who defected to fight for Hell in protest of the Ecclesiae's retention of the farmhouse, well...Turéada is among their number, and anything in Hell is unassailable. Were Turéada here, however, I believe that we would have little to do but sit and lounge while he and Father Luke took care of things. The alliance between the two would be unstoppable."

"Where was Father Luke in all of those wars?"

"Fighting alongside the Ecclesiae in the first war. He, Virgil and each of the twins were the Lord Generals, the commanders of the Foederati. Father Luke was the 'wild card.' In the second war he backed the Ecclesiae diplomatically, and it was he who won over the Bedouin. During the War that caused the Diaspora, well, he abstained. As far as I know. I have reason to believe that he supported the errant Wanderers' cause clandestinely."

"What makes you say that?"

"He was given the Tin Jewel of Joyful Noise."

"The what?"

"A small piece of tin painted green that adorned Turéada's mace. The other two jewels in the mace went to Hell with him. The Sacred Garnet of Life Everlasting was once worn around Pan's neck, but was claimed by Turéada's victory over the Old God in the Duel that settled the war. The Faithful Diamond was the mace's pummel, and was the size of your fist. Both are now embedded in the forehead of the statue of Samael that watches over the Hellforge."

"This is all a little much. What's the Hellforge?"

"The place that the shards are forged. Surely you know about the shards?"

"I do."

"It is where the weapons of the men in leather coats are created. A thoroughly evil place. I have only heard rumor of it in conjunction with the K'ung Wu."

K'ung Wu.

"*What did you say*?!" I cried, and startled him quite badly. "What is the K'ung Wu?" I demanded.

"It is the knife that the Shang dynasty…"

"I know that part. Why is it in the Hellforge?"

"It is the only knife that can cut the Divine Brilliance. The only knife that is sharp enough the form the shards."

I was silent for a moment. That was the K'ung Wu? What was it doing rattling around in my skull? I looked at Mr. O'Malley, who was suddenly regarding me very suspiciously.

"Where did you learn to move the way you did at the Threshold of Leviticus?" he asked me darkly.

"I don't know. How do you know about that?"

"Father told me. And what do you know about the K'ung Wu?"

I sighed and told him about the strange voice in my head. He looked, very suddenly, incredibly frightened. I tried to calm him down. "Look, I'm just me. I don't have explanations for things, don't try to explain them, but I'm a good guy, I swear it. Jesus. Have a little trust."

Mr. O'Malley procured a handkerchief and wiped a few beads of perspiration that had been squatting on his upper lip. "Yes. Yes, of course. Does Father Luke know about this voice in your head?"

"I don't remember whether or not I told him. Let me change the subject. Father Luke has the Tin Jewel of Joyful Noise. Is it possible he can still reach Turéada? Enlist him, somehow?"

"He would have, if he could have. Turéada is now fully a servant of the Enemy."

"Oh." I said quietly. "Rough deal."

"It is. And let me return once more to the previous subject. I would not mention to anyone else this strange voice. Folks are suspicious enough about the way you dispatched the demons at the Threshold of Leviticus."

"Why are they suspicious?"

"That is not for me to say."

"Fine. I'll ask Father Luke."

"If he wishes to tell you, he will."

We were silent for a moment and just stood there, eyes locked, searching each other, sizing each other up. *Do we trust each other?* I found myself thinking.

Do we have a choice? I thought I could hear him saying. Linda approached and took my arm. Vinaya came and took his.

"It's late." said Vinaya gently. "Let's take our leave."

"Yes, let's." said Mr. O'Malley, suddenly amicable again. His eyes seemed to plead with me not to let on to his wives what was going on. I put on my best happy face and clapped him on the shoulder. "An excellent night, folks. Thank you so much, Linda. And Vinaya."

Shortly the children and the wives were all around us, and we were ascending the stairs to the den.

I saw myself out. What the hell was that last little bit about? I don't understand anything any better than anyone else. I haven't even been here a full year. Why put me under the hot lights?

I got back to the Abbey late, found Father Luke snoring in his study. When I woke him up and asked him if he wanted to go to bed, he smiled and scratched his mustache, stretched, and passed out, head on desk.

Nope. He'd be sleeping in the study, tonight.

I went upstairs and crashed. An exhausting day. A baffling day. And I had some questions for Father Luke in the morning.

The Mustering of the Watchmen
Chapter 17

Just before lunch the next day, I broke our traditional small talk with the questions I needed answered.

"Father?"

"Son?"

"What, uh, what's the big deal with my...reaction at the Threshold?"

Father Luke was rifling through a cupboard but he suddenly stopped. I could hear him sigh, and then resume rustling.

"Well?" I asked.

"Innate." he said.

"Granted." I said. "No one taught me that. What's it mean?"

"It means that only Abaddon moves that way. Abaddon and Saint Michael."

I looked at him, saw that he was holding back. "Who else?" I asked.

"Saint Gabriel the Steadfast has, historically, displayed a level of skill that is comparable to yours, if slightly inferior."

"Who else?"

Father Luke sighed.

"Lucifer."

"Okay. Archangels."

"Yes. Well, and one other."

"Not an Archangel?"

"Not an Archangel."

"I'll save that for later. So I move like an Archangel. What's that make me?"

"Not a human."

"Untrue."

"How do you know?" he asked me.

"I just do. I *feel* you, Father Luke, like I *felt* Scholastica when she was near me. It's like a sensation behind my eyes. You know..." I trailed off, looking for the words.

"What?"

"You know when it's hot outside, and your pillow is sweltering, and you flip it over and its icy cool on the other side and how great that feels?"

Father Luke smiled.

"It's like that. Whenever I'm around an angel. Abaddon and Saint Michael, too. I'm not that. I'm a human. I can tell. I was around the O'Malleys last night and I could tell. I've been with you and the Ecclesiae, whatever they are…"

"Cherubim."

"Like you?"

"*Oui.*"

"Okay. I've been with you and the Wanderers and no one else since I got here. I was *home* with the O'Malleys. I know it's psychological, I know. What a field day Freud would have with that, huh? 'Man, if exposed to celestial beings, will feel better with fellow men than even with the elevated entities of angels and half-angels.' I could see it right now. I could see Herbert Marcuse writing a sequel to *Eros and Civilization.* He'd probably call it *The Human Animal and the Dominions Glorious* or some such nonsense."

Father Luke smiled again.

I sighed. "But, look. I know because I went there last night. So let's just consider that I look like Saint Michael and like Lucifer and that I'm a human being and that maybe, somewhere, there's a Nephilim that looks like us, too. Like there's a mold, or something."

Father Luke looked surprised. "Interesting." he said. "I hadn't thought of that."

"Well, I have. A lot. In fact, I think I've just been assuming it. Who is the other person that moves like me?"

"Turéada."

"Where is the Tin Jewel?" I asked, and it caught him off guard, because he shot straight up and looked at me incredulously.

"I'll return, shortly." he said. And he did. With the Prajna Khadga.

"What's that for? You want to fight?" I asked.

"No. Look at the underside of the pummel."

There, sure enough, was the Tin Jewel of Joyful Noise.

"That's it?"

"That's it."

"What's Turéada look like?" I asked Father Luke.

"Spanish."

"Can't be. He was around before the Moorish invasion of Spain made

Spaniards look like what they look like. Just like *you're* not really French, though God help me if I know what *you* look like."

"I do not remember that Turéada ever looked different than he does."

"Ahead of his time, perhaps? I think that Turéada made himself look Spanish, by whatever means he was able to. Angel magic or whatever. But I think he *really* looks like me. And I bet he looks like Mike and Lucy, too. There's something going on, there. I'll bet you."

"You can't just guess at something like that."

"I just did."

"Well, I suppose you did. Doesn't make you right."

Rat-tat-tuh-tat tat. Tat-TAT!

"Shave and a Haircut." I said. "The Bedouin."

———

We went to the front door and greeted the Wandering Bedouin, who embraced Father Luke warmly and just smiled sadly at me. We went to the kitchen and sat down at the table.

"Is it finished, then?" asked Father Luke.

"We are almost mustered. We wait only on the Frenchman." said the Bedouin.

"When is he expected?"

"Tonight."

"Is that so?" Father Luke glanced at me. "The O'Malleys will be here tonight. Shall I bring them over?"

"Do so. I will not say I am eager to get the war started…on the contrary, I dread it. But I am praying for a quick end, and looking very much forward to a time of peace, soon." He glanced at me. "One way or another."

One way or another. Either he wins or he dies.

"Hey." I said, softly.

The Bedouin looked at me.

"Father Luke talked you out of it in the Second War. Can he talk you out of it now?"

"I tried." said Father Luke.

"He can't." said the Bedouin.

"Why?"

"I swore an oath." he said flatly. "An oath before the Man."

I lowered my head, stared at my hands, which were folded in my lap. "Okay."

"Tonight?" the Wanderer asked Father Luke.

"Uh...*oui*. As good a time as any."

"For what?" I asked.

"Parley." said the Bedouin. If you have any ideas, any rules of engagement or special and circumstantial laws to be laid out prior to the outbreak of the conflict, bring them before us tonight. Your party and our party shall discuss things, celebrate our last night as friends, and afterward, we shall move into our towers. Provided that parley is concluded in orderly manner and with quickness, the war will begin tomorrow, although probably not until noon. And we will certainly not stoop to begin the violence until everyone is safely in their towers, Foederati assembled. I would be surprised to see a battle before a month is over and both parties have a detailed strategy. Unlike in other places where wars are fought, this conflict will always be a gentleman's war, unto the day that the Mountain is broken."

I nodded. So did Father Luke. The Bedouin stood up. "I will see you all tonight, then?"

"Indeed." said Father Luke.

"There will be great festivities. I planned them myself, with the Ecclesiae's food and your alcohol."

"What's left of it." I said, smiling through the fog of the solemnity of the occasion. The Bedouin and I laughed. Father Luke did not.

"We'll see you tonight." said Father Luke.

"Goodbye." said the Bedouin, and flashed his brilliant grin at us. It was not heartfelt, though. He exited staring at the ground.

When the doors closed behind him, Father Luke excused himself for a moment. When he returned, he had the chessboard and the pieces with him.

"Is there time for this?" I asked.

"*Oui*." he said, and set us up a game. He was white, I was black, and he opened his game not with the advancement of a pawn but of a knight, to the rook's side. "Watch me carefully."

"Okay." I advanced my king's knight's pawn two spaces.

"The mirror of the Heinrichsen's Opening. Seeking a limited occupation of the center before launching a queen's side attack."

"Okay." I said. "Your move."

"King's Knight's Pawn advances slightly. No threat. Called Bacza."

"Okay." I moved my queen's knight's pawn.

"Symmetrical. Interesting that you would choose that. I believe that they, too, will choose it."

"What?"

"Listen. Bishop moves into *fianchetto*. Originally meaning 'engagement' in Italian, from the Latin 'to flank.'"

"Okay." I loosed my knight to a mundane position. It couldn't threaten anything, yet, but it was free.

"You're playing defense."

"Yup." I said.

"Why?"

"Because I'm scared of you."

"Not very good defense. All you've done is extended some rigid symmetry, here. Granted, your knights are free, which is good. But I am directly threatening the main engagement area...here." He pointed to the center of the board.

"What's the point of this?"

"The Bedouin is scared."

"What?"

"He's scared. I don't expect you could have read him. But I smelled it. It clung to him like *shit*."

"I don't understand."

"You fear my prowess because I beat you regularly in chess, *non*?"

"That's right."

"So you extend this half-witted defensive game. Limited knight movement, no offense, pawns extended. You're moving your pawns out quickly."

"*What's* the point again?"

"So will they."

"Bullshit." I said, seeing what he was getting at and not believing. "What are they afraid of?"

"Me. And you. But me, especially. They've fought a Vicissitude. Hell, the Bedouin has *been* a Vicissitude. Never me."

"Okay..."

"Okay, so I'm a Cherubim of the Highest Order, God's own Warrior Angel. I have been called the Angel of Death, and also the Bringer of Plagues. Perhaps you know me by another name, but it changes nothing."

"You're...?" I was stricken speechless.

"Yes." said Father Luke, and his eyes flashed. "The Old Testament doesn't tell the half of it. Now be quiet. I believe that Virgil leans toward us. And there is a rumor that nearly a third of the assembled Wanderers plan to defect."

"Where did you hear that?"

"The Frenchman. He has not arrived, yet, but he will. And he will defect, if he can get enough of them to come with him. Otherwise he will remain in their ranks and work against them clandestinely."

"Sneaky."

"Indeed. I don't like it myself. But it may be our ace-in-the-hole."

"Um, okay. So they're losing Virgil, possibly, and a third of their generals."

"Right. Which makes the odds of us beating the foremost of the giants of old and the Ecclesiae, two full-fledged Warrior Cherubim like myself, just about even."

"Then what's to be afraid of?"

"They've never fought even odds before. Have you?"

I reflected that I had not, indeed, ever fought a war against even odds. Just a loose collection of insurgents. But by God, what damage they were able to do!

To what?

Our morale. Not as much to us. They were dangerous to our newly-trained comrades in the Iraqi National Guard, but they were no Viet Cong, it's true. When I went home we had suffered only one thousand deaths in a full year of fighting, a mere fraction of the fifty-odd thousand deaths my nation suffered in Vietnam. We were only truly in 'Nam for six years.

No, the Iraqi insurgents weren't comparable to my own country's armed forces. I'd never fought in a war where the odds were even.

Father Luke continued on. "So this will be a defensive war unless we threaten the center immediately and attack from the queen's side."

"Mr. O'Malley is the queen's side?"

"In a manner of speaking."

"The inventions?"

"Take out their 'pawns' quickly. Decimate their Foederati. They won't extend their 'knights' until their seemingly unimportant pawns are taking heavy losses. Call it the second lost battle. And they *will* lose the first two engagements, because we will have knights and bishops prowling, waiting for their Foederati to rear their heads."

"Uh...okay. I think I get it. Can we quit with the chess analogy?"

"I will try. Listen. A defensive strategy works only if an enemy is willing to attack, and they will undoubtedly employ no other. So we will take a few battles, and hold back. When their strategy seems to be changing, we'll unveil

Mr. O'Malley's inventions and make a hard push at the Rampart of the Cross."

"In the desert?"

"*Oui.*"

"How many of those contraptions are legal in the war?"

"Not the airships. But the sephirah and the Bolapults and grenades and the Arbalest are all sanctioned. So are many other of his inventions that he has not unveiled, yet."

"I thought that the sephirah used steam engines."

"The *Athenians* could have built a steam engine. They were just so fat and lazy and accustomed to their slaves that the concept of machine labor didn't make sense to them. Steam engines, if conforming to a certain standard of primitiveness, are allowed."

"We should get a hold of Mr. O'Malley."

"He is scheduled to be here for dinner. I did not tell you?"

"Nope. You told the Bedouin."

"I beg your pardon, O obtuse one. He and his wives and two oldest sons. I suppose that we shall dine at the farmhouse tonight. At the parley."

"Uh...okay. Okay. What's all this about the strategy? Why not wait for Mr. O'Malley?"

"Listen. You have a basic understanding of tactics and strategy, *non*?"

"Uh, modern tactics and strategy."

"I need not point out we are not fighting a modern war."

"No, you don't."

"So you will need to learn from me. Tactics are easy enough with graph paper. In discussing strategy I find chess a perfect medium."

"Uh...deal. When will the O'Malleys be here?"

"At dusk."

———

I remember sitting in my bedroom and hearing a great, full sound like a powerful wind outside, and then a great creak, like God's bones needed a little ointment. A cursory look out my window revealed only that it was dusk, and another sound like the releasing of air informed me that something hydraulic was being used somewhere near. I deduced (correctly) that the O'Malleys were now arrived, and that they had brought their airship with them. The hydraulics were part of a ramp lowered from the deck to the ground, so that they could disembark.

Mr. O'Malley wore a red-and-gold kilt, a fancy codpiece, a long knife and a short sword on his belt and a black dress uniform on his torso. Linda and Niwetúkame wore long sleeved, low cut black jumpsuits; Braunwyn had a long black empire dress and her pearls on, plus a bandolier, and Vinaya wore a black military uniform of dubious national origin. It was decorated in black and gold and bore several small stars on it, as did all of their uniforms, and each had a black-pummeled short sword at their hip. William and Patrick wore costumes identical to their father's, *sans* the long knife and with much more austere codpieces.

"Fancy." I said to Mr. O'Malley as he came in.

He grinned fiercely. "Valiant by sea and land."

"And air." I added.

"You've heard about the parley, then?" asked Father Luke.

"Silly question." said Linda.

"The Wandering Japanese came and notified us earlier. Can we postpone dinner?" asked Vinaya.

"Naturally." said Father Luke amicably, and he smiled. Braunwyn seemed twitchy, agitated. So did Patrick. He wore a string of Greek Fire grenades on his belt.

"It's a parley." I said to Patrick, trying to sound reassuring. "Don't be nervous."

Braunwyn shot a look at me, realized I wasn't talking to her, got her shakes under control and went to stand calmly in the Great Hall on Father Luke's tapestry with her co-wives and children, who were congregating over the depiction of the Third Angel of Judgment. Father Luke and I got ready.

I went to my bedroom, discarded my white clothing, attached the Prajna Khadga to a belt and slung it around black dungarees with pockets on the legs and threw on a black ribbed sweater. I went to the bathroom, shaved, brushed and braided my hair (getting quite long, by now) in tight rows and applied some ancient-smelling cologne that Father Luke had procured for me when I moved in here, after the Last Good Day of the Year. I decided, before going downstairs, to wear a black leather holster that Father Luke owned and to pack two of his big Desert Eagles. I strapped the guns around my chest and made my way to the stairs. Best to look fierce, even if there's no fighting going down tonight.

I came downstairs and received a shock. Father Luke had traded his priestly vestments for a sharp black uniform with gold stars all around the collar, and had fully extended, bright, glowing, beautiful white angel wings protruding from his shoulders. There were a few flecks of blood on the lowest feathers, but other than that they were as brilliantly pristine as freshly fallen snow.

"Pretentious, aren't they?" he asked, and he had a pained expression on his face.

"Did it hurt?" I asked.

"*Oui*." he replied.

"Let's go." said Braunwyn, and she led the way outside.

There, in the Abbey courtyard, was the magnificent *Autumnal*. On all sides of it stood ten thousand children, fully armored and armed to the teeth, the mass of which spilled out of the courtyard and into a great sea of rank and file surrounding the Abbey.

The red sails of the *Autumnal* rippled gently in the evening breeze, the breeze that whispered the rumor of war. I looked up and saw that the Tower of Babel, at last, was complete.

"Are they coming with us?" I asked Linda, who was closest to me.

"Yes. All of the Foederati will be there."

"Jesus." I whispered. "Seventy thousand kids?"

"They're not kids." said Linda.

"Well, at least we'll arrive in style." I said to Mr. O'Malley. He smiled mirthlessly.

What an exhilarating experience it is, a ride on an airship. The rotors turn soundlessly and the craft glides through the air with the ease of a paper airplane. I stood at the fo'cs'le and let the rushing night let her black hair down over me, watched the stars twinkle and shine on in their crazy old way, relished the last night of peace in the partition.

We flew over the great silver collection of Foederati already present, spread in six squares around the farmhouse, ten thousand strong each, and every twelve thousand square feet of child warriors made black by the twilight. It was simultaneously breathtaking and terrorizing. The war really was ready. The Towers were all finished, the Foederati were rallied. The parley was about to begin.

We landed in back of the farmhouse, between two of the massive armies, and saw assembled just near our landing site an audience of Wanderers. Foremost among them was the Wandering Japanese, behind him was the Wandering Frenchman, the Wandering Scot, the Wandering Jew, the Wandering Briton, the Wandering Maori and more, perhaps fifteen in total number, standing in a loose semi-circle around a large, crude wooden cross thrust into the soil of the Ager Epiphania. The Wandering Scot was holding a torch.

When the hydraulic ramp was safely extended, I proceeded off of the airship, before anyone else, and went and stood before the Wanderers alone. Vinaya was next to disembark; a hand held up by the Wandering Japanese stopped the descent of all the passengers on the ship.

"Good evening." I said.

"It is not." said the Wandering Japanese. "My heart is heavy this day." He looked from side to side at the great armies with morose eyes.

I stood silently, waited for the massive Oriental to speak. I searched his eyes, the eyes of his fellows, trying to glean some understanding of what was going on. Nothing seemed violent, nothing particularly confrontational.

Were they here to defect, as the rumor held?

At length the Wandering Scot approached me and handed me the torch. I took it warily with my shaker, traded it into my steady hand.

"This land, this Mountain…" he said in a thick, highland rasp, "has been under siege for well nigh two thousand years. Under siege by Hell, and under siege by the Connection."

My eyebrows furrowed a bit. It was true.

"Raise a summons. A summons to the clan, and to all kindred clans. Rally us to the cross for war."

What did he want me to do? Burn the cross? He looked at the torch, and then the cross.

That *was* what he wanted me to do. Isn't this what the Ku Klux Klan did? Hasn't the burning cross been the symbol of something horrible for years and years?

But isn't it older than America? Older than Scotland as a nation? This was a highland symbol. My eyes flicked back and forth across the many colors of the faces and bejeweled necks of the Nephilim standing before me. They watched back solemnly, expectantly.

According to Scottish ancient law, the cross could only be burned by the chief of the clan. Shouldn't Mr. O'Malley be doing this?

No.

Whether I was "Champion" by rules or not, I was Champion de facto, and it was going to be that way whether I delegated it or not. I was the Vicissitude. I was the chief of my clan.

I stooped slightly, thrust the torch into the middle of the cross, knowing that in doing so I committed myself and my kin to defend the Mountain unto death. The Wandering Scot had tears in his eyes.

The throng of giants knelt before me once, stood up. This was my clan and kindred clan. They had, indeed, defected. The Wandering Scot approached again and I gave him the torch, and then the semi-circle broke so that the cross could be seen from the farmhouse. Slowly, bewilderedly, Wanderers started filing out of the house to get a closer look, to discern the meaning of the flaming symbol not four hundred yards from their house. They gathered in the back yard, perhaps one hundred of them, and started making their way in an amoebic mass towards us. Father Luke and the O'Malleys disembarked and came and stood with us, and then Mr. O'Malley, Father Luke, the Wandering Japanese, Frenchman, Scot and myself stepped out in front. The Bedouin, at the head of his own gaggle of Wanderers, approached.

"Is it so?" he asked the Wandering Frenchman.

"*Oui.*"

"Then it is so." He dropped his eyes for a moment, sighed heavily. "Come inside. We are ready to parley."

———

The living room had been cleared of furniture, and a wooden table had been placed smack dab middle in the floor, set for twenty-six, with plates and silverware and wine glasses of the finest crystal. There were ashtrays in various positions, but as I had only ever known myself (and Father Luke, rarely) to smoke, I didn't see the point.

On each side of the table was twelve seats, with room for one at the head of each. We walked in, heads held high, and if the defected Wanderers did not make eye contact with their brothers as they entered I pretended not to notice. I went in confidently, stood behind the chair at the end of the table, waited for the procession to file around me. Mr. O'Malley hesitated as he passed the seat at the end of the table, continued on to sit at my right hand. Next to him were his wives, then his sons, then Father Luke, then the Japanese, Scot, Frenchman and Maori. The rest of our Wanderers stood patiently behind chairs, as space was limited in the room, which was not used to comfortably accommodating more than perhaps twenty.

It *was* a large living room. But there were nearly one hundred Wanderers plus Virgil, the Ecclesiae and an incredibly lithe man in regal red robes, with a grand crown and a priceless scepter in his hand, on the other side of the table. So the windows were thrown open, most of the Farmhouse-allied Wanderers were sent outside to the covered porch, and the table and standing room behind chairs was then filled. At the head, opposite from me, sat Virgil. *Diplomatic of them,* I thought. Give the devil's advocate their seat at the head of the table and win points from the get-go. I should have thought of it first.

Outside, the Foederati made not a sound.

At Virgil's right sat the Ecclesiae, then the Bedouin, then the Bony Prince of Nowhere (the man with the scepter) and then the Wandering American, the Wandering Ottoman, the Wandering Mongol, the Wandering Venezuelan, the Wandering Aztec, the Wandering Eskimo, the Wandering Samaritan and the Wandering Tutsi.

Father Luke passed a small piece of paper to me. *Two across from me: Knights.*

I looked over at the Venezuelan and the Mongol. They were furious, I could see, probably about the betrayal. Controlling it, but just barely.

Really? I wrote with a pen that Mr. O'Malley loaned me. When it got back to Father Luke, he nodded conspiratorially at me.

I motioned for the Wandering Briton to approach me, and he did, kneeling at my chair so that I could whisper to him. He walked around the table, knelt near Twin One and whispered to him, then disappeared into the kitchen. Twin One clapped and the Wandering Dutchman appeared from outside and followed the Briton into the kitchen.

We sat in silence, many of us sizing each other, many of us staring at the table, or at the wall. It was uncomfortable, to say the least. Here I was in the home of men whom had clothed and fed me, taken me in from my mundane life, freed me from the tyranny of my dull mind. On my left sat friends, the Wandering American and his cohorts, and a good friend, the Bedouin. And here I was leading a coalition of war against them. No one broke the silence until the Wandering Dutchman appeared with a cart and set fourteen bottles of Chateau Lafite, vintage 1787, on the table. The Briton laid a tub of warm water at my feet and also a white cloth. While the wine was being poured I waited silently, and then picked up the basin and walked over to Virgil. He knew what I was doing, and removed his shoes, and I cursorily washed his feet, dried my hands, then proceeded to Twin One and did the same for him. I progressed to every one of the guests at the table, washing their feet symbolically, and then moved outside and did the same for every single one of the Wanderers standing out in the night air.

The Foederati were silent.

When I returned, I set down the container of water and resumed my seat at the head of the table. The Bedouin rose, silently, and approached me. He took the basin and then washed my feet, as I had done for him. When he was through, he sat down and expelled a sigh, and then I broke the silence.

"I have been treated with nothing but kindness since I came here. Obfuscation, at time, obstacles at others, obtuseness at others, but all in the name of kindness." I cleared my throat, went on. "This...title and this war have been thrust upon me, and I do not relish them. I hope that every one at this table can take my meaning when I say that though I have enemies here, I have, indeed, no enemies here."

Silence again. Twin Two looked at me sadly. I realized, right then, that I didn't hate the Ecclesiae for the existence of the Basement, or the oppression of so many souls, or the myriad atrocities of the religions they represented. I understood the folly in their decisions, and understood also that I had no great solutions for their problems, myself. I realized then that I still loved them very much.

"Parley." I said. "This will be a short war, *Inshallah*, and if possible, as humane as possible. I hope you will all forgive that word, *humane*. I know no words in the English language that represent a similar sentiment pertaining to Wanderers and angels. *Nephilime* sounded silly, and anyway, I thought you'd all take my meaning."

Chuckles rippled softly through the Wanderers. I continued. "I regret also, that my Latin is imperfect as yet, and that we must hold the parley, in as much as is possible, in English, for my benefit. Maybe someday there will be such thing as a bilingual American; for the time being the concept is perhaps as mythological a character as the Wandering Jew."

More laughter, a bit more pronounced, a bit louder. The Wandering Jew waved, and so did the Wandering American, who apparently spoke no Latin, either.

"I propose, though I'm sure it is hardly necessary, that the concords laid down at the Geneva and Hague Conventions be immediately put in place."

Everyone present but William and Patrick started rapping the face of their palms on the tabletop, apparently expressing their agreement. Mr. O'Malley's sons caught on quickly, and were soon rapping, themselves. I doubt that they had ever heard of the Conventions, but it sounded good to them.

"I propose also that the articles contained in the 1968 United Nations Convention on the Non-Applicability of Statutory Limitations to War Crimes and Crimes Against Humanity be set, with the Geneva and Hague provisions, immediately to paper and signed by all present. I accuse none of intent or capability of war crimes here, of course. But medieval war was a brutal pastime. Nowadays, when you are shot lethally, you are dead. It does not take hours, weeks or days to die. Those who are able to healed are, those who are able to recover do indeed recover. War is no less horrible now, but its collateral damage has become easier to contain. We willingly enter into a war that is alien to some of us and familiar to many, but none here can contest that a medieval war is bloodier, more painful and less *humane* than today's somewhat more civilized conflicts."

"I second." said the Bedouin, and the table rapping commenced. The Ecclesiae gestured for the Wandering Dutchman again, seemed to communicate wordlessly with him and then sent him away.

Then Virgil took the floor. "This has been forced upon all of us, excluding myself, who willingly participates, in the name of either preservation or upheaval, whichever I deem necessary for the Connection. This *is* quite the responsibility. I am aware of this. The very future of spirituality could rest in my hands. Father Luke, of course, knows, as he has sat in this chair himself."

"Long ago." murmured Father Luke.

"But it should be known to all present that I am not alone in my decision making process, nor am I responsible to no one. Loth as I am to allow interference from other Plateaus in the goings-on of this, the First of the Glorious Plateaus, I remind us all that we are all beholden in one way or another to the Seventh Plateau, the Summit, and that the Governor of which has already interfered. It seems unlikely that He will elect to do so a second time, but I reiterate: If He chooses to, He will interfere through me. My decisions are my own until they are no my own no longer. Therefore, I will abstain for the larger part of the conflict until it becomes certain to me that the Will of God is that the fate of the war be indeed in my hands."

Thud, thud, thud, thud, thud. All were in agreement. Then again, we'd have agreed if Virgil was proposing a night of the long knives. This parley was as much a contest for Virgil's favor as a real convention.

Outside, not a Foederati was stirring.

I spoke up. "I propose, also, that overt strategic aggression in the form of sieges and capture of towers in particular be discouraged for the first fortnight. The parley came upon me fast, and I am led to believe that at the end of this meeting we will formally declare war. If it must be so, then it is. But I was unprepared, and I expect that Mr. O'Malley and the Ecclesiae (who have clearly not finished preparations, or else we would not be meeting here in the farmhouse) share similar inclinations."

Some thudded, some did not. Among those who did not were the Venezuelan and Father Luke, and Vinaya. Vinaya stood up.

"May I speak?" she asked me.

I nodded and sat down.

"I say that if we declare war, then war should be declared. We are civil, we are gentlemen and gentlewomen and are thus fair and decent beings, but to propose some extension of major combat operations until we are ready for the war…why declare war at all? Why not delay for some weeks until we are all prepared?" She sat back down.

The Bedouin and the Ecclesiae conferred for a moment, and then the Bedouin stood up. "We are in accordance with the Vicissitude in this matter. War must be declared, the war must begin, and soon, if we are to have a victor in any reasonable amount of time. Thus, we propose that Virgil settle it…"

"I agree." I interjected just before the Bedouin finished speaking. Virgil acknowledged me with a kindly nod before speaking. "War, in our hands, is capable of shaking off its most negative connotations and be stripped down to its barest evil. There are few opportunists in this room, and none among them would capitalize on an embargo on major combat operations. Reconnaissance, intelligence gathering and a minor skirmish are all that we can expect from a fortnight's moratorium. I am in concordance with the young Vicissitude in this matter."

Rapping on the table from everyone, if a little reluctant from some members and virtually absent but for a single rap from the Wandering Venezuelan. I think I threw a wrench in a plan of his.

Then again, I may also have screwed some of Father Luke's ideas. A good tradeoff? I thought so. Better that we rethink our own strategy and be saved from blitzkrieg that we are unable to defend ourselves from than gain a premature upper hand that may or may not affect the outcome of the war. Operations in the first semester of a war have never, it seemed to me, been as important as operations in the last.

"Are there any more items of business?" asked Virgil. No one spoke.

"Then war shall be declared at noon tomorrow. We will sign the Declaration upon the return of the Dutchman."

Not long after, the Dutchman did indeed return, with pieces of paper glued to a large posterboard that looked like they were ripped out of encyclopedias. Beneath the pieces of paper was a divider and on either side, thirteen hand-drawn lines for signatures.

"This will serve as a Convention and a Declaration." said the Bedouin. "And I would be honored to have the Vicissitude lay his signature first to the document."

"I thank you, sir." I replied. "But I respectfully decline. I would see Virgil sign first, and then I would be glad to do so."

The posterboard was placed in front of Virgil by the Dutchman, and he chopped it on the right side of the document, at the bottom. The Wandering Japanese then (quickly) picked it up and placed it in front of me. On the line right above Virgil's signature, I scrawled my own childlike autograph and felt as I did it a sudden pain, as if I was signing a will, in a way. There was an air of the awareness of mortality to the strokes of my pen.

It was passed around, then, and when it was finished it was push-pinned above the fireplace. Father Luke was looking at me slyly; he recognized my little tactic to ensure that Virgil's name was on the same side as ours as soon as I has implemented it.

I looked at the Bedouin, who had a single dark eyebrow cocked over one of his eyes and was smiling begrudgingly at me.

He saw it, too. Thirteen names on our side, twelve on theirs. It made the symbolism nice and clear.

The document had been signed. War had been declared. And from outside came a loud *clang*! When every Foederati, all seventy thousand of them, had beat their weapons against their shields once, simultaneously. It was a portentous clang, an ominous clang. And it broke my heart.

The wine was consumed, the tables removed, the furniture was replaced and chairs were situated outside. Liquor was made available, food was produced.

All of the veranda lights were thrown on and when there was room for all, the party began. Tonight, we would love life, love serenity, love each other, and leave the war for another day.

Tomorrow.

A Perfect Farewell to Peace
Chapter 18

There were, naturally, great waterfalls of fascinating dialogue and discourse that swapped like spit between the many mouths present that night. I could recount only the ones I was involved in or privy to, and introduce you thus to a puddle amidst a sea, or not. I could also simply illustrate only my conversation with Abaddon, who arrived with Saint Michael, Saint Scholastica and Saint Gabriel the Steadfast (who, like Abaddon, was black, and wore the most incredibly ornate set of silver armor I have ever dreamed possible) as this conversation was the only intellectual intercourse of the evening with any relevance to the advancement of the plot. Seeing as to how I've historically cared *so* much about not bogging you down with philosophical horseshit thus far (a joke, don't lynch me), I will try to remain focused in this chapter. The pacing is getting a little slow, it's true, what with the last few chapters having seen little to no action at all, but I promise at least one more action beat before the end of Volume I. Promise.

You see, I contemplated including as much conversation as I could to give you a clearer picture of the mental acumen of these giants, these Nephilim. Incredible stuff, would blow your little human mind to infinity and beyond if you let them. Unfortunately, I'm bound to tell a story.

Abaddon and the other angels arrived for this celebration of peace, this final celebration, to be with their friends in both camps and say final goodbyes to everyone, since it was impossible to forecast who would survive the war. They laughed and sang and danced and talked, just like all of us, except that like Father Luke they, too, wore their wings tonight. Scholastica, clearly not used to the formality of the feathered protrusions on her back, spilled several drinks and broke one vase by not minding them when turning corners or failing to retract them on trips to the kitchen, of which she made several. That was where drinks got refilled.

Our conversation, Abaddon's and mine, may have been considered a mere trickle in the shadow of the great cerebral Nile gushing forth that evening, but I encourage those six readers who have enjoyed the philosophy in this book so far to remember that I promised nothing. I encourage them also to think of

my poor acquisitions editor, who has already had to wade through mountains
of this pretentious, existential bullshit with a machete in one hand and a saw
in the other, hacking and slashing more than any horror movie had the
stomach for.

Pity my editor.

Here goes:

Abaddon came and sat by me, where I was listening in on one of the
Bedouin's conversations and contending with a slightly drunk Saint
Scholastica constantly wriggling on to my lap. I was trying to tag along with
my friend and spend as much time as much as possible with him before we
would become enemies, at noon the next day, but Scholastica seemed intent
on distracting both of us so much that we had winked and promised to meet
up later.

The most celebrated of Thrones plopped down on the couch next to me,
forcing a creak so loud you'd have though the Mountain was picking up its
roots and moving to Kansas, where there's always plenty of employment
opportunities for mountains. He ruffled my hair, smiled a lot, accepted four
drinks in less than fifteen minutes, proposed two toasts and then turned his
attention specifically to me. He leaned in close.

"You want to join me outside?"

"Uh…sure. Scholastica?"

"What?"

"I'll be right back."

"Bathroom again?"

"Uh, no. Boy talk."

"Okay." she said cheerfully, and hopped up and went over to molest
Father Luke.

I followed Abaddon outside and all the way to the *Autumnal*, where he
took me in his arms and flew us up to the deck. He set my slightly disoriented
carcass down and found a heap of rope to sit on, then began:

"Listen, son. Listen good. I know what you think about the men in leather
coats. The fallen angels. I know the misconceptions you have about them…"

"Misconceptions?"

"Quiet for a minute. Let me finish."

"Okay."

"They have a tactic they use that puts fear and evil images into people's
head. You've experienced it? Of course you have, you fought Moloch. Look,
it's just a minor bit of terrorism. All angels can and *do* use that tactic.

Everything you think you know about them is wrong."

"What?"

"They're not really evil, at all. That trick is the oldest in the book. I *still* use it, from time to time."

"Are you serious?"

"Yeah, listen to me. They used to work with God, then after the Big Idea and the Big Revolt they didn't. For a while. Then they were working with Him again, on and off, like thrones. The Man can't stay angry at anyone long enough not to be friendly, if they're sincere." Abaddon started playing with a little frayed bit of rope, twirling it in his massive fingers. "Look, I spoke to Lucifer."

"Uh...okay." I said, trying to be open-minded.

"And he wanted me to tell you that even though he doesn't give a shit what goes on around the Mountain anymore, he's rooting for you."

"Abaddon?"

"Yeah."

"The devil is rooting for me?"

"Sure. He hated the whole idea of organized religion to begin with. *Hated* it. Thought the Connection was much better served by Individual Worship and Personal Salvation. That's one of the major reasons he stopped working with the Man completely."

"Really?" I asked. That was a total flouting of all preconceptions I had about the Devil.

"Yeah. He cares about people. He *loves* people, even. That's why, when he left Hell, he didn't just take a cozy shack on the Fifth and exist there. He went to earth to play piano in seedy bars, where he could sit and be around humans all the time. The next best thing to Heaven is Earth, kid. I know you don't believe that; you're from Earth. But the Mountain's got nothing on Earth."

"Really?" I asked again, scratching my head.

"Yeah."

"Wow. Uh, as a matter of curiosity..."

"Who's watching the Abyss?" He finished the question for me.

"Yeah."

"No one." he answered. "Most of Hell is occupied on Earth right now, as I understand it, and the chances of them getting through the Abyss before I get back are so slight it's not even worth preparing for."

"How do you know it's not some kind of ruse?"

"I trust my own judgment. I've been guarding the passage to the Mountain a long time."

"You don't guard the passage to Earth?"

"Nope. Not my problem. I do my part by protecting the Mountain."

"So if you're…friends with these demons, how do you fight them and maintain a healthy, positive relationship?"

"It's all professional. I kick their ass and then, after work, go to their place for beers. We have an understanding, you get my drift? Things are different between angels, kid. Remember that."

"Uh, okay. So the devil's rooting for me and the demons are not bad guys."

"Correct. But they are antagonists. And there's more. You need to guard the Connection."

"Well, of course…"

"No, not of course. You don't believe in it. I see that. Look, it's better than direct governance, which means humans either having no part of the Boss or not having Free Will. I guarantee that the Connection is a more attractive option. Much, much better. So you need to guard it."

"Against Hell?"

"Yes. Be extra vigilant. They're plotting something so major, an invasion so big I'm not sure even I'll be able to stop it when it comes. And that's major shit, you know? *Me* not being able to stop it."

"When is this happening?"

"I dunno. Some time during the war. A while from now. Certainly not anytime soon."

"Fantastic. How am I supposed to commit resources to watching the phone lines?"

"Not the phone lines. The Endless Stair, the one you took to the Threshold."

"Oh…yeah. Okay. I can do that."

"We did blow it up. But they're crafty. I'll contact you when they start coming."

"Okay, Abaddon. Thanks."

"No prob. Let's get back. I'm getting thirsty."

"Uh, wait…" I said.

"Yeah?"

"Turéada."

"What about him?" asked Abaddon. One of his giant eyebrows was raised far above its natural resting place.

317

"Where is he?" I asked.

"Gone."

"I need him."

"I can't help you."

"Why?"

"Because he's gone." said Abaddon, with finality. "Besides, only Lucifer could help you with Turéada. That old fool does nothing without being absolutely convinced that it's in Hell's best interests. And Hell's best interests, to him, are Lucifer's."

"But the Devil endorsed me!"

"Wouldn't be good enough. If you meet Lucifer and can convince him to loan you Turéada, well…that'd be the only way. Anything else?"

"Uh, no. Just thirsty, myself." I kept the rest of my thoughts private. Maybe I'd already said too much. I didn't know his loyalties.

We returned and Scholastica was on my arm immediately and before long I was caught up with everyone else. I was drunk, myself.

We partied and laughed and danced and sang. At one point, the Bedouin stood up and gave a small speech, praising me and my "clan," detailing the accomplishments and exploits and titles earned by every one of my generals, including the O'Malleys. He had an intimate knowledge of their history; I expect that he had been friends with them before tonight.

I got cheered by everyone in the room when the Bedouin mentioned my victory over Moloch. In fact, Virgil and Saint Michael hoisted me up on their shoulders and they had all sang 'For He's a Jolly Good Fellow.'

It was wonderful.

I tried to give a fitting reprisal, to praise the other side as well, but I didn't know enough about all of them. Father Luke managed to take over for me with a tiny bit of grace, all he could muster, and delivered a rousing, convincing speech that almost had me rooting for their side, before I remembered that I was Lord General of the opposition. Father Luke then set aside a special segment for kissing Virgil's ass, and when he was done, he and I ran over and hoisted up Virgil on our shoulders, and the progressively drunker and drunker crowd sang a slightly different tune. 'Fur He's a Jelly Gud Fella.' Yeah, we were all slurring a little by that time.

A little later I had been approached by the skinny man in the red robes and we had gotten acquainted, seeing as to how we would be neighbors for some time. My tower, the *Shirivasta*, was right next to the Coenobitic Monastery, which was his domain. He was, of course, the Bony Prince of Nowhere.

Actually, he was the Lord of the Ecumenics, a King Monk, so to speak. Only he was no monk. The Ecumenics just took orders from him.

He was hilarious, an incredibly funny man, whimsical and assertive if effete, and I got the distinct impression that this Bony Prince seemed exactly the way I would imagine Oscar Wilde. He even looked a little like the old playwright. The Bony Prince and I had gotten ourselves into a 'shotgun' contest involving six ounces of brandy lined up in small one ounce shooter glasses in front of us that we would race to see who could finish first. I won, but only by a fraction of a second. He kept up admirably.

Did I mention that the whole farmhouse was alive with joy and celebration? That we partied and laughed and danced and sang like we'd never before? What a great night. A perfect farewell to peace.

As all good things must come to an end, four a.m. did eventually roll around.

I settled down on the floor with Scholastica, but it promised to be a sexless night, as she had passed out almost fifteen minutes prior and, anyway, we were in the living room surrounded by fifteen or more Wanderers camping near us.

The Bedouin came and made his bed on the floor next to us, and the three of us eventually fell asleep to the harmonious snorings of the myriad drunk giants we were surrounded by.

I dreamed of nothing.

—

I woke an hour later, at five a.m., to a slight tug on my sleeve. Startled momentarily, I calmed down when I found myself staring into the darkly lit face of Twin One (or Two, I couldn't tell.) I noticed that my other sleeve was being drooled on by an angel.

I disentangled myself from Scholastica and the Bedouin (whose arm had been resting protectively on my chest) and stood up. The Twin beckoned to me, and I followed. All the way upstairs, all the way to my old bedroom, where no one was sleeping. We walked in and there was his brother. He was standing over a few boxes of my possessions, the last items I had left there and had not moved out. I suddenly became very sad.

"Yeah, I guess I left these here, huh? I won't forget it, in the morning." I whispered.

They looked at each other, then me, then nodded.

319

"Hey, uh…I know I behaved pretty poorly the day I found out about…"

An upheld hand interrupted me, as if to say, "Don't apologize."

I did anyway. "Look, I'm sorry. About the war, and the changes, and the 'reprioritization' or whatever. I'm really, really sorry. I have nothing against the Church, never have. I love you guys, and I love your people, and your religions. I don't always agree, but I have nothing but love and respect for what you guys have done, and… well…"

They looked at me expectantly.

"Well, you guys should know that I love you."

They looked at each other, smiled, then embraced me, both of them.

"We love you, too." they said, in perfect, accentless English and in perfect, harmonious synchronization.

Shades of Mosul
Chapter 19

We woke in intervals, the Wanderers and others who were now at war with each other. We woke and stretched and yawned and our stomachs grumbled and none of us made any moves to strangle each other. Quite the contrary, in fact. We were all quite pleasant, given our respective post-alcohol conditions.

I walked out on the porch to have a thought and a smoke, to think about the coming war, to think about the preparations I had to make in the next two weeks. To think about my move up to the Shirivasta, and how lonely that was going to be, with only these Foederati, whom I did not even know how to communicate with.

It was a beautiful afternoon, the sun was high in the sky and shining and warm. Its rays reached down and kissed the Ager Epiphania, the gold and green tendrils of which were rustling in an early summer breeze. I saw the Mountain, leading up to where it led, I saw the rest of the sky, blue and beautiful, I looked out on the fields of the farmhouse. It was a beautiful afternoon, and as good a day to start a war as any other.

I had no sooner produced a cigarette from a pack in my pocket when the Wandering Japanese was outside with me, hand on his *odachi*, fully armored and eyes keen and alert.

"Is there really anything to worry about *here*?" I asked him.

"It is not my brothers I do not trust." he said. "There is a foul smell in the air."

"Uh, yeah. That's tobacco smoke, you know. Some people don't mind, others can't stand…"

"That is not what I am saying."

I watched him for a moment, then cocked my head to the side. "Did you sleep in your armor?" I asked him.

He nodded, scanned the collected Foederati, who had been standing outside all night, and then settled his eyes on the Wandering Turk, who was slowly making his way to the porch from the front yard. He looked a little edgy, and immediately a warning bell went off in my mind. Something was

321

saying *wrong, wrong, wrong.* The edginess of the Wandering Japanese bleeding on my senses? Or something older?

Something from...Iraq?

Something didn't smell right. Something definitely smelled like Iraq.

As I was still wearing my holsters, I unsnapped them and got my hands ready to draw.

"Good morning!" I cried, and the Wandering Turk looked up at me. He was dressed like the Wandering Turk always dressed, in his caftan, with his *boerk* tilted at a crisp angle over his forehead. He smiled at me, walked up the porch steps, spoke a few words to the Wandering Japanese privately and made like he was about to go inside.

That's when I noticed he wasn't wearing a necklace.

"Hey." I said, and touched his elbow.

He looked at me coolly, then looked at the Wandering Japanese, who was stroking the jewelry he wore around his own neck. Then he knew. And so did we.

This was not the Wandering Turk.

I grabbed his arms and held them high, put my knee forcefully into his crotch, then butted the bridge of his nose with my head. In a flash the tip of the Japanese's *odachi* was just centimeters from my stomach. The pummel was on the other side of the impostor, and the blade that had impaled him had black blood on it.

I pulled the now-lifeless body off of the sword and ripped open his garments, found several black legions and a very professional explosive device strapped to his chest.

Beneath his caftan the man wore a black leather coat.

Immediately the Wandering Japanese was inside and shouting in his native tongue, and immediately the Ecclesiae were outside, rifles in hand, joined by Father Luke with a shotgun and nearly ten other Wanderers brandishing various melee weapons: swords, spears, staves, halberds and axes were all accounted for.

Virgil appeared and swept up the body of the impostor Wandering Turk, and after he had dragged it inside, the real Wandering Turk emerged from the house with a shoulder mounted rocket-propelled grenade launcher.

Fucking Basement and it's fucking over-the-top weapons.

Close behind were the Archangels, Michael and Gabriel and Scholastica and Abaddon. They came out on the porch, all of them wingless but Gabriel and Abaddon, and stood surveying with us.

Our eyes nervously scanned the two great armies standing in front of the farmhouse, one army in blue standard, which were *my* Foederati, and the other in brown and khaki colors, which were the Bedouin's. They looked on guard, their weapons held ready, their own eyes searching and searching.

Abruptly, the Wandering Bedouin crashed out of the house with his staff and made a run for his army. "Seize him!" he was crying to his army. "Grab his arms!" I broke out in a dash, pursuing my friend, and the twins and Abaddon and Father Luke and several Wanderers followed, including the Wandering Japanese, who had never left my side. I saw a small being, dressed like all of the Wandering Bedouin's troops, struggling against a mess of soldiers in the fourteenth row of the ranks.

They did not stop him. They could not grab his arms.

The first explosion, however, did not come from the Foederati doppelgänger. It came from the farmhouse. The back of it.

A suicide bomber blew the entire back wall of the great grey and white house into pieces, and the blast shook the very foundations of this most important of structures, causing all of the windows to shatter and the living room to collapse on itself and bury several Wanderers. Then another explosion rocked our senses. The explosion from within the Bedouin's army.

The Wandering Japanese grabbed me and threw me to the ground as the shock wave rolled over us. It was massive, the equivalent of a brick of C4. With all of the bodies of the Bedouin's Foederati packed so tightly together, it must have killed hundreds. Maybe even a thousand.

And the Bedouin caught a piece of flying shrapnel, launched from the various armors wore by his troops, in his right eye. He spun, clutching his face, and fell to his knees. He roared, a roar the likes of I have no hope of describing, and writhed in agony, holding his wounded eye. The Ecclesiae ran to his side, tried to roll him on his back, but he resisted. He would not have them touch him. He fought them off, scrambled to his feet, and when he removed his hands his countenance was not the gentle, kind mien of the Wandering Bedouin that I knew. He was the most frightening thing I had ever seen.

Blood oozed out of his eye and into his mouth, open and curled over gritted teeth. His left eye was wild, wide open, insane. It scanned the porch, scanned me, scanned everyone, in three hundred and sixty degrees around him.

It settled on the Wandering Maori.

The Wandering Bedouin pulled the shrapnel with great effort out of his eye socket and with it came his eyeball. This he bit, right off the end of the shard of Foederati helmet that had punctured it, and swallowed. Roaring that inimitable roar again, he raised his staff up like a javelin, threw it in a high arch toward the farmhouse, and just as our heads turned to see that the projectile's final destination was undoubtedly to be about six inches deep in the Wandering Maori's chest, the Maori ripped open his shirt and revealed his chest, his bandolier of explosives, his necklace-less neck. He cried "Vengeance!" and detonated his device, incinerating the porch and all the Wanderers. The Archangels, who were of a constitution too resilient to be blown apart, were nonetheless propelled at incredible speeds out and away in every direction.

The Wandering Japanese, again protecting me, had flung his body over mine. I soon became aware of Father Luke near me, on the ground. He was growling and snarling, filled with a wrath not unlike the Bedouin's.

I felt it too. Poured into me was a red light that possessed my entire body. I started foaming and fomenting, snarling and shivering. I cast the Wandering Japanese off of me and got to my feet. The air was filling with a static, a rising tide of a voluminous, collective growl. It was a sound I'd never heard before, and a sound I would never hear again, but I knew it as the sound of a rage; I looked around and saw that every Wanderer and being around me was starting to retch and roar and grind his teeth. It was madness, pure chaos. It filled the air like a swarm of wrathful locusts and descended destructively on the composures of those collected in the shadows of the great army of children.

Another *boom*! and our boiling fury came to head, exploded in tandem with the sound of the latest blast. The Wanderers scattered and screamed. The frenzy was immense. Were one not in possession of his wits, he might have thought it was the Wanderers and I that caused that explosion. Were one to use just a little imagination, he could easily believe that our rage had caused it.

But that boom was *not* an externalization of the ire in the Wanderer's hearts. It was not a manifestation of the hatred, the black hatred that filled us up. It was not connected, indeed, to our anger at all.

It was a phone tower. A phone tower now in smoking, charred pieces.

And that's all it took, just one link removed in the Connection to fuck the whole thing up. The Connection was severed. The men in leather coats had achieved their goal.

Another boom, this time muffled. Where was that? Another phone line?

The *Autumnal*?

The human institution of religion was on its own, now. No more influence from the Mountain. No more nothing. From here it was God as governor or nothing at all.

And if I knew anything about the Man in the Yellow Polo Shirt, it was nothing at all.

I rose to my feet and ran, ran to the other side of the house to get sight of the *Autumnal*. I was still steaming and brewing and foaming at the mouth, and though I could see very little through the red zigzags in my vision, I was able to make out four figures tussling just outside the giant airship.

It was Mr. O'Malley and a Wanderer and they were fighting two men in black leather coats. There was also a great, gaping, smoking hole in the side of the *Autumnal*.

Whoosh! Air rushed by my ears and suddenly there was no sound. Time slowed, everything slowed, everything was infinitely slow but me. I was moving. *Moving.* I ran at the airship as men in leather coats began to emerge from all sides of the farmhouse, all brandishing sub-machine guns and all beginning to fire into the Wanderers and into the Foederati. I ran and ran, ran as fast as I could, and just as the flow of time came roaring and crashing down around me I finally reached Mr. O'Malley and the Wandering Dutch, who were battling with swords two men in leather coats. A moment later I saw that Abaddon, too, was by my side, and just as the Wandering Dutch lost his leg to a well-placed hack, Abaddon had destroyed utterly Mr. O'Malley's opponent and was turning toward the other. I jumped with all of my collected velocity in the direction of the man in the leather coat who had just administered the Dutch Nephilim's amputation. Time slowed again, slowed down to almost nothing, but I wasn't moving as I had at the battle near the Threshold. By contrary, I was moving almost twice as fast, relative to my time-sense.

I rocketed into the man in the leather coat and Time once again was Time, and we were flying at a hundred miles per hour, two hundred miles per hour, as fast as anything I could imagine. I had no speedometer, I had no way of telling anything. But within seconds I had crushed the man in the leather coat between myself and the partition wall, miles and miles away, the two of us slamming into the great stone structure with such force that the man in the brown leather coat actually exploded in my hands, leaving a great mess of black, acidic salsa all over my arms and chest.

I was not hurt.

Even though I, too, had collided with the wall at the speed of a bullet train, a subway, a jumbo jet, I was unhurt. Even though I was covered in molten black acid, I was not hurt.

I had no time to ponder, no time to wonder. I rushed back to the farmhouse with all of my will bent on moving progressively faster and faster.

In mere moments I was back to the farmhouse, where seventy thousand Foederati, one hundred Wanderers and several angels were engaged in a pitched battle with what looked like almost two thousand men in leather coats. Running away.

Abaddon had been fooled. They had been planning an invasion all along. They only waited for him to leave the Abyss.

I rushed into the fracas just as it succeeded in breaking up; the men in leather coats were in the middle of an extended retreat, with the destruction of the Connection complete and their objective clearly fulfilled. I swung left and right and brought damnation wherever I went. But it was wrathful, not fruitful. There was nothing I could do to prevent the men in leather coats from doing what they did. I could only exact revenge on as many as possible.

We pursued and "killed" as many as we could, but even I with my superhuman speed I could not stop all of them. The reason is very simple: I can not fly.

Most of the men in brown leather coats sprouted black, evil bat's wings and soared into the Second Plateau's mists, putting them far out of the range of everyone but Abaddon, who did, indeed, fly after them. But even Abaddon, the terror of all things evil, the avenger of Heaven, the scourge of Hell could not set things right. He could only pursue.

The other Archangels did not give chase. They were indisposed.

They had been standing right next to the suicide bomber that posed as the Wandering Maori, and were now lying somewhere in the Ager Epiphania, undoubtedly wounded, possibly dead. Or in Heaven. Or whatever happens to angels when they "die."

Saint Michael the Victorious could be dead. Saint Gabriel the Steadfast could be dead.

Saint Scholastica, my beautiful redhead, my beautiful Throne, could be in Hell.

And the Connection was destroyed.

And the Bedouin, King of Wrath and Justice, was blind in one eye.

And countless Wanderers were undoubtedly dead.

Where do the Wanderers go when they die? I don't know. But almost two dozen of them found out today.

———

It could not go unnoticed by anyone there that not a single Wanderer nor a single Foederati allied with the Abbey, Father Luke, Mr. O'Malley, or myself was harmed. It could not be overlooked that while my army was whole, our opponents' was decimated.

It could not be unspoken that I moved like an Archangel in the presence of thousands.

It could not be changed that the declaration had been signed, and that the war was on. It could not be denied that the defenders of the farmhouse were now at a serious disadvantage.

It could not be disregarded that the armies of Hell had won my first major battle for me.

———

We laid the Wanderers who perished that day to rest with the Kenyan in the Moslem cemetery at sunset. I took an extra few hours, and, with the Bedouin and Father Luke, built a small but functional fence around the burial site.

At the foot of every small, crude cross that served as a headstone was laid a little white flower from the Abbey's garden. Father Luke officiated the funeral services, which were simple. I cried and cried.

We returned with heavy hearts, Father Luke to the Tower of Babel, the Bedouin to the Tower of the Crescent and Star, Mr. O'Malley to the Turris Venti Mola, the twins to their respective ramparts. Virgil retreated to Salvation Rock and I left for my new tower, where I would be moving my things in and getting settled. Where I would prepare for the war. The Wandering Japanese refused to leave my side and came along, as well, with the Scot and the Frenchman and the other Wanderers allied with us. We would all be moving in to the Shirivasta, which would make my tower a juicy target, it's true. But with our presences there, it would also be the strongest fortress within the partition walls.

None of the Archangels were found, although a shred of Scholastica's gossamer tunic was found just east of the farmhouse. Smack in the middle of Devine Road.

The Road that cuts this Plateau in two.

The Road to Heaven. And to God.

The Road that burns the men in leather coats. The Road that led me to this Mountain. The divine Devine Road.

The war had officially started, and the first tragedy had been inflicted upon us before the first murderous thought entered any of our minds.

The war would go on, of course. The farmhouse had to have a new resident.

Who will guide the Connection when there is, again, a Connection? That's what the war was for. That's why we would be fighting. We would be fighting for religion, for spirituality, for mysticism, for witchcraft, for prayer, for worship of every mode and kind. We would be fighting for the Man in the Yellow Polo Shirt, and for the way that mankind could come to him. We would spill our blood all over the Mountain for the good of all mankind. For the glory of God.

We would march on a road of bones.

And Hell, one way or another, was coming with us.

To be continued...

Printed in the United States
51223LVS00003B/141

9 781413 797367